I0647144

GIRL, 7

A NOVEL

A.J. BASSLER

ISBN: 0615671659
ISBN-13: 9780615671659

Chapter One

When she was seven years old, her stepfather, drunk, beat her so badly that she almost died. Her sin was coming downstairs to retrieve her favorite doll from the living room once she had been put to bed. Her mother was on a beer run.

A neighbor heard her screams and putting aside her worries about being nosy, called 9-1-1. A police car was two blocks away. Officer Ray Jones, in his third year on the job, still had a crewcut from his stint in the U.S. Marines. He arrived at the house, got out of his patrol car and heard the stepfather shouting, the sound of a bottle shattering and a female scream, cut off abruptly. He was naive enough to be appalled. He grabbed his microphone and unholstered his nine-millimeter automatic pistol.

"Dispatch, this is Unit Sixteen-thirty-two on scene at Four-Twelve Eleventh Avenue. Female screams and sounds of assault. Request immediate backup. I'm entering residence by force."

Weapon out, he kicked in the front door of the house. He saw a blond child in a nightgown prone on the living room floor, a pool of darkness spreading under her. Over her stood a man, the neck of a broken Jack Daniels bottle in his hand.

"You! Drop it now!" Officer Ray ordered and the stepfather dropped the broken bottle and retreated to the far side of the room, hands raised.

With his right hand, Ray kept his weapon trained on the man. With his left hand, he reached up and grabbed the microphone clipped to his left shoulder epaulet. He turned his head just slightly, keeping his eyes on the stepfather.

"Dispatch, this is Unit Sixteen-thirty-two," he said into his microphone. "I need medical. Child down with severe bleeding and possible head injuries, I repeat, child down, possible DA situation. And send me backup."

Ten seconds later at the ambulance building 15 blocks away, a shrill alert tone sounded over the building's speakers, followed by the voice of the dispatcher: "Squad Fifty, report of a child down, repeat, child down, officer on scene reporting head trauma and hemorrhaging. Possible domestic assault. Address is Four-Twelve Eleventh Avenue, repeat, four-twelve, avenue eleven."

The paramedic and emergency medical technician on duty that night were in the lounge watching Emergency One reruns when the call came in. The EMT was a mother of three. When she heard "child," she bolted out of her chair and ran to ambulance Unit Five-ten, a boxy truck the size of a delivery van. She jumped into the cab, slamming the door that was left open to save precious seconds in case of an emergency just like this.

She had the diesel engine cranking less than 30 seconds from the alarm. Once the engine caught and roared, she punched dashboard buttons and the garage bay door in front of her began to clank laboriously upward and the red lights atop the ambulance's cab began to rotate, sending bright flickers off the ambulances parked in adjacent bays.

She grabbed the microphone.

"Dispatch, this is Squad Five-ten responding to DA with child down at four-twelve Eleventh Avenue."

When her fellow first responder did not immediately join her in the ambulance, she activated Unit Seven-ten's public address system, bouncing her amplified voice off of the building's cement-block walls.

"Squad Five-ten, we are exiting!"

She emphasized her words by revving the engine. A portly male white-shirted paramedic joined her in the cab seconds later, slamming his door.

"Jesus, Sue, what the hell?" asked the man who had just climbed into the cab.

Sue jabbed the accelerator and the ambulance surged out of bay. She immediately twisted a dial to activate the siren. A rising and falling wail accompanied the flashing red lights.

"Jim, didn't you hear the call? Child down." She glanced at him as they rounded the first corner. "You better buckle up."

Officer Ray kept his service automatic trained on the man who had stood over the girl.

"Don't move," he ordered. "Don't even move one inch and give me a reason."

Ray stepped closer and went to one knee. He risked a glance down. The girl lay unmoving, her hair soaked with blood, a patch of white skull visible. One arm was outstretched. The hand at the end of the arm was a tangle of blood, flesh and bone. Nearby were a broken whiskey bottle, shards of glass, a blue bowling ball and just outside the grip of the shattered hand, a pink-and-white cloth doll.

Officer Ray glared at the stepfather. With no backup present, he had a tough choice: detain the suspect or treat the injured. Knowing that the girl's lifespan was now measured in minutes, he made up his mind in an instant.

"Run, asshole," he said.

The stepfather hesitated a second, then ran from the room. Officer Ray noted the slam of a screen door as he holstered his weapon and bent over the girl. He performed a quick assessment, as he had been trained. Pupils dilated. Carotid pulse weak. Breathing very slow. He reached for his microphone. He gave dispatch his medical assessment, adding, "Tell that ambulance to expedite. This little girl isn't going to make it."

He began trying to find the place from where she was bleeding worst. It was hard to decide, but he did his best knowing that the girl's life was now in his hands.

Inside ambulance Unit Five-ten, Jim took the ambulance's radio microphone.

"Dispatch, this is Five-ten. Inform officer on scene that our ETA is under two minutes."

"Received, Five-ten," the radio responded. "Officer on scene reports severe hemorrhaging. Requests you expedite."

A car in front of the ambulance, a fat white Cadillac, was pulling slowly to the curb as if parking instead of yielding to an emergency vehicle. With red lights reflecting from the Cadillac's rear window and siren screaming, Sue jerked the wheel right, bouncing the ambulance over the curb and onto the sidewalk.

"Christ!" yelled Jim, throwing his arms out to brace himself.

Sue leveled three parking meters as she cut across the corner on the sidewalk. The ambulance slammed back down onto the street. The engine roared as she floored the accelerator.

"The city isn't going to be happy about those meters," Jim said.

"They can bill me," Sue said, gripping the wheel.

Just as the girl's mother pulled to the curb with a twelve-pack of beer and a carton of cigarettes on the front seat, an ambulance pulled away from her house, siren whooping and red lights flashing. She could see bright white lights in the ambulance's rear compartment and a figure bent over.

Two police cars were parked at crazy angles in front of her house, red-and-blue lights rotating. Two cops stood talking on her porch in the light of the open front door. Neighbors pulled their curtains aside and peered from their windows.

She lit a cigarette and decided to wait. She saw a young officer approaching, one hand on his holster. He stopped on the sidewalk near her car and bent over.

"Ma'am, do you live here?"

Well, this just shoots my evening all to shit, she thought. *I wonder what that asshole did now.*

Sue is working the ambulance through traffic, using her lights and sirens mercilessly. Cars pull onto the sidewalk to escape her relentless siren. She is focused on driving as rapidly as possible without losing control.

Jim yells to Sue, "Get us there! I'm losing her. BP is falling, pulse at one-sixty. I can't stop the goddamned bleeding!"

Sue turns her head to yell back into the compartment. "Hang on, honey," she yells. "Can you hear me? She can't hear me. Jim, tell her to hang on! Talk to her! Give her that doll. Talk to her! Hold her hand!"

"That's all I've got at this point," Jim mutters.

He takes a deep breath, then takes the girl's unmangled hand in his. His thin blue plastic gloves are covered in blood. He holds a large bandage on the girl's head with his other hand. It is soaking through with blood.

"All right, little girl," Jim says. "You just hang in there, like Sue said. See, here's your doll." He places the bloody doll beside the girl's head. "She's right here. Right here. Can you feel that?"

Jim glances at the monitor hooked to the girl. It shows her blood pressure stabilizing at 80 over 50 and her pulse holding at 120 beats per minute. It's not good but it's better than it was two minutes ago.

"We're going to the hospital and they're going to help you. OK?" Jim says. "You just hang on. I'll keep ahold of your hand. Don't let go. Keep listening to me. Can you hear me? Hold on to me. Don't let go. Don't let go, OK? Listen, I have a daughter. She's a lot older than you. She's all grown up now, but I remember when she was your age. How about if I tell you about her? You just listen, OK? Hang on, hang on. We're almost there."

He pauses.

"God, please get us there," he says to himself, then resumes talking to the little girl.

Chapter Two

The sliding doors to the trauma bay of the emergency department hiss apart as she hurtles in with Squad Five-ten pushing her stretcher hard. She is strapped to a plastic board, there are IVs in her arms, an oxygen mask on her face, blood splattered on the sheets, a cloth doll at her side and Sue is gripping her unmangled hand, talking to her. The stretcher is met by a team of nurses in teal surgical scrubs. There is a flurry of activity as the girl, limp, is transferred to the operating room table.

Inside, Dr. Jacobi waits, his glove-clad hands raised in front of him like he is appealing to heaven. As soon as she is on the table, he began running skilled hands over her body, assessing. He yells orders and nurses move.

On the admission form, under "Name," a night duty nurse scrawls, "girl, 7," because the emergency department is understaffed as usual and she has more important things to do than fill out forms.

After completing his initial assessment, Dr. Jacobi doesn't think that she's going to survive.

He despairs of his ability to undo what has been done to her.

Her stepfather hit her on the head so many times first with his fist, later with the whiskey bottle, that her brain has bled and swelled. Dr. Jacobi has to remove the top of her skull to relieve the pressure from the bleeding and swelling. The hospital keeps the top of her skull on ice in case she pulls through.

The major bones and knee of her right leg – shattered by multiple blows from a 16-pound Pearl Blue Brunswick bowling ball – are reduced to fragments.

Her right hand has been crushed and mangled, possibly by the bowling ball, possibly by a descending boot. The fractures indicate multiple blows, Dr. Jacobi guesses. Although the first blow crushed her small fingers, many blows – or stomps – apparently followed.

Her cheekbones have been smashed by something hard and unyielding. One eye is partially dislodged from its socket.

Dr. Jacobi doesn't know, but suspects internal injuries. He is right. Her liver, spleen and intestines are bruised. In the case of her liver, it is nearly torn from its internal moorings by multiple blows to her abdomen. These injuries were likely caused by hard punches to her 60-pound body.

Dr. Jacobi, with more than two decades of medical experience, has never seen such injuries outside of high-speed car accidents. He works as quickly as he dares, aware that the girl's chances for survival fall as each second ticks by on the large round white-faced clock on the trauma room wall. He focuses on stopping the bleeding first, then on her head and internal injuries. He does what he can for her mangled arm and knee. He is not a religious man, but in the silences between his barked orders, he prays as he works.

Dear God. She's just a little girl. What could she have possibly done to deserve this? Please, dear God, help me save her life. Give me strength. Help her find a way to live. Maybe one day she can set an example to keep people from doing this kind of shit to each other.

When he has done all he can, he issues a few more orders, strips off his gloves, washes up, walks rapidly to his office, closes the door, collapses into his desk chair and cries into his hands. He has never felt so helpless.

Chapter Three

The story of her beating trickled out into the community. A nosy local reporter got wind of it and bugged the hospital for details. Dr. Jacobi wasn't talking, but a nurse was. The reporter wrote what he could find out and the editor put it on the front page. The community was horrified.

The stepfather had already been arrested. Eventually, the district attorney filed charges and the newspaper had the whole story from the court documents. The story made the front page again.

A clipping service paid to be on the lookout for child abuse stories did what it was paid to do. A Philadelphia newspaper columnist paged through the latest pile of clippings sent to him and picked her case for a special venting of his outrage. He used her name, which was Cindy Phillips.

The columnist's column was syndicated. Newspapers all around the country could use the column if they wanted to. Many did. The columnist summoned a good head of steam for Cindy, and people across the country read her story. Some had tears running down their cheeks by the third paragraph. "Oh my god," they said. "God, that is awful. And they turned to others and said, "Did you read about what this guy did to his stepdaughter?" Others clipped the article and put it in their purses, although they didn't know why. Some read it and wondered what the big deal was. Kids got beat up by their stepparents all the time. Many didn't bother to read it at all because the columnist bored them.

On a farm in northwest Maryland, James Frederick Steele read the column about Cindy over his morning coffee. He wasn't a farmer – he'd never planted so much as a garden. But he did like quiet places and when he had visited the farm as a child, he had loved the way the sun broke over the hill behind the barn. He loved walking through the copse of trees that separated the two main fields, even if it was no longer the Amazon that he remembered from his childhood. Buying the farm hadn't been much of a financial strain for him, as he had figured out a way to get rich young. Mostly, he saw value in things that other people saw as valueless. Kind of like the farm.

When he noticed the column about Cindy, he put his coffee cup down. He read the column six times in a row, each time just as horrified. Each time, he felt something moving in his chest. He got up and got a pair of scissors from a kitchen drawer. Very carefully, he cut the article out. He retrieved a pen from a basket by the phone and wrote the name of the newspaper, the page and the date in the margin of the piece of newsprint. Then he placed the article in the middle of the breakfast table. He stared at it. His coffee sat steaming, untouched.

Something in his mind whispered *Here we go.*

Then part of him watched as another part of him balled up the rest of the newspaper and hurled it across the room. He turned around and kicked the chair he had been sitting in. It flew across the room and struck the cabinet, knocking off chips of paint and a chunk of wood. Too bad. It was older than he was. He turned and pounded both fists on the table as hard as he could. It hurt, but not enough. He shoved the table. It skidded into the stove, denting it. It still wasn't enough. He kicked the other chair, bouncing it off the door leading to the front porch. It landed on its side. He considered throwing it through the window, but the voice in his head whispered *Find something else.* He looked around the room. The phone offered an opportunity, but he knew that tearing it off the wall wouldn't provide satisfaction. There was no taming his furious rage. He knew that he needed to find something satisfactory fast or there would be trouble. He paused, breathing heavily, the need to pound and destroy possessing him completely. The woodpile behind the barn. At least a hundred logs needed to be split.

Go! the voice told him.

He went.

Where was the axe?

His coffee, spilled, cooled on the floor.

The memories came. His father coming home, smelling of gasoline and grease. If he came in the door and said how great it was to be home and smiled, everyone relaxed. But some days he came home with a scowl. Then he and his brother and his mother knew what was inevitable, but they hoped to avoid it nonetheless.

Dinner was usually the trigger. Something wasn't right. The peas were too crunchy. There was a dirty spot on his fork. His coffee was too sweet. His mother would try to head it off, scrambling to resolve the problems, one after the other, smiling a desperate smile that held no mirth. Finally, his father would start muttering, then growling, then something flew. A coffee cup. A plate. Sometimes a chair. "Upstairs!" his mother would yell, and the boys would scramble.

In the early days, they could hear her abuse – their mother's sharp cries, sometimes her begging. But she had learned that her cries terrified the boys, so she came to endure in silence. Sometimes they would hear the cracking sounds of blows delivered with precise repetition. Sometimes they heard nothing.

Set a log. Heft the axe, swing, strike the log. Wood chips fly. Heft, swing, strike. Chips fly. Heft, swing, strike. Chips fly.

When her turn was done, they would hear her pleading. "Please, please, honey, they've been so good today. They picked up all the sticks in the yard. Tomorrow they're going to pull the weeds. They gave me no trouble. Please. They're such wonderful boys. They're so good. You should see the pictures they drew for you. They love you. Please let them go to bed. Please. Please don't hurt them."

As he turned from her, a hulking and unstoppable force headed upstairs, she would be reduced to sobbing helplessly, wondering how she was going to explain yet another bruise to the butcher, who always asked and narrowed his eyes when she told him the usual lies and then somehow forgot to charge her for the pork chops.

The boys knew with sweaty dread what came after the silence downstairs. The creaks as their father climbed the staircase. He would get the top and pause, wheezing, waiting for a sound. They knew better. They held themselves motionless and dared not even to breathe. Then there were squeaks from the floor as he turned to his bedroom. The knob rattled. The door bumped shut. They knew that they had a respite as he stripped to t-shirt and boxers. More rattles and squeaks as he went into the bathroom. The boys lay in the dark, waiting for the inevitable but hoping nonetheless that it might pass, just this one time. It never did. Not when it had gone this far.

Always, something small. A toothbrush left out. A drop of urine on the toilet ring. The window left open. Came the roar: "Boys! Get in here and explain this!" They leaped out of bed for the time allotted for their appearance was never less than brief. Much, much better to appear when summoned than to have him come looking. They stood shoulder-to-shoulder before him in the narrow bathroom, one with his shoulder against the cold tall narrow metal medicine cabinet, the other with his shin pressed against the cold enamel side of the bathtub. Eyes downcast. Waiting for the unendurable.

Set. Heft, swing, strike. Chips fly. Heft, swing, strike. Chips fly. Heft, swing, strike. Chips fly.

"What is this?" their father would ask, voice full of menace. What "this" was did not matter. There was no explaining. They had learned not to try. Then it would come. There was no pattern; there was no anticipating. Ducking or avoidance would have only made it worse. The blow struck from out of nowhere, quick and mighty, like being hit with bag of wet sand.

When he was chosen, it felt like his head was jerked backward rather than struck from the front. He would fall into the bathtub or be driven to his knees. Bright, tiny lights would spin about his head. One part of his face would burn hot. The roaring in his ears would start. Then the grasp of his hair, like a merciless junkyard claw closing on his scalp. He would be lifted, arms and legs dangling helplessly, scalp bunched and stretched, carried through the hallway and to the bedroom. The windup, the stretching of the scalp as he swung, the pitch. They had both learned to position their pillows so that if they were lucky, they would hit the pillow instead of the wall. Sometimes they did. Sometimes they didn't.

There were quick bright lances of pain as strands of hair remained behind in the clutching claw. Then there was nothing but the ball. Curl up as tightly as possible and fight, fight, fight to stay curled. Self-preservation took over. There was no way the brain was going to convince the body to unwind and lay waiting for the punishment. Animal instincts called for the fetal position. So he tucked and held against the storm.

Set another. Heft. Swing. Strike. Chips fly. Heft. Swing. Strike. Cleaved. Set another. Heft. Swing. Strike. Chips fly.

Then the yelling and the threats and the pulling and tugging and the blows to back and head and legs. Even the blows to the back of the thigh that would produce agonizing muscle cramps later did not convince him to uncurl. But he always lost eventually. He found himself uncoiled, his throat exposed. Then came the worst.

Sometimes it was with hands, sometimes it was with the pillow that a few seconds (minutes? hours?) ago had been an ally. It arrived. The removal of his ability to breathe. Again, self preservation took over. He knew better than to strike his father, but he thrashed and kicked and punched in desperation as his brain screamed that oxygen was needed NOW and damn the consequences but the pillow was inexorably pushed down harder or the fingers tightened until there was nothing but a high keening in his ears and crazy frantic desperation, a red screaming siren in his brain and then, then just when it was too much to take and something inescapable and awful was going to happen, it ended.

The pressure vanished; he gasped and gasped, nothing in the entire universe but the need to get sweet air into his lungs again and again and again. In the far, far distance, he could hear the bellowing. This time he better have learned his lesson and that would show him and did he think he was smarter than his father and if he thought this time was bad wait until the next time when he would really be taught a lesson. The great empty spots before his eyes would grow and grow until one of them swallowed him. Then he was gone to blackness.

Set another. Heft. Swing. Strike. Chips fly. Heft. Swing. Strike. Chips fly. Heft. Swing. Strike. Wipe the sweat stinging his eyes. Heft. Swing. Strike. Chips fly. Heft. Swing. Strike. Chips fly.

He would awaken to a dark quiet house, which seemed impossible because only moments before the world had been filled with fury and noise and pain. The clock would tell him the truth. Hours had passed since he first stood with his brother in front of his father, wondering whose turn it was.

Then, as he breathed, nothing on his mind but sucking good oxygen into his lungs, feeling stings and burns on his face, throat and body, his mother would appear, furtive, crying. Whispering: "Oh, honey, I'm so sorry, I'm so sorry, are you OK, you know he loves you he just has that temper" and on and on, the words meaningless. She would put a cool cloth across his burning neck and stroke his hair back and kiss his forehead and he couldn't hate her because in the light from the hallway he could see the purple around her eye and the bruises on her cheeks, the marks on her neck and arms. She would caress him and whisper to him and soothe him until sleep was the best alternative and he would give in to it, to his welcome friend nothingness.

There were no more logs.

He straightened, his back creaking. At his feet were chips and split firewood. His left hand stung. He looked at it. Sweat was running into a bleeding gash. When did that happen? How? Tiny wood chips stuck to his sweaty arms. With muscles protesting, he chunked the axe into the splitting stump. He looked at the sun. It was late morning. He was still in his bathrobe. He turned and walked back toward the house. He felt the calm that follows exertion. The rage was gone, burned up. Inside the house, he righted the chairs, sopped up the coffee, moved the table back into place, threw the newspaper away. He shook his head at the chunk taken out of the cabinet. The clipping seemed puny and vulnerable on the floor. He placed it on the desk in the next room and went upstairs to shower.

After his shower, he felt numb but clean. His brain was a blank page. As he toweled off, thought began to return. He made a cup of coffee and drank it slowly. He made four telephone calls. One was to his office. One was to his stockbroker. He asked a few questions and performed some mental calculations that would have amazed his high school algebra teacher, who had told him, "If you'd just pay attention, you would be a great student." He gave a few orders. He hung up. He retrieved the clipped article from his desk. He called his lawyer and issued more orders, glancing at the article. Then he called his mother and told her that he loved her and that he would stop by for a visit and asked if she needed anything.

Chapter Four

Dr. Jacobi was irritated. He had a double caseload because Dr. Rebecca Confer was off this week, his right hip was bothering him again, his wife was not talking to him over something he'd said and that seven-year-old girl who'd been beaten practically to death had taken a bad turn. He'd requested help from some specialists, but few had responded because she had no medical insurance.

Now there was someone insisting on seeing him right now and waiting in his office. Now was as good a time as any. He sighed as he pushed open his office door.

The waiting stranger was standing. Dr. Jacobi didn't know much about clothing, but he could tell that this man was no stranger to custom-tailored suits. He wore a deep blue suit, a very white shirt and yellow tie with tiny blue polka dots. He had a neat goatee and glasses with tiny lenses. The stranger put out his hand. Dr. Jacobi took it and said, "I am Dr. Jacobi, sir, but I have to tell you that I don't have much time today."

The stranger didn't give his name. He apologized and said he would only need a minute.

"Literally, doctor. I know your time is valuable," he said.

The stranger asked if Dr. Jacobi was Cindy Phillips' primary physician. Dr. Jacobi said that he was. After saving her life in the emergency room, he had taken a personal interest in Cindy's case.

The stranger produced a very white, very stiff business card. On it in black serif type was the name of a man and two telephone numbers.

"From this point on, she is to get nothing but the absolute best care," the stranger said. "There is to be no concern about cost. During her recovery, there is to be no concern about any specialist or what he charges. There is to be no concern about cost at all. If you have to fly a specialist in from Europe, then do so. All you have to do is authorize the treatment – you, Dr. Jacobi – just sign off on it. And fax an itemized bill to the bottom number."

He waved the business card between two fingers.

"All the bills will be paid. All of them. With no questions and no quibbles. The goal is to see that Cindy gets world-class care. Cost is not to be a concern. Am I being clear?"

Dr. Jacobi looked at the stranger. His eyes were calm and serious. Dr. Jacobi believed him. He didn't take the stranger's last question as an insult. He knew that it wasn't intended to be.

Dr. Jacobi said, "She's getting very good care, but –" The stranger cut him off.

"Of course she is. You're doing the best you can. But we all know that there are patients and then there are patients. There's health care and then there's health care. And Cindy's family, we gather, is not in a financial position to do much for her."

They were not. Her stepfather was in jail and her mother was back on welfare. There had never been much money and there was certainly none for world-class health care, although there was always enough for cigarettes from what Dr. Jacobi could discern.

"I promised only a minute of your time and I'm afraid I have taken twice that. If you have any questions, doctor, please call the first number on that card."

They shook hands again and the stranger was gone. Dr. Jacobi tucked the card in his shirt pocket. He would be seeing Cindy later. He'd have to test the truth of that card.

The hospital administrator looked at Dr. Jacobi across the top of his half-glasses. He liked to do that, Dr. Jacobi knew, because it intimidated many people. But Dr. Jacobi had worked the emergency department long enough to remain un-intimidated by the likes of Calvin Simmons, hospital administrator.

"All expenses?" Calvin asked. It was the tone he used when people asked him if he liked football.

"All," Dr. Jacobi said firmly.

"But he didn't give you his name. Odd that a complete stranger would take such an interest in her case. An interest to the extent of paying her rather substantial bills."

"It is odd. But we've got nothing to lose. We'll fax an itemized list of everything that we've done for Cindy over the past two weeks. If they pay, they pay. If they don't, then I'll throw his card away and we're no worse off than we were before."

Calvin's head and eyes had not moved since he had peered at Dr. Jacobi over his glasses. He didn't move for ten more seconds, his eyes fixed on Dr. Jacobi's.

"Well," he said, breaking off his gaze and looking down at his papers. "That is true. Although whether they continue to pay after receiving the first round of invoices is another matter. Nevertheless ...."

Dr. Jacobi knew that was as close to a go-ahead as Calvin would give. He had to retain his deniability for the board of directors.

"Thanks, Cal," Dr. Jacobi said, standing, although it hurt him to thank Calvin for anything. If he could get someone to pay for world-class treatment for Cindy, it was worth a ding in his pride. Besides, he knew that Calvin hated being called Cal.

Within fifteen minutes, he had the fax machine running. Single-spaced and itemized to insurance company standards, the list had taken fourteen and three-quarters pages. It covered everything from Band-Aids to surgeon's fees from the moment Cindy had been brought into the emergency room.

Dr. Jacobi surprised himself by whispering a little prayer as the fax machine buzzed and digested his list, digitized it and sent it out over the phone lines to a man with the ridiculous name of Peter P. Pannington.

Please, Lord, I know I'm a pretty pitiful penitent to be asking for a favor. But please give this little girl something she hasn't enjoyed yet in her life – a break. Please let this not be a hoax.

Two weeks later, Dr. Jacobi found a copy of the fax in his mailbox. A yellow sticky note from accounting was attached to it. The note read: "Dr. Jacobi. FYI. All charges paid by cert. check. Check cleared."

Dr. Jacobi was thrilled. On the strength of his gut feelings and Calvin's lukewarm approval, he hired the best. The world's experts were called in to repair Cindy. A German neurosurgeon was flown in to repair her skull and assess her brain injuries. Her right leg was rebuilt with metal rods. Her new knee had been designed at MIT. It was an intricate plastic marvel. "Better than God's design," the inventor had once joked. The highly skilled plastic surgeon nearly gave up on her cheekbones. They had fallen victim to both the bowling ball and the whiskey bottle.

"There's nothing here to work with!" the plastic surgeon cried in despair during the operation. The nurses kept their heads down and waited and eventually the surgeon sighed and resumed her work. She did a good job, but she was right. There wasn't much to work with.

The surgeon who repaired Cindy's hand shook his head while reviewing x-rays of the damage.

"I have seen worse, but not often," he said. "Usually industrial accidents. Crushing incidents involving machinery. And this was done by her father, you say?"

"Stepfather," Dr. Jacobi corrected. "He used a whiskey bottle and a bowling ball. Maybe his boot."

"Hmm." said the surgeon. "A challenge."

A few weeks after Dr. Gruber's brain and skull surgeries, Cindy's hair began to grow back in, two shades darker. She had a scar around the crown of her head – there was no avoiding that – but her hair would cover it.

A month after that, she began squeezing back when her hand was squeezed. Three weeks after that, she opened her eyes for the first time since she had closed them to duck a fist. Or maybe it had been a whiskey bottle. No one would ever know.

Chapter Five

Two months later, Dr. Jacobi sat before Cal again. Cal carefully maintained his skeptical attitude but his attention was riveted on the sheets of paper in front of him.

"All of them?" he asked.

"Every dime," Dr. Jacobi said. "By certified check. And they always clear."

"And this Dr. Gruber?"

"Neurosurgeon from Germany. He's the best the world has right now. He's recognized and cataloged and successfully treated conditions that most other neurosurgeons are still trying to learn."

"We put him up at the Pittsburgh Hilton, I see."

"Yes," Dr. Jacobi said with secret delight. "Three hundred a night or something like that. For a suite. But you don't get someone like Gruber to fly over here for a week, perform an operation and get him to agree to come back in six weeks and put him up in a Motel 6."

"And this Mr. Pannington paid."

"Hilton, first-class flight, Gruber's fee, yes, they paid everything. Everything we send them is paid to the penny in two weeks. They never even squeak."

"Unfortunate that insurance companies don't share this attitude. Hmm. Well," Calvin said, looking up from his papers. "I guess we can assume – for now – that Mr. Pannington is 'for real,' as my daughter would say."

"I suggest that we continue with the present course," Dr. Jacobi said. "Cindy has finally started to come around. She's responding to voices and touch."

"You sound positively optimistic, Dr. Jacobi."

"For the first time since they brought her in here, yes, I'm beginning to think she has a chance."

"Hmm, yes," Calvin said, shuffling the papers together. It was a sign that the meeting was over. "But what kind of life is it going to be?"

Dr. Jacobi had no answer for that. In his estimation, the beating that Cindy had received had set her development back at least a year. She was no longer able to walk. She would have to relearn. Her right arm and hand did not exhibit the proper response to nerve stimuli. Her facial expressions were limited. It was possible that her mental processes had been affected.

Whether she would ever be normal was a question he had asked himself many times over the past few weeks. It was a question he now asked God when he went to church every Sunday and prayed for Cindy.

He left Cal's office without offering an answer.

Chapter Six

"Thank ... you," Cindy said to Dr. Jacobi.

Her facial muscles still wouldn't allow her a full smile, just a lopsided imitation of one. It looked insincere. Maybe 'wistful' was a better term. Simply getting her to the point where she could interpret a social situation and respond was a minor miracle. Her speech was halting, but appropriate to the situation she was in. There was clearly coherent thought behind her words.

Dr. Jacobi thought that overall, she was doing very well. Gruber was either a miracle worker or Cindy had an incredible constitution.

"I've ordered you a rack that will fit over the bed here and allow you to read these," Dr. Jacobi said, his hand resting on the box of books. Don't overdo it. If you start to feel tired, stop. You'll have plenty of time to sit in bed and read."

As soon as he said the last part, he regretted it. She might have the rest of her life. But Cindy took no offense. She seemed genuinely pleased by the books and she had yet to crack a binding on one.

"Thank ... you," she said again. "Who ... from?"

"I don't know, Cindy," Dr. Jacobi said. "They came FedEx and there's no return address. I guess a secret admirer."

That earned him another smile. He'd take those smiles over a hundred-dollar bill any day.

Dr. Jacobi had ordered the best reading rack he could find. It had cost $275 from one of the many catalogs he had stored in the lower-right drawer of his desk. He had ordered it shipped overnight for an additional $67. Many of the catalog companies considered him a premier customer. He had added it to the itemized list he sent to Pannington and, as with every other bill he had ever sent, it was paid in full and without comment by certified check two weeks later.

Cindy carefully placed the first book onto her reading rack. Her right thumb didn't always do what she told it to and at first the book slid off and onto her lap. It struck the stainless steel brace screwed into her pelvis to hold her new metal hip in place. She winced. It hurt. But she soon forgot the pain as she gazed in wonder at the book. It had a brightly colored cover, a swirl of pinks and yellows. It was a design, not a picture or photo. A big pink "1" was set in the upper right corner. She had looked – there were 20 books in the box and they were numbered in order. The title of the first one was "The Young Princess," across the top. In the lower right corner it read, "For Cindy Phillips." For her! The book was for her! She opened it and began to read.

"Once upon a time, there was a beautiful princess named Cindy. She lived in a castle beside a bright shiny river ...."

"I tell you, they were written for her. About her. They're all fairy tales about this little princess named Cindy. She was a beautiful little girl – in the books I mean – and she has all these adventures."

Dr. Jacobi was talking to Dr. Rebecca Confer in the physician's lounge.

"And?"

"And – what. What can I say? The books tell the story of this young princess named Cindy. She is a wonderful little girl. One day, a big bad evil magician puts a spell on her to cause her pain and make her life difficult. All the best white magicians in the kingdom – all the good ones – can't undo the spell of the evil one. So this princess is stuck with her problems. But she keeps persevering, keeps having adventures, never turns bitter and keeps being kind to others. She rescues puppies and such for the children of the village."

"Sounds like a fairy tale, for sure," Dr. Confer said, sipping her coffee.

"But who did this?" Dr. Jacobi said. "Someone studied Cindy's situation and sat down and wrote these stories, apparently to encourage her – to make her feel like her life is still worth living. Who would do that?"

"Or who would pay to have it done?" Dr. Confer asked, sipping her coffee.

"I know what you're thinking," Dr. Jacobi said. "It's the same guy who's paying for her treatment. I agree. It has to be. But it still amazes me. Who is this guy and why does he care so much about this girl he's never met?"

Dr. Confer shrugged. "I think we should just be happy that she's found her prince charming or guardian angel or whatever. It seems like it's just part of the treatment that this fairy godmother is already paying for. First, he paid to fix her body. Now he's paying to fix her mind. You know how victims of abuse may recover physically but never get over it mentally. How many kids like her never find the help they need? How many grow up to beat their own kids, just keeping the cycle going? Look, she would probably still be on a feeding tube if fairy godmother hadn't shown up and agreed to pay for Gruber and all those other high-priced asswipes that tied up the OR for weeks. Don't look a gift miracle in the mouth, Ron."

Dr. Jacobi shook his head. The whole thing was like Cinderella. Cindy's life had been poverty, then pain. And now miracles.

The night duty nurse sat down on Cindy's bed though it was against protocol. She had been on duty the night Cindy had come in to the emergency room. The night-light between the bed and the bathroom spilled a half-circle of light on the floor. The moon added white bars that fell across the floor and the foot of Cindy's bed through the mini-blinds. The floor was as quiet as a hospital floor ever is.

"Oh, honey," the nurse said when Cindy asked her a question. She took Cindy's hand. It was cold. There was a white scar that ran along one finger and up past her wrist.

"What." Cindy asked again. "What ... happened ... to me?"

The columnist had predicted that this moment would come. The night-duty nurse had taken to reading his columns, along with most of the rest of the staff.

She gripped the cold hand tightly.

"Oh, dear, I'm not sure if I'm the right person for this," the nurse said. She felt the pressure of tears in her eyes and blinked them back.

"Please," Cindy said. "Why ... am I ... here?"

Cindy deserved the truth, the nurse decided.

"Cindy, honey, you ... your stepfather beat you up," she said. "He hit you and...." Then the tears came, though she had seen much that was grim and sad in her 17 years of nursing and had learned to handle it. Most of it. Some things still got through her defenses.

She realized that Cindy was patting her hand.

"It's ... OK, all right," Cindy said. "I just ... wanted to ... know. I'm OK."

The nurse could only bite her lip and grip the cold little hand tighter and run a gentle hand through the thin, fine hair on Cindy's head. She fluffed Cindy's pillow and gave her a smile. She hoped Cindy couldn't see her tears.

Cindy had been moved to a rehabilitation hospital so she could re-learn how to walk. Nine months, two weeks and four days after she entered the emergency room with a faint pulse, unresponsive, covered with blood and suffering from massive trauma, Cindy took her first step without assistance. The physical therapist – assigned to Cindy full-time – was delighted.

"Cindy! Way to go!"

Resting on her aluminum crutches, Cindy beamed. Her smile was getting better.

Later, they had cake and ice cream. Cindy cut the cake and insisted on serving everyone. No one minded that the pieces were all different sizes and that the icing got smeared. Dr. Jacobi couldn't stop smiling. The staff chattered happily. Dr. Jacobi paid for the cake, the ice cream and the "Congratulations, Cindy!" banner.

Over cake, the physical therapist told Dr. Jacobi that she had never worked with a patient with so much determination.

"She has no doubt that she's going to walk again," he said. She honestly believes that it's just a matter of time. Sometimes I have to end her sessions even when she wants to keep going."

"She's tough all right," Dr. Jacobi said. "Or she wouldn't be here."

The boxes of books, one per month, followed Cindy to her new hospital. Always 20 books. Always with "Princess" in the title and always with "For Cindy Phillips" at lower right. They were illustrated and hardbound and Cindy loved them. She read them over and over.

One day, Dr. Jacobi picked up one of the books and took back it to his office to read. He was no teacher, but he was pretty sure that the books were getting more sophisticated in writing and content.

Cindy's appointed county caseworker visited Dr. Jacobi regularly. Upon learning that she was not likely to leave the rehab hospital any time soon, the caseworker arranged for a tutor three times a week. Cindy was learning multiplication and history and reading. The tutor was mildly interested in Cindy's princess books, but seemed to think that they were rather light reading, being fairy tales and all. She launched Cindy into books she considered to be more appropriate for Cindy's age, like "Ramona The Spy" by Beverly Cleary. Cindy read them willingly, but a stack of the brightly colored books was always at the side of her bed.

Chapter Seven

James Steele is sitting on the front porch of his farmhouse, drinking coffee. The summer evening is cooling, the sun slanting low across the fields. The big oak tree in the yard casts an elongated shadow that seems to stretch for miles. He is suffused with happiness. The reason for his happiness is peeking at him from behind the big tree. In a yellow sundress, barefoot, she has her palms pressed against the tree's rough bark and her forehead resting on the backs of her hands. She is counting.

"Seven ... eight ... nine ... ten! Ready or not, I am coming!" She looks up from the tree and scans the yard, pretending not to see him on the porch. "Daddy!" she yells. "Where are you?"

He remains silent, smiling, sipping his coffee. She begins to prowl the yard, looking in improbable places. "Are you in this flower? Are you under this leaf? Are you a bug?" She moves closer and closer to the porch steps. "Where are you, daddy?"

She climbs the steps slowly, carefully avoiding looking at him directly. "Daddy!" she yells. "Where are you?"

He puts the cup of coffee on the floor beside his rocking chair. He waits for her to come close enough to grab. Once he gets her, he is allowed to tickle her until she squirms out of his grasp, giggling. Then they do it all over again. These are the rules of the game. He has never violated the rules since she laid them down.

She is coming closer, her blonde hair swinging as she turns her head from side to side, seeking him. Closer. Her feet are grass-stained, her legs tanned, one knee still bearing the speckles of a scab from a fall a week ago.

Another two feet. He is ready. Another foot – she's almost close enough....

"Daddy! You are just too good at hiding!"

He waits until she is fully within range. He wants to be able to grab her bodily, not just grab an arm. He doesn't want to hurt her. She is there. He pounces, looping an arm out to scoop her onto his lap. When he grabs her, she whoops, then begins laughing. Her bare legs kick.

"No daddy, no daddy, no daddy!"

"Here I am!" he yells. "Ha! I was invisible! I've got you now!" He tickles her where he knows it gets her worst – on the back of her neck and in the middle of her rib cage.

Her giggles turn to laughs, then to screams of delight.

"Daddy! No, daddy! No, daddy!"

Her scream changes to one of terror. "No, daddy! Please stop!"

"No daddy!" There is fear in her protests. She is frightened and hurt. He looks down at his hands. They are bloody. His nails are torn.

She twists and thrashes in his lap. "Daddy, stop! Daddy, that hurts! Daddy, why do you hurt me?"

He wants to help her but he can't. Every time he touches her, she screams in agony and twists to escape. His rocker crushes the coffee cup with a sickening crunch.

"I stopped! I'm not hurting you ... honey, what is hurting you?"

Then she is gone. He looks out into the yard. The sun has gone down. The air is chilled. The moon has risen and it is watching him. On the lawn, robbed of its color by moonlight, is a small coffin. He knows that it is pink.

He rises to his feet, then falls to his knees. One knee lands on a shard of coffee cup and a pool of blood spreads rapidly. It reaches the steps and he can hear it dripping, dripping, dripping.

"What?" he cries in anguish. "What did I do? You can't take her from me! I love her! She is my life!"

The lid of the coffin begins to rise, slowly. He is seized with terror, but he cannot move. In the yard, just beyond the shadows, he feels the presence of something of awesome power, something so powerful that it might extinguish life with a gesture, something so terribly mighty that it cannot be human. He wants to scream, but he cannot. He knows what he will see inside the coffin and he knows that it will shred his sanity if he does. He calls on his very deepest will to lower his head. He cannot. The coffin lid is nearly fully open; inside something is dark and gleaming.

He finds that he can move his eyes and he casts them downward just as something in the coffin rustles and snaps.

"Daddy," rattles a small voice.

He cannot form words; he screams in despair.

"You know who put me into this box, daddy." The voice hisses with a shriveled tongue and missing teeth.

He feels a gaze on him. He does not know if it is the thing in the coffin or the other thing that is ambling about his yard. He wants the nightmare to end.

"I do, I do, I do."

"Tell me."

He can imagine moonlight shining from the dead eyes in her emaciated skull, stringy strands of blonde hair dangling from her peeling scalp.

"I know this! I know I am not worthy! Why do you torture me? You know I cannot bear to look at you. What do you want? Please."

"If you want peace, speak."

"Me! It is me! Daddy! James Frederick Steele! I put you in that coffin! I am sorry, I am so sorry, don't you know ... You were my life, my light, my heart, my reason for living! I would never have hurt you..."

Something with a black heart laughs, unconcerned with his despair. His blood has spread to cover the porch. It drips from all the edges. The laughing thing laughs again, closer. He tries to rise to his feet; he must escape, but he cannot, he cannot rise, his blood has stuck him to the porch; his own blood is holding him down.

The laugh is behind him, he can hear the porch boards groan and splinter under the weight of something enormously heavy; something splatters on his neck.

He sits up in bed, sweating, his heart pounding. He looks wildly around the bedroom, terrified. Shadows threaten; he gasps, he cannot breathe. The room is quiet. Downstairs, a clock chimes gently four times. The spell is broken. He is in his bedroom. He does not have a child. He did not kill his child. His breathing slows.

He gets out of bed slowly and goes to the bathroom. The old faucet creaks as he swings its handle. He swallows cold water. Outside the window, the moon is up and bright.

He walks slowly downstairs, still fragile from his dream. He makes coffee. He does not want to sleep again that night. Not ever. Out on the porch, he cannot bear to sit in the rocking chair. He thinks that he might take the axe to it. Sitting on the swing, he looks out at the big tree where she is not. His heart aches for something that he never had.

He wishes he could see her for just an instant, even just a flash of tanned legs under a dress, a shining whirl of hair. But he knows that he cannot; he must not. His dream told him what he always feared: that he is not worthy because his rage is his master and when in its thrall he might do the unspeakable.

His punishment is his feeling of aching loss. He deserves his punishment. He deserves his fate. He deserves his nightmares. He deserves everything he has, including his empty life.

His life's successes are dust in his hands because his lack of temper has denied him the thing that he wanted most: A family. A wife to share his life. A little girl to tickle until she giggled. To greet him joyfully at the door when he comes home from work. A little girl to spoil with too many toys. To buckle little feet into little white sandals. To wipe tears when knees are skinned. To tell stories to under the big tree on a lazy summer day.

He looses one bitter thought for his father. *You put this into me. You planted this seed.* But he cannot sustain his anger because he knows that the abuse started long before his father. His father suffered, too. There is no point to that chain of accusation, no resolution, no answers.

Sipping his coffee, he ponders that he owns a car that cost more than most people make for two years of work. He paid the equivalent of the lifetime earnings of five men for a condominium in a fashionable part of the city. He eats at the best restaurants and does not even glance at the bill. He tips heavily even when the service is lousy. He scatters dollars to the wind, spending carelessly on meaningless toys that those with fewer resources lust for. He knows that his wealth means nothing because it cannot buy him what he really wants.

He sits on the porch trying not to think or remember, just to be. Just to be a piece of the world; nothing more. Eventually, he realizes that the air has become still and damp. He clears his mind and enjoys the gray quiet of dawn. The birds awaken and keep him company until the sun breaks over the hills, chasing away the night's chill. An old red pickup truck comes down the lane, trailing dust. It stops with a clatter. He watches through the gentle mist of the morning that softens corners and blurs details.

An old man in a blue denim coverall climbs out and begins unloading tools from the back of the truck. It also carries a heap of topsoil. The man has a red bandanna stuck in his back pocket. Every now and then, he grabs it and snorts into it, then stuffs it back into his pocket. It is such mundane gesture that Steele appreciates it for its very ordinariness. He remains quiet so as not to startle the man.

Eventually, the man turns to walk toward the house carrying a shovel and a hoe. He spots Steele and stops an instant, then resumes walking.

"Morning, Mr. Steele," he says. "Didn't expect to see you up."

"Had a bad dream, Charlie," Steele says. "Couldn't sleep."

"Happens to us all, Mr. Steele."

"Yes it does, Charlie, doesn't it? We all have those things that keep us awake at night. Can I get you some coffee?"

Charlie stops at the porch steps and leans the tools carefully against the banister.

"To be honest, sir, yes, I could use a cup. I usually stop and get some, but I only had a dollar in my wallet this morning."

"Coffee's always free here, Charlie. Come on up and sit a while. I'll get you a cup. The yard work can wait."

Charlie hesitates, then says, "Well, sure. That sounds fine." He starts up the porch steps.

"Charlie," Steele says, pausing at the screen door.

"Yessir?"

"This sitting on the porch stuff is never going to work if you don't start calling me Jim."

Charlie sits down carefully in the rocking chair. "Well, OK ... Jim. I guess I can get used to calling you that."

Jim smiles and goes inside for the coffee.

Chapter Eight

The day came when Dr. Jacobi could no longer justify keeping Cindy in the rehab hospital despite the punctual certified checks. He refused, however, to send her home. He had a long and unsatisfying conversation with the rehab hospital's administrator, then sat in his office for an hour, thinking. Finally, he turned to his computer and composed a letter. He fed the letter into the fax machine with his next invoice to Pannington.

"Your honor, I am here to represent Cindy A. Phillips in the matter of her custody." The lawyer's voice rang from the back of the courtroom.

The county judge managed to look perplexed and irritated at the same time.

"Young man, this had better be good," the judge said. "This court has better things to do than listen to frivolous challenges from those with no legal standing. Miss Cindy Phillips has an attorney, appointed by the court, who is also her mother's attorney."

The young attorney at the back of the court-room smiled a predatory smile. He was not there to represent Mrs. Phillips. He was there to represent Cindy Phillips.

The attorney for Cindy's mother was a harassed-looking, nearly bald man wearing a red, white and blue tie and a cheap suit. He had been appointed by the court when the Phillips family pleaded poverty. He had felt despair when he saw the law firm he would be going up against. He felt greater despair when he saw his opponent in person.

The confident young attorney, just a few minutes late for the hearing, was from a law firm in Washington, D.C., that had on its client list the speaker of the United States House of Representatives, the CEOs of several multi-billion-dollar corporations, two Supreme Court justices and half of the president's cabinet. He had graduated first in his class from the University of Pennsylvania law school. The young attorney had not yet lost and was pretty sure that he would never lose a case during his career. This little custody case wasn't to be his first loss, that was for sure.

He would have considered the case beneath his talents, except for a handwritten request from an A-list client of his law firm. Which was accompanied by a firmly worded yellow sticky note from a senior partner. Which was why the very skilled young lawyer had researched this case more deeply than any other to date. Which is why he had employed the services of a very good private investigator. Which is why he was today standing in the courtroom of a small rural Pennsylvania city, facing an ancient and crotchety judge, fully and completely prepared.

The young lawyer's suit was of French cut. His white shirt gleamed. His tasteful tie, perfectly tied four-in-hand, was of woven silk and cost more than the opposing lawyer's entire suit. His briefcase bulged.

"Your honor, my appearance and my plea are neither frivolous nor brought without standing," he said, the absolute confidence of the young and bright in his voice. "If I may ...." He approached the bench, fat briefcase in hand.

Forty-five minutes later, having seen certain documents, photographs and private investigator sworn statements and having listened intently to the young attorney, the judge signed an order removing Cindy from the guardianship of her natural mother Mrs. Phillips and placing her in the care of a foster family recommended by Dr. Jacobi.

The harassed-looking lawyer threw up his hands. On a bench in the courtroom, all alone, Mrs. Phillips showed no emotion. When the judge stood, she stood and left the courtroom.

Fourteen months later, now eight years old, Cindy still needed crutches to walk. But the braces and racks and supports screwed into various parts of her skeleton were gone. She got awful migraine headaches that she described as "whanging." She had learned the term "whanging" from a Kurt Vonnegut story her tutor had read to her. She didn't understand all of the story, but it was funny and Mr. Vonnegut seemed to her a sad but warm person.

Her right hand still didn't always do what it was told. There were scars all over her body, some large and some small. She had asthma, which she never had before. There was a constant low level of pain in her body, like a radio tuned between stations. But she was alive and she had a resilient nature, a sunny disposition and a pretty good brain, despite all that the three had been through.

Sixteen months after he beat her, a jury found Cindy's stepfather guilty on seven counts after a one-day trial and thirty-seven minutes of deliberation. The charges included attempted murder and aggravated assault. Charges of torture had been dropped. The district attorney showed the jury 26 photos of Cindy's injuries, blown up to 10 times life size.

Officer Ray Jones testified. He showed up a half-hour early in hopes of talking to Cindy, but she did not attend and was not called as a witness. The DA was certain he could get a conviction without putting her through the ordeal, although he was prepared to have her limp down the aisle in front of the jury if necessary. The defense did not dare call her.

Emergency Squad Five testified. Sue didn't cry on the stand, but did when she heard the verdict, which she had stayed to hear.

Dr. Jacobi was a key witness. The jury found him fatherly and believable and they sensed his outrage. Upon hearing the verdict, he closed his eyes and said a little prayer of thanks.

The judge spoke at the sentencing of her stepfather.

"Your crime is of the most despicable known to man," the judge intoned. "You violated every civilized expectation for a child placed under your care. You betrayed society, your stepdaughter and yourself when you savagely and without mercy attacked her. It would be difficult to be more harmed than this child was and not be dead. You have shown no remorse. This court has no sympathy for your position or your excuses."

The judge gave him seven years, the maximum under state sentencing guidelines.

When the sentence was announced, the stepfather flew into a rage, shouting obscenities at the judge and swinging at his lawyer. He was subdued by three deputy sheriffs and led from the courtroom in handcuffs. Sitting on one of the benches, Mrs. Phillips showed no emotion. When the stepfather was led away, she got up slowly and walked out of the courtroom.

The judge announced that the stepfather would do his time at a state maximum-security prison. He would be eligible for parole in two years.

The Philadelphia columnist wrote another column about Cindy and the outcome of the trial. He pointed out that while Cindy still had trouble walking and was in a state of constant pain, the stepfather would get three meals a day, have a TV in his cell, have exercise facilities available and would have a pain-free body that could make use of them. He was in prison for seven years – he would be 51 at most when he got out – but he had condemned Cindy to a different kind of prison for a full lifetime.

Some people who read the column thought that the stepfather got off easy. Some thought that he got what he deserved. Some hoped that he was put into a cell with a homicidal maniac who stayed awake at night, staring and polishing a shiv. Others thought that the columnist should really get off this child abuse kick. It's not like the topic was going to win him a Pulitzer or anything.

Chapter Nine

Cindy is walking down the empty hall of her high school. Classes are in session, but she has permission to go to the library to work on a report. Coming toward her, she sees three girls that she doesn't like. Cindy keeps her eyes down and moves to one side of the hallway.

"Oh, there she is," one of the girls says. "Watch this." The girl, tall and athletic, breaks away from the other two and moves to intercept Cindy. The other two stop and lean against lockers, smirking and watching.

The big girl walks directly toward Cindy, a snarl on her face, her eyes cold. Cindy tries to speed up to get past her, but the girl stops in front of Cindy.

"Hey, little miss A-plus." She looks angry, ready for a fight.

Cindy stops. She says nothing. She hates confrontation. She knows that this girl could hurt her.

"I have something for you. Look here."

Cindy raises her eyes. The girl is drawing her arm back. She brings it forward rapidly *you little shit* and Cindy flinches violently. Her books tumble to the floor. When she recovers, the girl is standing with her arm out as if to shake hands. A huge grin is plastered across her face.

"Howya doin?" she says. "I just wanted to shake hands. You're awfully jumpy."

The other girls laugh. The big girl walks away laughing as Cindy bends to pick up her books. "She was scared shitless," she hears. "Did you see her face?"

As she gathers her books, Cindy can feel the adrenaline receding from her system. She knows it will probably trigger a headache.

The incident upsets her. She thinks that she should be able to stand up to such bullying. *Why didn't I take a stand? Why didn't I just keep walking? Because I'm weak, she thinks. I allow myself to be abused. I deserve it.*

Upset by the incident and her response to it, she sits down at a table in the library, her enthusiasm for her research project evaporated. She puts her books on the table and decides to look for some fiction to distract her. She has found that libraries are a good place to find something to distract her from the various failures, pains and difficulties of her life. She begins cruising the aisles. Nothing catches her interest. She keeps moving, scanning titles, occasionally pulling a book from the shelf and looking it over. But she returns each one. Nothing is striking her. Her mind lingers on the incident.

If only I had stood up to her. What was the worst that could happen? She might hit me. It would hurt. Maybe she would knock out a tooth or blacken an eye. So what? Wouldn't that be worth it to stand up?

For a moment, she considers what might happen if she tapped into her internal anger. *Wouldn't that be something?* She is certain that if she grew angry enough, she would be able to fight back, to strike out, to do damage. But almost as fast as the idea arrives, she rejects it. She has promised herself that her internal resource of fury will never be used to lash out, to harm, to hurt. That's how it was used against her. She refuses to use it for violence. She only wants to tap its energy to do good things, positive things. At worst, she burns it off with long walks, even though the walks leave her with an aching hip. At best, she transforms the anger it into energy for good things. Like research projects.

As she pulls a book from the shelf, a slim, small volume falls and strikes her on the foot. It is too small to hurt. It seems more like a request for attention. She bends and picks up the small blue book. It is "The Diving Bell and the Butterfly" by Jean Dominique Bauby. On the cover is a picture of a lonely lighthouse. The picture and the title intrigue her. She opens the book to its cover flap and reads that the book is about a man who is trapped inside an unresponsive body following a stroke. No, it's not about him, she reads, it was written by him. Bauby dictated the book by moving the only part of his body that he had control over following the stroke: his left eye. He wrote the book by having someone read the alphabet to him and blinking when the reader reached the letter that he wanted. She is fascinated. She takes the book back to her table, sits down and begins to read.

She is astonished at the man's perseverance and courage. Nearly completely paralyzed by a stroke, he wrote a book. He tells of his experiences in the hospital, visits from his friends and family, how he is treated. He relives high points of his un-paralyzed life and describes the occasional misery of his current situation, but never with self-pity. She finds his writing clean, refreshing and invigorating. She reads and reads. She is amazed that a man struck so low could still somehow retain the joy of life. Even the worst parts of his descriptions of his paralyzed state are written so that they come across as irony, not pathos.

Eventually, someone touches her shoulder. She breaks from the book and looks up. It is the librarian.

"Honey, I think you're going to be late for your next class," the librarian says, smiling.

It seems to have been only minutes since she discovered the book. Strange how it actually seemed to find me, she thinks. But she knows that she's late; now pulled back into the current world, she remembers hearing the distant ringing of a bell. She grabs her books and checks out "The Diving Bell and the Butterfly."

"That's a wonderful little book," the librarian says. "Very inspiring."

She runs to class. On her way, she thinks about how brave Jean Dominique Bauby was. How being nearly completely paralyzed would send most people into a downward spiral of hopeless despair. He somehow managed not only to avoid despair, but also to create a work of art to thrill and inspire others.

On her way to class, she finds that the book has banished her despair. How can she dare to feel despair over a simple high school bullying when someone like Bauby stared down a true terror and won by force of will? How petty and small her sadness seems now. How silly. If Bauby can find the will to survive having his fully aware brain locked inside an immobile body, then surely she can survive a little humiliation.

On the way to her class, late, her steps are light and the small blue volume is not an added weight at all. Instead, it is like helium, lifting her body and her thoughts as she dashes down the corridor. The bullying incident has receded. It is insignificant. The day is beautiful and tomorrow is full of promise.

Cindy is in gym class. The class is running laps around the gym, timed by a sturdy-looking teacher in a gray sweatsuit. The teacher has a stopwatch and a clipboard and she makes a note as each runner completes a lap.

Cindy is at the rear. She is sweating. Her gait is uneven. Her face is pale.

She has been lapped several times by the best runners. Sometimes they snicker and look back as they pass her.

The teacher holds up her hand as Cindy approaches. Cindy steps out of the running lane and stops, bent over, breathing heavily. Sweat drips from her head and splatters on the gym floor.

"Cindy," the teacher says. "You can stop. You don't have to do this."

Cindy takes three deep breaths, then looks up. The teacher is taken aback. Cindy's eyes are aflame and her jaw is clenched.

"Oh yes I do have to do this," she says. And she's off again.

She completes three laps in the allotted time. The best student completes 14.

After the run, Cindy stands for a long time under the hot shower water, face lifted, eyes closed, willing the pain in her hip to go away. It doesn't. She's grateful for the water running down her face because it hides her tears.

Chapter Ten

As a junior in high school, her tutor encouraged her to go into social work. Dr. Jacobi encouraged her to go into medicine. Her foster parents wanted her to enter academia. But Cindy surprised them all.

"I think I'm going to study politics," she said.

One night before bed, her foster mother eyed the stack of books by Cindy's bed. It contained biographies of Harry Truman, John Adams, Richard Nixon, Olympia Snow, Winston Churchill, Martin Luther King Jr. and Margaret Thatcher. There was a book on the world's greatest speeches.

Cindy, sitting on the bed, was reading a book on Shirley Chisholm.

"Honey," her foster mother said, "don't you want to read something besides biographies?"

"Mom, these books are great. These people were so ... brave. When the time came, when they had to make a tough decision, they did it. They didn't try to duck out of it."

"Who is Shirley Chisholm?" her mother asked. "I've never heard of her."

"She was the first black woman elected to Congress. She ran for the Democratic presidential nomination in 1972. Guess what her slogan was?"

Cindy's foster mother shrugged.

"Fighting Shirley Chisholm – Unbought and unbossed. Isn't that great?"

"It certainly sounds determined."

"She was also a great speaker," Cindy said. "Listen to this, mom."

Cindy read:

Eleanor "Ellie" Smeal, publisher of Ms. Magazine, worked on Chisholm's presidential campaign as a member of the National Women's Political Caucus, organizing speaking events and campaigning for Chisholm door-to-door.

Chisholm and her opponent George McGovern were each invited to speak at a presidential debate at Carnegie Mellon University in Pittsburgh. Smeal introduced Chisholm and then watched the debate. Smeal said that although McGovern eventually won the Democratic nomination, that day in the auditorium, the audience clearly belonged to Chisholm.

"I lost count of the number of standing ovations she got," Smeal said. "McGovern got no standing ovations. Chisholm didn't have a chance to win. But she absolutely took that audience into her heart. She spoke so dynamically. She had a lisp but it didn't matter. She taught me one thing about speaking: It's what you say and if it's coming from your heart."

Cindy looked up from the book. "Isn't that great? She won over that audience by speaking from her heart. She must have been so brave!"

"You're right, honey, she must have been very brave. But I think that in the here and now, it's time for you to turn out your light."

"Maybe I'll even run for office one day," Cindy said. "How does 'President Cindy' sound?"

Her foster mother smiled from the doorway with her hand on the light switch.

"I think that has a very nice ring to it."

At the very bottom of the pile, waiting patiently to be re-read, was a thin volume with a worn pink-and-yellow cover. It was so thin that it escaped her foster mother's notice. Its title was "The Princess Who Was Elected President."

Chapter Eleven

Cindy sits in a neurologist's office with her foster parents. Her foster mother holds Cindy's hand. The white-coated doctor stands before two whitely glowing viewing boxes mounted on the wall. They look out of place against the dark wood paneling and hunter green of the office. On the glowing boxes are images of Cindy's skull, front, rear and side.

With a thin chrome pointer, the doctor traces lines on the images visible only to him.

"Here is indication of the reattachment of the top of the skull," he says. "Perfect match. Here and here and here are healed fracture lines. Good knitting. Your surgeon was very skillful. There is no compression nor indication of pressure points. No malignancies; no aneurysms. Other than the healed fracture, nothing abnormal at all."

He snaps off the light box and the sudden absence of a buzzing sound makes the room seem very quiet. The doctor turns to Cindy and her family. He telescopes his pointer back to pen size with a series of tiny clicks.

"I can't see any physical reason for the headaches. This is the same situation indicated by the CT scan and the MRI," he says.

The family is silent. Cindy's foster mother squeezes her hand.

"I can prescribe a painkiller," the specialist says. "That seems to be our only alternative at this point."

"They make me dizzy," Cindy says. "Thank you anyway."

Chapter Twelve

One day when Dr. Jacobi was sitting at his desk, staring out his window into the parking lot, his phone buzzed and the receptionist told him that a "Cindy" was here to see him. He hadn't seen her in a year, since she'd talked to him about seeing a specialist for her migraines.

"Cindy? Send her in!" He was enthusiastic about seeing her again.

His door opened slowly, tentatively. She peeked inside. Her hair was cut very short. Her eyes and smile were as bright as ever. "Doctor? Are you busy?"

"Cindy! Never, ever too busy to see you." He leaped to his feet and pulled out a chair. "Please come in. What are you up to?"

He noticed a slight limp as she walked in. She was slim and dressed in jeans, a white t-shirt and a light yellow cardigan. She was long gone from the little girl who had come into his hospital bloody, battered and nearly dead. Ten years had passed since she had walked out the doors of the hospital – defiant of the "wheelchair exit" rule – with the staff cheering, clapping and crying.

A few minutes of small talk followed. He tried to keep the focus on her. He didn't want to talk about himself. He was divorced; he had a girlfriend who was 10 years younger. He'd bought a sports car and was trying to convince himself that his life to date had not been without purpose. Over the last year, he had become obsessed with disappearing without a trace, of being completely forgotten the moment that he was dead and buried.

She held out an envelope, ripped open on a short side. He raised his eyebrows and took it.

"I applied to four colleges," she said. "University of Maryland, University of Pennsylvania, Georgetown and the University of Virginia. I was really pulling for Georgetown and Maryland because they have great poli-sci departments."

"That's quite an impressive collection of schools," he said. "And ...?"

She nodded at the envelope. "My foster parents don't even know yet. I wanted you to be the first."

He turned the envelope over. There was a University of Maryland seal on the front. He slid out a piece of folded stiff paper.

"Dear Cindy," he read aloud, more delighted with every word, "As the Director of Admissions for the University of Maryland, I am pleased to offer you admission to the university's Political Science program. As you know..." He broke off and jumped to his feet, coming around the desk. "Cindy! Congratulations!"

She stood to accept his hug.

"You go get them, girl," he said. She hugged him tightly, surprising him. "Go show them what you can do," he said fiercely into her hair, which had grown two shades darker but still very fine. In his arms, she was surprisingly thin and frail.

They sat down again. He adjusted his tie. "Well. Political science, huh? You'd make a great doctor."

"I know that's what you wanted," she said. "But I'm all caught up in the idea that I can do something to make people take child abuse more seriously. I think it would just break my heart to be a doctor and have to treat them after the damage is done. I want to try to stop it up front."

"So you're going to take political science classes to learn how to be a lawmaker? You know that most of your colleagues are going to be headed for academia, not Congress."

"I know."

"And you know that the world of politics is pretty rough. People generally either love you or hate you. And it's harder than you think to get things done. It can take years just to get one piece of legislation passed, and it always gets corrupted ...." He stopped. "I'm sorry. Here you are with great news and a brand-new life and I'm pooping on your party. I'm sorry."

She smiled her million-dollar smile. The right side of her smile didn't turn up quite as far as her left. But what's-her-name, that plastic surgeon, had really done a first-rate job on her teeth, he thought. He knew that the ones in front weren't real, but there was no way to tell.

"Well, we must celebrate," he said. "Lunch? Dinner? Catch a plane to the Bahamas?"

"I can't stay today. I have to get back to work. But, yes, let's do lunch."

"Said like a true politician," he said as they stood. He put out a hand awkwardly, but she came to him for a hug.

"Thank you for everything you did for me," she said softly to his shirt collar, just below his ear. "I wouldn't be here without you."

He hoped she wouldn't see the tears that abruptly welled up. They came more easily the older he got.

"Hey. I didn't do anything. You're the tough one. I never saw anyone fight like you did. No one in this hospital thought you'd ever walk again," he said.

"Except you," she said.

After she left, he sat at his desk for a long minute, then pulled open a desk drawer. He pawed through the jumble until he found it, there at the back, under a clear acrylic paperweight emblazoned with "Many Thanks."

It was a stiff white business card with two phone numbers and the ridiculous name of Peter P. Pannington on it. Holding the card, he thought about how quickly ten years can pass. He turned the thought over and over until there was a rap on his door and an irritated voice told him that he was late for the staff meeting.

Chapter Thirteen

Cindy is a junior in college. She is behind the podium in a classroom. Behind her is a chalkboard erased blank except for "Dr. Stanger Politic and the Amer Exper papers to TA in 343" scrawled in a corner. Her hair is gelled down conservatively. Her suit is navy blue. Her manner is formal. She is addressing the class, which sits in rows of seats at semi-circles of desks that rise toward the back of the room. The lighting is dim. The class is almost in darkness; only three lights at the front of the room are on. One of them shines down just in front of Cindy and her podium. It highlights her cheekbones.

Her professor sits off to her left, chewing on a pen as he listens to her. He's wearing khaki pants, a yellow shirt and an ugly brown striped tie. He occasionally makes notes on a pad he has in front of him.

"Victims of child abuse deserve more than simple acknowledgment," Cindy says, index cards before her on the podium. "Victims of child abuse need ways to find closure to their experiences; they need help to find ways to redirect their energies to positive pursuits. Otherwise, they are likely to live lives filled with rage. Many will be unable to handle the burden; many will be unable to come to terms with what happened to them." She glances down at her cards.

"As a result, they will not be able to contribute their full measure of skills and talents to society, and society will suffer as a result. Many will turn their repressed rage on their children, perpetuating the cycle of violence. This cycle will not be ended until the importance and severity of child abuse is recognized and acted upon at the federal level, preferably with a constitutional amendment."

She looks up to indicate that she has finished. The class applauds dutifully.

She glances at her professor, who is chewing thoughtfully on his pen.

A friend, Evelyn, leans forward as Cindy sits down.

"Nice job," Evelyn whispers and sits back.

"OK, OK," says her professor, seeming distracted. "Nice job, Cindy. Thank you. Next is Brad. Brad, are you ready?" A broad young man in a suit and tie rises from a back row and begins descending to the podium.

"Oh, Cindy," says her professor, "Would you see me after class?"

In the professor's tiny office, Cindy sits nervously in the only chair available. The office is filled with stacks and stacks of newspapers, magazines and buff-colored folders full of paper. A huge plastic chart on the wall traces the results of every presidential election in the U.S. from George Washington. Memos from the political science department head are taped above the desk. One, she notices, is four years old. A plant in a red plastic pot is dying on the windowsill.

Her professor, balding, fortyish, is silently reading a printed copy of her presentation.

"Cindy," he says, "Your logic is impeccable. Your sources, your research – fabulous. This is obviously the result of a lot of work." He hands the printout back to her. "But that's not why I wanted to see you."

She tenses. Her headache gets worse. She tries to smile. The old familiar fear of inadequacy rises in her. *I'm not good enough and never will be.* She can't keep up in the class. It is a struggle. Many of her fellow students seem to be grasping the material much faster. They make incisive comments in class while she's still thinking it over. She often gets lost. Sometimes she can't see the connection between the class discussions and the reading assignments. Her frequent migraines keep her from studying. He's about to ask her to drop out of his class.

"Relax, please," he says. "You're doing fine in my class. You're actually fun to have around because you really care about this stuff. My concern is with your presentation skills. Now, don't get me wrong, you're good. You're better than average, actually." He pauses and smiles. "OK, you saw Brad, who presented right after you did. Now, come on."

She can't help but smile back. Brad had been awful. He had started strongly, but lost track of his notes in the middle of his presentation. There had been a full minute of painful silence while he shuffled index cards, trying desperately to get back on track. Once he found his place, his confidence had been shattered and he mumbled the rest of his presentation. It was a relief for the whole class when he finished and bolted from the podium.

"Brad lost his place," she says.

"It's very kind of you to cut him slack," her professor says. "But a really good public speaker doesn't need notes. A really good speaker doesn't even memorize his speech. Or her speech. A really good public speaker speaks from the heart and it shows. The words just flow; the logic is implicit because the topic is so well known. The facts have been absorbed and dissected and re-assembled, not just memorized and typed out neatly for recitation. Do you know what I'm talking about?"

She thinks of Bill Clinton. Of Winston Churchill. A crying Jimmy Swaggart. John F. Kennedy. Martin Luther King Jr. In her head, she hears: *When we let freedom ring, when we let it ring from every village and every hamlet, from every state and every city, we will be able to speed up that day when all of God's children, black men and white men, will be able to join hands and sing in the words of the old Negro spiritual, Free at last! Free at last! Thank God Almighty, we are free at last!*

Her head rings with the power of the words. *How do I know that?* she wonders.

"Yes," she says to her professor, snapping back to reality.

"I'm giving you an A for your presentation," he says. "It was very good. But I'm going to be tougher on you for the next one. Your research and writing are fine; keep up the good work there. But for the next one, I want you to focus on your delivery. I want you to build some fire. I want to see you banging on the podium. I want to see you holding your audience in the palm of your hand," he says. "Find something that fires you up and blow us away with it."

"OK," she says. It's all she can think of to say. She thinks she's terrible at public speaking. She's frightened of getting up before an audience.

"I wouldn't even have asked you up here if I didn't see that potential in you," he says. "It's just a hunch, but I see the potential in you for a really good speech. A barn burner. A stump speech. Something inside you wants out. Am I right?"

She doesn't believe him, but she says, "Yes, sir. I'll focus on delivery."

He eyes her for a few seconds. "I can see that you don't believe me. Well, you just need to find that one thing that really motivates you. What angers you? What pushes your buttons?"

"There are a couple of things," she says.

"Whatever those things are – whatever they might be – pin them down. Think about them. Build a speech around them. It doesn't have to be the pinnacle of logic. What I want to hear from you is something that demands attention, something that fires people up, something that convinces through emotion, not recitation of fact. Do you have any idea what I'm talking about?"

"I think so," she says. She just wants to be gone.

"Listen to me," he says kindly. "Cindy, you've got it in you. I can feel it. I just want to see you show it. With your next one, pull out all the stops, OK? Blow me away."

"OK," she says.

Chapter Fourteen

She pulls away abruptly, pushing, pushing, she has to be clear, she's suffocating; she can't stand it. She kicks, pushes herself up, slides down the bed. He falls on the floor, astounded. She pulls her t-shirt down and huddles at the end of the bed, clutching a pillow. She's not crying, but it's hard to breathe. She's gasping. From the floor, in his underpants, he looks up at her.

"What? What did I do?" he asks.

She wants to cry but can't. Her eyes are dry. There's something thrashing around inside of her that she can't identify. It gave her the strength to reject him. But she is afraid of the rage that she feels. It doesn't seem controllable.

"I'm sorry. It's not you. It's not you. It's ... I just ... I can't ...," she says. There are no words.

He looks at her. He can make out the shape of her breasts through the thin t-shirt. She has pink panties on. There's a long thin scar down her leg. He wants to ask her about it. He wants to trace it with his tongue. He wants to hold her. He wants her so badly that it's a taste in his mouth. He can't believe that she has just rejected him. Everything was going right. Everything was on track. And now he's sitting on the floor with his underpants in a tent and she's freaking out.

"I'm so sorry. I just ... can't." she says. She clutches the pillow tighter and gets smaller, if that's possible.

He considers being cruel, then decides to keep his options open. "OK," he says carefully. He stands up. "I'll, uh, just go then."

She can't look at him. "OK. I'm sorry," she says into the pillow.

He pulls on his jeans, buckles the belt, pulls on his shirt, finds his shoes.

She's rocking back and forth on the bed.

He stops at the door. "Hey, we don't have to ...."

"No. Just go. I'm sorry."

When he's gone, she needs to move, she needs to take action; she needs to make something happen. The thing that she can't control lashes her. She wants to run, she wants to smash something but instead snaps on her desk light and sits down at the computer. She opens a text file and begins to type rapidly.

The very term child abuse is limiting. It leads us to believe that the effect is only upon children. But as experts and victims know, the effects extend far into adulthood. In fact, it might be fairly said that an abused child is never fully free of the devastating effects of the abuse and that every aspect of the victim's life is affected from the time of abuse onward through adulthood.

Victims find that the most elemental aspects of their lives are corrupted. Their sense of self-respect is damaged; their self-confidence is often destroyed. They find it difficult to trust others. Often, the abused find it hard to express themselves even with those they love. They seek to minimize their emotional involvement with anyone and everyone. Sometimes they can trust only themselves. They become withdrawn; it is difficult for them to extend the hand of friendship.

Because they experienced pain at the hands of those they trusted implicitly, they fear ever again permitting another human to occupy such a position in their lives. This limits their ability to bond, to accept, to love.

Others might find child abuse victims to be cold or distant. If so, it is because they cannot understand the turmoil within the victim: the self-criticism that evolves into self-hate, the utter lack of confidence, the confusion in simple social situations, the inability to just smile and make a friend.

She reads it over. Tears running down her cheeks, she saves it and goes to bed.

Chapter Fifteen

She takes long walks around the campus, in the fog, in the rain, composing her thoughts, imagining scenarios, working out bits and parts and sections. Sometimes she feels in her gut that they work. Other times they lead her down dead ends. Those she reworks or discards. After she has nine or ten defined segments, she organizes them in her head like fitting a puzzle together. Then she practices saying them out loud in front of a mirror and in front of Evelyn.

She practices tapping into the feelings of rage and fury that child abuse ignite in her. She has found that if she concentrates, she can tap into the rage like plugging into an electrical socket. The rage provides energy. She has learned to focus the energy into something positive instead of something destructive. When she speaks before her class, she finds that the energy helps her speak loudly and clearly. When she speaks the truth, she feels unstoppable.

After many walks and practices, her thoughts, reviewed, coaxed, cajoled, finally fall into a semblance of order and she is ready to face her audience.

Now again she stands at the podium before her class in the darkened room. She has no index cards; no notes; no crutches. She inhales deeply and thinks of the collection of articles that she has clipped from newspapers over the years. Children locked in cages by their parents. Children bound with duct tape and tortured with cattle prods by those they loved and trusted. Children burned by cigarettes; starved, beaten bloody. She grows furious. She feels the pressure of tears, but grits her teeth, wipes her eyes and refuses the tears their exit. This energy must be focused for good. She has been practicing this.

She closes her eyes, takes a deep breath and imagines her anger as an electrical current. In her mind, she grabs it and twists it into a yellow stream of power. She plugs it into the back of her head. She releases her breath. She opens her eyes.

She is ready. Her audience is before her.

"I come before you today to speak of the human spirit," she says, walking away from the podium, using the surging power within her to project her voice. "The spirit that drives us to our highest accomplishments and survives our worst defeats; the spirit that motivates the greatest and the least among us. I speak of the spirit that we draw upon when our greatest effort is required, when history calls upon us. I speak to you of those who find that spirit within themselves and who triumph despite formidable obstacles. I speak to you today of the bravest of mankind."

She pauses. Her ears tell her that she's speaking too loudly, so she knows that she's at the right volume.

"I ask you, when one of mankind survives despite overwhelming odds, when a man or woman refuses to accept a grim fate, do we not instinctively celebrate such strivers, whether they ultimately fail or succeed? Were George Mallory and Sandy Irvine cowards because they dared to climb Everest in the 1920s but failed to reach the peak?"

She faces her audience, her eyes roving across them. They watch her.

"When has mankind accomplished the most?" she asks, pausing at a desk. "When have we made God most proud of us? How did Lincoln inspire a young nation to forgive and forget after a horrendous, divisive war? How did Martin Luther King Junior strike a chord that still resonates today? How did Gandhi defeat the British Empire without firing a shot? How did Barbara Johns ignite a spark that did not burn out until it had ended segregation? How did they do it?

"I will tell you. They did it by tapping into a great spirit of mankind, a force that cannot be denied once it is loosed. I tell you that this spirit is available to us all, when we need it, if we are brave enough, if we dare to reach out and grasp it and turn it to good use.

"Why is Hitler reviled? Because he killed people? No. No. Nothing so simple. He is hated because we know that he attempted to deny this spirit of humanity. In his gas chambers at Treblinka and Auschwitz and with his tanks in the Warsaw ghettos he and his henchmen tried to erase that which is greatest in humans – our ability to strive, to achieve, to become more than the sum of our parts, more than dumb animals."

She pauses. She appears to ponder.

"What are the greatest achievements of humanity? The Senate of the Roman Empire? The Renaissance? When Neil Armstrong took mankind's first step on the moon? The American and French revolutions? These are indeed shining moments for mankind.

"But for each moment of triumph comes the times when we found that our reach exceeded our grasp, as with Mallory and Irvine. Why do we feel that odd mixture of despair and awe when things go terribly wrong, as when the space shuttle Challenger exploded minutes after liftoff? How did you feel when you heard that a brave band of men and women sent a hijacked airliner plunging into the Pennsylvania soil rather than let it strike the White House? Would anyone here say that Neil Armstrong is a hero but that the people on Flight 93 were not?

"Today, we must take our heroes where we can find them. Our heroes of the human spirit are not the superhuman heroes of myth. We do not have Hectors and Helens. Video cameras and 24-hour news cycles have cut our heroes down to size. But our modern heroes are no less great because they are not giants.

"Today, we think of a tired Rosa Parks on a bus in Alabama who refused to give up her seat to a white man because … finally, ultimately, it just wasn't right. Today, the heroes of the human spirit are these such as Rosa Parks. And the man who stopped the line of tanks at Tiananmen Square. Remember that photograph? Our heroes are the ragged Afghans on horses driving the armored Soviets out of their homeland. Our heroes are the ordinary Germans on both sides of the Berlin Wall, tearing it down with their hands, brick by brick. Today, the heroes of the human spirit are the New York City firefighters who on nine-eleven were running up the World Trade Center stairs to rescue while everyone else was running down to escape.

"What is the common element here? What spirit ties New York firefighters and Rosa Parks to Lincoln and Gandhi and Martin Luther King Jr.? I will tell you. And it is simple. In each instance, human beings drew upon their spirit to say: No. Stop. This evil shall not pass me."

She looks at her audience. No one moves. Her professor is sitting absolutely still, his attention riveted on her. He is not chewing on his pen.

"This spirit that I speak of today is not exercised only by the Lincolns and the Gandhis, brave as they were. In fact, I submit that the very bravest, the most important, the most essential exercise of this triumph of the human spirit – this innate human desire to be hold the line against what is wrong and evil – is exercised at the basic unit of human existence: the family."

The eyes of the class follow her as she strides again past the podium. No one fidgets; there are no side conversations. *I have them,* she thinks. *I hold them in the palm of my hand. Their emotions, their thoughts, their opinions are mine to mold.*

"I ask you: Who is braver and more noble than the man who has suffered abuse at the hands of his father and who refuses to pass the evil on? How brave is the man, ridiculed as a child, robbed of his confidence, belittled and crushed, who somehow survives and rises up and who as a father cradles his tiny, vulnerable son in his arms and swears before God Almighty that the life of fear that he led will not be the life of the fragile one that he holds? Never will this child flinch when I raise my arm. Never will this child fear his own father.

"I ask you – How great is this man? How amazingly brave is the man who makes good this promise, who swears by God that the cycle of abuse stops cold and dead with him? How powerful is this man who stays his thundering hand when his child infuriates him, who withholds his wrath when his overwhelming anger urges him to strike and punish? How powerful – no, how brave – is this man? How dare he defy his fate? How dare he reject the legacy of punishment and abuse that was his to inherit and pass along?"

There is not a stray noise in the classroom. The class waits for her words. Her professor's eyes are wide and fixed upon her. Power surges through her. The words come and she cannot rein them because they are her truth.

"So, today, I ask you to celebrate this man, this woman, who epitomizes the human spirit of triumph, of refusal to surrender to fate, who stands before a mighty evil force and resists, perhaps for only one simple goal – to give a child a chance to live a life free of fear. Today, I ask you to celebrate every man and woman who, despite abuse at the hands of someone they loved and trusted, stands up and says in ringing tones, No, by God, the cycle of abuse stops here with me."

She pauses.

"Today, I ask you to celebrate with me that human spirit. I propose that the same spirit that drove Gandhi, the same spirit that lifted Martin Luther King Junior, the spirit that stopped the Nazis, the spirit that ended segregation – this human spirit that instinctively turns against evil – this spirit is present in every man and woman today who survives and struggles but triumphs by being a kind, loving parent every single day despite the past inflicted hell of child abuse.

"This great nation must recognize and acknowledge this spirit and celebrate it. This brave spirit must be celebrated in every village, in every state and in every city. Only then will we as a nation reach the heights – and indeed, deserve the fate – that God has intended for us, and be able to unite our hands in protection of our children, the very greatest resource of this great land."

She pauses.

"Thank you."

There is a moment of silence, then as one the class stands and applauds. She leans on the podium, exhausted, sweaty, suddenly embarrassed, looking at her professor. He is seated, scribbling a note. *I must have blown it,* she thinks.

Too much emotion. Too wild. Not logical enough. I think it fell apart in the middle.

When she collapses into her seat, Evelyn leans forward and says, "Holy shit, girl!"

"Cindy," her professor says. "Can I see you in my office after class?"

She again sits before her professor in his office. He is making notes on the blue piece of paper that holds his assessment and her grade.

"Your logic, solid, but not unassailable as your previous pieces," he says, making a note. "Your research – minimal. You could find the information that you used in any encyclopedia." He makes another note.

She looks away. *I knew it. Too much emotion. I went overboard. I blew it. I'm not cut out for speechmaking.*

She raises her eyes. Her professor is smiling. The look he gives her is one of pride.

"But who cares about logic?" he says. "That was a *speech*. That's what I was looking for from you – that's what I wish everyone in your class would deliver. But I know from experience that no one else in your class is going to give a speech like that. You've set the bar impossibly high, I'm afraid."

He is delighted, she realizes.

"Cindy, you will convince more people with that speech than you ever will with a hundred dry, well-reasoned, fact-filled speeches delivered calmly and neutrally. You were on fire! That part in the middle about 'how dare this man' – the hair on the back of my neck stood up. That is the kind of speech that moves people, Cindy. It moves them emotionally. They believe you; they literally love you. When you're done, they want to act, to follow your lead. They will ask you what you want them to do next."

He pauses.

"Cindy, if you go into politics and you deliver speeches like that, you are going to be one very successful politician. You'll have people lining up to work for you and follow you."

He hands her the peer evaluation sheets and his grading sheet. On the blue grading sheet are a grade of A+ and the words: "You made me believe you."

She pages through the stack. Her peer comment sheets include such comments as: "You opened my eyes," "You changed my mind," and, most rewarding to her, "You made me think about child abuse in a whole new way."

"Cindy," her professor says. "Don't ever forget this. Don't forget the power of a great speech, well delivered. Speeches have changed the world."

Chapter Sixteen

She goes to Florida on spring break with her poli-sci friends. Five of them rent a two-room beach house near Miami. The day that they arrive, everyone dumps their bags into the house, jumps into their bathing suits and heads for the beach. Cindy and Evelyn are changing in the same room. Cindy envies Evelyn's curves and smooth brown skin. As Evelyn pulls up the straps of her bikini, she notices that Cindy is getting into long jean shorts and a t-shirt.

"Oh, no, you don't, girl. Where's your suit?"

"Ev. You know I can't go out there with a bikini on."

Evelyn glares at Cindy, hands on hips. "You're afraid of people seeing those scars, aren't you?"

Cindy shrugs. "I didn't even bring a suit. I don't look good in a bikini. Too skinny."

"So get a one-piece! Girl, you are not going to sit on the beach and read. Not while I'm around. We're here to swim and surf and get drunk and check out cute guys. Studying time is over."

Cindy smiles. "I'll be OK. Please."

"Cindy, no one else even sees those scars. You see them, but no one else even notices."

"I know. But I ...." She trails off.

Evelyn gives Cindy the eye a minute longer, then relents. "All right. But you're going to have fun here, you understand me? Studying is over!"

That night, as Cindy is unrolling her sleeping bag on the living room floor, she notices that the bag contains a lump. She is puzzled. She didn't pack anything inside her sleeping bag. She shakes the bag until the lump falls out. It's a package, wrapped in beachy blue-and-white striped paper. Puzzled, she tears open the paper. Inside is a brand-new one-piece bathing suit in her size. And a huge beach towel. She unfolds the towel. On it is a badly drawn bust of Martin Luther King Jr. At the top, it reads "I Have A Dream ...." She unrolls it completely. At the bottom of the towel it reads ".... of finding the perfect beach."

"I know that's unbelievably tacky, but I couldn't resist," says Evelyn from behind her.

Wordlessly, Cindy stands and goes to her for a hug.

"Now, I'm going to see you on the beach tomorrow in that thing, right?" Evelyn says.

"Yes. I promise." Cindy steps back, wiping her eyes. "What did I ever do to deserve such a good friend?"

"You were just yourself. And you keep doing that," Evelyn says, smiling. "That's payment for getting me through Polls and Stats. Now get your sleep. We're going to be rowdy tomorrow. Goodnight, Cindy."

"Goodnight, Ev."

Chapter Seventeen

Cindy graduates from the University of Maryland with a 3.86 GPA. Her junior-year speech professor is on the stage. After she accepts her rolled scroll, he hugs her instead of shaking her hand.

"Use that power you've got wisely," he whispers before he releases her.

Dr. Jacobi and her adoptive parents are in the audience, beaming. Her stepfather is still in jail. Her natural mother is not there.

Afterwards, Dr. Jacobi and her adoptive parents take her out for dinner. They focus their attention on her the entire evening and she can see the pride in their eyes. She chats and fulfills her role in the celebration, but she's thinking about her professor's whispered comment. Those six little words brought into focus something she had been thinking about, but had found elusive.

She realizes that she does indeed have a power and that she should indeed use it wisely.

Her desire to return to Pennsylvania coupled with the lack of demand for political science majors results in her acceptance of a low-paying job with a social services agency. She takes a job as a caseworker for a not-for-profit agency that works to improve the lives of poor families and prevent child abuse. The agency depends upon state funding, grants and donations to survive.

Her salary is barely enough to live on but she is inspired by the dedication she finds in her co-workers. Like her, they care far more about the goals of the organization than the size of their paychecks.

She finds a cheap and amazingly beautiful apartment in the forlorn downtown of Altoona, a small city in southwest Pennsylvania. Her third-floor apartment offers light blond polished wood floors, arched doorways between white-painted rooms and a glorious view of the ancient, wooded, ever-present mountain ridges of the Appalachians. She moves in a mixture of her college dorm room furniture and some items rescued from the local Goodwill store.

Chapter Eighteen

She is walking along the sandy shore of a gold and glittering sea, the heavy ocean breeze ruffling her hair and fluttering the sweatshirt tied around her waist. He walks beside her close, but not touching her. She is happy. She does not turn to look at him. Her eyes are on the horizon. The sea crashes beside her.

"And we can get married," he says. "And have children."

She is filled with joy. She reaches out to touch him, but he's not there. He has stopped walking. He is behind her, poking at the wet sand with his toe. His form is unclear, blurry. She steps toward him and speaks his name. He looks up, but she can't make out his face.

"I'm sorry," he says, receding.

Clouds roll in. The sea turns dark. She is splashed with cold spray.

"But," she says, her joy destroyed in one stroke and replaced with hopeless despair. "But our children ... our happiness."

"It is no longer possible because you..." he says, and his next words are lost in an angry buzz, rendering his words as indistinct as his form.

She is helpless, her world is rent, her destruction complete. She cries out, but he is ever more distant, his words buzzing, buzzing, buzzing ....

She snaps awake. At eye level, her pager is vibrating itself toward the edge of the bedside table, its small green screen lighted. She grabs it. The number is the state police dispatch. She fumbles for her bedside phone, rights it, dials the number. The ring tone purrs once, twice, three times, then a click.

A crisp and efficient voice: "State police dispatch, may I help you?"

"Uh, yes, this is Cindy Phillips from, um, Family Services. Uh, I was paged."

"Miss Phillips, we have an officer requesting your presence at the scene of a possible domestic disturbance, child abuse suspected. Child welfare is already on-scene. Can you respond?"

She is fully awake now.

"Yes, I can. What is the address?" She grabs the pen and pad of paper kept at her bedside just for this. "Uh-huh. Fifteen-oh-six North Eighth Avenue. OK. Thank you. Please tell the officer that I'm on my way."

Twelve minutes later, she is starting her Honda. When the engine catches and turns, she notes in her log that the time is 4:17 a.m. She drives toward the address she was given, taking corners too quickly and running red lights on the deserted streets. In the dark, she nearly misses the street. Not all the streets at this end of town are well marked. She slams on her brakes. The rear tires of the Honda lock up and squeal. She slams the car into reverse, backs up 40 feet and swings onto a dead-end street.

Halfway down the block, under the pool of a streetlight, she can see a state police car parked at the curb. Behind it is a small red car. An ambulance is parked in the middle of the street. Only its parking lights are on. A paramedic and an EMT have unloaded a stretcher and stand beside it, waiting.

Light streams from the first-floor windows of a nearby dilapidated two-story house. She parks 20 feet behind the red car, in front of a battered old green pickup truck. She grabs her shoulder bag and exits the Honda. She has a quick impression of a nearby dark and wooded area. The air is damp. She smells dog waste. Shouts are coming from the house.

As she approaches, the paramedic tosses a glowing cigarette into the middle of the street.

"Hey," he says. "You from county children and youth?"

"No, I'm from Family Services. Non-profit agency. Not the county. What's going on?"

"Ha. You tell me. Statie just told us to stand back. The county social worker guy is already in there, but he doesn't seem to be doing much good. From the conversation they're having, I guess someone was beating the shit out of a little girl. Girl is hiding. We got a call for a domestic, but they told us to stage until the officer gives us the all-clear."

"Do you know the names of the parents?" she asks.

"No. We don't get that from dispatch. Just an address. You want me to call in and ask?"

"No, that's OK. Thanks," Cindy says. She smiles and walks toward the house.

The porch is long unpainted, the floorboards worn gray and smooth. The steps creak and groan. The voices grow clearer. The door is open. A greasy smell emanates from the house. Inside is a living room with stained yellow carpet and dark paneled walls. She sees a state police officer in gray and black near the door, clearly identified by his Smokey the Bear-style hat. Beside him stands a redhead. Must be the county Children and Youth caseworker. On call, like she is. She wonders if he volunteered for the on-call duty as she did.

The county caseworker holds a clipboard. He and the police officer are talking to a man and a woman who stand with their backs to a sagging gray couch. At one end of the room is a staircase; at the other, a soundless TV showing a Steven Seagal movie.

" – And you can just get the fuck out of my god-damn house!" the male shouts.

He's wearing a black t-shirt with a Pittsburgh Steelers logo on the front. He's in a pair of sagging gray boxer shorts. He's thin and wiry. His receding gray hair is slicked back on his head. His mouth is twisted in fury. At his side is a pudgy woman in a faded ankle-length nightgown. She has one dirty pink slipper on. She looks more scared than angry. The couple and the trooper are about 10 feet apart.

"Mr. Edinburger," the red-haired caseworker says, "I believe I've been quite clear. I can't leave until I see your daughter and make sure that she's OK."

The man's eyes are wild. "Look, you goddamn neb-noser, I told you that everything is just fine here! You got no goddamn business here and you can just take yourself right back out that goddamn door and drive the fuck away! We'll handle our own family business right here without you sticking your goddamn nose –"

She knocks politely on the open door. Four pairs of eyes turn to her. She can see that the state policeman recognizes her status instantly. He's tall, broad and dark-haired. He looks to be about 40. She senses that he's frustrated but is too professional to show it.

"And who the fuck are you?" the skinny man asks with the exaggerated indignation of the intoxicated.

"Cindy Phillips, Family Services. I was paged out by state police dispatch. May I?"

The man's eyes widen. His mouth opens. "Oh, that's just great! Another professional neb-noser in my house! Just what I ordered!"

"Mr. Edinburger is reluctant to let us verify the condition of his daughter," the redheaded caseworker says to Cindy. "I was thinking that maybe a woman's touch ...."

"Get the fuck out!" the man yells. "That's the only touch I need!"

Cindy turns to the angry man. Her eyes connect with his with an almost audible click.

"Mr. Edinburger, may I come in?"

"Well, shit, half the damn town is in my living room, you might as well come in, too!"

She looks at the couple. The man is defiant. The woman, eyes down, shifts from slippered foot to non-slippered foot. Cindy steps inside the door and speaks without breaking the eye contact with the man.

"Mr. Edinburger," she says, "the best way to get this situation taken care of is for some talking. Now I know that you're frustrated and you would like everyone to leave –"

"Goddamn right!" he yells.

"– but I think you know that if you will give me a few minutes of your time, we can get this situation resolved a lot faster. Because, to be honest with you, Mr. Edinburger, if the caseworkers can't resolve this, then the police officer will have to."

She shifts her eyes momentarily but significantly to the state trooper, who inclines his head slightly. "And I don't think we want that to happen. Not tonight, do we, sir?"

The angry man narrows his eyes, glaring, but then drops them.

"Whadda you want?" he asks.

"Mr. Edinburger, I just need a few minutes. Please give me a minute to talk with these two gentlemen. I think I can get them to leave. Then I need to talk with you. Please."

"If it'll get everyone out of my house, then ...." He makes an aimless gesture and then shifts his eyes to the TV. He picks up a silver beer can from a small table and takes a swig. He sits down on the couch, eyes on the TV, pointedly ignoring his home's intruders. The woman sits down beside him.

Cindy, the caseworker and the officer step outside onto the porch. The young caseworker holds out his hand to Cindy.

"Frank James, Children and Youth. Nice work there."

"Cindy Phillips, Family Services. Maybe I can unwind this a little if you and the officer would step outside for just a minute," she says.

The officer extends a giant hand.

"Palin," he says. She takes the hand and shakes.

"Cindy Phillips, Family Services. Thank you for the page."

The trooper shrugs his broad shoulders. "We can't haul everyone off to the tank."

"Can you give me ten minutes with Mr. Edinburger and his wife? I'll see what I can do."

"Kid's hiding in that closet," Palin says, gesturing to a closet door underneath the staircase. "Neighbor heard crying and screams and called it in."

"Isn't this in the city?" Cindy asks. "Why didn't the city police respond?"

"This is actually just outside the city, in the township. No local police," Palin says.

"Well, Officer Palin, thank you for responding. I think I can resolve this if I have a few minutes with the couple."

"That's not his wife," the young caseworker says. "Not legally, anyway. Girlfriend or common law. The child is his, but that's not her mother."

"Thank you, Frank," Cindy says.

"We've been here before," Frank continues. "He's always here, but with different women." He lowers his voice and leans toward Cindy. "He's the abuser. The girl is five, she's from a failed marriage. No siblings. We think that he takes out his frustration on her. She showed up at a daycare two weeks ago with bruises. The director called us. We didn't have enough evidence to remove her. No signs of sexual abuse, just physical and psychological. If you can find justification to get her out of here, we have a foster family lined up."

There is a moment of silence, then Frank says, "OK, well. We'll just step out for a minute. As I said, maybe a woman's touch ...." He is smiling.

She smiles back.

"Thank you, Frank, Officer Palin. I'll try to move this forward."

The two men leave the porch, squeaking down the creaky wooden steps.

"They can just keep walkin'!" Mr. Edinburger shouts, rousing himself from his feigned attention to the TV.

Once the two men are off the porch, Cindy re-enters and introduces herself to the couple. The man's hand is hard and he eyes her as he shakes. She can smell alcohol on him. The woman's hand is damp and limp. The man introduces himself as Gene and "his woman" as Greta.

"May I sit down?" she asks. The man gestures toward a black battered rocking chair in a corner. She drags it over and sits on it in front of the couch, facing the couple.

"Now, Mr. Edinburger, I didn't get any details when the dispatcher asked me to come out here. So maybe you could just tell me what's going on."

He licks his lips, glances at the TV, and looks down at his hands.

"Well, I always said that a father got to be firm. So when Brittany started actin' up, I had to straighten her out." He looks up at Cindy. "She's got a mouth on her. She knows words I didn't teach her."

"Children can be frustrating," Cindy says.

He looks at her. It doesn't seem to be the response that he expected.

After a moment, he asks, "You got any of your own?"

Cindy smiles. "No. I just got out of college. But I hope to start a family soon."

He eyes her. "College girl, huh?"

"In this field, if you want a job, you pretty much have to," she says.

"Never got there myself. Went to the school of hard knocks, like my daddy did."

"What do you do, Mr. Edinburger?"

"Laid off right now. I work for a sawmill upcounty. McClatchy's." He holds up his right hand so she can see that two joints of the little finger are missing.

Knowing he wants a reaction, she winces. "Ooh. That looks bad. It must be dangerous work. Did it hurt?"

"Never even knew it happened till Sonny looked over at me and said, 'Gene, why you got blood all over you?' I looked down and sure enough there was blood all over my coverall. We found the finger layin' there in the sawdust. But the foreman wouldn't let me take off to go to the hospital. Doctor said later if I'd-a got to the emergency room right away, they might of saved it."

"Oh, that's terrible," Cindy says. "Do you miss it?"

He chuckles. "You'd be surprised. You don't use that finger for much."

"Mr. Edinburger, you must be pretty tough to handle the loss of a finger like that."

"Well, hell, like I said, I didn't feel nothin'. It just must have sliced it off clean."

There is silence. The TV buzzes. There is a scuffling sound to Cindy's right. She glances over and sees a bar of light from under the closet door under the staircase. A section of the light is blocked out.

"Mr. Edinburger, Greta, you know why I'm here."

"Because one of our goddamned neighbors can't mind her own business," he says.

"I understand your frustration, Mr. Edinburger. But these days, there are certain laws to protect children and once someone calls the police – well ...."

"You can call me Gene."

"Thank you, Gene. Please call me Cindy. So you understand that we have to accomplish certain things tonight."

His eyes return to the TV. "Whatever." He takes a swig of his beer, then swings the can from side to side. "Greta."

The woman takes his empty can, gets up silently and walks to the kitchen. When she opens the door of the refrigerator, Cindy notices that the entire lower shelf is stocked with silver cans. Greta selects one, pops the top and walks back. She hands it to Gene. She sits down again, eyes directed to one side.

"Gene, Greta, I need to talk to Brittany. I need to see her."

Both of their eyes slide to the closet, then back. Greta's then slide to the TV. Gene meets Cindy's gaze.

"And what if I said that girls like her just don't get to talk to people who barge into my house?" He slurps from his beer can.

"Gene, I know that you want to be a good father –"

"And I am!" he says.

"– and that you want the best for Brittany –"

"She'd do a lot better without that mouth."

"– and that you want to get me out of your house." She smiles. "And I would like to leave you alone. But I can't until I see Brittany."

"She's all right. She's always all right. She just needs straightenin' out."

"Gene, did you hit her tonight?"

Greta glances quickly at Gene, then away. His eyes slide to the side.

"I might of grabbed her. You know, to control her. She's uncontrollable when she gets goin'. She's got too much of her mother in her."

"Gene, if you grabbed her and left marks, then that might be considered abuse. In that case, I might have to remove her."

He looks up, his bloodshot eyes meeting Cindy's. "Remove her for what? For having a smart mouth and not listenin' to her daddy? Is that a crime all of a sudden?"

"No one is talking about a crime here, Gene. That's for Trooper Palin outside. In here, we're talking about what is best for Brittany. And for you. And for Greta. Maybe it would be best if Brittany were away for a while. To give you a chance to think things over."

"What kind of things? I don't have nothin' to think over."

"Well, your feelings toward her. Maybe she does remind you a little too much of her mother. Maybe you don't have all good feelings toward her mother. That's normal, Gene. It's hard to handle breaking up with someone. But sometimes kids get caught in the middle and they get hurt when it's not their fault. Sometimes kids get hurt and parents don't mean to hurt them, but it kind of just happens."

Gene is looking at the TV.

"Gene, it might be best for everyone if Brittany had a little break from this family."

Gene is still watching TV. Greta is watching her hands in her lap.

"You don't even know her. How do you know what's best for her?"

"Gene, I don't. I don't know. That's why I need to see Brittany."

He sips from his beer. "She's around."

"Gene, I know she's around. But I need to see her in privacy. Somewhere where I can talk to her."

"She's got a room upstairs. Right top of the stairs."

"Gene. Greta. Thank you."

Cindy stands up and pushes the rocking chair back. She walks toward the closet door.

"Well, Christ, woman," says Gene behind her. "Turn the goddamned volume up."

Cindy sees that a small silver sliding-bolt lock has been placed on the closet door. It is crooked. The bolt slides into U-shaped piece of metal screwed into the doorframe. It is in its locked position. Cindy puts a hand on the door. "Brittany?"

The volume on the TV behind her goes up. She hears televised gunshots. Someone shouts.

"Brittany? I'm here to help you. Will you talk to me?"

Inside the closet there is a shuffle, a floor squeak. Cindy crouches down, facing the closet door.

"Brittany, I know that you heard what I said to your father and Greta. My name is Cindy. I'm here to help you if you need help."

Silence.

"Brittany, if you got hurt, if someone is hurting you, it's really important that I talk to you. I can help you. I know you're scared. But daddy is watching TV. We can talk. We'll go up to your room and talk, just you and me. Just girl talk."

Silence. Then a sob. "I want my mommy!"

"Brittany!" Cindy leaps to her feet and slides the lock. She opens the door. Hanging inside the closet is a profusion of jackets, sweaters. Crushed shoes clutter the floor. Sagging cardboard boxes are stacked around the sides. A single naked light bulb illuminates the closet. Underneath, in the shadow of the hanging garments, on a scratched wooden floor, is a small girl, dark-haired, barefoot, in a thin white nightgown. Her head is down and she's hugging a purple-and-white cloth doll.

A vision explodes before Cindy. She is looking up at a male's distorted, angry face.

I just wanted my dolly.

I don't give a good goddamn what you wanted! You stupid little shit! Get back up to your room before I kick your skinny little ass!

But Miss Pretty is right over there!

It so unfair. She just wants Miss Pretty so she can sleep. She is right there on the living room floor. She takes a step toward the doll. Maybe she can — from nowhere, a blow to her head. Her head snaps to the side; her body twists; her cheek burns.

Didn't you hear what I said? A voice tight with fury. Get goddamned upstairs or I'm going to hurt you so bad you wish you'd never got born!

Her arm is grasped with a jerk. Her shoulder snaps. A jolt of pain shoots down her arm and across her chest. She cries out. Something slams into her ribs. Suddenly it is hard to breathe. By her hurting arm, she is lifted with irresistible force. Something slams into her belly, stealing the rest of her breath. Then again. Her wind is gone. She is gasping. At the junction of her ribs and her belly, a blow. Something clicks in her chest and a red burn spreads from there. She can't breathe. She twists, suspended by an arm. Someone is screaming. Her vision spins and blurs. Pain shoots through her body; she cannot escape; she swings and twists, her shoulder snapping painfully, the blows to her body come again and again ....

Cindy realizes that she has slumped against the doorframe. The little girl is looking up at her with concern. There are tracks of tears down the girl's cheeks, but she's not crying now. Cindy notices a purple bruise on her left arm, just above the elbow and below the frilly sleeve of the nightgown. It's a strange shape, a wavy line with three narrow humps. Cindy recognizes it instantly as the bruise left by fingers when someone grabs and squeezes hard.

"Are you OK, lady? You're not my mommy. I thought maybe you would take me to my mommy."

Cindy crouches down to be at the girl's level. She has a wide face, curly brown hair. Her eyes are dark. There is pain in them. Her nightgown is too small and threadbare. Her toenails are too long. She clutches the doll, but Cindy notices that she's tentative with her left arm.

"Hello. What is your name?"

"Brittany. Who are you?"

"Brittany. What a pretty name. My name is Cindy."

"I heard that."

"Brittany, I would really like to talk to you. Can we go up to your room?"

"I'm not in trouble?"

"No, Brittany, you're not in trouble. I just want to talk to you."

"But my daddy is in trouble, isn't he? There was a policeman here."

"No one's in trouble yet, Brittany, and no one has to be in trouble. But I'd like to talk to you alone, without your daddy around."

"Did Daddy say it's OK? If he gets mad at me, he hits me."

"Oh, Brittany, I'm sorry to hear that. But your daddy said it's OK for you to talk to me. Can we go up to your room? Just you and me."

The girl puts one dirty finger in her mouth.

"Can I bring Dolly?"

"Of course you can. I wouldn't want you to leave her here. She might get scared."

Brittany looks around the closet and shivers.

"This is where daddy puts me when he's really mad at me. He says I'm supposed to be in here and think about how bad I am."

Cindy touches the girl's shoulder. "Oh, Brittany. You're not a bad girl. Sometimes you might make your daddy angry, but that doesn't make you bad. In fact, that's why I'm here. I want to help you and your daddy get along better."

"Will he stop hitting me?"

"Well, that's what we want to do, Brittany."

"Will I have to stay in the closet any more?"

"I hope not."

"Daddy says I'm a little shit and I need to watch my mouth. But I just want to go see Mommy. Why can't I go live with Mommy? She doesn't hit me."

"Brittany, I don't know your mommy. I don't know why you can't go see her. But I think –"

"I do go see her. Down at the jail. I get to see her in the place where you eat. But I can't sit on her lap. The policemen there won't let me."

"Brittany, I just want to talk to you a little bit and see if we can help you get into a situation where you're happier."

"What's a sitch-you-son?"

"Situation. A place. A place where you can be happy and where no one hits you or hurts you. Can we talk?"

Brief silence. "OK. Let's go up to my room."

Cindy helps the girl to her feet. She notices another bruise on the back of Brittany's leg, just below her left buttock. That bruise is yellow streaked with brown. At least a week old, Cindy thinks. The bruise is huge on the child's skinny leg, the size of an adult hand.

Cindy lets Brittany take the lead. Clutching Dolly, Brittany peers carefully around the closet door. Gene and Greta are pretending to watch TV. Brittany scuttles to the stairs, then darts up. Cindy walks to the steps, catching a glimpse of Frank and Palin outside. Frank gives her a thumbs-up from the sidewalk. Palin is sitting inside his cruiser, door open, the interior lights on, talking on the radio.

Cindy walks up the worn and creaky wooden stairs to Brittany's room. Brittany has not turned the light on. Cindy stops at the door and looks inside. She can't see Brittany. She knocks lightly on the open door.

"Brittany? Are you here?"

"Shh!" comes a hissing whisper. "Over here. Under the bed. Don't let Daddy see you."

Cindy enters and goes to her hands and knees to look under the bed. Brittany has pressed herself as far under the bed as she can get, back against the wall. She is holding Dolly to her chest, stroking the doll's yarn hair.

"Brittany, I think it will be OK to talk out here. Can you come out?"

"If Daddy sees me out of the closet, he'll smack me."

"Brittany, Daddy said it was OK for us to talk up here. He knows you're out of the closet."

Long pause. "Are you sure?"

"Yes, Brittany, I'm sure. Your daddy won't hit you as long as I'm here."

Brittany scuttles out from under the bed and Cindy finds herself powerfully clutched by the little girl. "Then you don't ever leave."

Cindy moves so she can sit on the floor. Brittany pours herself onto Cindy's lap, still clutching her. Cindy strokes the girl's hair. It is greasy and unwashed. She can smell that Brittany could use a bath. In her arms, the girl is light and thin and fragile.

Cindy begins rocking, stroking Brittany's hair. Without meaning to, she finds herself singing quietly.

On yonder hill there stands a maiden, who she is, I do not know.
I'll go and ask her hand in marriage, she must answer yes or no.
Oh, no, John, no John, no John, no.
My father was a Spanish captain, went to sea a month ago.
First he kissed me, then he left me, bid me always answer no.
Oh, no John, no John, no John, no.

Oh madam in your face is beauty, on your lips red roses grow.
Will you take me for your husband, madam answer yes or no.
   Oh, no John, no John, no John, no.
Oh madam since you are so cruel, and that you do scorn me so,
If I may not be your husband, madam will you let me go?
   Oh no John, no John, no John, no.
Oh hark, I hear the church bells ringing. Will you come and be my wife?
Or dear madam have you settled to live single all your life?
   Oh no John, no John, no John, no.

When the song is over, she realizes that Brittany's breathing has become slow and regular. "Brittany?"

The child is asleep.

Cindy sighs deeply.

Chapter Nineteen

On a Friday, Cindy's supervisor finds her in Family Service's small lunch room. She pulls out a chair and sits down. Cindy pushes aside the slices of apple she was eating. She was warned by Dr. Jacobi to never bite into an apple because her front teeth aren't real and she might dislodge them. "You had some pretty good dental work done there, but don't go asking for trouble," he said.

"Vivian," Cindy says to greet her boss.

"Cindy. How's lunch?"

"Good."

Vivian sighs. "About the Edinburger case."

"I know," Cindy says. "The placement recommendation isn't going to hold."

"Cindy, it's true that Brittany is bruised. But five-year-old kids get bruises. They fall out of trees, they –"

"They don't get bruises that look like scallops from falling out of a tree."

Vivian sighs again. "Cindy, I –"

"And what about her statements? She's terrified of her father. She lives under her bed. She never knows what's going to set him off. Did you read my report? He hit her because she got up too early one morning and turned on the TV and woke him up. It was only noon. What an ungodly hour that is."

"Cindy, of course I read your report. I understand that you're trying to help Brittany. I believe you. But if this case goes to a hearing, there's just not enough evidence to support removing Brittany."

"Not enough evidence? Bruises, the little girl saying how she gets hit at least a dozen times a day, the fact that I found her locked in a closet. None of that matters? No judge is going to think that's enough to get her out of that horrible situation?"

"Cindy, parental rights are strong and hard to overcome. There has to be very strong evidence of unusual abuse before we can even hope to win a removal case. And even then, we lose too many of them."

"And Brittany's statements to me don't mean anything? Just because she's five doesn't mean that she can't count how many times a day she's hit!"

"Cindy, please calm down. I'm on your side here. I'm just telling you that there is no way we can defend removing her from the home right now. If we do, and her father gets a lawyer, she'll be back in his custody within the day."

Cindy opened her mouth to protest, but Vivian continued speaking.

"And, Cindy, if we do place Brittany with a foster family, and then she ends up going back to her natural father, it's just that much more traumatic for her. You know that a lot of kids get blamed for all the hassle and expense when they get returned to their natural parents. And then the abuse is even worse."

Cindy felt like crying, but she fought it back. "So you're telling me that it's better for Brittany to stay there and get smacked a dozen times a day than to go to a foster family. Because if, God forbid, some judge decides to send her home, Gene will beat her even harder. So Brittany has the choice between being abused and being abused worse. Is that what you're telling me?"

"In so many words, yes."

"That's insane. That's just insane." Cindy can't meet Vivian's eyes. She grabs a slice of apple and chews it furiously, just for something to do. "What a life. She's certainly going to grow up to be a kind, well-adjusted adult."

"Cindy, we're still waiting on the x-rays. If it turns out that her arm is fractured, I'll support you a hundred percent for removal to a foster family. But even then, I warn you, it might not be enough. Kids do break their arms falling out of trees."

"Yeah. And their parents don't take them to the hospital and just let them suffer. That's normal. It's normal when a little girl hides under her bed and only comes out when a stranger tells her that it's OK and then she falls asleep in that stranger's lap because it's the first time she's felt safe in God knows how long. Tell me that's normal."

Cindy's eyes are blazing. Vivian is unsure of what to say. There is an awkward silence. Cindy closes her eyes, breathes deeply, then opens them.

"I'm sorry. That was uncalled for. I know you're just doing the best that you can. I know you have tons of experience in this and you're trying to guide me. I'm sorry I'm such a pig-headed idiot. I just –"

"Cindy, you can't save them all."

Cindy looks into Vivian's eyes.

"You know, that's it," Cindy says. "That's my problem, isn't it? I want to save them all."

Vivian pats Cindy's hand.

"The reality of it is, honey, you have to pick your fights. You save the ones you can. Some you lose no matter what you do. And you just learn to live with that because you know that if you lose five but save one, at least that one was saved."

"That's a horrible ratio," Cindy says.

"It's horrible but it's accurate," Vivian says. "Cindy, you're great at this job. I've never seen anyone with your rapport with kids. They just take to you. And you're good with clients because you show them respect. But you have to realize that you're going to lose some of these kids. And it's going to break your heart. But if you don't just move on and try again and again, then you burn out and then ...."

"And then the abusers win," Cindy says. "Because then you're not saving any of them."

"In this business, you need to find a reason to get out of bed every morning," Vivian says. "You have to be ready to fight the battle all over again every day. Every day, you have to be able to answer the question, 'why do I keep doing this?'"

"You do it because it's infinitely better than not doing it, no matter how many you lose. Right?"

"Right," Vivian says. She pats Cindy's hand again and stands. "Let me know when you get those x-rays."

As Vivian leaves, Cindy chews another apple slice. She can't stop thinking.

There has to be some way to save more children. Some way to protect more of them. Some way. There has to be a way. Even making a small difference in the system would make a big difference to the kids. We can't keep doing what we're doing and hope that things will get better.

Back at her desk, her phone rings and Cindy picks it up.

"Family Services, this is Cindy Phillips."

"Mrs. Phillips, I'm calling from Altoona Hospital radiology. We have results on Brittany Edinburger. We can confirm a greenstick fracture to Brittany's left humerus, about ten centimeters above the elbow. We estimate the fracture at two to three days old."

"I'm sorry. Can you translate that middle part for me? I'm afraid I'm a medical moron."

The woman on the other end of the line chuckles.

"Certainly, Mrs. Phillips. Brittany's left upper arm was fractured – broken – about two days ago. But it wasn't a break all the way through the bone, as you would normally think of a break. Instead, as with many children who are still growing, there is damage only to one side of the bone. Like if you try to break a stick that's still green. You know, if it's dry and old, it snaps. But if it's still green, it just splinters but it doesn't separate."

"Is there any sign that it was treated?"

"Well, we don't have any records that she was treated here. But even if she was taken to another hospital, there's often not much you can do for a greenstick fracture except tell the kid to take it easy. They usually heal pretty much on their own."

Cindy felt her case for removal collapsing.

"So, even if Brittany's arm was technically broken, and she was treated by a doctor, there's not much that he could have done."

"Probably give her something for the pain. Maybe put her arm in a simple sling. Told her parents to try to get her to take it easy. No tree climbing, that kind of thing."

"How do kids usually get these kinds of breaks?"

"Greenstick fractures? Oh, they're pretty common with kids. They get them from anything. Taking a tumble off a bike. Falling out of bunk bed. Out of a tree. Wrestling. You know, typical kid stuff."

"I see. Well, thank you. Can you send those records over?"

"Sure. We'll get them right over to you."

"Thank you so much. You've been very helpful."

"Glad I could help."

Cindy walks to Vivian's office with a heavy heart.

Chapter Twenty

Cindy parks her car outside City Hall. She walks two flights of stairs to the police department. At the window, a policeman with a bulging belly asks her what she wants. She shows her Family Services ID card and asks if she can see any records that the department has on Eugene Edinburger of 1506 North Eighth Avenue.

He eyes her ID with suspicion, his chair creaking as he shifts. "Official business?"

She nods.

"All right. Door over there to your right. Go back in. Tell 'em Roger said it's OK."

Cindy thanks him and walks to the door indicated. It looks like it has been painted too many times. The current color is black. The window is frosted and sectioned into diamonds by thin wires in the glass. In chipped gold leaf, the door reads "Records."

Cindy pushes it open. It groans.

Inside is a short hallway. A battered gray coat rack to her right. Doors open to the left, right and straight ahead. "Detectives" reads the door on the right. The door is open and two untidy desks are inside. The door on the left is unlabeled. Filing cabinets fill it. The carpet under her feet is threadbare and orange. She walks down the hallway into the doorway straight ahead. Inside are two army-issue green desks. On one is a putty-colored computer monitor with fingerprints along its sides. To her right, a fax machine sits on a small table before a bricked-in fireplace. Two floor-to-ceiling windows overlook the downtown. The same hideous carpet covers the floor. There is no one in the room.

"Hello?" Cindy says tentatively. No answer. The is a door out of the room to her right and she can hear someone tapping on a keyboard.

"Hello?" she asks again.

There is a squeak of chair and a short, portly woman in a gray police uniform walks through the doorway and into the room. Cindy notices that she wears a badge and the standard black leather police belt with handcuff pouch, holstered automatic handgun and snapped-closed pockets holding magazines for the gun. Her brown hair is pulled back in a bun. She is chewing gum.

"Can I help you?"

"Yes. I'm Cindy Phillips from Family Services. I'm looking for information about Eugene Edinburger. The officer at the front desk sent me back here. Roger."

The woman chews her gun, eyeing Cindy. "You got ID?"

Cindy shows her the Family Services card. The woman inspects it briefly, then hands it back. Her gum smells like spearmint.

"All right. Yeah. Whaddya want to know?"

"Well, I'm looking for any records on Gene – uh, Eugene. Arrests, DUI, that kind of thing."

The woman pulls a pencil and a small notepad from her belt. "Spell it."

"Ee-dee-eye-en-bee-you-are-gee-ee-are. Eugene. Goes by Gene."

Address?"

Cindy gives it to her.

"Aliases? Former addresses?"

"None that I know of." Cindy tries a smile, but the woman is impervious.

"Yeah. All right. Have a seat over there. I'll be right back." She leaves the room by the door Cindy came in.

Cindy perches tentatively on a battered office chair in front of the desk with the computer on it. The monitor gives off a hum. The chair abruptly lists to one side, threatening to dump her on the floor. She grabs the desk to keep from tipping over. The chair is unbelievably uncomfortable. Despite a fabric covering, the seat is hard as steel. Cindy has to sit straight upright or the chair tips precariously. It feels like it balances on a needle point. Maybe they make bad guys sit here to psych them out, she thinks.

Somewhere someone is talking on a phone. A radio crackles and a voice says something. None of it is understandable. She waits. The room's ceiling is high, the many-times-painted walls showing relics of art deco. The building was probably built in the city's spurt of commercial and civic enthusiasm during the 1930s, she thinks. Little did the city know that it was about to be blindsided. Built on the railroad industry, the city had prospered from the expansion of railroads from the mid-1800s through World War II. Then came Truman and the national highway construction program. Suddenly, people were shipping by truck, not by rail. People began driving their own cars, not taking passenger trains. The town's fortunes plunged rapidly. Its population peaked at 90,000 in the late 1940s. But today, fewer than 40,000 people lived within the city limits.

An officer walks into the office, gray-haired, with what looks like sergeant's stripes on his shoulder. He hangs his flat police hat on a rack in the corner, then notices Cindy.

"Can I help you?"

She smiles. "I'm waiting for some records. Someone's helping me. Thank you."

"Who you waiting on?"

Cindy is confused. She didn't notice the name of the female officer who was helping her.

"I, uh, didn't –"

The female officer walks into the room reading from a red folder. "Edinburger, Eugene G. Uh huh. Last year, assault reduced to disorderly. Judge. Hmm. Shoplifting – jeez, that's old. Well, not much here." She closes the folder and hands it to Cindy. "You can write down whatever you want, but you'll need –" she notices the sergeant. "Oh, hi, Rob. Well, you'll need his permission to copy anything." She looks at Rob. "And you can't take the folder out of this room. If you want the full records, you can access them on that computer there." She points to the smudged monitor. "He's on the screen. I called it up for you. Anything else?"

The folder holds maybe 20 sheets of paper.

"No, if I can just look at that and the computer records, that should be OK. Thank you."

"All right. Leave the folder on the desk when you're done. I'll log the computer out." The woman nods at Cindy, says "Rob" to the male officer and leaves the room.

"Is that Gene Edinburger, North Eighth?"

"Yes," Cindy says, apprehensive about his intent. Maybe he doesn't want her to see the file.

"Oh, yeah, Gene," the officer says, shaking his head. "I busted him for a DUI, what, maybe three years ago. It's a Saturday night out on Logan Boulevard. Oh-four-hundred. He's driving maybe 30 miles an hour. I figure, this has to be a drunk, right? Most people do fifty, maybe push sixty on that road."

The officer sits down on the desk beside Cindy, one foot on the floor, one raised. "I mean, who the fuh — who drives thirty? Ever? So I hit the lights and pull him over. He's perfectly courteous, you know, officer this and officer that. Yeah. He says he had a couple beers at a friend's house a few hours ago, but he's sober as a judge now. Right. So I get him out and make him walk the line. Well, it's borderline, I'll admit. I mean, if you met the guy walking down the street, you'd think, OK, he's drunk. I could fuh– I could smell it on him. You know. But he does OK on the field test. So I gave him the breathalyzer. Damn if it don't come back right on the line of legal. I know this guy's drunk, but what am I supposed to do? I let him go and he kills someone, that's on me. But if I run him in and he lawyers up, I'm going to lose in the courtroom. So ...." The officer lifts his hands and moves them apart. "Whaddaya do? I ran him in. Hospital, blood tests, the whole shebang.

"Well, the guy was borderline to start with and by the time those asswipes at the hospital can give me a minute of their precious time, he's pretty well below point-one. That's back when point-one was the legal limit, you know."

Cindy nods.

"So I cut him loose. I pretty much forget about it, you know. I write it off. I figure one day before long I'll be called into court and he'll have some asshole lawyer there who'll make me look like an idiot and he'll get off. But that's the job, you know? Comes with the territory.

"So, anyway, I'll be damned if I'm not sitting at the same spot about three weeks after I pull ol' Gene over, and here he comes again, chugging along at thirty down the boulevard. Only this time, it's broad daylight. I was real careful timing him. He wasn't doing a mile over thirty-one. He still drive that piece-of-shit green pickup?"

Cindy nods.

"Well, anyway, here he comes, still doing thirty. He waves to me. You know what I think? I think that guy just fuh– just drives like that. That's his normal speed. He just chugs along. In no hurry."

The officer snorts a laugh.

"So that's Gene Edinburger. Right there."

"What ever happened with the DUI?" Cindy asks.

"Oh yeah. That's the hell of it. Court date gets set, right? I show up, badge and shoes polished, all that. I figure I'll do the best I can. Well, he's got this slippery local lawyer. Beck. Asshole. Can you believe the guy's case? He goes after cause!"

Cindy widens her eyes, but she's not sure what the officer means.

"Cause! He questions my reason for pulling the guy over in the first place! I tell him, well, the guy's driving thirty in a stretch where most people do fifty, fifty-five. At four in the morning. You know, most bars finally decide they better quit serving at three-thirty.

"And this lawyer says, well, your honor –" the officer draws himself up as if addressing a judge "– my client usually drives at that speed, so the officer's basis of reasoning for pulling him over is moot, ipso facto, or some shit like that.

"And the judge gets Gene up there on the stand and asks him, so, Gene, do you usually drive thirty? Now, remember, Gene, you're under oath. Like that would matter to Gene. Gene, who's not the sharpest knife in the drawer, but who's not that stupid, says, why, yes, your honor, I drive thirty everywhere I go. I'm in no damn hurry.

"And so the judge lets him go! I mean, I fully expected to lose that one, but not on the grounds that Gene drives like a damn farmer!"

The officer laughs. "So there, that's Gene Edinburger for you." He stops to eye Cindy as if he just noticed her. "What's your interest in Mr. Edinburger?"

"I'm from Family Services," she says.

"He still smacking around that girl of his?"

"Wife, daughter or girlfriend?" Cindy asks.

The officer laughs, mistaking her question for an inside joke.

"Right! Gene's an equal-opportunity abuser!"

"Did he ever hit his wife?" Cindy asks seriously.

"His wife? The smack-addict? Oh, hell. You can ask the county welfare workers, but I'll bet that they made trips out to his house monthly if not weekly. He starts drinking, he gets pretty slap-happy."

"And his daughter?" Cindy asks, afraid of the answer.

The officer turns serious. "That little girl. What is she now?"

"Five."

"Five. Right. Yeah. Well, we don't get up there much because that's outside the city limits. But I did an assist with the state boys out there two years ago. The place was a mess, people screaming, neighbors out on the porches. He was having a fight with his latest camping partner." The officer nudges Cindy on the shoulder. "Know what I mean?"

She nods. She's not sure what the officer means, but she can guess.

"Little girl's in the closet, he's toasted, his woman is in bra and panties, they're outside on the sidewalk screaming at each other. Yeah. Real quality people. Just the sort you want next door."

The officer's belt beeps stridently and he says, "Excuse me." He pulls a walkie-talkie from his belt and walks to the other side of the room, muttering into the radio.

Cindy turns to the folder. She pages through the police reports, typed up on pages lined with black boxes requiring certain pieces of information. She's amazed that the officers can manage to collect such detail on what must often be chaotic scenes. Eye color. Type of clothing. Nearest cross street. Lots of dates and times. In a big box taking up the bottom half of each page is where the officers type their description of the incident. The report on top is a dozen sheets of paper related to Gene's arrest for assault of a woman last year. The papers on top are court documents. She skims them. Gene apparently "lawyered up," as the sergeant had said and the judge reduced the charge from assault to disorderly conduct. She pages toward the back of the packet, finding the original officer's report. An officer Steven showed up at Gene's house on a domestic assault called in by a neighbor. *Wonder if it's the same one who called in Brittany's abuse?* Gene and a woman fighting outside on the sidewalk, as the officer had said. Both arrested; apparently both had been drinking.

She looks deeper into the folder. Eight years ago, Gene was arrested for shoplifting from a sporting goods store. He apparently tried to walk out without paying after putting on a fishing vest. Various lures and a folding knife were found in the pockets. There was no paperwork on the resolution of the case. The other pages are related to the DUI arrest that the sergeant described. Nothing new there. That is all.

Cindy closes the folder and turns to the computer monitor. Its screen is covered with green words that take her a few minutes to decipher. Following commands listed at the bottom of the screen, she scrolls through Gene's criminal record.

There are more details than in the folder, but nothing striking. Cindy stands up, not sure if she is relieved. Gene has had a few scrapes with the law, but he isn't a routine criminal. He isn't showing up in the police reports over and over. That fits with her perception that Gene is basically a decent guy, but whose temper sometimes gets the best of him. She leaves the folder on the desk, mouths a "thank you" to the sergeant, who is still muttering into his walkie-talkie, and leaves.

Chapter Twenty-One

On her way to work, she suddenly veers off her normal route. She realizes that she's heading for Brittany's house. Technically, she's not due for another visit for two weeks. But she wants to check.

Pulling onto Brittany's street, she sees Gene's battered green pickup truck parked in front of the house. She parks behind it and gets out. She sees that the bed of the truck, usually empty except for a spare tire, dry leaves and crushed beer cans, is nearly filled. There are two of what look like long cases for rifles. A tent packaged in a large vinyl drawstring bag. Several ugly bright blue tarps. A pile of logs, all about nine inches in diameter and about two feet long. A shovel. Two blue-and-white plastic coolers each large enough to hold two cases of cans. The driver's-side window of the truck is down.

The front door of the house is open. The TV is blaring. She walks up on the porch and knocks. There's no answer. She knocks again. No response. She hears a noise from behind the house. She walks around back. In the rear is a wooden garage, once painted yellow. Its roof is sagging, a rusted gutter dangling. The door is open and Gene comes out carrying four fishing rods in a bunch. Their lines are snarled. Brittany is right behind him. She is pushing Dolly in a battered plastic stroller sized for dolls.

"... and can I go swimming?" she asks, excited.

"Yeah. Whatever. They'll be a lot to do – goddammit!" Gene tries to put the fishing rods down but the line of one has wrapped around his head. He tries to pull it off, but it snags his ear. "Goddammit!" he swears again. "Motherfucker!" He untangles the fishing line from his head and heaves the cluster of rods across the yard. They land with a clatter. His face is red. When he throws the rods, he notices Cindy. He stops and inclines his head as if he's trying to place her.

"Oh. Yeah. Hi." he says.

"Hello, Gene. Looks like you're planning a trip."

"We're going to the lake!" Brittany yells, running to Cindy. "Hi, Miss Cindy! We're going to the lake!"

"Wow!" Cindy says, bending down to hug Brittany. "That sounds like fun."

"Yeah. Well. We got a little place up north," Gene says. "Share it with a couple other guys. Hunting cabin. There's a lake there, a couple-a nice streams. Nice and quiet. You know."

"Sounds great," Cindy says.

"And our cabin has Jesus in it," Brittany says.

"Jesus?"

"Yeah, Jesus lives with us in the cabin and he's always with us. He protects us."

"One guy is a Jesus freak," Gene says. "He put a cross up on the door. She asked him why and that's what he told her."

"Well, it sounds like you're going to have lots of fun."

Brittany's eyes are shining with excitement. "I get to swim in the lake and Daddy said that he might even take me out on the boat. I love to go out on the boat. There are fish! Daddy paddles and I watch the birds!"

Brittany does a little dance, twirling. She's wearing a dirty t-shirt that's too small and jean shorts. "It's lots of fun up at the lake!"

Cindy stands. "Which lake is it, Gene?"

He has retrieved the tangle of fishing rods. He sits down on a rusting folding chair. He's cutting the fishing lines with a pocketknife.

"Uh. Elk. Elk Lake. Elk County," he says. "You gonna take Brittany from me?"

His eyes are downcast, focused on the fishing gear.

"Gene, I don't have the authority to do that. I just make a recommendation. It's up to the county Children and Youth Department."

"Well, what'd you tell them? You tell them to take her from me?"

Brittany is singing and pushing Dolly in the stroller in a figure eight. She's in her bare feet and Cindy is worried that she might cut her foot. There are rocks and what looks like broken glass in the yard.

"Gene, I think that you and Brittany are – well, you're gas and matches. I think that she sets you off."

"She's got that mouth."

"Yes, Gene, I understand that. But she's five. She doesn't know how much she upsets you when she says certain things."

"Bears!" Brittany yells. "Miss Cindy, we saw a bear up at the lake! It was eating our garbage. Daddy said to stay away from it but he tried to walk up to it."

"Last year," Gene says, tugging at a loop of line. "Bear got in the garbage dump bin."

"Don't worry, Dolly! I'll keep you safe!" Brittany yells, grabs her doll and runs into the garage.

"Gene, things would go a lot easier for you if you could try not to hit her," Cindy says. "Maybe when she's really bothering you and you know that your anger is rising, maybe you could just send her to her room."

Gene looks up, stopping his work.

"You people are all alike," he says. "That's what that asshole from the county told me too. Send her to her room." He spits. "You guys don't get it, do you? That's what I do!" He is yelling. "I tell her to go to her goddamned room and she won't. She don't! Or she comes right back down the stairs with that mouth going about how her mother ain't mean to her and she wants to go live with her mother and how mean I am! Well, shit!" He spits again and begins tugging at the fishing line. "I told her that her goddamned mother is a piece of trash that can't keep a needle out of her arm, but that don't do no good. She still wants to go live with that bitch. Why, I don't know."

He turns his attention to his work.

"Gene, I'm sorry. I know that you try not to hit her."

"Bears! Rar!" Brittany is peeking from the garage door, holding her doll out. "Daddy is a bear! No, Dolly, I'll save you!" she pulls the doll back and disappears into the garage again.

"That's why she ends up in the clos–, in trouble. She don't listen and she don't do what she's told." Gene tugs and one fishing pole is free. He places it on the ground next to him. "That's what the trouble is. She just don't listen."

"Well, Gene, maybe since you're going on this special little trip, you could do something special. I mean, Brittany obviously likes going to the lake, right?"

"Yeah. She loves it up there."

"Well, maybe you could make it really special for her and decide that no matter what she does, you're not going to hit her. Or grab her. Or anything like that. You're just going to keep away from her when she's making you angry. Maybe you could just walk outside and throw rocks into the lake or something."

Gene chuckles. "Yeah. Like that would help."

"Well, anything's better than hitting your little girl, right?"

Gene is silent. He tugs and a second rod is free. He places it on the ground next to the first one.

"Going to have to put new line in all of these," he says.

"Gene."

He looks up and meets her eyes. "I don't want to hit her. I really don't. I just ... she's just ...."

"Gene, I know. I know. Kids can make you nuts. But you're so much bigger and stronger than she is. When you hit her, it really hurts her. And what if you hit her too hard and put her in the hospital or ...."

"Or killed her, yeah, I've thought about that." He looks rueful. "Guy at work's brother smacked his kid, knocked him off a porch. Kid hit his head and died right there. The guy's never been right since."

"It's the anger, Gene. You're not a bad man. I see you right now, sitting here, patiently untangling those fishing rods. I'm sure that you can be that patient with Brittany."

Gene smiles. "Yeah. I guess you're right. Never thought of that. I can be pretty careful when I want to be. That's why I work the front end up at the mill. Boss said I'm reliable. This was just a freak thing," he says, holding up the hand with the missing finger.

"Gene, you're a good man. And I know that you can be a good father. And the best way to do that is to stop letting your anger control you when it comes to Brittany."

"Bears!" Brittany shrieks from inside the garage. She runs out, holding Dolly close to her chest. She runs to the stroller, throws Dolly into the seat and runs toward the house, pushing the stroller ahead of her. "No bears are going to eat us, Dolly! Daddy will protect us! We run away from bears!"

Cindy watches Gene watching Brittany. He is smiling.

"You see?" Cindy says quietly. "I know you love her. I know you want to take care of her. She's a precious little girl. I know that you guys will have a great trip up to the lake. And I know that you won't put your hands on her. Right, Gene?"

He takes his gaze from Brittany. "Yeah. I've been trying to work on that. I'll ... I'll try to make this ... uh, a good trip. You know, not to hit her or nothing."

"Thank you, Gene. I hope you have a good trip."

Gene is back at work on the remaining rods. Cindy turns to leave.

"Hey. Miss Cindy," Gene says.

She stops and turns.

"I didn't mean that when I said that you're like all them other caseworkers. You ain't. You're different."

"Why, thank you, Gene. I appreciate that," she says.

He nods, flushing, then begins tugging on the lines again.

Brittany comes running up to Cindy. She holds a purple flower.

"Miss Cindy, this is for you," she says. "Isn't it pretty?"

Cindy crouches down to be at Brittany's level. "Why, thank you, Brittany. This is a beautiful flower. Thank you very much. It looks like a violet."

"It's a real pretty purple. That's my favorite color, so I wanted to give it to you," she says. Her dark eyes are glowing; her dark hair frames her face. She has a kid's summer tan. *She really is a pretty little girl,* Cindy thinks.

"Thank you so much, Brittany. It's beautiful."

Brittany turns to run away. "Brittany," Cindy says. The girl stops.

"Brittany, can you promise me something?"

The girl comes back. "What, Miss Cindy?"

"Brittany, when you're up at the lake, can you promise me that you won't talk about your mommy to daddy? Just don't talk about her at all."

"Daddy gets mad when I talk about mommy."

"Right. Exactly. When you talk about your mommy, it makes daddy sad. And that's why he gets ... sad."

"And then he smacks me," Brittany says.

"Yes. When your daddy is feeling bad about mommy, he might hit you. So if you don't talk about mommy, then he won't hit you."

"He hits me for other stuff, too. Like one time I dropped Dolly in the potty."

"Well, sometimes those things make big people mad. Because then they have to clean up a mess. Right?"

"Right. Daddy hates it when I make a mess. He gets mad."

"So can you be really careful up at the lake and be nice to daddy and do what he tells you to do?"

"There's no closet up at the lake. So daddy makes me sit in the boat's house. Where the boats stay when we're not there." She wrinkles her nose. "It smells funny in there."

"Well, maybe if you're really nice to daddy, he won't have to yell at you and he won't have to make you go to the boathouse. Can you try to be nice to your daddy and not talk about your mommy?"

"OK!" Brittany says, enthusiastic.

Cindy puts her arms out and the child comes to her for a hug.

"I love you, Miss Cindy. You're nice to me. You talk to me. Nobody ever talks to me. So I talk to Dolly."

Cindy holds the warm, frail little body close to hers. "Oh, Brittany. You're such a wonderful little girl. You just behave for your daddy this weekend, OK?"

They break apart and Cindy can't resist giving Brittany a kiss on one dirty cheek.

"You have to kiss Dolly, too!" Brittany runs to the stroller, retrieves the doll and brings her back. Cindy dutifully kisses the cloth doll on one dirty cheek.

"Dolly likes you too, Miss Cindy," Brittany says.

"And I like Dolly," Cindy says. She ruffles Brittany's hair and then she has to go before the girl sees her tears. As she walks to her car, she can hear Brittany singing.

Once upon a little star, there was a maiden.
Oh, maiden, can I marry you?
Oh, no John, no John, no.

Chapter Twenty-Two

Cindy sits at her desk, surrounded by stacks of reports. Her head is in her hands. Vivian is at her door.

"Cindy?"

Cindy straightens up, wipes her eyes. "Oh. Yes. Vivian. Hi. Come in."

Leaning against the doorframe of Cindy's office, holding a cup of coffee, Vivian says, "Still waiting to hear on the Edinburger case?"

Cindy sighs. "Yes. Frank James caught the case, which is good news, but I don't know how far he can take it."

"What did you recommend?"

"That they do weekly visits. I told them all about her bruises and being locked in the closet. It's all in my report."

"Do you still think she needs to be removed?"

Cindy sighs. "Viv, I just don't know. Gene is such a nice, calm guy ordinarily. I mean, every time I talk to him, he's completely rational and calm. He just doesn't seem like the kind of person who would beat his own kid. But then I look at the bruises on

Brittany and I listen to her stories, and I get a completely different picture of him. It's like he's Jekyll and Hyde. When I'm there, I can see how much he loves her. I can see it by the way he looks at her. But there must be times, late at night, when things go wrong – I don't know. He obviously has a temper. But I think he could learn to control it. I mean, when he sees me coming, he just clamps down on it. But Brittany is just – she's a trigger for him. And it's worse when he drinks. And I think he drinks a lot. You know, the old, 'It's after noon, so it's time for a beer' mentality."

"I've subscribed a few times to that mentality myself," Vivian says.

Cindy laughs. "Well, I can't say that I haven't had a few of those days, too," she says. She sobers. "But in Brittany's case, it just leads to her getting abused."

Chapter Twenty-Three

On her voicemail one day is a message from Frank James, the caseworker for the county Children and Youth agency. She hasn't seen him for weeks.

"How about lunch?" he asks on his message. "I have a case here that requires your special touch."

She calls him and they make arrangements to meet at a downtown cafe that has tables on the sidewalk, a rarity in this blue-collar town. Rumors are that the owner is gay, that he's French, that he's gay and French. She doesn't really care because she loves having lunch outside on a summer day.

The day of the lunch date, she feels sophisticated and European and digs out of the closet a hat that someone gave her in college. "You'd look good in this," the girl said. "I look like an old aunt."

It's a summery straw hat with a blue-and-white polka-dot band. She pairs it with a blue dress and examines herself in the mirror. Still too skinny. Bony hips. Breasts too small. Too pale, but there's not much time for sun tanning with her job. She turns and twists before the mirror. She doesn't like her shape. Is the hat too much? She takes it off and the outfit loses its zing. She puts it back on and gives the mirror the kind of glance that she imagines Parisian women give their lovers when they meet clandestinely at a cafe. She decides to wear the hat, but only for the lunch date. She can't imagine trying to explain it to the people at work.

Later, she is at a tiny round table, sitting in the sun, sipping lemonade. Frank is late. She tells herself that it's OK because this is a working lunch, not a date and he probably got held up at work. She glances at her watch. He's now 15 minutes late. She'll give him 20 minutes, then she'll leave.

She wonders about the hat. Maybe it's too much. After all, this is a working lunch. Frank will get the wrong idea. Or he'll think it silly. Or worse, unprofessional. What was I thinking? This is Altoona, not Paris. Suddenly embarrassed, she pulls the hat off and stashes it under her chair. Maybe she should take it to the car. But now she has hat head. Maybe a visit to the ladies room, maybe she should just leave....

"No, please, leave it on," says a voice behind her. "It's perfect."

She turns and Frank is there. He's in green khakis, a short-sleeved taupe button-down shirt with one front pocket. His wavy red hair is combed back and his little goatee/mustache combo is neatly trimmed. His eyes are green. He is grinning widely.

He walks to the table, one hand behind his back.

"I'm late," he says. "I'm an ass. I'm sorry." He brings his hand out and he's holding a bunch of daffodils wrapped in green paper. She takes them, making an appreciative noise.

"Thank you," she says. "They're very pretty. Would you ...." He bends down and retrieves her hat from under her chair. He holds it in both hands.

"May I?"

She nods.

He places it gently on her head, then steps back. He raises a hand to his chin and adopts the pose of someone examining a work of art.

"Hmmm." he says. "Wait." He reaches out and taps the hat a fraction lower over her brow. He steps back and eyes her again.

"Perfect!" he exclaims. He pulls out a chair and sits down.

"As I was saying, I'm late and I'm sorry," he says. "My father always told me never to keep a pretty woman waiting."

She blushes; she can't help it.

"Frank."

"Oh, right," he says. "I'm sorry again. That was my dad's second rule: Never make a pretty woman blush." He leans toward her across the table. "Unless you want to see her even prettier."

"Frank!"

"Oh, OK, right!" he says, pulling back and snatching a paper menu from between the salt and pepper shakers. "Business lunch. Right." He straightens his back and pretends to focus on the menu. "Well, what's good here? I don't get out much."

"Frank." She can't help smiling at him.

He doesn't turn his head but looks at her from the corner of his eyes. He too is smiling. "I hear that the crab cakes are great. Of course, I don't know how they could be when we're about a ten-hour drive from the ocean. You don't suppose they trap them in the Juniata River, do you?"

"I'm sure the crab cakes are delicious. Everything here is and nothing is fried. Would you please look at me?"

He puts the menu down and turns. He looks directly into her eyes. "Yes?"

"Thank you for the flowers, Frank. They're very nice. They almost make up for your being late."

"Well, actually, they're the reason I'm late," he says. "I realized that I couldn't arrive here without some token of my appreciation. You've really done marvelous things with Gene Edinburger."

"Really?"

"Really," he says. "I was up there late last week and ...."

A waiter appears at their table bearing a pitcher of lemonade.

"More?" he asks Cindy.

"Yes, please."

He pours.

"Sir?"

"That looks great," Frank says. "I just need a glass."

"And are you ready to order?"

Frank looks at Cindy. "No," he says. "We need a few more minutes."

The waiter nods and departs.

"Anyway, I was up there last week and every-one was getting along fine. Gene wasn't exactly happy to see me, but he let me come in and talk to Brittany. She really likes you, you know."

"I like her. She's a beautiful little girl."

"Little girls and butterflies need no excuse," Frank says.

"What?"

"Little girls and butterflies need no excuse. Something Robert Heinlein wrote."

With her eyes and hands, Cindy indicates that she has no idea who Heinlein is.

"Science fiction writer. Wrote great stuff. *Stranger in a Strange Land*. Dead for 20 years. Anyway ...."

The waiter appears with a glass for Frank and pours him some lemonade. Lemon slices and ice tumble from the pitcher. The waiter tops off Cindy's glass.

"A few more minutes, please," Frank says. The waiter nods and departs.

"As I was saying, Brittany thinks you're quite something. It was 'Miss Cindy this' and 'Miss Cindy that' the whole time I was there. And she insisted on singing me this song that you taught her, something about a maiden getting married."

"On yonder hill, there stands a maiden ...." Cindy sings quietly.

"Yeah. That was it." Frank takes a drink. "Very pretty song." He pauses. "You have a beautiful voice."

She looks down. "Thank you."

"Well, I did an assessment and Brittany had no fresh bruises and her arm seems to be fine. She said that Gene hadn't hit her in 'a while,' but she's five, so 'a while' could be hours, days or weeks. No way to tell."

"When I last saw them, they were getting ready to go up to the lake," Cindy says. "I asked Gene not to hit her and I asked Brittany not to agitate Gene. I hope it worked out."

"It seemed to. Brittany said that she had a wonderful time at the lake and that daddy didn't smack her at all or something like that."

"Isn't awful that she's so matter of fact about it? Daddy smacked me for this and daddy will smack me for that. She just accepts it – accepts the abuse as part of her life."

"That's the sad part with these kids," Frank says. "They just assume that getting hurt all the time is normal. They assimilate it. Then they grow up and smack their kids around because they think that's the way things work. It just gets passed down. I haven't been at the county all that long, but Norma, my boss, is going on 40 years in the Children and Youth office. And she'll tell you that she's seen it go from generation to generation. Dad smacks the kids around; they grow up and smack their kids around."

He stops and takes a drink. "Well, unfortunately, this is a working lunch and ...."

The waiter appears at their table.

Frank laughs. "OK. I'm sorry. We're being terrible lunch customers. If you come back in three minutes, I promise" – he puts his hand over his heart – "that we will be ready to order."

"Oh, it's OK. Take your time." The waiter smiles at them and tops off their drinks.

"OK, menu time," Franks says. They both study the paper menus.

"Seriously. What's good?" Frank asks.

"Seriously. I don't know," Cindy says.

Frank flaps his menu shut and sticks it back between the salt and pepper shakers.

"Then crab cakes it is."

"Make it two," she says. "If they're horrid, we can order something else next time."

Whoops.

"Next time?" Frank raises an eyebrow. The he strikes a Shakespearean pose, one hand on his breast, one arm outstretched, his gaze on the horizon. "Madam, you assume much!" He looks at her from the corners of his eyes. It's a strangely appealing look. "But not too much," he finishes.

She laughs. He laughs with her.

"I'm a goober. I can't help it. Especially with you."

The waiter reappears, smiling.

"OK!" Frank says in a hearty voice. "We are ready. The lady will have the crab cake sandwich. As will I."

"Cocktail sauce?"

Frank looks at Cindy. She makes a gesture as if placing something to the side of an imaginary plate in front of her.

"The lady will have hers on the side. Mine is fine on the sandwich," he says. The waiter nods and vanishes.

"You were saying about this being a working lunch..." Cindy says.

"Yes. Actually, it was a pitiful excuse to spend time in your presence. I admit that. So shoot me.

But I do have something work-related to tell you. Forgive me."

"OK."

"OK. It's this. I have a case that – well, do you remember when I paged you out on Brittany, the first time?"

"Actually, the state trooper paged me out."

Frank knits his brow.

"Right. Well, I think it was my idea. Anyway. You remember that I said I thought a woman's touch would help. Well, this is the same kind of case. But completely different. Does that make sense?" He picks up his glass and shakes it slightly so that the ice cubes clink. With her hat on and the sun warm on her back, the sound is the essence of summer.

"What do you have, Frank?"

"I love the way you say my name. Most people say it like FRANK, like the sound of something going wrong with your transmission. But you say it, Frank, like the sound of someone being honest."

"Are you honest?"

"With everyone except the IRS," he says. Their eyes meet. She has to look away.

He takes a drink; there is a pause not quite filled by the laughter of others at a table nearby.

"Uh. As I was saying. There's a case that I think could use a woman's touch again. But it's not at all what you would think."

She sips her lemonade. "OK. I'm interested."

"Sixteen year old. Husky kid. Dad is a big local businessman, very successful. Big house up on the mountain. Dad drives a Caddy. Mom drives a Lexus. Big man around town, all that kind of thing.

Would seem to be the perfect family. The kid is on the football team. He's a left tackle. He's talking to his coach about the upcoming game, you know, they're sharing a little intelligence on the upcoming team. This is last fall."

Frank sips his drink.

"Well, in the middle of a discussion about the upcoming game, the kid breaks down and starts bawling. I mean, this is a six-two high school junior, jock-around-town, big hit with the ladies, all that kind of stuff. And he's suddenly bawling like a baby to his coach. Well, I know Coach Fisher and he's a good guy. So he closes the office door and says, son, what is it? What's bugging you? To make a long story short, it turns out that the dad is really hard on the kid. Really hard. I guess dad played football in high school and college and wasn't bad. Got scouted by the pros, but never quite made the cut. But he knows football. So he critiques the kid's every move. I mean, every move. Like when the kid gets home after a game, he's beat. He's tired, he just wants to go to bed. But the dad keeps him up and just ... berates him. No matter how the kid does, it's never good enough."

"Not good."

"No. Definitely not."

"But, Frank, I'm not sure that ... I never thought I'd say this. But when you look at a case like Brittany's, where her dad is hitting her ten, twelve times a day and she's five years old ... does this kid's case rise to the level of abuse? I mean, it is. It is abuse. But if we have limited resources, shouldn't we be spending them on the Brittanys of the world?"

Frank is silent. He stirs his lemonade by whirling his glass in a small circle until the ice cubes swirl.

"Well, that's not all. It's not just verbal. The kid says that every now and then, in their 'sessions' where the dad is critiquing his performance, he gets physical. Violently physical. I mean, the dad played football at the college level, so you know he's not a small guy. And I guess he just comes after the kid if he doesn't get the response he wants. You know, 'You're right dad, I suck and I'll try harder next time.'"

Cindy is silent. She can imagine the scene. The enraged father, with all the psychological advantages, pounding verbally and physically on his son, pounding him down and down and down. She closes her eyes.

"The kid has bruises," Frank says. "Because he plays football, nobody asks questions. But he told Coach Fisher that most of them are from his father, not from the game. As far as I know, nothing has been broken yet."

Cindy is very still. She is managing her reactions and controlling her emotions. She takes a deep breath and looks up. Frank is looking at her. The twinkle in his eyes is gone. He meets her eyes.

"I don't know where to go with it," he says. "I got an informal referral from Fisher, but the kid begged him not to make it official. Fisher is torn. He wants to help the kid, but he's not sure that having Children and Youth climbing all over the family is going to help much. Plus, the dad's rich. He'll hire a great lawyer. He can cause us a lot of trouble. And you know that if a fuss is raised, the kid will pay for it."

Cindy narrows her eyes. "There's this thing – this 'acceptable' level of abuse that goes on. Where we just say, oh well, as long as the kid isn't beaten too badly, it's OK. It's better than what will happen if we intervene. Then the kid will really get beaten. So we better just stay out of it. God. That is such ...." She runs out of polite words.

"Bullshit," Frank says. "I know. I completely agree. And ...."

He is interrupted by the arrival of two plates of crab cake sandwiches with sides of cocktail sauce and coleslaw. It gives them a chance to not talk and to think, as they unfold napkins and prepare their sandwiches. Frank slathers the cocktails sauce on his and takes a big bite. Cindy puts a dab on her sandwich, takes a tentative bite.

"Spicy," Frank says.

"It's a little different than the usual cocktail sauce," Cindy says, opening up her sandwich to put more on.

"They probably have their own recipe. This is that kind of place."

They both chew quietly for a few minutes.

"When I say a woman's touch, I don't mean to offend you," Franks says. "I'm not being sexist. I hope you don't take it that way. I just mean that I think – honestly – that women have better instincts when it comes to certain things. These child abuse cases are so delicate. One wrong comment to a parent, and suddenly a minor problem blows up into a big deal. So when things get delicate, I just think that it's better to bring in someone who has a lighter touch."

"Surely there are a lot of women at your agency," Cindy says.

"There are. Most of the caseworkers are women. But ... well, how can I put this nicely? Most of them are county lifers. They've been there a long time. Don't get me wrong – they know the system and they've seen it all. Their experience is invaluable. But with that longevity comes ... sometimes, well, they get a little cold. A little jaded, I guess. I mean, I don't blame them. Ten, twenty years of dealing with kids who get hurt by people they trust most ... well, I guess it's probably a defense mechanism."

"Vivian told me about that. About growing a shell to protect yourself."

"Actually Vivian has managed to stay fresh," Frank says. "In fact, when I had the state trooper page someone from your agency, I thought she might come out."

"She tries not to take pager duty," Cindy says. "But we're short-staffed, and sometimes she has to."

"Yes. Exactly. That's why I wanted someone from your agency, someone who isn't quite as hardened. Your caseworkers are usually younger. And since you don't just do child abuse, it takes longer to burn out. We might still be able to save Brittany. So I wanted – I was hoping for – someone who could handle it." He gives Cindy a big smile. She notices that he has nice teeth. White, straight, proportioned. "And I lucked out. I got you. And you handled Gene like a pro. I was getting exactly nowhere with him and I think that the trooper was just about to make things ugly."

"Well, I'm glad I caught the call. Even though waking up at four-thirty isn't my idea of fun."

He grins his agreement at her and takes a drink. He looks at her over the top of his glass. She smiles back.

"So. About this kid," Cindy says.

"Oh, yeah. Right. Well, I was hoping that you would agree to talk to him. I don't know where to go. I won't make it official unless Fisher asks me to. I've tried to talk to him. The kid, I mean. He just grunts at me, pretty much."

"What makes you think that I'd have any better luck?"

"I don't know," he says seriously. "You just seem to be pretty good at understanding kids. Maybe you can get through to him. Convince him that he needs to do something."

"What do you think he needs to do?"

"Honestly, I don't know. All I got is the bare-bones assessment from the coach. Maybe someone could approach the dad – oh, that sounds stupid. I don't know. I'm saying 'I don't know' a lot. I guess I'm counting on you to work a miracle."

"I'm willing to give it a try. How should I approach him?"

"Set it up through Coach Fisher. He's in the phone book at the school, athletic department. Tell him you're the one I suggested."

"The one what?"

He smiles. "The expert. The empath. I don't know. There! You made me say it again."

The waiter appears. "Can I recommend a dessert?"

Frank glances at Cindy, who gives the slightest of head shakes.

"Nothing, thank you, but those sandwiches were delicious. Can I ask about the cocktail sauce?"

"Michael's own," the waiter says, gathering their plates. "Came to him in a dream. He mixed it up the next day and liked it. So he put it on the menu. It's been a hit."

"He ought to bottle it and sell it," Frank says.

"He does," the waiter replies. "Along with his steak sauce and his salad dressing. Would you like a bottle?"

"Actually, yes," Frank says. He looks at Cindy and raises an eyebrow. She nods.

"Two. Please."

The waiter nods and departs with their dishes.

Frank is suddenly fidgeting with his cloth napkin.

"So. Business lunch or not. Can we do this again?" His expression is serious. "Maybe uh, dinner?"

"You were actually worried about asking me that," Cindy says, smiling.

Frank stops fidgeting. He smiles back, but a touch warily.

"All through lunch, you were just the epitome of confidence," Cindy says. "You order for me, you keep the conversation going, you're so kind to the waiter. And it comes time to ask about dinner and suddenly you're five years old and on Santa's lap and about to ask for a really expensive present."

Frank grins. "OK. You nailed me. You're right. Everything was going according to plan right up there to the dinner question."

"And then what happened?"

"Well, to be honest, the game plan didn't go that far. I never thought I'd get to that point."

"Why on earth not?"

"I don't know," he says. "Lack of confidence, maybe. Uncertainty about how you ... think about me."

She meets his gaze. "Do you think about me?" she asks.

"Every damn minute of the day," he says, his eyes locked on hers.

A chill runs through her. She holds his gaze, then breaks it to drink the last of her lemonade.

"I've been thinking about you, too," she says.

His eyes widen. "So then dinner ...."

"Sounds very nice," she says.

On the way back to the car, her step is light. Her hat is just perfect. She's glad she wore it. He even paid for her bottle of cocktail sauce.

Chapter Twenty-Four

Surviving a challenge from the rent-a-cop at the main entrance, and after checking in at the front office, Cindy walks down the highly polished hallways of Hollidaysburg High School. Narrow yellow lockers line the sides of the halls, their ranks broken by the occasional blond-wood classroom door. Inside, students sit and teachers gesture.

There's a smell that is found only in schools. Cindy follows the directions to the gym from the friendly woman at the front office.

She turns right, walks down another wide, long corridor. This one is a little darker; there are fewer windows. The locker color changes from yellow to beige. The walls change from yellow and white to brown and white. Now she can hear the squeaks of rubber-soled shoes on a gym floor. She can smell chlorine and the dirty-socks smell of a locker room.

For a moment, she is back in gym class, in a baggy sweatsuit, grittily determined to finish her run. Her memories of gym class are not good ones. She was usually last. Most of the activities were physically painful for her. Mentally painful too, when other students laughed and whispered when she couldn't get more than two feet off the ground in the rope climb. Or when she felt that grating in her hip when she ran ... or when a hurled rubber ball would catch her in the belly during dodge ball ....

She snaps back to the present. She's standing before wooden double doors with a worn and tarnished brass push rail. Inside, there are the squeaks, yells and an occasional whistle, the sounds of a basketball game. She takes a deep breath. She's here to help someone. A victim of abuse. Time to pull it together. She pushes on the rail and the door swings open.

Inside is a huge gymnasium with varnished wooden bench seats pushed back against the walls. The floors are marked with lines incomprehensible to someone who doesn't understand basketball. Perhaps two dozen boys are playing the incomprehensible game. They're clustered around a basket across the gym from her. They all wear white t-shirts and shorts. Some have loose red jerseys over their shirts. They're yelling. One boy raises his arms and shoots the ball toward the basket. A taller boy in front of him slaps it aside. It bounces across the court, striking the bleachers. There are shouts, hand slaps and the cluster falls apart, with the boys moving back to pre-determined positions.

A surprisingly short male coach in a blue sweatsuit and red baseball cap retrieves the ball. He wears a silver whistle around his neck and has a clipboard in his hands. He sweeps the ball under the arm with the clipboard, a practiced gesture.

He's probably done it thousands of times, Cindy thinks.

"Now, what went wrong?" he asks. His voice echoes and re-echoes across the court, muddling it.

Cindy begins walking, following one wall around the gym.

One boy says something too low and muddled for her to make out.

"Right!" the coach yells. "Bret needed to charge, not plant and shoot. Bret, you're not going to get the ball over Chris. He's got a good foot on you."

For some reason, there are snorts of laughter from the boys at this.

A boy says something.

"Anybody have an answer for Bret?" the coach asks.

"Knock him on his ass!" someone yells clearly.

"OK. Move on him aggressively, good." the coach says. "It repositions you. Sets up the pass. And it gives you the momentum to get the ball moving toward the basket if you're going to take the shot. Right. Good answer. But next time, let's lose the profanity, all right, Todd?"

Cindy is close enough now to see nods.

"OK, red ball in," the coach says, tossing the ball toward a husky kid. It's apparently some kind of signal because the kid catches the ball and the boys fall into attentive positions. The coach blows his whistle and lets it drop back to his chest. The kids begin to move around, apparently seeking a positional advantage. They yelp and yell. The coach is watching attentively.

"All right, all right, there you go!" he yells following a pass that doesn't appear remarkable to Cindy.

Cindy walks up tentatively. For a minute, the coach doesn't notice her. He yells and gestures, waving the clipboard. The kids squeak on the floor. There's a flurry of action. The ball is launched; it arcs through the air and snicks through the net. Half the kids cheer. The other half looks disconsolate.

One kid catches the bouncing ball and looks toward the coach.

The coach blows his whistle, two short sharp tweets.

"All right. All right. Good hustle. Nice shot, Chris. OK, you guys. Hit the showers."

The ball comes bouncing toward the coach and the kids stream off the court, chattering, pushing each other, laughing.

The coach turns toward her.

"Can I help you?"

"Cindy Phillips, Family Services," she says, holding out her hand. The coach takes it. His hand is dry and rough, his grip firm.

"Oh, you must be the girl that Frank told me about." He looks her up and down. He gives his head a little twitch.

"Well. All right. You come highly recommended," he says.

"Thank you, coach."

He eyes her a moment longer. She meets his gaze. She's not usually comfortable in a gym, but she's not afraid of his appraisal.

"Brian's in a bad spot," the coach finally says. "How much did Frank tell you?"

She briefs him.

"Right. So." he begins walking toward the doors that the boys disappeared through. "I'd like to help him get straightened out, but ... well, he doesn't seem to want help. But the situation has to be moved forward. No kid should have to take abuse like that, even if his dad did play college ball."

As they walk, they make arrangements for Cindy to see Brian during gym class the next day.

"He doesn't need the 20 minutes of activity that they actually get anyway," Coach Fisher says. "He's in tip-top shape."

They arrive at the double doors. "Locker" is printed on the left wooden door in square black type. "Rooms" is on the other. The coach pushes the bar and holds the door open for her. It leads to a narrow, dim corridor of beige brick. At the end are two doors. In the same black block type, one reads "Men" and the other "Women." The air in the corridor is musty and damp. The coach walks halfway down the corridor, then stops and turns.

"All right." He looks around. "Brian needs to do something, but no one seems to know what. The abuse he's taking just can't go on. No kid can handle that. No kid should have to. I don't want to get involved directly. That won't do any good. I know the kid's dad pretty well, but just socially. There's no way I can go to him and say, 'George, you've got to quit beating the crap out of your kid.' That's not going to work. If I make an official complaint with Frank, then the county gets involved and –" He snorts. "I don't know everything about George, but I can tell you that if someone accuses him of abusing Brian, the sh–, uh, the stuff is going to hit the fan. Real fast. And in a town like this, that can make a lot of trouble for a lot of people." He pauses and looks down the corridor at the two locker room doors. "Myself included."

"Coach, I think just bringing it up to Frank was the right thing to do. You know football; we know child welfare. We'll take it from here," Cindy says.

Coach Fisher releases a gusty breath. He turns his eyes to Cindy's. "Well, I'm very glad to hear you say that, Mrs. Williams."

"Phillips."

"Phillips! Right. Sorry." He pauses. "I try to be good to these kids. You know, not all of them have the best family lives. For a lot of them, I'm the best father figure you're going to have. It breaks my heart sometimes, seeing them. I mean, they take showers right in front of me. I can see it. All the phys ed teachers do." His gaze wanders down the hallway again.

"Coach? See what?"

"The bruises. The cuts. You know." He shifts his clipboard to the other hand. "I know what it looks like when a kid's been hit with an extension cord. Or when there are big bruises all over the kid's ribs and you know damn well that the most physical activity he gets is running home ahead of the bullies. Those are no football bruises."

"Coach. You see cuts? Bruises? Regularly?"

He looks at her. "Oh yeah. There's always a few. Every year. You know who they are. You see the bruises go from being fresh to yellow and green – then they're gone for a while. Then a couple of weeks later, they're back."

"Coach, what do you do? When you see them, what do you do?"

The coach lets out a short laugh. "What do we do? Well, we tell the school nurse, of course. Then it's out of my hands. That's not my call, by the way. That's policy. School board. Athletic director down in Bedford County pushed a case too far a few years ago. It cost him his job."

"What does the nurse do?"

The coach shifts his clipboard again. "You'd have to ask her that." He puts out his hand. "I better get in there before the towel snapping gets out of hand."

Cindy takes his hand. "Thank you, coach. You've done the right thing."

"Lord, I hope so." He walks down the corridor and opens the door to the mens' locker room. Steam rolls out and Cindy can hear cracks and yelps. Coach Fisher yells something coachlike. The door thumps shut.

Chapter Twenty-Five

Cindy drives to Brittany's house. She didn't call; she wants to surprise Gene. The green pickup isn't parked in front of the house. Maybe it's in the back, she thinks. As she walks up on the porch, she can hear the television. She knocks at the door. No answer. She knocks again. She knows that the door-bell doesn't work. She can see a shadow approach through the door's frosted glass. The knob rattles and the door opens a crack. She can see a sliver of Greta's face.

"Hi, Greta. Is Gene here?"

Greta's face is closed. "Nope. Got called back to work."

"Well, that's great! So he's back at the sawmill."

There is no discernable response from Greta.

"Well, can I see Brittany?"

Greta's eyes shift briefly down and right. "Sleeping."

"She's napping?"

"Yeah."

"Well, that's good. Girls her age need a nap."

No discernable response from Greta.

"Well, Greta, thank you very much. Please tell Gene that I'm glad he's back to work. I'll stop by another time."

"Call first," Greta says.

Cindy pauses. "Call before I come up?"

"Yeah." Greta hasn't moved the door by even a fraction.

"Well, I hope I'm not intruding. I'll be happy to call."

"All right," Greta says and closes the door. Thump, click.

Cindy stands on the porch a moment, then turns and walks to the car. She's not sure that Brittany is in great hands with Greta. But if Gene gets back to work, his attitude might improve. If he's more satisfied with things, maybe he won't drink as much, or get as angry. All of those would be good things for Brittany.

She drives away, hoping good fortune for Brittany. Then she laughs. During their entire conversation, Greta didn't speak more than a dozen words. Well, as long as Brittany isn't getting hit, she thinks.

Back at the office, there's a message from Frank on her voice mail. She can tell right away that he's all business.

"Cindy, this is Frank. It's about twenty after one. I have the entire case file on Brittany right here and I'm wondering if you want to schedule a hearing in front of a judge. It'll take about two weeks to get a hearing. If Gene has a halfway decent attorney, he'll probably be able to get it put off another two or three weeks. So, if I file today, we probably won't actually get into court for at least a month. But you know that filing will set off fireworks, so I don't want to file unless you want to go that route. Thanks. Call me."

She returns his call and of course gets his voicemail.

"Frank, this is Cindy. Thanks for your call. Sorry you missed me. I was up trying to visit Brittany, but Gene got called back to the sawmill and Greta said Brittany was sleeping. So I didn't see her. Give me a chance to do an assessment and I'll let you know. Thanks for your help." She hesitates, then says, "I'm looking forward to dinner" and hangs up.

Maybe I shouldn't have said that, she thinks.

Chapter Twenty-Six

James Steele was outgripping the commercial real estate broker when his pager went off, the tiny one that buzzed only when it was something serious.

"Terry," James said, ratcheting up his handshake pressure another notch, "I'm glad we got together on this one."

Terry was good. His cheesy smile didn't fade at all, but Steele knew that his hand had to hurt. He had felt tiny snaps and pops from Terry's hand. If the bastard wants to play this game, he'd better spend a little more time in the gym, Steele thought.

"Back atcha!" Terry said, his grin holding, barely.

James let him go. He wondered if he did so because he wanted to answer the page or because there was some mercy in his soul.

Terry gave his crushed hand one quick flick, but that was all.

"Need me to see you down?"

"Nah. I'll be all right. I've been here a few times before," James said. Terry gave a quick fake laugh that sounded like a bark.

James opened the dark-wood door of the boardroom. The light of the hallway was subdued, but it still seemed bright after the dark, macho black-and-gray of the boardroom with its high-backed black leather chairs around an obsidian rhombus table.

Rhombus, James thought. *That sounds like what I'll be calling Terry when I buy the drinks tonight.*

Terry followed him to the elevator anyway. The stainless steel door swept open noiselessly. James stepped in. Terry stood grinning like an idiot as the elevator doors closed.

"See ya," Terry said.

James gave him a nod, his cell phone out. The doors closed and James forgot about Terry.

"Mr. Steele," his assistant Julie said when she picked up. "Your mother had a stroke. She's over at General, room 340."

Numbness gripped James, but he had long experience in dealing efficiently with sudden and startling information. *This is no different than when you get last-minute deal-breaking info,* he thought. *Handle it.*

"How long ago?"

"I beeped you as soon as the hospital called. I don't know how long she's been over there. But ... James, it sounds serious."

"Cancel everything for the rest of the week. Call the hospital. Tell them I'm on my way."

"James. They wanted to know ... she has a DNR order on file."

"I know." The elevator was taking forever to get to the garage. "That's what she wanted. It's legal. I'm not going to try to countermand it."

"OK."

"OK." He broke the connection and fished his electronic key out of his briefcase. At last, the elevator stopped and the door slid open, revealing a dank garage reeking of exhaust fumes and rubber.

He chirped the Porsche's tires pulling out of his parking space, then put the car's thrust and handling to good use as he sped to the hospital.

At the hospital, his suit, his demeanor and his courtesy got him to room 340 with minimal fuss. A hospital security officer took him right to the room. He entered. The lights in the private room were dim. His mother lay quietly, connected to machines. Something beeped discreetly.

She was sleeping. Or unconscious. Her face was slack, her thin arms outside the blankets, at her sides. He hung up his jacket, loosened his tie, pulled a chair close to her bed and sat down. He took one blue-veined hand gently.

"Mom?"

No response. He didn't know what to do. He tried to pull the sheet a little higher on her chest, but it was tucked and resisted him. He watched her breathe. Her chest rose and fell slowly but steadily. Her mouth was slightly open. He looked at her closed eyes. He remembered the bruises he used to see under those eyes, the deep purple-black where the skin would turn shiny. Then, later, the color would go to a yellowish green and then disappear except for a few dark crescents that always seemed to linger and linger. He thought about how her eyes got deeper and sadder as he got older.

He remembered.

Clutching his mother's denim-encased thigh, face pressed against her buttock. Hoping, praying that she could save him. She stood, arms out, a guardian angel between him and his furious father.

"Quit trying to hide the little bastard!" his father growled, his anger a palpable presence.

"You have no argument with him," she said. "Leave him alone! He's just a child! Let him go to his room!"

"That little shit is going to learn a lesson," his father said, stepping closer, his face red and ugly.

Clutching, praying, he felt only terror because he knew that his mother was physically no match for his father. He would be next. Wordlessly, his father grabbed one of his mother's arms and twisted. She shrieked with pain and went to one knee. He clung to her, eyes closed, still praying that she would somehow save him.

He felt her body rise as with desperate strength she lunged up, grabbing his father's free arm. "Run!" she yelled, and he abandoned the warmth of her body to scramble out of the room.

He never knew exactly how his mother bought him the time to escape, but he was sure it was ugly. Behind him, as the screen door slammed, he heard a scream. Then a thump. Something shattered. He ran and ran.

There was a polite cough from the doorway. He realized that he was kneading his mother's hand. He turned. A white-coated doctor stood in the doorway. He had dark skin and gold-rimmed glasses with tiny lenses. His head was shaved.

Steele stood.

"Mr. Steele? Doctor Karanjia."

They shook hands. Steele could see the doctor appraising him, his suit, his watch. He studied the doctor, mostly his eyes. Each silently came to a decision about the kind of man he was dealing with.

"Mr. Steele. Your mother had a severe stroke. She is only lightly sedated now, and it's unlikely that she will regain consciousness. Unfortunately, there was apparently a significant time lag between the onset of the stroke and when help arrived."

"How long?"

"We can't be sure exactly. Based on the extent of the damage, I estimate that it was at least two hours from the onset until she received medical assistance. During that time, her brain was partially deprived of oxygen. Her basic functions are continuing, but ...."

"There's no hope."

"Very little. Even if she were to regain consciousness, she would likely be ... impaired. Significantly. I'm sorry."

"She's not on any sort of life support?"

"None. She had a do-not-resuscitate order on file. We stabilized her in the ER, but did nothing else. As you can see, she's breathing. Her heart is functioning normally. It's the higher functions of her brain that were affected."

"How long might she remain alive in this state?"

"I'm sorry to tell you that I don't know. It could be just a few more hours. It could be days. Weeks. I've personally witnessed people in this state remain for months. Medical literature has cases of people remaining in this state for years. There's no way to tell."

The doctor stepped to the foot of the bed and picked up the aluminum-cased report that hung there. He flipped through the pages.

"She's on a blood thinner. Without continuing to take that, she could be at danger of a second stroke. In that case, it would likely be fatal."

"Is that something that could be administered to her in in her current state?"

"The DNR doesn't specifically address that, but generally, the interpretation would be not to administer any medication whatsoever." The doctor closed the aluminum chart case. "Of course, you are listed as the POA. If you believe that her wishes included continuing her medication, it can be administered intravenously."

"But that would do nothing to improve her current state."

The doctor shook his head. "No. The damage is done, Mr. Steele. I'm very sorry."

Steele could think of nothing to do but walk to the bedside and take his mother's hand. He sat down in the chair.

"She was a wonderful woman. I wish that I had been able to say goodbye."

"Did you ever tell her that you loved her?"

Steele was startled. He looked up to see if the doctor might be kidding. But his eyes were dark and serious. Steele looked back at his mother's sleeping face.

"I didn't for a long time. Not like I should have. Then I had this dream. I was, I don't know, in my late twenties. You know, that time when you usually finally figure out all the things that your parents did for you. You begin to appreciate their sacrifices. I had this dream that she died and I realized I had never told her that I loved her. Not since I was five, anyway. In my dream, I was terribly upset. Completely anguished."

He paused, holding his mother's limp hand.

"I woke up in the middle of the night. I was so rattled by the dream that I called her right then and there. At 3 a.m. I woke her up. I said, 'Mom, I just want you to know that I do love you and I thank you for everything you ever did for me.' " He fell silent. The doctor didn't move.

"After that, I made it a point to say it to her every time it occurred to me."

"Then you said your goodbye and more," the doctor said. "That's all a mother ever wants to hear from her child – those three little words. They mean a lot when she hears them when her child is thirty-five."

Steele smiled at the doctor. "More like forty-four."

"If you were still telling your mother that you loved her at forty-four, then you are in an elite class of American sons," the doctor said, smiling back. "She must have been quite a mother."

"She had more guts than any person I've ever known," Steele said.

The doctor left quietly and Steele spent the next four hours holding his mother's hand. He talked about his life, remembering the good times he had spent with her, just in case some part of her could still hear him.

After a time, he said, "Mom. I never said this before, but it wasn't your fault. It wasn't your fault. None of it was. You did what you could. I couldn't have asked for more. You were my guardian angel. You saved me. You really did."

Then he was silent but he didn't let go of her hand.

Chapter Twenty-Seven

Three days later, Steele was still keeping a vigil in the hospital room. He was awakened by a gasp. He roused himself quickly, scooted his chair over to his mother's bedside and grabbed her hand.

"Mom?"

Her eyes were open but sightless. Her eyes widened and a convulsion shook her. He felt her body go taut. She began breathing rapidly.

"It's OK to let go, Mom," he said, squeezing her hand. "Go ahead. Let go. Find your reward. No one deserves a rest more than you. I'll be OK. I promise. I love you."

Her hand tightened on his, then relaxed. The light left her eyes. He didn't even have time to summon a nurse. The discreet beeping device abruptly gave off a shrill tone.

He reached up and closed her eyelids as two nurses rushed into the room, pushing a cart bristling with medical instruments.

They eyed James, ready for action. "Sir, there's a DNR, but if you ...."

He shook his head. "No. But thank you."

They shut off the squealing machine, then pushed the cart back out of the room. He sat there, remembering and thinking. And realizing how alone he was.

Chapter Twenty-Eight

Cindy sits in Coach Fisher's office with Brian. The door is closed. She let him take the desk chair. He's slumped, wearing a ragged yellow t-shirt advertising a rock band that she's never heard of, baggy oversize blue jeans and huge sneakers. His blonde hair is cropped short. His left earlobe is pierced with a tiny diamond stud. His eyes are brown and wary. He is husky and handsome.

"Brian, I'm just going to let you talk. I have nothing to say right now. I have some information from other people, but it means nothing to me right now. All it did was get us into this room. If you want to stop talking, or leave, or anything, at any time, you just do it. I'm just here to help if you ask for it. That's it. That's all."

He doesn't look at her. He has one leg across the top of the other and he's picking at his huge sneaker. She waits. He picks.

"I don't know."

She waits.

"Maybe this isn't such a big deal. Maybe it's nothing."

"Brian, if you're being hurt, then it's not nothing."

"I can take it."

"Brian, I have no doubt that you can. The question is whether you should have to take it."

He says nothing.

"Brian, let me tell you something about me." She puts an edge in her voice. "I'm not just some ditzy guidance counselor here hoping that a big bad football player will cry and reveal his true feelings and we can hug each other. To be honest, I'm not really concerned about your feelings. I'm concerned about whether you are being abused."

He looks up and meets her eyes but his walls are still up. She sharpens and projects her energy at him, trying to penetrate his defenses.

"Brian, when I was seven years old, my stepfather beat the living shit out of me." His eyes widen briefly. She knows she's struck something. "He beat me so badly that I had to re-learn how to walk. I lost a grade in school, not just because I was unconscious but because he literally beat my brain back a grade. If it weren't for a certain doctor, I'd probably still be wearing leg braces and talking funny. What was done to me was wrong. It was beyond wrong. It wasn't fair. It messed me up. I'm lucky I survived, not just physically but emotionally. A lot of kids like me end up committing suicide as adults. Do you know what I'm talking about?"

He nods, his eyes fixed on hers. She can see the wall crumbling. She rolls up her sleeve and extends her arm, palm down, fingers out. "Do you see that scar, Brian? The one that starts at my ring finger and runs up almost to my elbow? That's the scar that the surgeon made when he rebuilt my hand, my wrist and the bones of my arm. He had to rebuild them because my stepfather basically crushed the bones to sand."

He winces. She is glad.

"It still doesn't work right," she continues. She closes her hand into a fist. "That's a pretty loose fist. That's the best I can do. See how the middle finger doesn't close down like the others do? That's not all. My hand doesn't always do what I tell it to. It's not very strong. I drop stuff all the time. You should see me trying to open a can with a manual can opener, when I have to coordinate my two hands. Notice I wear slip-on shoes. That's because I can't tie laces."

Brian glances down at her shoes. She rolls her sleeve back down.

"Child abuse is wrong, Brian, whether it's as bad as I had it or whether it's just a kid being smacked around now and then. Or whether it's a parent making a kid feel worthless. No child should feel that way. No one has the right to make anyone else feel like that, especially a parent. Parents have the responsibility to raise their children the best they can. Give them the best start that they can. Most do. Most try, anyway. That's what parenthood is all about. But if something is going wrong, something needs to be done about it.

"I can tell you for a fact that any kid ..." she pauses and drills him with her eyes – "any kid who suffers abuse is going to pay for it later in life. It's a debt that has to be paid some time, somewhere. All too often, the abusive parents are not the ones who repay it. It's the kid. The kid suffers. Sometimes for his entire life. He always looks back and wishes that someone had saved him. Or someone had spoken up. Or that he himself had done something to stop it."

She stops. She softens her voice.

"Brian, it's not fair when a father abuses his son. Dad has all the advantages. Most times, he's bigger physically, but even if he isn't, he's got the psychological edge, doesn't he? He knows the tricks, where to insert the knife to lever out those insecurities. He knows which buttons to push. He knows how to intimidate. But that's still abuse. It's still wrong.

"Now I know that you're tough. You think that you can handle what you're going through. You're right. You can. For now. For now, you can handle it. But Brian ...." She pauses until he meets her eyes again. "... if the abuse isn't stopped, I guarantee – I absolutely guarantee – that down the road, the price will be paid. And it won't be your dad who picks up that check."

Brian is silent, his eyes back on his shoe. She waits. Finally, he sighs.

"My dad's pretty hard-core about football," he says. "He played in college. He almost went pro. He knows all the moves. All the tricks, the helmet-slaps and stuff like that. He thinks I should still be doing them. But ...."

She waits.

"Some of them are illegal now. Or nobody does them anymore. The game has changed."

She waits.

"He seems to think that every play should be some Super Bowl thing, some perfect play that goes off just like coach diagrams it. But it just doesn't work like that. It's..." He pauses, groping for words. "It's a messed-up game. When that ball is snapped, you know what you're supposed to do and you do the best you can, but it doesn't always work out that way. Sometimes something happens and you're a little slow catching on, and you can make the adjustment. I'm not saying that I can't, but I just can't always be so lightning quick. Sometimes the game gets ahead of you and you're just trying to keep up and ...."

He looks up at her quickly and she sees anguish in his eyes. "I just don't think I should have to pay for that. It's just part of the game. I do the best I can, every play. But he just doesn't understand that."

"Brian, what happens?"

"Well, I usually look at the quarterback, because what he's doing tells you a lot about –"

"No, I mean with your dad. What happens when he's not happy with your play?"

"He's always not happy with my play. It doesn't matter what I do, I always missed all these opportunities." Brian drops his leg to the floor and leans forward, an imaginary remote control in his hand. "Like here, can't you see this guy coming? And here, what did you think he was going to do? Look there, you missed a prime turnover opportunity, they almost handed you the ball!" Brian jabs with the imaginary remote, stabbing at an invisible television. "Look at that! You missed that! Look here! You missed that, too! And here and here! And there! Again!" He slumps back in his chair.

"Where does he get the tapes of the game?"

"Tapes them himself!" Brian says with the tone of someone who is trying to convey the depths of someone else's obsession. "Sits there the whole game with a camcorder glued to his eye, zooming in on every damn thing I do. So then we go home and he pops the tape in the VCR and it's three hours of 'you fucked up this and you fucked up that –' " He stops and looks at Cindy in horror. "I'm sorry. I meant …."

"It's OK. I understand." She gives him a smile. He smiles back, but it's perfunctory.

"I just …."

"He hits you?"

Brian closes his eyes. He breathes deeply several times. "Yeah," he says without opening his eyes. "Somewhere around the review of the third quarter, he usually loses it. He just wings out on me. Instead of yelling, he comes after me."

"What does he do?"

Brian's eyes are still closed. "Throws punches, mostly. Shoves me. Taunts me. You know, 'Oh, look, mister big tough tackle can't stop this little pussy guy here. You can't stop him, huh? You think you can stop your dad? I've been out of the game for twenty years, but do you think you can stop me, huh? Come on, try and stop me. Come on, what are you, some kind of little pussy boy?' That kind of stuff. Then he hits me. Body blows, mostly."

"What do you do?"

Brian opens his eyes and meets Cindy's.

"What do I do? I take it, of course. I block a few, but I don't hit back. I just take them. I just …." Cindy sees that the slightest gleam of tears in the eyes of the husky kid and suddenly he's not seventeen, he's seven. "I just take them. I take them. What else am I going to do? He's my dad."

Brian closes his eyes tightly, then opens them and takes a quick wipe at each eye.

"I just take it. Like in practice, you know. Sometimes it hurts, but you just take it and don't show it. He wears out. He dies down. Then he waves an arm at me and I know I can go. He's still pissed but he's done. So I go upstairs and go to bed. And lay awake half the night."

"Brian, are you a good football player?"

Brian's eyes are still moist. He blinks several times and sits up straighter in his chair. "Not according to my dad, I'm not."

"I didn't ask you what your dad thought. Are you a good player? What does the coach say? What do you teammates say?"

Brian sniffs and looks around the cluttered coach's office. It smells of chlorine, gym socks and old sweat. Dusty golden trophies are clustered on top of a battered green filing cabinet.

"Coach Fisher tells me that I'm one of the best he's ever coached at tackle. He has me explain stuff to the other guys in practice. My moves. Why I do what I do. What I'm thinking."

"And your teammates?"

"I get respect. I mean, everyone gets joked now and then. Practical jokes. You know." He looks at Cindy and she looks back. "But I think I'm respected."

"So you're respected by your coach and your fellow players for what you do out on the field. When you're out there, you're trying your best. Other people see that; they understand that you're not always going to be perfect. Other people who understand the game say that you do a good job out there. Am I right? Is that a fair assessment?"

Brian smiles a small smile. "Assessment. Yeah. Now you sound like a guidance counselor."

"Brian, my advice for you is very simple. You're not going to get this advice from anyone else. Not even from Coach Fisher, although he'd love to tell you what I'm about to say."

His attention is riveted on her.

"Can you take him?" she asks.

"You mean …."

"Strip away the fact that he's your father. Subtract that out. I mean, if he were just some other guy who was bugging you, and you looked at him, would you think, 'I can take this guy?' "

Brian looks off into space. "I ... well, he's getting a little slow."

"You take his punches. Could you hit him back harder?"

Brian looks troubled. "Well, yeah. I think so. I don't know if he's giving me everything he has, though."

"Brian, the next time your dad starts hitting you, hit back."

Brian opens his mouth, then closes it.

"You're young. You're healthy. You're a good football player. You can take a hit. A punch. Your dad is twenty-five years out of the game. He's lost touch. He's trying to make you pay for every mistake he ever made, for him not making the pros, for every fumble, every time that he wasn't perfect. But that's not your problem, is it? That's not your fight. What he's doing to you is wrong and unfair and down the road it's going to mess you up. You need to stop it now. Right now. And there's only one language that your dad is going to understand."

Brian sits up straight, his eyes looking right through the walls. He's almost not there with her.

"Brian, the next time he swings at you, grab his arm. Stop the punch. Look into his eyes. And say, 'Dad, this has got to stop.' And hit him back. Hard. Knock him over. If he comes back at you – and he will, and he'll be mouthing off – hit him again. Again, if you have to. Stop him. Make him think. Don't taunt him – that's stooping to his level. But let him know that you're not a punching bag and you're not taking the hits for his failures. You have your own lessons to learn and your own life to live. What he did or didn't do is gone. It's past. It can't be recovered."

She pauses.

"Brian, my sense is that your dad doesn't even realize what he's doing, the effect that he's having on you. When he hits you, he sees himself, twenty-five years ago. He sees his mistakes, his screw-ups. He wants to punish himself for those. Maybe he had one shot in front of a pro scout and he slipped and fell and never got a second chance. He's been punishing himself for it all these years. But that's his fight, his loss, his failure. Not yours. From what I hear, he's done OK in the business world. He was a good college player. He needs to come to terms with all that without making his son pay for his failure."

Brian is still staring through the wall.

"Hit dad?" He turns to look at Cindy. "Hit him. Hit back." He turns his eyes to Coach Fisher's cluttered desk. His right hand curls into a fist. He slams it onto the desk and the coach's clipboard and photos of his children jump impressively. A pen bounces and drops to the floor. "Hit him back," he says.

"Yes," Cindy says. "Hit him back. But Brian. Brian!" She reaches out and touches his knee. He turns toward her like a searchlight seeking a ship. She leans toward him, intent. "Brian. Listen to me. This is very important. Hit back only enough to show him that you're a real person who can defend himself. He's hitting you because he sees you as himself twenty years ago, not as you, not as Brian, his son. Don't get angry. Don't let anger or revenge drive you. That's wrong. That will take you down the wrong road. You just want to get his attention, wake him up. Be cold. Be calculating. Stop when you've made your point. Then never hit him again. I don't think you'll have to."

Brian's eyes clear and in them she can see power and resolve where before there was confusion and defensiveness. He looks into Cindy's eyes. He blinks slowly and she can see the power recede but not vanish.

"No one else will say that to me, will they?" he says. "No one else is going to tell me that. Not even Coach Fisher."

"No, Brian, no one is going to even hint at that solution. Because it could go very wrong. But I think you can handle it. I know you can. And I think it's the only real answer to your problem."

"Coach said you were worth listening to. I didn't believe him."

"For the record, Brian, I told you to engage your father in constructive dialog in a non-confrontational manner at a time when tensions between you were at a minimum."

Brian grins. "Right. What you just said."

Cindy hands him her card. "Call me any time of day or night. I mean that."

As they leave the office, Cindy sees Coach Fisher standing at the other end of the vacant gym, too far away to have heard anything. But she can tell just by his posture that he's concerned. She suspects he's been hovering, waiting for the meeting to end.

Fisher yells. "Hey, Brian."

Brian stops, looks and notices. "Coach."

"Everything OK?" Coach asks.

Brian glances back at Cindy. She gives him a goofy little wave. Brian smiles a big genuine smile. "Yeah. It's all OK."

"All right, kid. See you at practice."

Brian jogs casually out of the gym. Cindy admires his complete lack of affect, how his body moves; how his coordinated motions exude a deep-seated physical confidence that she will never have.

Coach Fisher gives her a wave and disappears through the set of double doors.

Walking to her Honda, she hopes that she gave Brian the right advice. If she was wrong, the outcome could be catastrophic. And it would be all her fault.

Chapter Twenty-Nine

The man with the neat goatee looks over his tiny glasses at James Steele.

"Jim, you're worrying me. This all looks like a man who is wrapping up his affairs."

Steele, who has signed a hundred pieces of paper this afternoon, chuckles without looking up and keeps signing.

"It's about time I got some of these things straight, that's all," he says.

"Does this have anything to do with the death of your mother?"

Steele stops and looks up. "Well of course it does. What else can get you thinking so much about your own mortality than the death of a parent?"

When the goateed man's worried expression remains, Steele adds, "Look. I've got some serious assets here. I could be hit by a bus tomorrow. With no heirs, I just want to make sure that all this goes to the right places. I've been in business long enough to know that if I don't get all this down in writing and notarized and whatever else, it's just not going to happen. Not the way I want it to, anyway." He scrawls another signature and moves another piece of paper to the "done" stack.

"I figured this ought to make you guys happy, anyway," he says. "You've always on me to keep everything updated and tight as a drum."

"Well, Jim, you've ... well, let's just say that we at this law firm are well aware of your tendency to shoot first and ask questions later." Both men laugh.

"That's the nature of the commercial real estate business," Steele says. "I learned a long time ago that if I see a fifty laying on the sidewalk, I'd damn well better jump on it right away. If I don't, someone else will. And I guarantee that anyone who stands there amazed that a fifty is laying there is lost."

He completes the "to do" stack, moves the last sheet to the "done" pile, caps the heavy green-and-gold pen and tosses it to the lawyer, who, startled by the toss, catches it clumsily.

"There! Done." He hands the stack to the lawyer, who places it carefully inside a folder.

"If you do get hit by a bus, you're going to make some people very surprised and very happy," the lawyer says.

"That ought to even out my karma then. I can tell you there are a lot of people out there who curse my name."

"Only those stupid enough to underestimate you."

Steele stands and puts out a hand. The lawyer takes it and receives a firm, reassuring handshake. "Thanks for all the times you pulled my nuts out of the fire."

"And for all the times to come," the lawyer responds.

After Steele departs, the lawyer sits a while, tapping a pen against his cheek and swinging back in forth in his chair, thinking.

A tall, gray-haired man sticks his head into the room. "Hey. Was that Jim Steele I just saw leaving?"

"It was."

"What's he up to now? Raping and pillaging another real estate firm?"

"No. Strangely, he seems like he's ...."

"He's what?"

"Ahh. Never mind. His mother just died. He's getting some things in order."

"Always recommended. Especially when we can bill by the quarter-hour for it," the gray-haired man says and walks on.

At two a.m. that night, Steele's alarm goes off. He slaps the snooze, but as always, once he's awake, he's awake. He briefly questions the wisdom of what he's planned to do, but then shrugs it off. In the bathroom, he looks into his own eyes as he brushes his teeth. *Who's really in there?* he wonders, not for the first time. And, not for the first time, he has no answer.

He dresses comfortably in jeans and polo shirt and exits his condo for the elevator to the underground garage. He hesitates between the Harley-Davidson and the Porsche, but finally selects the car. He puts the top down and starts the car. As always, it leaps to life, then settles into a deep purring that speaks to him of hundreds of fine-toothed gears meshing perfectly, everything in synch. *Seventy years of German engineering tells,* he thinks.

He steers the car out of the garage and into the urban night, enjoying the cool night air and the scenes of a city at night. Each streetlight is a tiny universe, illuminating some segment of a life. There are two guys sitting on the porch steps of a row house. A third man stands in front of them, gesturing urgently. The two sitting seem bemused. He wonders what the story of the encounter is. What their lives are like. At another light, a dog sniffs the lamppost. It seems casual and unstressed. Must be in its own neighborhood. Whose dog is it? he wonders. Under another pool of light, a tall thin kid with a basketball under his arm makes no attempt to hide his interest in the bright red Porsche 911 passing before him.

Steele reaches the beltway entrance and accelerates. As usual, there is traffic, but not the gridlocking masses of cars that clog the highway during the day. The beltway was built to move huge numbers of cars, unlike the autobahn, which was built for high-speed travel. Tonight, for Steele's purposes, that difference is irrelevant.

As he catches second gear just onto the highway, he can feel the car pushing at his back like the thrust of a jet fighter. Many years ago, trying to put off returning home for as long as possible, he would ride for hours on his bicycle on nights just like this, with the night air cool on his face, streetlights flashing by. On those nights, he would imagine that he was piloting a jet fighter on a mission to rescue his buddies who were outnumbered in a dogfight. As he swooped around the corners of the dimly lit streets, he would play out the scenario in his head.

Delta team leader, this is Delta Seven. I'm launched and inbound. My ETA is under ten minutes.

Scratchily through his headphones the voice of one of his teammates comes through, his voice betraying tension and fear.

Delta Seven, that's not good enough! We're getting chewed up here! We need you now!

Roger, Delta team leader. Delta Seven going to afterburners. I'll be there in three.

As he tops a hill and starts down, gaining speed rapidly, he pushes an imaginary button. The afterburners kick in, slamming him back in his seat.

Whoo-hah! he yells, pumping a fist in the air. He does a barrel roll just for the hell of it.

Back on the aircraft carrier, the commanding officer would throw his unlit cigar onto the deck and stomp on it.

Goddamn it! Delta Seven, you might be the best damn pilot I've got but you're not authorized for bullshit!

He shifts crisply into fourth gear, plenty of muscle there. The car's reserve of power is like an immense body of water behind a dam – overwhelming force, instantly available. The speedometer hovers at 90. He is unable to restrain a grin has he depresses the gas pedal slightly. The steady growl from the engine behind him deepens a note and the speedometer needle moves rapidly right, passing 100. He gives the engine a break, shifting into fifth. The tachometer needle drops but the engine is still in its power band. The slightest touch of the throttle and the car responds.

He moves over, staying to the left, flashing his headlights as he overtakes car after car. Occasionally he darts to the right when someone is slow to move out of his lane. The speedometer needle moves steadily right. 110. 115. 120. He lets the engine relax into sixth gear. Streetlights flicker by, shadows race through the car. Nothing matters but the unrolling strip of highway before him. At this speed, it requires his full attention.

The car is rock-steady, perfectly at home at this speed. The engine is singing, the steering wheel responsive to his every nudge. There is just a trickle of sweet night air past the windshield. He punches the play button on the CD player without looking down. The car's speakers blast Eric Clapton's cover of Robert Johnson's "Hellhound on my Trail."

He depresses the accelerator a bit more. He is pressed back in his seat, the car still willing and able. This strip of highway and night sky, these flickering streetlights, the snarling beast that he rides, these are his only reality.

Now this is why you pay two-twenty grand for a car, he thinks.

To his dogfight buddies, to his mother and his brother, he says, *Hang on. I'm coming.*

Chapter Thirty

Cindy pulls up behind the now-familiar battered green pickup truck. Its bed still contains the remnants of the trip to the lake. Two coolers. A blue tarp, now rumpled and muddy. A dozen or so logs. A pile of leaves. She peeks into the cab as she walks by. Bits of dirty yellow stuffing erupt from the cracked blue plastic bench seat.

She has intentionally arrived on a Friday afternoon, hoping to catch Gene when he's home from work but before he goes out drinking.

She walks up the now-familiar worn steps and pauses to listen before she knocks. The ever-present sound of the TV. Nothing else. She knocks. Footsteps. The door's curtain is flicked aside. She can't see who did it. Then she hears the squeal, "Miss Cindy! It's Miss Cindy!" She looks down and sees Brittany through the curtain, hauling hard on the doorknob. The door swings open and Brittany rushes out. Cindy crouches down to catch her hug.

"Miss Cindy! It was great up at the lake! I caught a fish! Daddy helped me! And Dolly fell into the lake, but Daddy got her out with the paddle! And we had marshmallows one night except Daddy's kept catching on fire and he would say bad words! And then we saw the bear again, except this time it was bigger and Daddy didn't try to get close to it! And this woman parked her boat at the same place we did and she said that I should be a nurse when I grow up because I'm so good at helping people because I helped her clean out her boat!"

"Wow," Cindy says, pleased at the healthy glow to Brittany's skin and the light in her eyes. "Sounds like you had a blast."

"Went OK," she hears Gene say and she looks up. He stands in the middle of the living room, a silver beer can in his hand. He is wearing a sleeveless t-shirt and his scalp, face and arms show the red of too much sun.

Brittany looks at Gene, then back at Cindy. "And Daddy didn't smack me at all!" she says. Gene winces, but Cindy speaks immediately to cover his embarrassment.

"I'm glad that things worked out so well. It sounds like everyone had a great time."

"And the Jesus man was there and he told me that God will save us all and all I have to do is ask him into my heart. So I think I'm going to ask him to be in my heart tonight," Brittany says, growing serious.

"That's a great idea, Brittany," Cindy says, still crouching. "Brittany, I really want to hear all about your trip, but can I talk to your daddy for a few minutes? Just me and Daddy. Then it can be just you and me. OK?"

Brittany looks at Gene, who shrugs and takes a noncommittal swig.

"OK," she says. "I'll go out on the porch with Dolly." She picks up her doll from beside the couch and retrieves the battered pink stroller from a corner. She plunks the doll into the stroller and heads out the door to the porch. "And then we will talk, right, Miss Cindy? Just you and me, right? Girl talk?"

"Yes, for sure," Cindy says. "Girl talk. Just you and me."

Brittany smiles and wheels her doll onto the front porch.

"Can I come in?" Cindy asks Gene.

"Sure," he says. He seems calmer than usual.

There is no screen door, so Cindy leaves the front door cracked so she can keep tabs on Brittany, who is wheeling her doll back and forth and singing. Cindy and Gene perch at opposite ends of the couch. Cindy can hear someone clattering in the kitchen. She assumes that it is Greta.

"So things went OK up there," Cindy says.

"Yeah. I did what you said. I tried to think about not hurting her. And she didn't get real mouthy, so it went OK."

"Gene, it sounds like you did more than just not grab her. Taking her fishing. Marshmallow roasts. It sounds like you really tried to make it fun for her. Really made an effort."

Gene flushes and looks down at his beer can.

"I know what you mean when you say she's like a ... like a diamond. She's ... she's ..." He seems to run out of words. Cindy waits, keeping her expression neutral.

"I guess I don't think of her as a little kid. A lot of times, I just think of her as a damn – as a ... as a ... I just think about how she's keeping me from doing what I want to, like going fishing or having a beer and watching a race, you know what I mean? But I ... I should try, I guess, to take her along more. Don't hurt none."

He looks up at Cindy abruptly with a worried expression. "I don't mean that I take her drinking or nothing. I wouldn't do that. I mean like taking her fishing. We did that. Up at the lake. It wasn't so bad. She was OK. It was all right."

"Gene, I think that's great. You did a great job. I know that you have good fatherly instincts."

Gene flushes and looks down at his beer. He tries to swig, but it's empty.

"Greta!" he yells.

"Gene, I'm going to be straight with you," Cindy says. "Right now, the county Children and Youth agency has paperwork ready to file to remove Brittany. But nobody wants that. I don't. I know you don't."

Greta appears with a can of beer. Eyes downcast, she replaces Gene's empty and leaves without a word. Gene cracks the fresh one open.

"I really don't think that it is going to do anyone any good to remove Brittany," Cindy says. "I would only do it if there's no recourse. But if things keep going like this ...." She stops.

Gene takes a swig and swallows. "Uh, yeah. Geez. I didn't know it went that far. Having papers ready and all."

"Gene, that doesn't mean anything definite. It's just preparation. In case. But it looks like we won't need to go forward in that direction if things keep going well."

"I don't want you to take her," he says.

"I don't think anybody wants that," she repeats. "I hear you got called back to work," she says to change the subject, thinking that she has made her point.

Gene brightens. "Yeah. Got a new order in for pallets. So I'm back at work. First shift, too. Big order. Ought to keep us going for a couple of months anyway."

"Well, that's good news."

"Yeah, things are just all bright and sunny around here," Gene says, taking a drink from his can. Cindy isn't sure if it was irony or sarcasm or if he was being honest.

Cindy stands and extends her hand. Gene seems surprised, but stands, switches his beer to his left hand, wipes his right on his jeans and shakes.

"Gene, I'll check in now and then but I hope things keep going this way. If they do, I think you and Brittany – and Greta – can have a nice life together."

Gene snorts but looks pleased. "All right." He takes a drink. "Guess you want to talk to Brittany," he says.

"If you don't mind."

"Naw. I don't mind at all. She likes you a lot." Gene meets Cindy's gaze. "She talks about you a whole lot. Says you're her girlfriend and all."

"Well, Gene, if she sees me that way, I'm very pleased. I hope she can trust me."

"So you ain't gonna take her?"

"Not if she doesn't get abused. And if you keep thinking of her as your little diamond."

Gene nods. "Guess you can go talk to her now."

Cindy gives him her most encouraging smile and he retreats to the kitchen. Cindy hears muttered conversation. Greta seems displeased with something.

Cindy opens the front door. Brittany is sitting in a corner with Dolly on her lap. She holds the doll by its neck and she is shaking a finger in its face.

"Now, if I told you a thousand times, I told you once, you are supposed to keep your mouth shut!" she admonishes the doll.

"Brittany, are you being mean to Dolly?"

"Miss Cindy, sometimes she just won't shut her mouth!" She gives an exaggerated sigh and rolls her eyes.

"Is that what daddy says to you?"

"Sometimes. And Greta, too. Greta's mean. She makes me eat lima beans."

Cindy sits down on the porch next to Brittany.

"Does Greta ever hit you?"

"Nope. Just Daddy. But he didn't the whole time we were up at the lake."

"Do you know what really helped?"

"I didn't talk about Mommy."

"Right. So do you think you can keep doing that?"

"Not talking about Mommy?"

"Yes."

"I guess. But sometimes Daddy is so mean."

"Can you tell me about this lady you met up at the lake?"

Brittany grows excited. "She is a nurse at a real hospital. And I was helping her clean out her boat. Well, it's not really hers. It's hers and her ... her ... the man she's married to."

"Husband."

"Yeah. And they have the same parking place we do. You know, that long wooden thing where you park your boat."

"Pier."

"And I was helping her clean out her boat. And she was so nice. And she was telling me that when you're a nurse you help people all the time like I was helping her." She pauses and puts a finger in her mouth. "Except that you help sick people. You don't help boats."

Cindy smiles. "When I was little, I was very sick for a while. And nurses helped me a lot."

Brittany turns to Cindy, eyes wide.

"They did? Really?"

"Really."

Brittany looks away, nodding her head. "Then I will have to be a nurse when I grow up. So I can help people like you, Miss Cindy. I would like to help you."

"That would be wonderful. I bet you would be a very good nurse."

"I try to help Greta, but she just yells at me. She doesn't want me to help her. She's so mean. So now I don't help her any more."

"Well, Brittany, some big people get impatient when children try to help. That's just the way they are. If Greta doesn't want your help, then you should just leave her alone. That's probably best."

"Daddy sometimes calls Greta the b-word, but he says that she does a good job around the house so he'll keep her."

"And what does Greta say when daddy says that?"

"He doesn't say it to her. Just to his friends. When they're drinking beer. Then they laugh."

They talk for a few more minutes. Brittany wants to hear the "maiden song" again. Cindy resists, but Brittany pleads. Cindy sings it again, softly. Brittany calms down and rests her head against Cindy's shoulder. She strokes Dolly's yarn hair as she listens.

After she's done, Cindy says, "Brittany, I have to go now. Will you promise me that you will be nice to Greta and not talk about your mommy to Daddy? If you want to talk about your mommy, wait until you see me. Then we can talk about your mommy all you want."

"When will you be back, Miss Cindy? I don't like it when you leave. Daddy's always nice when you're around."

"I have to go back to my job, Brittany. But I will be stopping in now and then to check on you and to talk to your daddy. So you'll see me regularly."

"What's a reg-are-lee?"

"Often. A lot."

Brittany leans over and wraps her arms around Cindy. "I like to see you, Miss Cindy. I like it when we have girl talk. Just you and me."

"I like it too, Brittany. Just you and me."

Back at the office, she calls Frank.

"I don't think we're going to have to remove Brittany. Gene's back at work and things seem to be going pretty well. I don't think Greta likes me much, but it doesn't look like anyone has been hitting Brittany."

"So you want me to just hang on to this filing?"

"Yeah. Put it in a drawer. I hope we won't need it."

"Me, too."

Chapter Thirty-One

On her way to work weeks later, thinking about what she has to do that day, she sees a strange-looking blob on the highway. As her car flashes over it, her brain processes the image and she realizes that it was a turtle, crawling slowly across the road.

He'll never make it, she thinks.

She goes to slam on her brakes, but a glance in the rear-view mirror shows her an orange pickup truck close behind. She settles for slowing and taking the next exit. She waits impatiently at the light at the end of the off-ramp, knowing that the turtle's chances for survival are less with each passing minute. She remembers reading an article about a psychology student's Ph.D. thesis on how some drivers aim for animals trying to cross the road.

She endures endless delays as she circles to get back on the highway the way she was originally headed. As she approaches the spot where the turtle was crawling, she slows. She peers frantically through the windshield, slowing to a crawl. Other drivers zoom past, their horns blaring.

She spots it – a dark lump. She pulls to the side of the road, puts on her flashers and exits the Honda. The turtle is near the white dotted line, in the center of the busy highway. He's not moving and looks like he's pulled back into his shell.

Well, I would too, she thinks.

She glances toward oncoming traffic. A cluster of cars including a tractor-trailer is headed her way but she has a moment. She darts to the middle of the road. Arriving at the turtle, she is devastated to see spherical bright red splatters of blood around him. His shell looks cracked.

Minutes too late, just minutes too late, she thinks. She grabs the turtle and runs back to her Honda as the cluster of vehicles rushes past her. The huge semi roars by, slapping her with a wind, snapping her skirt against her legs and shaking her Honda. She places the turtle on her hood and peers at him. He is closed up, head and legs pulled inside. Blood oozes from a broken place on his shell. She pops her trunk open and finds a plastic bag. She puts the bag on the floor of the passenger side and places him on it. She gets back in her car and drives to work, thinking how silly she is for risking her life to save a turtle. The turtle does not move and does not emerge.

She parks the car under a tree and rolls her windows down so he won't get overheated and goes in to work.

At lunchtime, she goes back to check. He's gone. There's a smear of blood on the plastic bag and no turtle. She opens the door and looks under the seat. There he is, about a foot from where she left him. He's still tucked inside his shell. She picks him up carefully. His head is still tucked inside his shell, but she can see his face. His eyes are open and he doesn't move. The bottom of his shell is smeared with blood and a yellowish fluid with black specks in it. She realizes that he's dead. He probably lived only minutes after she arrived at work. Hit and crushed by a tire, he retreated into his shell to die. Moving off the plastic bag to under the car seat was his last action, an instinctive desire to die in a sheltered place.

She quietly curses the driver who hit him, thinking how unfair it is that turtles have survived for hundreds of thousands of years with a simple defense – a hard shell. But now they find themselves helpless before the hurtling steel monsters that heartless humans have invented. She replaces him carefully under the seat.

After work, she stops at a home improvement store and buys a small shovel. She pulls out of the lot and keeps driving, drives out of town. She drives to a nearby state park, parks and gets a pair of battered sneakers out of the trunk and replaces her work flats. Carrying the turtle and the shovel, she takes a slow hike to a creek that runs through the park. There, by the chuckling water of the creek, she digs a hole.

I'm sorry, she thinks as she digs. *I'm sorry I couldn't get there fast enough to save you. I tried. I did. I'm sorry I didn't stop when I first saw you. I could have saved you if I had acted fast enough.*

She carefully places the turtle in the hole, shovels the dirt back and leaves. On the way home, she plays the radio loud so she doesn't have to think.

Chapter Thirty-Two

The night of her dinner date with Frank, she worries about what to wear. She has a little black dress but it's a bit on the sexy side and she doesn't want Frank to get the wrong idea.

What wrong idea?, she thinks. *That you like him?*

She finally talks herself into the black dress because it fits so well. She adds a fine gold necklace and a small black clutch. She tries to do her hair a little differently, but decides that it looks stupid. She washes it again and settles for her standard workplace gel-and-hairspray. She adds a little more gel and puts a little more spike in her hair. Too much, she knows, and her scalp will show. She wants to look different but not too different. Looking at herself, she has to admit that the change is subtle. She's satisfied with it but not pleased.

She's ready an hour early and feels silly, so she sits on the couch and dives into a John Irving novel so she doesn't have to wait and think about being so over-anxious that she's ready an hour early. Irving is describing a sun-dappled New England college campus when her doorbell buzzes.

Frank is in an obviously new white polo shirt and crisp green cuffed khakis. He greets her and leads her out to his little red car that isn't really a sports car. It's more like an economy car with some sporty options, she notices. He opens the door for her. The car is low and a little awkward to get into with a small, tight dress, but he helps her in and waits until she's settled. He closes the door and returns to his side.

"OK, since we liked Michael's for lunch, I figure it's worth a shot for dinner," he says, pulling away from the curb.

"Fine with me."

"By the way, you look stunning," he says, turning to look at her. "I'm going to make all the other guys jealous."

She opens her mouth but isn't sure what to say. She finally settles on, "You look nice, too."

On the short drive to Michael's, they talk about work, but keep it light. Frank drives right past the restaurant. He seems to be watching the sidewalk for something, but it's clearly not open parking places because he drives past several. Finally, he seems satisfied, pulls to the curb and shuts the car off. They are blocks from Michael's.

He opens her door and helps her out into a warm summer evening. There's a soft breeze and the sound of outdoor music, blues, not too far away.

"OK, I'm sure you have a good reason, but ...."

"But why the heck did I park way down here?" he asks as they stroll. He hasn't tried to take her hand but she wouldn't mind. The blues music gets louder.

"The reason is right here," he says.

The commercial storefronts lining the sidewalk have given way to a small open plaza, paved with brick. There's the standard municipal fountain and a small stage beside it. On it is the source of the blues music, five men illuminated by colored lights, four of them in front of a glittering drum set, one behind. They're all in white suits, black shirts, skinny ties, black fedoras.

A small group of people sit and stand around the plaza, most facing the band and listening, but some off to the sides talking and laughing, sitting on benches. Frank walks up to a vendor who has a small trailer on wheels behind him.

"Two chairs, please," Frank says. The vendor produces two folding chairs from the trailer. Frank hands the man his money and takes the chairs.

"Shall we?" he asks.

They walk to a place near the back of the crowd, off to the side. Frank sets up the chairs and they sit.

"Blues might not be your favorite, but there's nothing like music outdoors in the summertime," he says. "I hope you're not too hungry to listen a little."

"It's wonderful," she says, and means it.

The blues being pounded out by the band has a beat to it. She finds herself moving her foot to it; the band breaks into a jam and some people start dancing. Frank is tapping his hand on his leg.

"Blues fan?" he asks her.

"No, but I don't mind this. It's fun."

"I'm one of those people who likes it but I don't know much about it," Frank says. "That is, I know what I like, but I can't tell you who the big influences are or who was important or anything like that."

"Blind Lemon," Cindy says, the words popping out of her mouth.

Frank smiles. "What?"

"Wasn't there some big blues guy named Blind Lemon. Or Blind Melon?"

"Oh yeah," Frank says. "He was very famous. And then there was Blind Cantaloupe, Blind Pear and Not-blind-but-can't-get-a-driver's-license Kumquat."

She laughs and he smiles.

"No, I'm serious."

"I know there was a guy named Blind Lemon Jefferson," Frank says. "I don't know much about him, but I've seen his name on some of my CDs."

"And Muddy Waters?"

"Oh yeah. Everybody knows Muddy Waters. Mannish Boy. Dah-dah-DAH-dah-dah dum."

"Isn't that a great name?" she asks. "Muddy Waters. I always wished I could have a really cool name like that."

"Cindy Phillips is a perfectly nice name. Besides, you might have trouble getting a job if your name was Stagnant Pond or something like that."

She laughs again.

"You're funny."

"Thank you."

"Would you really give me a name like that?"

"Like what?"

"Stagnant Pond."

"Oh, no," he says.

The singer on the stage stops dancing, grabs the microphone like he's about to fling it like a discus and growls the lyrics.

"So what would my name be, if you were going to give me a cool name?"

"Now you're really putting the pressure on here," Frank says. "How long do I have to come up with one?"

She pretends to look at a watch; she's not wearing one.

"Thirty seconds."

"Hey!"

"Twenty-eight seconds," she says, smiling and keeping her eyes on the non-existent watch.

Frank knits his brow in a look of frantic concentration.

"Thank you, thank you," the singer says to scattered but sincere applause. "That was a nice little tune, *Boom, Boom* by John Lee Hooker. Hope you liked it."

Behind him, the drummer starts up and the lead guitar player plays a rolling little riff. They run through a couple stanzas, then the singer grabs the microphone like he wants to hurt it and snarls another set of lyrics.

"Time's up!" she says.

"Arg!" Frank says. "That's a tough assignment! Thirty seconds."

"Cuts to the essentials," she says. "So, what would it be?"

"Come on. I don't have a good one."

"Well, what was the best one you came up with?"

"The Terminator," Frank says.

She laughs and slaps him lightly on the shoulder. "No, really."

"Well, the first part was 'pretty,' " he says, catching her hand. She hopes he keeps it.

"Pretty Baby?" she asks. "That would be cheating. The singer just said that."

He keeps her hand and she feels a tingle.

"How about Pretty Lady?" he says. "Now, remember, I only had thirty seconds. But Pretty – well, I don't need to explain that one." She blushes and has to look away. "And Lady," he says quietly, when she turns back. "Because there aren't too many of those left. We have to value the ones that are."

She smiles.

"Thank you, Frank. I'm sorry. That was mean. Fishing for compliments. Putting you on the spot like that."

"Ha!" he says. "That's nothing compared to what Norma does to me at work."

"This is really nice music," she says, although they're not watching the band any more. She's looking at him, his nice teeth, his neatly trimmed beard, his warm, sparkling eyes.

"Glad you like it," Frank says. "I'd hate to get you out here and find that you hated the blues."

"Anything is nice on a night like this."

Frank agrees silently and they listen to the music.

The band is picking up speed on a jam and people begin dancing again. An idea occurs to her. She rejects it as too audacious but it boomerangs right back to her, whispering, *But it feels right, doesn't it?* She gives in.

"Come on!" she says, standing, and pulling him by his hand.

"Dance?" He looks terrified.

"Dance." she says.

"I don't ...."

"Come on! Dance with me!" Still holding his hand, she spins, wrapping his arm around her waist. Suddenly, she's very close to him, her legs touching his. He's looking up at her. In his eyes, she sees the decision made. She stands back to give him room and he stands up. They walk to the area right in front of the stage cleared for dancing. There are only a few other couples there, but they're moving. The band is keeping the rollicking beat going.

They face each other and begin to move. Frank isn't graceful or smooth, but he keeps the beat. He's very tentative at first, but the beat is infectious and he soon loosens up. They come close, they touch; they keep each other's hands, then they split apart. She can see genuine enjoyment in his eyes. She wonders what he sees in hers.

The band plays on. At one point, she catches the lead singer's eye and he gives her a wink. She supposes he's happy that his music makes people want to dance.

At last, the music stops and the singer says, "All right. Thank you. We're going to take a little break. See you in ten."

The drummer taps out a little flourish and the band leaves the stage to applause. Standing, Frank looks at Cindy. They're both sweaty but she feels like she's glowing. She feels very comfortable with Frank.

"Whew," he says. He pulls out a white handkerchief folded into a square. "Wow. I don't dance much."

She is thrilled when he offers the handkerchief to her.

"You did fine."

"You looked pretty nice yourself," he says.

She dabs her neck and brow, then hands it back to him. He puts it up to his head like he's going to wipe his forehead, then stops. He carefully places the handkerchief into a back pocket.

"I'll never wash it," he says.

She puts her hand in his. His hand is smooth and warm.

They walk to Michael's through the soft summer air.

At the door, it's clear that Frank has done his homework. The maitre' d gives Frank a nod, says, "Sir," and pulls two menus and leads them to a quiet corner. On the tiny round table is a flickering candle and a single rose, wrapped in white paper.

"Frank," she says. She feels the tingle again.

He pulls out her chair. "Please," he says. She sits.

"Now, I've done some serious research," he says. "I'm told that the stuffed shells here are the best you'll find outside of Italy."

"Do you think stuffed shells are from Italy?"

"Well, from what I hear, this place is second-best only to the place wherever they were invented. Maybe Denver. I don't know."

She giggles. "Stuffed shells. Invented in Denver."

Frank pretends to be wounded. "Well, I don't know! Where do you think they're from? I figured pasta, so, you know, Italy."

"You said Denver!"

"Only after you shot down Italy!"

He orders wine for them and it is light and delicious.

He raises his glass to her.

"Call me a silly romantic, but I must offer a toast. A private, intimate kind of toast. Not like the Elks do."

She raises her wine glass. "And this toast is because …."

"Because I never, ever thought that I would find someone like you in Altoona," Frank says. "Whatever the future brings, let us always be friends and comrades in the good fight. Let me always remember and be thankful for the day I met you."

They clink glasses and drink.

"Thank you," she says. "That was very nice."

Frank smiles. "Ahh, it was clumsy. It came off a lot better in rehearsal."

"It was fine."

The stuffed shells are delicious, but they could have been cardboard and she would have endured it for the pleasure of Frank's company.

After the meal, they walk hand-in-hand slowly back down the street to Frank's car. As they arrive at the plaza, she sees that the blues band and its audience are gone. Not surprising, since they spent more than three hours at dinner. The plaza looks lonely in the cold streetlights, with the band, its dancers and its colored lights gone.

"I didn't think that you could dance to the Blues," she says. "I always thought of it as kind of slow and sad."

"Well, you have to remember," Frank says, "that the Blues is very much a music of the people, if I can use a stupid sociology phrase. Back in the early part of the 1900s, if you were a black bluesman traveling around cheap bars in the deep south, or singing in some gin joint in Chicago, you had to be able to make people dance. True, the blues is sad, soulful music. It's about being sad, but the music itself isn't sad. I think that's what has kept it alive. The lyrics are about things that make you blue, but the music is about accepting it as part of life and trying to move on."

"You know, it makes me think about how we spend our lives looking for a place to fit in," she says. "We're always looking for a place to take us in, a place where we're accepted for who we are. We take different jobs, we move in and out of different circles of friends. We're always looking. We want to find that one place that feels like home."

Frank is looking at her.

"We look and look, but it's mostly random, isn't it?" she says. "I mean, what really are the odds of you finding a group of people who really accept you for who you are? There are always so many distractions. Even if you do find a good group at work, someone takes another job and somehow something's missing and the group falls apart. Or someone gets a promotion and now he's a boss and suddenly all the dynamics change and it just doesn't work any more. You know, people form book clubs and volunteer for charities and do all these things in groups but I think that a lot of time, we just want to find that group where everything fits and everything makes sense and where we can make a real contribution."

Frank does not speak.

"How many people look and look and never find a group to fit in, a place where people say, 'hey, we value you for who you are and what you've done and we'll overlook your faults. And we really, genuinely, like you, too.' How sad is it that most people look and look and never find it?"

They've stopped walking and she's frustrated by her inability to express her idea more clearly, but Frank turns to her and takes both her hands in his.

"That's both a sad and beautiful thought," he says. "It's poetry, in its own way."

She looks into his eyes, wishing to see something, confirmation, acceptance, something definite. But his eyes although deep are unreadable.

"Are you looking for that? Is that what you want? A place to fit in?" he asks.

They're all alone on a city street lit by the orange glow of sodium bulbs.

"Sometimes I think we're all just alone and we just have these very brief moments where we connect with another person," she says. "The rest of the time, we're just pretending. We really are like ships on a dark ocean. Love is lie. All we ever do is just try to make the best of it. We just get by for most of our lives. We just get by."

"That's bleak," he says.

She searches his face. She's afraid that she's ruined the evening, taken it in a direction that will drive Frank away and leave her alone again. But she wants desperately to complete her thought and earn his agreement.

"I mean, you see these parents who harm their own children and I'm not even talking about abuse. Even in a divorce, you get these spouses who are intentionally cruel to each other and who allow their kids to get caught in the middle." She pauses. "I can't imagine anything more baffling to a seven-year-old than to be told that Mommy and Daddy don't love each other any more and Daddy is going to move away. Kids just don't have a frame of reference for that. It's just not something that makes sense to them. People are so mean in a divorce, fighting over stupid stuff, looking for revenge. An attorney once told me that you see good people at their worst." She trails off, stops and looks down.

"I'm not being very coherent here, am I?" she asks, looking back up and meeting Frank's eyes. "Too much wine, maybe."

"However you are saying it, I know exactly what you're talking about," Frank says. "That's what my stupid toast was about. I was hoping ... oh, I don't know ..." His gaze goes above her head to the blank windows of an office building across the street. "I was trying to say, I guess, that there's a connection here that I don't want to lose, ever, no matter what might happen. You're right, we don't know what's coming. The stupidest things can come between two people, no matter what their intentions are. So, I was just hoping that maybe, somehow, this connection that we've found can somehow beat the odds and last. I don't know. That sounds stupid."

"No, not at all," she says quietly.

Abruptly, he pulls her close for a hug. He grips her tightly and she holds on as if she might slide off the earth if he lets go.

Then there is a crackle of tires on gravel and Frank releases her. She dabs the tears from her eyes and sees that he is doing the same. A blue-and-white police cruiser has pulled to the curb near them.

"Everything OK here, folks?" says the officer from his open window.

"Just great," Franks says, finding a smile. "Just taking a little walk."

"All right," the officer says and drives on.

They walk silently to Frank's car. The evening seems colder. He opens the door and helps her in. As he drives her home, shadows moving through the car, the only illumination the green lights of his dashboard, she says, "Thank you. I had a wonderful evening."

Frank doesn't look at her. He shifts the car. For a moment, she's afraid that she did indeed ruin everything. Then he turns and looks directly into her eyes.

"Does it have to end?"

She is relieved. She grasps his hand, which is still on the gearshift. He lets her take it and place it on her lap.

"No," she says. "It doesn't have to end. Not yet, anyway."

His eyes back on the road, he smiles.

Chapter Thirty-Three

As usual, Brian is sitting on his father's circular footrest, staring at the television. His back hurts. His knee is sore from a fall. He's fall-asleep-in-the-car tired. But he's again suffering through his father's post-game analysis. His father stands on his left with the remote control.

"Now, look at this!" his father says, freezing the picture. "Right here! There was a clear lane to the quarterback. What the fuck were you thinking? Were you asleep? Jesus Christ, you could have driven a goddamn truck through that fucking hole and you stand there like a stunned sheep. Jesus."

Something clicks and suddenly, Brian has had enough.

"Dad, would you lay off the profanity? Please."

He keeps his eyes on the screen but he can feel his father's attention swing to him. There is a moment of charged, stunned silence. Then his father says, in a voice almost a whisper, "What did you say?"

It's now or never, a voice says inside Brian. Just the way he makes decisions in a game, he decides that it's time. He swivels on the footrest and looks up at his father.

"I said, 'Dad, would you lay off the profanity?'"

The blow comes quickly and without warning, but he's ready for it. As his father's right hand streaks toward his head, he comes up off the stool *twinge in the knee* and blocks the blow with his forearm. He stands upright. He realizes that he's a good three inches taller than his father.

His father's eyes narrow and his mouth twists. "Oh, now you're going to stand up and do something. Now you're going to try to be a man about it."

Brian remembers Cindy's words: *Be cold. Don't get angry. If you do, he wins.*

"Actually, Dad, I'm going to bed. Thanks for your advice, but I'm beat."

He moves toward the steps.

"Take one more goddamn step and I'll rip your fucking head off, you rotten little bastard," his father says.

Brian turns.

"Dad. Please. Back off. I'm tired. I'm going to bed." He turns back toward the steps, but he's ready. He hears the quick rush of steps behind him.

"Why you rotten little ...." He turns as his father, very close, swings for his head with his right fist. Brian grabs his father's wrist and calls on the reservoir of strength he uses during games. He stops his father's swing, halts it in mid-air. Then, looking into his father's eyes, he very slowly bends his father's arm back and down. In those eyes, he sees blind fury.

Abruptly, his father lunges, catching Brian off-balance. Brian stumbles backwards, trips on the carpet and falls. His father wrenches his wrist from Brian's grip as his son goes down. He stands over his son, his eyes flashing. He rolls up his sleeves.

"Get ready to get hurt," he says. "I always knew you were a pussy."

Brian scuttles backwards, but his father is on him quickly. One kick knocks Brian's legs aside, ending his scuttle. His tailbone hits the floor painfully. Another kick comes. Brian rolls left, taking it on his thigh. There's immediately another kick square in his back, a hammer-blow of pain.

That's not fair, he thinks. *You don't kick in a fair fight.*

He rolls rapidly, coming to his feet near a wall. His father, his face distorted with rage, is on him immediately. While Brian finds his balance, a blow hits him in the stomach. His breath leaves him and he bends over. His father's hands close around his neck and shove him upright, slamming his head back against the wall. Brian sees bright sparkles around the edge of his vision. He can smell onions on his father's breath.

"You little shit," his father hisses and spit sprays Brian's face. His head feels like it's expanding, tightening. "I'll show you what happens when you disrespect me."

Something is screaming in Brian's ears like the whistle of a tea kettle. His vision narrows to his father's red sweaty scalp, the strands of hair combed over it. Now his breath comes only in gulps and the air is hot and thin.

His father shifts his weight without lessening his grip. Without knowing why, Brian twists slightly to the side and his father's knee hits him hard in the upper thigh.

He tried to knee me in the balls, Brian realizes. *That's not fair.*

He gasps again for air as his father hisses, "You're not much of a man and you're not much of a football player. I hoped for more from my son. You can't even beat your old man."

He slams Brian's head against the wall and the sparkles return, brighter this time, closing in on the center of his vision. They appear against a background of blue. He can't breathe at all. He considers surrendering, giving up. Then something deep inside him uncoils.

This whole fight wasn't fair, he thinks. *Dad's cheating to win. The bastard.*

He's suddenly furious. His father has no right. Cindy's words come to him again: *Be cold.*

He brings control to his hands and grabs his father's wrists. He slowly but steadily pulls outward, like one of his weight-lifting drills. His father's skin is clammy and sweaty, but Brian's hands are big enough to lock around his father's wrists. The muscles in his father's forearms bulge and then quiver as Brian downshifts and applies more torque. Slowly, his father's hands come off his neck. Brian looks directly into his father's eyes as he slowly, steadily pulls the hands outward. As the last touch of red-hot fingers leaves his neck, he sees the fury in his father's eyes fade. As Brian pulls his father's hands completely off his neck, he sees confusion emerge.

Brian pulls his father's arms together in front of him, between them, and pushes them together until his father's wrists are almost touching each other. He holds his father's hands there, locked, as if handcuffed. He is in control. Their faces are close. He looks directly into his father's eyes. He thinks he sees a glint of fear.

"Dad," he says carefully. He coughs. His throat is sore; his voice is rough. "I. Said. Back. Off."

His father struggles to separate his hands, but Brian's arms and heart are made of steel. Gathering his strength in his hips, Brian takes a half-step forward and shoves his father as hard as he can. His father stumbles backward, arms flailing. He loses his footing and falls hard on his back. Brian sees a quick grimace of pain as he hits the floor and slides a foot.

Brian walks over to where his father lies. His father winces and wedges a hand between the small of his back and the floor. Brian looks down at him. His father's face is pale; his scalp is mottled red and white.

"I played a good game tonight, Dad," Brian says, his voice raspy. "I had two sacks. I can't get one on every play. Eight tackles. I played four quarters as hard as I could. We won."

His father turns his head away, one hand still under his back.

"Dad," Brian says.

His father's head doesn't turn.

"Dad." Brian says. "Look at me."

His father slowly turns his head. With reluctance, he meets his son's eyes. Brian allows their gazes to lock, then bends down and extends a hand, fingers curled, thumb up, ready to grasp.

His father looks at the extended hand, then into Brian's eyes. Brian looks back.

Slowly, his father removes his hand from his back, reaches up and grasps Brian's hand. Brian roots his feet, crouches and pulls his father up as he does so often for his teammates.

His father arrives on his feet unsteadily. His hair is mussed into wild spikes. His expression is neutral but his face is drawn. Brian can smell his sweat. Brian holds onto his father's hand a moment longer than is standard. He claps his father on the shoulder.

"Dad. I'm tired. I'm going to bed. You should, too."

He walks to the steps, then stops and turns around. His father stands unsteadily, his gaze unfocused, one hand on the small of his back.

"I'd love to talk about the game tomorrow, Dad," Brian says. "You've got great insights."

Then he turns and walks up the steps, to a soft bed and calm dreams.

Chapter Thirty-Four

Frank puts the cardboard box down on the dining room floor. It has many companions. "There," he says. "That's the last damn box." He wipes sweat from his forehead with his arm.

"Then it's official," Cindy says from the kitchen, where she was putting utensils away. "We're living in sin."

"Well, technically, I have three days left on my rent this month," he says, coming into the kitchen. He swings the front door shut with his foot. "So I could still move back. My landlady loves me. She'd let me move back in, no questions asked."

Cindy pauses in her task and narrows her eyes at him. "Typical guy. Short attention span. I thought we agreed that this was our new life together. That means, since you weren't paying attention, shacking up."

"Well," Frank says with his sideways look that tickles her, "We're not an official household yet. We never did sort out the chores. Who's going to do laundry? Who's going to take the garbage out? Who will put the cat out?"

"Silly," Cindy says. "We don't have a cat. You can do all that stuff. I'll be on the couch with my chocolate."

"Typical woman," Frank says. "Always ready to give orders from the couch."

"What?" Cindy asks, outrage in her voice. She raises a plastic spatula menacingly.

Frank says "Yikes!" and runs. She chases him. She catches him in the bedroom, where she can block the door, trapping him on the far side of the bed. He crawls onto the bed looking wary, seeking an exit. She says "Grrr!" and jumps on him. They wrestle for a minute, then he pins her. He straddles her, holding her wrists above her head.

"Release the spatula, wench!" he orders.

"Never!"

"Then you force me to use drastic measures." He lowers his head and nuzzles her neck. She shrieks and struggles. "Stop! OK! OK! You win!"

"Then surrender the weapon," he says, his lips almost touching her ear.

"I think I dropped it. I don't know where it is," she whispers back.

"Then just surrender," he says and moves his lips back to her neck. His beard tickles but she closes her eyes and doesn't move.

Later, lying still, he says, "I think it was the bandanna."

She opens her eyes and looks at him. He rests with his hands locked behind his head. The light from the window catches his beard and his hair, making them a translucent amber.

"The what?"

"The bandanna on your head. I think that's what made you so cute."

It had fallen off or been removed some time ago. She doesn't know where it is at the moment. Probably on the floor.

She laughs. "So all I have to do is put on a bandanna?"

"Oh yes," he says. "Especially if that's all you're wearing."

"Stop. You're bad," she says.

"What's the point of shacking up if not the frequent wild and crazy sex?" he asks.

"Define frequent," she says.

"Well, let's see," Frank says, shifting onto his side to look at her. She stays cuddled around a pillow. "My definition would be … oh, three times a day."

She purses her lips and looks at him.

"Oh, OK, you win," he says. "Six times a day."

She laughs. "My god, that's all we'd get done."

"And that's a bad thing how?" Frank asks.

She smiles, but her gaze drifts and Frank knows that she is thinking. He gives her three minutes by the red numbers on the clock behind her. Then he asks, "What's thrashing around inside there now?"

He frees one arm to run his fingers through her hair. If he pays attention, he can just feel the ridge around the top of her skull. He never mentions that to her.

"Do you really find me that attractive?" she asks.

"You mean, like six-times-a-day attractive?"

"Like even one-time-a-day attractive," she says.

Frank knows to be careful with his answer. "If we didn't have to go to work and eat and stuff like that, I'd be content to stay right here for the fore-seeable future," he says.

"But I'm so … how can you –" Frank interrupts her.

"You and a bandanna, that's all it takes. I think you're very sexy," he says. "I swear. Do you think I'd shack up with someone I didn't find attractive?"

"But I'm –" He interrupts again.

"So cute, yes," he says. "And perky."

She blinks and sits up. He levers himself up onto an elbow.

"Perky?" she asks, narrowing her eyes.

"Yes, perky."

"Perky?" she yells and hits him with her pillow. "You like perky?"

He grabs the pillow, pitches it aside and wrestles her down again.

"Twice," she says, breathless, on her back.

"Four to go," he says.

Then they don't speak for a while.

Chapter Thirty-Five

"**D**id you pay the renter's insurance?" she asked as soon as he came in the door. He hated it when she did that, but he mentally wadded up his frustration and threw it away. She was standing at the kitchen counter, her purse and a pile of mail beside her. Some of the letters had been torn open. She was holding one folded bill and peering at it with a knitted brow.

"Hello to you, too," he said.

She looked up. For an instant, she looked at him as if he were a stranger. Then her face softened.

"I'm sorry," she said. "But the stupid premium is way overdue and they're going to cancel us and …."

He went to her and got a kiss.

"Much better," he said, smiling. She smiled back. He took the bill gently from her hand and put it on the counter.

"We're not married yet. Let's save those stupid fights for married life."

"I wasn't fighting. I just wanted to know –"

"I know," he said. "I just wanted to cut it off before anything got started." He picked up the bill and slipped it into his breast pocket. "I'll take care of it tomorrow. I promise."

"Thank you," she said. "But what about the rest of them?"

"They can wait," he said, putting a hand on her waist. "For now, let's change our clothes, sit down, have a drink and decide what we're going to do about dinner." He kissed her on the brow. "How was your day, honey?"

"Honey? You just called me honey."

"That I did. Seemed the right thing to say."

"If we're at that stage, am I supposed to be in the kitchen with pearls and heels on and have dinner hot and ready?"

"And I can toss my fedora on the hat rack," he said, putting his other hand on her waist. "Where are those darn kids?"

"Oh, little Billy's doing his homework and his big sister Sally is helping him," she said, smiling.

"Mmm! Dinner smells delicious, honey," he said, pretending to sniff the air. "What's cooking?"

"What's cooking is that I think you're going to do the cooking tonight," she said.

"What? I cooked last night."

"Yeah, but you still owe me one from last week."

"Well," he grumbled, "then it's macaroni and cheese and peas again."

"Not fair! That's what you made last time."

"And it was delicious, wasn't it?"

"Mac and cheese only goes so far," she said. "I'm kind of in the mood for something a little more adult."

Frank smiled.

Chapter Thirty-Six

She became aware that Frank was holding her tightly, rocking her and muttering something soothing. They were in bed; the room was dark, the covers were twisted. She was sweating. When she tried to talk, her voice failed. Her throat was raw and dry. Frank pulled back from her a little so he could look into her eyes.

"OK now?" he asked. She could see deep concern in his eyes.

"Drink," she croaked. He nodded, got up and walked to the bathroom. She looked around the room. The pillows were scattered. The blankets were twisted into a giant rope and were mostly off the bed.

Frank came back with a plastic cup of cool water. She drank it, handed it back to him. He placed it on the bedside table and sat down near her. He reached for a foot and began to massage it.

"Are you OK now? You had me scared."

"Oh, god, what did I do?"

"You just sat straight up and started screaming. Your eyes were wide open. It was like some kind of horror movie. When I first grabbed you, you didn't respond at all. You just screamed this long ...." He shuddered. "This long, awful scream. For a second or so, I really thought that you might have slipped out of your sanity."

His warm pressure on her foot calmed her.

"I ... Let me think."

She frowned. Frank rubbed.

"Oh god. Now I remember. Did I just say god? How appropriate. I don't remember any of my dream except the end ... and that was the part that made me scream."

"What was it?"

"This sounds ... stupid," she said.

"No. You know me. I know you. Nothing's stupid between us."

"I was watching a sunrise. I was sitting in a field. The sun was rising over some hills. Except that when the sun came up, it wasn't the sun. It was the eye of God." She looked at Frank. "I told you it was stupid."

"That's not stupid," he said. "That's frightening. I can see why you freaked."

"I was sitting there. I was thinking about my life, and all these kids, and how sometimes it seems like we just can't do the right thing. I started thinking about my life and whether it is worth it or not. Whether I should be doing something else. Then I felt this warmth and I looked up, expecting to see the sun and ...." She shivered. Frank stopped rubbing and began to untangle a blanket. When it was unwrapped, he placed it around her shoulders. She smiled her thanks.

"So," Frank said, "what is it like to look into the eye of God?"

"I know exactly what they mean when they say that you can't look God in the eye and lie," she said. "That eye was so penetrating. I was completely exposed. I had no secrets. I could no more have said a lie to that eye than I could break my own neck. The power that was there, just this force, the gaze was like a physical force, like a wind screaming down a tunnel, but focused right on me. Right on little me." She paused. "You know how when you look up at the stars and sometimes you start thinking about how big the universe is and you start thinking about how insignificant you are – how silly all human stuff is, our ambitions, our plans. You know that feeling?"

Frank nodded. He found a foot under the blanket and began to rub again.

"It was like that, except a hundred times worse. A thousand times. I felt so completely pointless, useless. I was less than an insect to that eye. It could have done anything it wanted to me and there was nothing I could do. I was completely powerless. You know, we like to think of God as this kind old man with a beard. Maybe he would present himself to us that way so he doesn't scare the wits out of us. But the truth is, I think, that he – it – is an intelligence far beyond our understanding. We can no more understand God than a flea could understand international finance."

"I admit to struggling with international finance myself," Frank said with an almost imperceptible smile.

"Oh, you know what I mean," Cindy said. "We have no idea. No idea what God is like."

"So, was this eye looking at you with hostile intent?" Frank said. He took on a look of extreme caution and began edging away from her. "Like, there might be a bolt from the blue here or something?"

She leaned over and slapped his leg. "Quit it! You're goofy. No, I don't know. It wasn't hostile, it wasn't terrifying because it was hostile. It was terrifying because it was just so cold and alien and penetrating."

"But did you get the impression that God was pissed at you? Or was he just being God?"

"He was just being God. That's what was scary about it. He was just being Himself and I almost lost my sanity. Who knows what would happen if he had been mad at me?"

"So, do you think that you've been warned? Or something? I mean, you said that you had been thinking about whether your life was on the right track. Did seeing this eye change that? Bring something into focus?"

She thought a minute. "I don't know. I don't know. I know that if I do something else, it's going to be something less meaningful but much less stressful. Like I'll go be a bank teller or –"

"Car washes are always hiring," Frank said. "I could give you a great reference."

She laughed. "Car wash. Jeez. Frank! What's wrong with that? People need to have their cars washed. Some people want a low-stress job. Why do you have to be mean?"

Frank pretended to be appalled. "Mocking them? Who was mocking? I just said that car washes are always hiring – which is true – and that I'd give you a reference if you wanted one. It was your nasty little brain that denigrated the job." He sniffed as if wounded. "Perfectly fine career choice if you ask me."

"Frank. Honestly. What do you think about God?"

"I was raised Roman Catholic," he said. "So, my god is that pissed-off, irritable guy in the Old Testament. You know, the one who warns cities to shape up and when they don't, he nukes them in good Old Testament style. Plagues of locusts. That kind of stuff."

"But you're not a kid anymore. They fill your head with that stuff. But somewhere along the line, I think most people arrive at a different conclusion. Didn't you?"

"I don't know. There are a lot of people out there who seem to have swallowed what they were taught in grade school. What did they call it? In my day, it was CCD. They changed the name, but it's the same thing. They indoctrinate you."

"Yes, but even those people who go to church and seem to have swallowed it whole – don't you think that they have sort of let their beliefs settle a little? Kind of like, they might agree with 95 percent of what the church teaches, and they believe in the overall picture, but in their hearts, they believe things that are just slightly different?"

"You mean like Catholics who realize that the rhythm method doesn't work, that four kids are enough, and they start using condoms?"

"Yes! Exactly like that. It doesn't mean that they're bad Catholics. They still believe, they still go to church, they still teach their kids to believe, but they make a few little adjustments in the own lives and their own beliefs. You know, they figure that if they follow most of the teachings, God will look the other way at a few transgressions."

Frank chuckled. "Transgressions. Now you sound Catholic."

"You know what I mean."

"Yes, I do. And I agree with you there."

She turned to look at him. "So, Frank, what do you believe? Surely you're not one-hundred-per-cent Catholic anymore."

"No. I can't say that." He smirked. "Exhibit A – I'm in bed with a woman who is not my wife."

"Yes, you're very naughty that way," she said.

"We could make it worse," he said, sliding a hand up her leg.

She narrowed her eyes, grabbed his hand and pushed it back.

"Behave yourself. Not until you answer my question," she said.

"Geez," Frank said. "Echoes of Sister Ursula in fourth grade. You going to crack my knuckles with a ruler?"

"Frank."

"All right. I believe in God. With a capital G. But I think that he keeps out of our daily lives. He set up the universe and then went away. Or watches from a distance. For example, if you're praying to him to get you through an algebra test or to get a raise, forget it. He's not interested. You're on your own. Free will. That's how he set us up."

"Do you think he loves us?"

"Loves. Hmm. Well, like in your dream. I think that he might 'love' us in a certain sense, but not in the same way that we humans love each other. Our closest approximation here on this globe might be relationship between a man and a dog. You know, dogs just love humans. They worship us. But I'm damn sure that they don't understand us. Trips to the vet must be a complete mystery. They love us so much that they tolerate those trips, even though they usually end up with the dog getting a painful shot or having to gag down a pill. It's the same way with God. We wonder why he lets bad things happen to us down here. But we're missing the big picture. Unfortunately, there's probably no way that we can ever understand the big picture. Just like there's no way that a dog is ever going to understand why it has to go to the vet and get a rabies shot."

"So is religion a waste of time?"

"Geez, woman, it's four in the morning and you're running me through Philosophy 101!"

"Does God care if we worship him or not?"

Frank sighed. "I don't know. I admit that I haven't given this the deep thought that it deserves. I apologize. I'm usually too busy trying to remember if we need milk or not and what your bra size is and how I'm going to handle a particular nasty case that Norma just gave me."

"Why are you worried about my bra size?"

"Because in day-to-day life, that's a more important question than whether religion is a waste of time or not. Especially if it's near Valentine's Day."

"So is it? More important, I mean."

"I don't know," Frank said. "I tend to think that God doesn't really care if we adore him or not. If he's really such an advanced intelligence, then our pitiful little songs and prayers just don't mean that much. Like I said, praying to pass a test or get a raise or not get stopped for speeding – or even for the health of someone you love – it's all pretty much water under the bridge for Him. Our lives will take their course and that's it. God maybe watches it unfold, but he's not going to step in and heal someone who's sick. The illness of one person here on Earth probably consumes less than a billionth of a billionth of one percent of His mind. He's got the whole universe to keep track of. Maybe we're not the only beings that he created. Maybe there are trillions and trillions of planets out there with intelligent beings on them and he's got to keep track of them all. Or maybe, hell, there are planets filled with bears and tigers and dolphins and no really highly intelligent life. Maybe He likes them better. I bet those planets don't have problems with pollution and overpopulation. I bet dolphins don't rip each other off in big investment scams."

"So religion is useless?"

"Now, I didn't say that," Frank said. "You're really setting me up for a tough confession next time I go." He paused. "Religion has its value, at least for us as human beings. I don't know if it does that much for God, but it certainly can be a powerful force for good here on this planet."

"You mean like how the Catholic church helped high-ranking Nazis escape after World War II? Or the priests who abused kids while the church looked the other way?"

Frank pursed his lips. "Now, the pope apologized for both of those."

"But you can't say that religion is always a force for good. As you would say, 'Exhibit A: The Inquisition.'"

"Yes. I admit that bad shit has been done in the name of the church. But you also can't deny that religion tries really hard to bring out the best in people. Think of the Ten Commandments. It seems pretty basic stuff to us today, but to people two thousand years ago, it was a code of conduct. It was a blueprint for a better society. You know, don't kill each other. Don't envy what your neighbor has, or you might be tempted to steal from him. Thus violating one of the other rules. Fear me, for I am a jealous god and I'll kick your ass if you step out of line. He had to put an enforcement clause in there or no one would have listened. How about the one that says, behave and listen to your parents. How smart was that?"

"Proof right there that God must be a parent in some sense," Cindy said. "No one but a parent would put into a set of rules for society that you have to listen to your parents."

"Right. Exactly. Either God is a parent in some sense that we can understand, or He had such a deep knowledge of human psychology that he knew that human kids were going to drive their parents nuts."

"And this was before cruising and malls were invented," Cindy said.

"No wonder that parents sent kids to the factories in the 19th century," Frank said. "Got them out of their hair for twelve hours."

"Oh, that's just mean! Those poor kids."

"Yes, I know. I'm sorry. I shouldn't kid about that."

They were both quiet for a minute.

"What do you believe?" Frank asked. He moved closer.

"About God?"

"Yeah. Who is he? What is he? Why are we here?" Frank asked.

"Oh my," Cindy said. "First of all, this could take a while. Second of all, I'm not sure about a lot of it. I'm still sorting it out, I guess."

"Well, why don't you give it some thought," Frank said, leaning closer. "Meanwhile, I think I need to check on your bra size again." His hand was warm on her. She put her hand over his.

"But …."

"Shhh," Frank said, kissing her very softly.

"Vivian always tells me I don't know when to stop talking," Cindy said, relaxing as he gently pushed her back.

"This is one of those times," Frank said.

Chapter Thirty-Seven

She stops at the big box discount store outside of town after work. She hates the store and its ever-present crowds and indifferent employees, but it has the best price on an asthma medicine that works for her and which her health care plan doesn't cover.

Because of the usual discount store crowd, she's forced to park at the far end of the four acres of asphalt that make up the store's parking lot. She's getting out of her car when he hears the loud blare of a horn from the nearby busy commercial street. She looks up. A battered green pickup truck has skidded to a halt just inches from the rear of a car whose driver had stopped to turn left into the discount store's gigantic lot. She hears an exchange of yells, tinny with distance, and a grey-haired man in the truck flips the finger at the car's driver. With a roar of his engine and a squeal of tires, the pickup truck driver lunges onto the shoulder, bypassing the line of cars. The pickup truck, with two wheels still on the shoulder, accelerates, engine roaring.

Cindy shrugs at what must be an every day occurrence on the busy road and begins to walk toward the store. Then she stops and turns.

Something about the skinny arm that was extended out the window and which now hangs out the window, something about the driver's profile. Gray hair. Green pickup. She catches the briefest glimpse of a blue tarp flapping in the bed of the pickup before it tops a hill and vanishes.

Was that Gene? Now why would he be driving like an idiot? He's usually such a slowpoke, she thinks. She turns back toward the store, shrugging. Discount store traffic seems to bring out the worst in everyone. She's been frustrated by the drivers who seem to be in a great hurry to experience the discount store's so-called "extra-special low" prices.

Ten steps later something whispers *Brittany* and she stops. Then she's running back to her Honda, keys out, digging in her purse for her cell phone.

Part Two

Chapter Thirty-Eight

"Nine-one-one, what is your emergency?"

"Dispatch, this is Cindy Phillips, I'm a caseworker with Family Services. I have reason to believe that a girl has been physically abused and needs medical care urgently. Would you please dispatch an ambulance to Fifteen-oh-six North Eighth Avenue?"

"Ma'am, are you at the scene?"

"No. But I'm headed there."

"Ma'am, who called you to the scene?"

"No one."

"Ma'am, then how can you be sure that there is a medical emergency?"

"I can't be sure. I'm not. But I have a feeling."

"Ma'am, I'm very sorry, but I cannot dispatch an ambulance on the basis of a feeling. It's required that you be a witness or have first-hand knowledge of the emergency."

"Please," Cindy said. "Just send the ambulance. If it turns out that there's no emergency, I'll pay the entire cost of the run. Please."

"Ma'am, I can't just –"

"Look. Haven't you ever had a feeling, just known for sure about something? Had a premonition? You're female – do you believe in female intuition?"

"Ma'am, you're getting rather personal. I don't think –"

"OK. I'm begging. I'm officially begging. Please. I just saw a man driving out of town like a maniac. He usually drives like a turtle. I know for a fact that his daughter – that he abuses his daughter. I'm the family's caseworker. I strongly suspect – no, I know that Gene Edinburger is trying to get out of town because he's done something awful to his little girl. Please. Please. Please send an ambulance to her house. Like I said, I'll pay all the expenses if it turns out to be nothing."

"Ma'am, I – please stand by." Click.

Click. "Ma'am?"

"Yes?"

"I checked with my supervisor and I am absolutely not permitted to dispatch without you having direct knowledge of the emergency situation. I'm sorry."

"I'm sorry too. Look, I have to go. I'm trying to drive and talk, and doing both just isn't working."

As she accelerates down the street honking her horn, a wail begins behind her. She glances in the rear view mirror. Sure enough, a city police car is behind her, red and blue lights flashing. Far back, she can see other cars that have pulled to the curb to let the police car by.

As she approaches her next left turn, she makes sure to turn on her signal. She slows, corners, then steps on the gas pedal again and the willing Honda accelerates. The police car comes around the corner rapidly, wailing and flashing. She grabs her cell phone with her right hand and, risking a glance down, locates the 9 button. She pushes it, then as she speeds up the street, feels up the matrix of buttons with her thumb for the 1 button. She pushes that twice, then raises the phone to her ear.

There are two rings, then a click.

"Nine-one-one, what is your emergency?" A male this time.

"Dispatch, I am Cindy Phillips, a caseworker for Family Services. I am currently northbound on North 18th Street, headed for a suspected severe case of child abuse at Fifteen-oh-six North 8th Avenue. A city police officer is behind me. I can't see the number of the car. Would you please contact the officer and tell him what I am doing?"

"Ma'am, do I understand that you are being pursued by a police car?"

"Yes, I am –" she breaks off to signal a right turn and make the turn. She is almost there. Back on the gas. "– I am being pursued by the police car. But I'm responding to an emergency. The officer can help by ending his pursuit of me or by escorting me to the residence."

"Ma'am, stand by."

Almost there. Almost there. She swerves around a slow-moving driver, taking the phone from her ear to send a blast of rapid horn honks.

"... in pursuit. You are advised to pull to the side of the road and stop," the dispatcher's voice says when she returns the phone to her ear.

"I can't. I need to get to the –" The dispatcher interrupts her.

"Ma'am, you are advised to pull over immediately. You have already been identified as fleeing from an officer and other units are responding to your location."

"Look, there is probably a little girl up there in a pool of blood. I couldn't get you to dispatch an ambulance, so I had to go myself. I'm trying to get there because this little girl probably has only a few minutes to live. Yes, I am speeding. Yes, there is an officer chasing me. I am responding to an emergency and I don't happen to have red and blue lights for my car."

"Ma'am, the officer in pursuit suggests that you pull over immediately. Once he has verified your situation, if it is as you describe, he will escort you."

"There is no time for me to pull over and describe my situation to the officer. Don't you see that? There is a little girl dying on North 8th Avenue and – oh, hell!"

She throws the cell phone down on the passenger seat, signals a right turn, slows, and pulls onto North 8th Avenue, the officer right behind her.

There are no cars in front of Brittany's house. She slams the car to a stop, jams the gear lever into park, leaps out and runs for the house, leaving her door open. As she reaches the porch steps, she hears, "All right, lady, stop right there!"

She is at the front door. She tries it. Locked. She takes three steps backward, turns her shoulder toward the door and runs at it. Behind her, she hears, "Lady, I need to talk to you!"

She hits the door hard and something cracks. She hits it again. It holds.

"Goddammit!" she swears and hits the door again. This time, a sharp pain shoots through her shoulder. She backs up for another try.

Behind her, a voice says, "All right, lady, let me try."

She turns. The officer is there. He shakes his head.

"You're here for a kid, right?"

She nods rapidly. "Please!"

"All right." He kicks the door near the knob and it pops open.

Cindy runs inside. Living room. TV on. A woman in a low-cut dress is kissing a man in a suit. Soap opera. "Brittany!" she yells. No answer.

She runs up the steps, taking them two at a time. Brittany's door is open. Her bed is unmade. She drops to her knees and looks under. A rumpled blanket. She isn't there. Back down the steps, leaping, almost losing her balance. *If I catch a heel now ....*

"Brittany! Where are you, honey? It's Miss Cindy!"

Where could she be? Kitchen? Basement? Where would she go if she were hurt?

Cindy starts for the kitchen, then stops. The closet under the stairs is just ahead on her right. From under the door runs a thin line of dark fluid. It is the most horrible thing she has ever seen.

Oh dear god, no, please god, no, no, no, she whispers.

The closet door is locked. Cindy slides the lock and pulls the door open. She smells excrement.

There is Brittany, sprawled, arms out, legs crossed, in a too-small pink t-shirt and panties with little purple bears on them. A black trickle runs from an ear, along her jawbone with a purple-and-yellow bruise *she's got that mouth on her* down her neck and to the floor and out the door. Her mouth and one eye are open.

Cindy bends down. *No, no, no, Brittany! Not you!*

She can feel the police officer right behind her. Two fingers to the carotid artery. No pulse. She grasps Brittany's arm. It resists her effort to lift it. Rigor mortis has started. Of course the closet stinks. Brittany soiled herself when her muscles relaxed upon death. Cindy tries the carotid again. Nothing. No pulse.

Cindy sits down on the floor beside the body, numb. *Brittany, I'm so sorry. I'm so sorry. You never even had a chance. This is my fault. I didn't save you. I didn't do enough.*

She feels the police officer recede, then hears him speak.

"This is Unit Sixteen-twelve. I'm up on Eighth Avenue with the flight suspect. She's here at the house. She's a social worker." He pauses. "Uh, fifteen-oh-six, I think. Fifteen hundred block. We need a medical response for a child with a head wound. Request homicide unit up here, too. This is a probable ten-five."

Brittany. The violet. She was going to be a nurse so she could help people.

Without warning, Cindy is seized by great sobs. Her body shakes as they surge through her body from deep in her chest. There is no stopping them.

She suffers them for a minute, then two, as they wrack her body, then she takes control of herself. She reaches and closes Brittany's open eye. She very carefully leans over and kisses her on one bruised cheek.

"Oh, Brittany. What can I say? I'm so sorry, Brittany," she says. "This was my fault. All my fault. I'm so useless." Anger seizes her. "But right here, I swear – I swear to God above that you didn't die in vain. This has got to stop. This has got to stop."

She stands up, takes one last look, then wipes her eyes and steps out of the closet. The police officer stands in the middle of the room, eyeing her, obviously unsure of himself. She doubts that he feels that way very often. Don't they train police officers to be certain, to be sure, to be in control?

"Officer," she says. "We're not going to need an ambulance, we're going to need the coroner. You might want to put out an APB or whatever you call them for Eugene Edinburger, white male, early 40s, approximately five-eleven, about 170 pounds, thinning gray hair, missing two joints of the small finger on his right hand. He'll probably be driving a dark green Ford pickup, no hubcaps, wheels painted silver. It's from the late 70s or early 80s. This is his house."

The officer pulls a notebook from one of his belt pouches as soon as she starts to speak. He scribbles as she speaks.

"Gene might be accompanied by Greta Dolan, female, about five-four, 180 pounds, shoulder-length brown hair, no distinguishing features that I know of. Gene is the natural father of that little girl in there." She gestures to the closet. "There's a history of abuse, including a fractured arm and frequent serious bruising. I can verify all of this through official reports at Family Services."

She pauses until his scribbling catches up.

"My guess is that they'll head north to Elk County, where Gene shares a hunting cabin with three other men. I don't know their names, but I know that the cabin is on the north side of Elk Lake. It has a cross – a religious cross – on the front door. The cabin, I mean."

Far away, she hears the wail of a siren. She takes a deep breath. The officer is still writing.

"My guess is that this was accidental. Gene drinks and he has a temper. Brittany reminded him of his first wife. They got divorced when Brittany was two. Brittany's mother is a heroin addict and has been in and out of jail and treatment programs for the last ten years. She's not a fit mother, so the courts gave custody to Gene. Brittany never understood that she couldn't be with her mother, so she gave Gene a hard time. She was only five, for god's sake. If he was drunk, he'd get mad and smack her around. He broke her arm once when he grabbed her too hard.

"What happened here – my guess is that she made him mad and he hit her with something. Probably just something he had in his hand at the time. A phone, a bottle, I don't know. He probably didn't mean to kill her – he was probably just trying to shut her up."

The siren outside gets louder. Now she can discern two separate wails. One long, rising and falling and one short, whoop-whoop-whoop.

"Gene's not real bright, but he knows death when he sees it. I saw him zooming north out of town past the big discount store. He almost rear-ended somebody. My guess is that he'll run to the cabin and try to think of his next move. That's why I was in such a hurry to get here. Once I saw him driving like that, I knew something was wrong. He usually drives like a farmer in the big city. Slow and steady. I didn't see Greta in the truck, but she might have been bent down."

She sighs deeply. "And you might as well arrest me or whatever you're going to do for my speeding incident. I was just hoping that I could get here fast enough. You know, if someone can give first aid fast enough, there's this thing known as the golden hour for trauma victims."

She closes her eyes. "Once, a long time ago, someone did get there fast enough ...."

She opens her eyes.

"Never mind. She's been dead for at least an hour. I'm way too late. What do you want me to do?"

The officer meets her gaze. "I'm sorry," he says.

"It doesn't matter," she says. She pauses. "No. That was wrong. I'm sorry. I'm just very upset by this. It does matter and thank you for your condolences and your help." She smiles. "I guess you could have shot out my tires or something."

The officer smiles back. "Well, you were using your turn signals. So I figured you weren't Al Capone or anything. Fleeing criminals usually don't let us know which way they're going to turn."

She laughs and he joins her.

He holds his notebook up. "Let me call all this in and then we'll talk."

"OK. I'll go wait in my car. I don't want to mess up the crime scene. Just come get me when you're ready."

They walk out to the porch. He lets her go first. As she walks down the steps and along the sidewalk toward her car, she hears him on his radio, regurgitating everything she'd told him.

There is an abruptly loud siren whoop that startles her. She sees an ambulance turning the corner and heading down the street, lights flashing.

There have been way too many ambulances in my life, she thinks.

Chapter Thirty-Nine

Late one night Cindy is sprawled on the couch, aimlessly changing channels, afraid of going to sleep. She's afraid that Brittany will visit her in her dreams. Frank is sound asleep in the bedroom. She can hear his occasional snoring. Clicking through the channels, she hears the phrase "battered child" uttered by a talking head. She stops and backs up to the channel. It's an early-morning rebroadcast of an 11 p.m. local news program.

A man with silver hair, wire-rimmed glasses and a gray suit reads to her. Over his left shoulder appears an image of a blindfolded statue of Justice holding up a set of scales.

"In court today, Cambria County Judge John Sheldon said, 'This little girl deserved a better life.' But he also said that doctors believe that the five-year-old girl's life had already ended after an alleged beating at the hands of her mother and stepfather."

Cindy sits up.

The newsman continues. "Judge Sheldon then ordered that life supports be removed from the little girl. The request for removal of life support came from the Cambria County Children and Youth agency, which is in charge of her case. Doctors testified in court that the girl was left severely brain damaged by a beating that one doctor described as 'savage.' The doctor from Cambria County Medical Center testified that the girl has lost nearly all detectable brain function."

The remote falls from Cindy's hand. She feels tears well up.

Over the news reader's shoulder there appears a fuzzy picture of a young girl, smiling widely, butterfly barrettes in her hair. Before her is a pink birthday cake with four candles. Under the picture is the name "Tawnya Johnson."

"The five-year-old girl was admitted to the hospital August 18th with head trauma, a broken pelvis, a broken arm and broken ribs. Her mother and stepfather, Hope and Jason Johnson, are lodged in the Cambria County Prison on felony child abuse charges. County Prosecutor Harold Reese said that if the girl dies following removal of life support, charges against the parents will be changed to murder. Channel Eleven Action News will keep you informed about this important story."

Cindy closes her eyes, feeling despair. *Will this ever end? What will it take to stop it?*

The news reader places a piece of paper that he has not looked at to the side and brightens noticeably. A photo of a smiling silver-haired man appears over his left shoulder.

"Philadelphia Mayor Donato Pacifico, who is running for one of Pennsylvania's U.S. senatorial seats, visited Cambria County today, pledging to work for job growth and economic development if he is elected senator in next November's election."

The TV picture changes to video of a silver-haired man in a gray suit smiling widely and shaking hands with men in yellow hard hats who were leaving an industrial complex. As the video runs, the news reader's voice says, "Mayor Pacifico, who is running on the Democratic ticket against incumbent Republican Robert Walker, said that Walker hasn't been back to Pennsylvania for more than three years. He called Walker a 'classic Washington insider.'"

The video switches to a head-and-shoulders shot of Pacifico, who appears to be leaning toward the camera. Cindy watches, still numb from the previous story.

"My opponent has completely lost touch with the people of Pennsylvania," Pacifico says. "He has no idea what is important to people here. He hasn't even been back to the state in three years. I'm here to tell the people of Cambria County that I'm the candidate who will bring good jobs to this area. I have a proven record of job creation. My opponent has a proven record of caving in to special interests."

The screen changes back to the news reader, who says, "Senator Walker's office did not return a call asking for comment."

The news reader places another sheet of paper to the side. "In other news, a woman has sued Cambria County government over losing her job ...."

Cindy is sitting up, thinking. She goes to the dining room, sits down at the computer, flips it on, opens a word processing program and begins to type.

Something has to be done. Something drastic. The abuse has to stop. What will stop it? County agencies like the one I work for just respond to the after-effects. We're not proactive. We have programs to try to prevent child abuse, but we work within the existing structure. What's needed is a whole new structure – a structure that holds abusers responsible for their actions. A structure that discourages. A structure with weight. Why do people worry about speeding? Because they don't want a ticket. They know that if they do speed, there's a chance of being caught. And if they do get caught, they're as good as convicted. And the fines are nothing to sneeze at.

The problem with child abuse is that although the penalties might be severe, there's a good chance that you'll never get caught. The county agencies that investigate child abuse are understaffed and the workers have too much on their plates. So cases of severe abuse don't always get the attention they need. Sometimes the caseworker is distracted by an excessive caseload and doesn't have the time to investigate properly.

Caseworkers aren't trained to be investigators. They're trained to be social workers – they clean up the mess after it's already made. What's needed is a serious investigative presence, an agency with the experience to investigate and aggressively prosecute child abusers.

There has to be education. Child abuse has to become better understood by the general population and more feared as a crime. Ordinary people don't hold up a bank when they need money. But some will lock their kid in a basement or burn his hand on a stove when the want to teach him a lesson. Why? They know it's wrong to hurt a kid that way. Any normal person knows that such abuse is wrong. But what are the chances of getting caught? Minimal. And if you do, who handles the investigation? An overworked caseworker untrained in sophisticated investigation techniques.

Murder cases get investigated by serious professionals who are backed up by laboratories and forensic experts. So does rape. So does bank robbery. So that's what we need in child abuse cases: serious weight.

She pauses, thinking of the implications.

What would it take to bring such investigative weight to child abuse cases? Who would do it? Local police forces usually take child abuse seriously these days, but don't have the resources or the time to look into the cases extensively. They're more worried about catching murderers and keeping drugs off the streets. Or, in small towns, enforcing the speed limit. Sure they go after those who kill children. But it shouldn't require a child's death to bring the big guns to bear.

She feels an idea forming, something fighting to be born, but she can't clarify it. She saves her typing and goes to bed.

Chapter Forty

"**C**indy?" Frank yelled as he came in the door. He closed the door behind him. Her car was in the parking lot, but there was no response to his call. By reflex, he hung his brown leather jacket in the hallway closet and put the brown-bagged remains of his lunch into the refrigerator.

"Cindy?" He called again. He heard a muffled noise. Alarmed, he ran to the bedroom. The door was locked. *Dear god,* he thought. *What is wrong?*

"Cindy? Are you OK?" He paused with a hand on the knob, his ear close to but not touching the door.

"Cindy?"

"I'm OK," he heard, but the voice held tears and he knew that she wasn't.

"Bad day?"

He heard soft footsteps, then the knob clicked in his hand. He pushed the door open a foot. She was standing barefoot in pajama bottoms and an old white dress shirt of his. She had been crying but she wasn't now.

"You OK?"

She smiled and wiped her eyes. "Yes. I'm much better now that you're here."

He went to her and she held him tightly. He stroked her hair. He didn't know what else to do.

"Bad day?" he asked again.

"I started thinking about Brittany again," she said. "I thought I was handling it OK. But then ... I just got to thinking about how she never even had a chance. She never even got to get out of child-hood. In the end, Gene was a selfish asshole and nothing else. He hit her because he wanted to and damn the consequences for her, the child. When are people going to get it?" Cindy said, falling back-wards onto the bed. "When you abuse a child, you create a monster. Or, if not a monster, at least a very mal-adjusted human adult. Why don't we take this more seriously? Why don't we understand it better? Why do we permit parents to beat and abuse their children?"

"You know that I wish I had answers for you," Frank said.

"Here's a crazy idea I've been kicking around," Cindy said. "What if – just what if – the federal government got involved in stopping child abuse?" Cindy asked. "The federal government should let more decisions be made at the state and local level. I believe that. But there are certain times when the feds should get involved, when something is serious enough."

"The FBI investigates bank robberies, no matter where it happens," Frank said.

"Right!" Cindy said, sitting up. "And why is that?"

"Because deposits are federally insured," Frank said. "At least that's what my bank tells me."

"And why is the federal government so worried about our deposits?" Cindy asked. "They don't insure the cars we buy. The feds wouldn't insure our dishwasher, if we could afford one."

"Ahh, but they do inspect our meat," Frank said, glad that the conversation was trending away from Brittany.

"OK. Good point." Cindy looked at the floor and Frank could almost hear her brain buzzing. He knew to just go along when she got like this.

"So what do bank deposits and meat have in common?" she asked, finally.

Frank, distracted by trying to find a way out of the conversation, said, "What?"

"Meat. Money in the bank. Why do the feds care about those two things?"

"In the case of meat, it's because the private sector can't be trusted to police itself," Frank said. "If it were up to them, we'd be eating stuff scraped off the slaughterhouse floor. Sinclair Lewis, investigative reporting and all that. What was that book he wrote? The Jungle?"

"I hear we still eat that stuff in hot dogs," Cindy said.

Frank made a face. "That's why I don't touch those things," he said.

"So, what's so bad about eating bad meat?" Cindy asked.

"Uh, people would get sick and die," Frank said with the tone of someone who had just been asked if he was sure that two plus two was really four.

"Right. And what about money? The federal government has a vested interest in people believing that their money is safe. If people don't trust banks, all kinds of problems erupt."

"Depression, circa 1929," Frank said.

"The feds don't want great masses of people getting horribly sick over bad meat. So in both cases, the federal government believes that first, there is an important public matter at stake, and two, that federal oversight – not state oversight – is the best way to keep things under control."

"Right," Frank said. "So what does this have to do with the price of tea in China?"

"Child abuse," Cindy said. "When child abuse rises to a certain level – when it is particularly horrendous, or when it goes on for a long time, don't you think that society has a vested interest in having things change for the better? A change in the child's life situation. Which is not having him remain with his abusive parents. And having those parents punished. Right? Isn't that what needs to happen?"

"Well, yes, given the psychological problems that adults who were abused as children have," Frank said. "There's a pretty high cost to society there, in terms of drug abuse and crime."

"So, why doesn't the federal government do something about it? When it reaches a certain level, why doesn't the FBI investigate? If you even try to rob a bank, there'll be cop cars everywhere and FBI guys helicoptering in. But you can beat the crap out of your kid his entire life – until he finally snaps or runs away – and what happens? Nothing."

"Now, just a minute," Frank said. "You're on my turf here. That's what I do all day – try to stop that shit from going on and on."

"OK, but what if the abusers, the parents, pack up the kids and move to Utah? Then what will you do?"

"You know goddamned well that I'll call Utah children and youth and tell them."

"OK. Bad example," Cindy said. "Let's say that the parents just disappear, taking their kids with them. You have no idea where they went."

"Not much I can do there," Frank admitted.

"Ha!" Cindy yelled, startling Frank. "Exactly! And let's assume that they just keep abusing their kids like they did before. Why would they change? Now who can do anything? The authority of the state of Pennsylvania ends at its borders," she said. "All we could do is politely ask other states to be on the lookout for the family. How much attention is that going to get when cops are also looking for escaped killers and murderers and bank robbers on the loose? Not to mention all their own local crimes and criminals."

"Actually, it's the 'Commonwealth of Pennsylvania,'" Frank said. "And most cops hate child abusers as much as we do. I get great cooperation from them, except for the guys who are assholes to everyone."

Cindy waved a hand at him. "Right. Commonwealth. Whatever. My point is that any attempt by a state to find a fleeing child abuser is going to be pretty difficult when you don't have jurisdiction beyond your own borders."

"I see," said Frank. "That's why you're thinking FBI."

"Yes! The FBI can cross state borders. And you know what? I bet they'd be willing to do so to catch child abusers. I bet they hate them as much as regular cops do. Even if the abusers stay within a state, there's no standard for child abuse investigations. The local cops might be untrained, or distracted by another crime – or god forbid, maybe they just don't think it's a real crime."

"There are some national child abuse laws," Frank said. "Didn't Clinton pass one?"

Cindy waved again. "They're toothless. They mostly authorize the creation of databases, require federal agencies to share information and come up with annual reports. How typical of the federal government. Let's solve the problem by collecting statistics! There's nothing that lets the FBI move in on actual individual cases of child abuse."

"Oh, I bet local cops would love that," Frank said. "The local guys already get big-footed by the FBI any time a criminal crosses state lines. Or robs a bank. I bet they'd just love it if the men in black showed up every time someone cracked a kid too hard."

"No, no, I said already – the FBI would only get involved if it was a really serious case. Like ongoing abuse, or the horrendous cases that make the news," Cindy said. "Then the local cops could refer it to the FBI to be sure it gets investigated by those with training and serious resources. They could create a special unit – The Child Services Unit."

"You'd have to establish some kind of stand-ard," Frank said. "How bad would it have to be before the FBI flies in and takes over?"

"Oh, that's for the goofy lawyers to work out," Cindy said. "Or it could just be a local option. The DA makes the call. It's not unheard of. Geez, you get threatened with jail and a fine by FBI every time you spin up a DVD. That screen that comes up and tells you you're not allowed to copy and sell the DVD. If the FBI is so worried about illegal DVD sales, you think they could get worked up about child abuse!"

Frank moved over onto the bed with Cindy. Her eyes were bloodshot, but they were shining with excitement over her idea. The top three but-tons of the white shirt were undone.

"Speaking of worked up," he said, "you're really cute when you're intellectually stimulated," he said.

"You're really obvious when you're horny," she said, smiling.

He tried his best smile. "Well, maybe we can turn a bad day into a better one. With a distrac-tion," he said reaching for her. She didn't skitter away.

"It's going to take quite a distraction to improve this day," she said, closing her eyes as he began to kiss her neck.

"Give me a chance," he said, his voice muffled.

"OK," she said almost inaudibly. "Help me forget."

Chapter Forty-One

Cindy realized that she was clutching Frank and was practically in his lap. He held her hands tightly. His eyes were dark and serious and his brow was furrowed.

The specialist took a pen out of his pocket and began to play with it, turning it end over end. He frowned at his desk.

"The results are ... as expected," he said, his attention still on his desktop. "Miss Phillips, I'm sorry, but it appears that you are ... will be unable to conceive or carry a child to term."

Even though she was expecting them, the words still tore a hole in her world. She closed her eyes and fell through it, only Frank's cool, firm grip keeping her from exploding and dissipating into nothingness.

Frank cleared his throat. "Any artificial means that could –" The doctor cut him off. "No. There has been damage to the womb that is irreversible and final. The only real alternative would be to find a surrogate mother, have an external union of an egg and sperm and allow the surrogate to carry the child to term." He paused and looked up to meet Frank's eyes. Cindy's were still closed. "I'm very sorry," he said. "I have to deliver this news a few times every month and it never gets easier."

She could feel her grief swelling, forcing out tears and threatening to take her voice. Suddenly she was furious. She opened her eyes and sat up straight. She glared at the doctor, realized it wasn't his fault, shifted her gaze to his window. Cindy heard her voice.

"It's not fair! It's not fair! I never asked for this, I never did anything to deserve this. Why is the one thing that I wanted more than anything, a child of my own, why has this been taken from me? It's not fair!"

The doctor looked pained and Frank made soothing sounds.

"I –" the doctor started, but she cut him off. "This is ... there's no word for the ... rottenness of this crime," she said, her voice rising in volume. "This is about the worst thing that you can do to a woman short of killing her and he's ... he's not suffering enough for this crime. There should be some ... nasty, horrible ... some ugly ...." She pounded on the arm of her chair, sending a spike of pain through her hand. "Some nasty, ugly punishment for this! Something of equal value should be taken from him! He stole so much from me and he got to sit in some room with a bed and three meals a day, watching TV and laughing ... It's not fair! It's not right! He stole so much from me ... he stole my belief in myself, my self-worth, he stole ... something that can't be replaced! Just like that!

Just like that! He ruined me! He ruined me for a lifetime and he got seven lousy, stupid years in jail! Where is the justice in that?"

Then the rage gave way to a deep, deep grief and she found herself leaning on Frank, sobbing, her tears wetting his shirt. After a moment, she pushed herself away, stood, and found that her hands were balled into fists. The doctor's office swelled and bulged in odd ways as tears flooded her eyes. She felt them, full and fat, run down her cheeks.

"I wanted a little girl. I wanted a little boy of my own. Is that so much to ask? I see so many kids, every day, their parents neglect them and abuse them and they just completely fail to understand what a gift they've been given. They have something that I never can, and they don't even care. They have zero appreciation for the greatest gift possible. Zero!"

She stopped, breathing hard. "I swear by God that I'm going to do something about this. I swear, right here before you two that I'll have my revenge. I'll have it! Someday, people who steal like this will face real punishment, not some crummy little jail term."

The futility of her rant occurred to her and she sat down abruptly. Frank put a hand out. She took it gratefully. She steadied her breathing. Frank produced one of his ever-present handkerchiefs and she dabbed at her eyes.

"I'm sorry," she said, feeling used up. "That was out of line." She turned to the doctor. "Doctor, I'm sorry. You've been wonderful. I know that this isn't your fault." She forced a smile. "It's just very hard news to take."

"Yes," the doctor said, apparently not willing to venture further. His pen lay on his desk.

"Cindy," Frank said gently.

"Yes, I know. We should go," she said. She turned back to the doctor. "He's terrified of being improper. Very British of him. Well, thank you, doctor." She stood. The doctor nodded and nodded. They both shook hands with the doctor.

During the walk down the white corridors of the clinic, the hallways seemed to have altered subtly, almost imperceptibly. Yet they were different. So was the unfairly brightly shining sun when they left the building. So was Frank's little red car, waiting for them across the parking lot's hot asphalt.

It's not the world that's different now, a voice told her. *It's you.*

She knew that it was true.

Chapter Forty-Two

Cindy has a copy of Brittany's autopsy on her desk in front of her. There are photos at the back of the report but she can't bring herself to look at them. She was hoping to find out exactly what killed Brittany, but she can't get more than a general idea of what happened because of the dense medical language used in the report.

"Indications are that death occurred from injuries to the cervical spine with vertebral fracture and brain hemorrhage," the report read under the "Cause of Death" heading.

Cindy tried to plow through it: "A forceful blow was delivered by a hard, somewhat rounded and unyielding object causing a right frontal temporal paretal subdural hematoma. Significant swelling of the soft tissues of the scalp resulted from the blow. The blow caused a midline frontal skull fracture and post-mortem examination revealed a right subdural hematoma, resulting in a midline shift."

What does this mean? Cindy wondered. *She was hit over her right eye. But what killed her? Did it kill her right away?*

She turned back to the unhelpful autopsy.

"Post-mortem examination further revealed a posterior dislocation of C1 with tearing of surrounding ligaments, fracture and displacement of C2 with tearing of surrounding ligaments, contusions of the spinal cord and significant hemorrhage at the base of the skull."

This is hopeless, she thinks, and reaches for the local phone book. She pages through the report, skipping the photos with a shiver. On the last page of the autopsy, she locates the name of the doctor who performed the examination.

She calls the doctor's office and identifies herself. The receptionist promises to page the doctor. While she waits, Cindy thinks about how unreal the autopsy seems to her. It's like reading an autopsy in a detective novel. How can Brittany be dead when just the other day she was telling Cindy how she was going to be a nurse and help people? Her heart tells her that Brittany has just gone away for a while and will be back. But her brain whispers the truth.

The doctor comes on the line and Cindy thanks him and starts asking questions. At first, he frustrates her by using the same language as the autopsy. Cindy tries to cut through the foreign language and get an answer in English.

"I guess what I'm really looking for here, doctor – and please pardon me, this is kind of personal – did she suffer?"

Cindy's heart aches at the thought of a critically wounded Brittany dragging herself across the floor, crying in pain and no one there to help. Cindy squeezes her eyes shut and swallows the lump in her throat that the thought brings on.

"No, I don't believe so," says the doctor reassuringly. *I wonder if they teach them to answer like that – so convincingly, leaving no room for doubt,* Cindy wonders.

"Most likely, she died almost instantly upon being struck," the doctor says. "The force of the blow was such that her head snapped back, cracking vertebrae and severing her spinal cord. There was reduced bleeding from what was a serious head wound for that very reason – her heart stopped beating almost immediately."

"So she was hit and just dropped, ah, dead?" Cindy asks.

"Most likely," the doctor says. "She was probably technically dead upon hitting the floor or very shortly thereafter. The coroner believes that she was placed in the closet by the father. There was no indication that she was mobile following the blow." He pauses and then says in more gentle voice, "Miss Phillips, I truly don't think she felt a thing. One second she was there and the next she was with God."

Then her tears come.

Behind her closed eyes, she sees a wide-eyed Brittany, finger in mouth, Dolly clutched under one arm, looking up at an indistinct but glowing human figure. The figure's arms are outstretched in welcome. "Come to me, my child," the figure says. "Your suffering is over." The horrible wound is absent from Brittany's face as she walks unhesitatingly, unafraid, toward the figure. She disappears into the warm glow.

Cindy grabs a tissue.

Please let it be true. Please let it happen like that. Brittany, please forgive me.

"Miss Phillips, are you still there?"

Cindy tries to keep her voice from cracking.

"Yes. I'm sorry. Doctor, you have been so helpful. Thank you very much."

"Miss Phillips, I'm sorry. This is terrible."

"Thank you. That is very kind of you."

She says goodbye, hangs up, bolts for the bathroom and turns the water on to hide the sound of her sobs. She cries not just for Brittany but for all the children who are at that very moment suffering, crying, wondering why life is filled with pain and not love.

Chapter Forty-three

Cindy was placing a box of Cheerios on the supermarket checkout conveyor belt when her pager buzzed. She glanced down and saw "911" followed by a phone number that she recognized as the county's emergency dispatch number.

"I'm terribly sorry, but I have to leave right now," she said to the bored checkout clerk, a 16-year-old with her bangs in her eyes.

"Ah, yeah, all right," the girl said and cracked her gum.

Cindy didn't think the clerk was getting it. Cindy pointed to her shopping cart, which was loaded with groceries.

"No, I mean that I have to leave this cart. If you push it to the side, I'll come back later and pay for it, but right now, I have to go."

"Yeah, OK," the girl said, her eyes still not showing comprehension of Cindy's situation.

Cindy couldn't help but roll her eyes as she began picking items off the conveyor belt and replacing them in her cart.

"Hey!" the checkout girl said. "What're you doing?"

Wordlessly, Cindy finished replacing the items in her cart. She gave the girl the best smile she could find and pushed the cart to the side. The girl watched, cracking her gum, as Cindy pulled out her cell phone and walked rapidly out of the store.

"Hey, lady!" the clerk yelled. "Hey, lady!"

Mercifully, the automatic door hissed shut behind Cindy, cutting off the clerk's baffled yells.

"Nine-one-one, what is your emergency?" the voice asked after Cindy dialed the number on her pager.

"This is Cindy Phillips of Family Services. I'm responding to a page."

"Mrs. Phillips, please stand by."

Cindy heard the dispatcher's voice recede as she finished a conversation with a police officer: "Unit Seventeen-oh-nine, that is correct. We have an outstanding warrant on that suspect, dated oh-four of last year. Instructions are to detain and notify."

The dispatcher switched back to Cindy, her voice now louder.

"Mrs. Phillips, we have a Logan Township police officer at the Logan Valley mall requesting your presence. Situation involves an altercation between a man and woman. A child is involved."

"Where in the mall?"

"The officer is reporting from just outside the food court on the second floor. Can you respond?"

Cindy was walking rapidly toward her Honda.

"Yes, please tell the officer that I'm on my way."

"Can you provide an ETA?"

"Approximately ten minutes."

"Thank you, Mrs. Phillips. Dispatch out."

After she got the car started and moving toward the mall, she called 911 dispatch back.

"Dispatch, do you have any details of the situation?"

"Officer on scene is reporting a female with a young boy, approximately six years of age, was accosted by a male. Male is claiming to be the boy's father. An altercation ensued. The officer has the situation under control but is requesting Family Services to advise on the custody issue. County children and youth is on another call and unavailable."

"Thank you. I'll, uh, sign off now," Cindy said.

"Dispatch out."

Cindy navigated her way to the mall, got to the food court and began walking around. It wasn't too hard to find the scene. A uniformed police officer stood at the edge of the food court area, talking into his walkie-talkie. Near the officer was a woman with a boy on her lap. They were playing a game with their hands. The woman was dressed in high heels, tight pink jeans and a sleeveless white t-shirt. She had large breasts and an enormous pile of blonde hair. The boy, in new jeans and a Teenage Mutant Ninja Turtles t-shirt, shared the woman's hair color, although his was cropped short.

Three tables away sat an obviously uncomfortable male who kept glancing at the woman and the boy. The man wore jeans, a white muscle shirt and had dark curly hair under a baseball cap. He had a thin moustache. His right leg jittered up and down as he switched his glances from the officer to the woman. It was clear to Cindy that he had been told by the officer to sit there and behave.

Cindy approached the officer, who despite having white hair and appearing to be in his fifties, had a tight, trim body. He was standing in a military stance, his legs apart, having placed himself between the man and the woman with the boy.

"Ma'am?" he asked politely as Cindy walked up to him. She put her hand out.

"Cindy Phillips, Family Services. I was paged," she said.

He extended a large, big-knuckled hand and shook. "Lt. Clark Bonner," he said. "Thanks for your response. We've got a little paternity case here. I think everything's OK between these two now, but both are asking some questions I can't answer. Maybe you can help."

"I'll be happy to try," Cindy said.

Bonner pointed to the woman with the antennae of his walkie-talkie.

"She's apparently got custody of the kid. He's six. She says she's a waitress." Bonner raised an eyebrow. "Said she was walking through the mall, just shopping with her kid, when the male here –" Bonner switched his antennae to point at the restless male – "apparently just walked up to her, grabbed her by the arm and went off. Started yelling about how the kid is his and she's withholding visitation rights. Said he just wants to see his son. She started yelling back. The male made a grab for the kid and the female went nuts, according to bystanders. There was a scuffle and she ended up with the kid. She picked him up and started running, but you're not going to get far in those shoes." He raised an eyebrow again.

"The male went after her. About then, mall security showed up and separated the two. They called me in. He claims that she told a judge that she was going to leave the area so he couldn't see the kid. She says that the courts gave her custody and denied him visitation because he's got a record."

Bonner paused. "She's right about that. I was calling him in when you got here. He's got two recent priors, one for drunk and disorderly outside a bar. One a little older, still pending, is for marijuana possession. There's more, but I didn't want to tie dispatch up for too long."

He looked at Cindy. "So what do you think?"

"Well, officer, I should talk to them both. Separately, of course. So if you could stay a little longer, I'd appreciate it. And maybe when you go, you could escort the male off the property."

"I can stay as long as I don't get another call," he said. "Go ahead and do your stuff."

She smiled a thank you and walked over to the woman. The woman carefully avoided looking at Cindy and concentrated on playing with her son.

"Rock, paper, scissors, shoot!" she said. Her son held out scissors. She held out a rock.

"Ahh, mommy!" the boy said. "You beat me again!"

The woman laughed, then looked up at Cindy. Cindy saw something flicker through the woman's dark eyes. Her mouth tightened. Her eyes were hard.

"Can I help you, miss?" she said. The boy turned and looked at Cindy. His eyes were a beautiful pale blue. His gaze was frankly appraising.

"My name is Cindy Phillips. I'm with Family Services of Blair County," Cindy said, extending her hand. The woman looked at Cindy's hand, then back up at her eyes.

"I don't need any family services," the woman said.

Cindy kept her hand out for a count of three, then lowered it.

"Can you please tell me your name?" Cindy asked.

"Betty Grable," the woman said.

Cindy kept her eyes fixed on the woman's. "My. What an amazing name," she said.

"Yeah. My parents knew I was going to grow up to be something special," she said.

The boy abruptly ended his scrutiny of Cindy and turned to his mother.

"Mommy, who's this lady?"

Without taking her eyes from Cindy's, the woman said, "Someone who's not our friend, Hunter. Someone who wants to take you away from me."

The boy jumped from his chair and scrambled onto his mother's lap. He clutched her tightly. She patted his hair and whispered in his ear without breaking her lock on Cindy's eyes.

"Now, Mrs. Grable –"

"Miss."

"Miss Grable. That wasn't very nice," Cindy said softly. "That's not helping."

"I can tell you what will help," the woman said. "The biggest help that I can get is everybody quits trying to help me raise my little boy. I'm doing just fine."

"I'm sure you are, Miss Grable. But there was an incident here, and the officer –"

"To be honest with you, lady, I don't much care what you or the officer think. I didn't commit a crime. A man who has no rights to this boy tried to take him away from me. I responded like any mother would. I protected my son. I'm only sitting here now because the officer asked me nicely. If you don't have anything to help keep that creep over there away from my boy, I'm going to get up and go home. And if you want to stop me, you're going to have to arrest me."

Cindy took a deep breath. "Miss Grable. This is a situation involving a child. That's my field. The officer would like to know the status of your boy and –"

"The status of my boy is that he's just fine," the woman said, wrapping her arms around him. "He's growing bigger every day. He's a smart boy. He's got everything he needs. He's well fed, he's got new clothes, he gets all the love he needs. He's doing fine in school. He has lots of friends. He's fine." She broke her gaze from Cindy's to lower her head and whisper into her son's ear. He nodded vigorously, his back to Cindy.

She smiled as false a smile as Cindy had ever seen. "Anything else, honey?"

Cindy held the woman's gaze for five beats of her heart, then said, "You'd best check with the officer before you leave," she said. "I can't arrest you, but he can."

"No one is going to arrest me," the woman said. She stood effortlessly, still holding her boy, his head on her shoulder. Cindy was impressed by her steadiness in the stiletto heels. "I'm leaving now."

She turned and walked toward the exit doors. Cindy caught Bonner's eye. She raised her hands in a "nothing I can do" gesture. The officer shook his head and moved to intercept the woman.

Cindy turned toward the man. He was still nervously shaking his leg up and down rapidly. He was biting a thumbnail as Cindy approached. She noticed that all of his nails were bitten painfully short. When he looked at her, Cindy could see where Hunter got his eyes. The man's were an almost startling pale blue.

"What?" he said, looking at Cindy. "What? You going to arrest me?"

"I'm not a police officer," Cindy said. She extended a hand. "Cindy Phillips, Family Services of Blair County. I'm a caseworker."

"Caseworker?" the man asked. He took her hand mechanically while still seated and gave it the briefest of clasps. His hand was work-hard but his grasp was limp.

"May I sit down?"

"Sure," he said. His leg had stopped vibrating but he still looked extremely nervous. "What's a caseworker doing here?"

"We're generally called in when children are involved," she said. "The officer had some questions about Hunter and he thought that I might be able to give him some help."

"So what do you want to know?" the man asked.

"We could start with your name," Cindy said.

"Oh yeah. Sorry. I'm Steve. Steve McCarr."

"Mr. McCarr, is it OK if I call you Steve?"

"Uh, sure. Steve is OK."

"Thank you. Can I also ask what you relationship is to the boy who was sitting over there with the blonde woman?"

"Hunter? He's my kid!" the man yelled. "Christ!"

Cindy put out a calming hand.

"Steve. Please. I'm just trying to sort his out, OK? No one is making any accusations. No one is blaming anyone. No one is doubting you. I'm just asking some questions because I don't know what is going on here and the officer asked me to figure it out. OK?"

Steve's leg started vibrating again and he resumed chewing on his thumbnail.

"Steve? Is that OK?" Cindy asked.

He looked at Cindy as if seeing her for the first time.

"Yeah. Sure. OK," he said.

"So Hunter is your son. Is the blonde woman Hunter's natural mother?"

"That bitch is –"

"Please, Steve. Can we keep this calm?"

"Yeah. OK. Sorry." He composed himself with an obvious effort. He stopped his leg. He put his hand on the table. "Yeah, Bobbi is his mom. Hunter's."

"And you are his natural father?"

"Yeah."

"Were you and Bobbi ever married?"

"Uh, no."

"Did you live together?"

"For about six months. Then I got sick of her bullsh–, uh, her attitude."

"Who moved out?"

"She kind of … made me."

"How long ago was this?"

"Well, she was pregnant with Hunter. I don't know. I guess about five years ago. Maybe a little longer."

"How did you meet her?"

Steve looked at Cindy. "Didn't she tell you what she does?"

"She told the officer that she's a waitress," Cindy said.

Steve snorted. "Ha. Yeah, that's real funny. Waitress."

Cindy kept her expression neutral.

"She dances. What do they call them – ah, exotic dancers. Yeah. She dances naked."

"Is that where you met her?"

"Yeah. Place over near State College called Out of Bounds."

"Does she still dance?"

"Far as I know. That's all she's ever done."

"Where were you living when you moved out?"

"Here. Altoona. Her little house."

"And she got pregnant?"

"Yeah. That was stupid. I thought she was protected. You know, being a dancer and all, I thought that was, like, part of the job. You know? So I didn't bother. And then one day she tells me that she's late. So she goes to the drug store and buys one of those little sticks that you pee on. Right?"

Cindy nodded.

"And it came out positive. Two blue lines or whatever. We were excited at first. At that point, we still liked each other. We had even talked about buying a house together."

"Ever discuss marriage?" Cindy asked.

Steve gave her a blank look. "Naw."

"So, you were excited about her being pregnant. And then?"

"And then … things just went south. She got all uptight about stuff. Wanted me to quit smoking. Shit like that. She's not an easy person to live with," Steve said. "She started laying down all this shit, like about me staying home Saturday nights and stuff. She wanted me to quit riding my Harley. And going with her to the doctor. Like I need to go with her to the goddamn doctor. I mean, as far as making a kid goes, my job was done, right? I mean, I'd be a good dad and all, but for Christ's sake, I didn't need to be going with her on those appointments where she puts her legs up in those stirrups and –"

"So you broke up," Cindy interrupted.

"Yeah. We had a couple fights." Steve flushed. "A couple of those types where the cops show up. She's a bit— she's got a temper. Then she made me pack up and move out. And that was it."

"After you left, did you try to find out what happened to her?"

"Kind of. We still had friends who knew friends, you know? So I heard about her a lot. This town ain't that big. So I still heard about her a lot. I heard she had a boy. So I went over. She let me in and showed me him."

"Did you talk about visitation then?"

"Nah. I didn't want to deal with that baby shit, you know? All that bawling at night and stuff? I figured she could deal with that. But then he got a little older. A couple years ago, I ran into her over at Kmart and saw him – Hunter – and he was like a little guy, you know? And I thought, well, I can deal with that. He was out of diapers and stuff. Not a baby anymore."

"Did you talk to Bobbi about wanting to see him?"

"Yeah. I said I wanted to start seeing him. You know, just now and then. No big deal."

"What did Bobbi say?"

"She said OK. We were cool. Or I thought we were."

"It didn't work out?"

"Like I said. She likes to be in control. She wanted to say when and where and how I could see him. It didn't always, you know, fit my schedule. I work construction, masonry, so my days can be pretty long in season. And I'm out of town a lot. I wanted to see him when I could, you know, when I could fit it into my schedule. But she wanted to lay down this plan, this regular kind of thing. It just didn't work for me. And she had all these goddamn rules, like no smoking around him. I couldn't take him on my bike or nothing. I've been riding since I was thirteen. Never had a wreck."

"Did you work it out?"

"Shit, no. That's the whole thing. A buddy of mine told me about this lawyer, so I hired the guy and tried to get – what do they call it? Visitation rights. Goddamn lawyers are expensive." Steve looked around. The officer was talking with Bobbi near the exit doors. She was still holding Hunter.

"What did the judge say?" Cindy asked.

"Fu—jerk. Jeez. I wish I could have a cigarette."

"Would you rather talk outside?"

"Nah. I'm OK. We're almost done, right?"

"Well, that depends upon what I can find out about your situation," Cindy said.

"Well. Yeah. The judge. The asshole says that she gets possession of Hunter just cause I've had a couple minor arrests. Bullshit stuff that any guy gets hit with."

"Can you give me an example?" Cindy asked.

"Uh. DUI a couple of years back. That was just stupid. I worked it off. It's history now. But those judges don't forgive."

"The officer told me that there had been a few incidents recently," Cindy said.

"He did?" Steve looked down. "Well, yeah. Some guy gave me a hard time at Winchester's the other day." He looked up at Cindy. "Well, what the hell am I supposed do, let some guy beat the shit out of me? So there was a little action. Cops showed up. I got busted. Yeah, I'd had a few, but so did everybody. Winchester's is a bar, for chrissake. What do people think you do there, drink tea?"

"And there was something about a possession charge," Cindy said.

"Aw, for – Jeez. Doesn't everybody smoke a little dope now and then?"

"Maybe so. But you got caught," Cindy said. "Whether it's common or not, it is an illegal drug. And a judge is going to take note of that."

"That shit was all after the judge made up his mind," Steve said.

"So the judge's decision was that Bobbi got to keep Hunter?"

"Yeah. I had to work out visitation with her. It was only what was called – supervised. Supervised visitation. Which meant that either Bobbi or her sister had to be there or I had to do all the visiting at Bobbi's house. Which sucks because of all her bullshit rules about smoking and stuff. I couldn't take Hunter out or nothing. We couldn't do anything without Bobbi or her goddamned sister there. It was just bullshit."

Steve sat back in his chair, felt for his cigarettes in his breast pocket, realized where he was and stopped. He put his hand back on the table and his leg started vibrating again.

"So, even though there are all those rules you have to follow, have you seen Hunter?"

"Shit, no! I ain't gonna put up with all those stupid rules. If I can't see my own son the way I want to, well, then I don't need to see him, I guess."

"So, today in the mall, was this the first time you've seen Hunter in a while?" Cindy asked.

"Yeah. All that stuff with the judge was about a year ago. Then I hear that Bobbi told the judge that she's moving to Florida and she doesn't want me to have any rights to see him at all."

"Hunter, you mean," Cindy said.

"Yeah. No rights at all. The judge sent me this big long letter. I showed it to my lawyer. That cost fifty bucks right there. He said it meant that I wasn't allowed to see Hunter at all unless I went down to Florida and asked some damn judge down there to let me see him. Complete bullshit," Steve said. "So I figure she's gone and Hunter's out of my life and I'm just not going to get to see my son. And then I see that bitch walking through here with my little boy."

"Here at the mall, you mean."

"Yeah."

"And what happened?"

"I already told the cop all this."

"I didn't get any details from the officer. Would you please re-tell it for me?" Cindy asked.

"Well. Yeah. So I see her walking down there with that walk she has. You know."

Cindy kept her expression neutral.

"And there's Hunter. All I can think is that she's supposed to be in Florida. Gone. Not my problem any more. So I went up to her. She sees me coming, and I can just see that she's not happy. She pulled Hunter over to her. I went up to her and asked her what's going on. Like, you're back from Florida, huh? I can see from her eyes that she ain't never been in Florida. So I asked her about that. She gives me some bullshit answer. And I said, well, then, I guess I can come over and see Hunter. And she said that I had to go back to that judge and get permission. Then I said, well, so what's up with this Florida stuff? Did you ever really go? And she says that her plans changed."

Steve snorted. "Yeah. Her plans changed all right. She lied. Then she ran into me. That's what happened."

"The officer said that there was a scuffle," Cindy said.

Steve looked away. "Well, there was a little of that," he said.

"Did you touch Hunter?" Cindy asked.

"Well. I guess I did. I mean, I have the right to touch my own son, don't I?"

"And when you tried to touch Hunter, what happened?" Cindy asked.

"She flipped out," Steve said. "She just went nuts. She swung at me and then grabbed him and started running."

"Did you go after her?"

"I was just trying to get things straight," Steve said. "I was – I had a lot of questions for her. I wasn't getting no answers at all. I just wanted to know certain stuff. Like is she back in town for good or what? And was I going to be able to see Hunter or what?"

"Did you chase her?"

"I kind of went after her. I mean, I followed her, yeah," Steve said.

"Were you yelling?"

"That what the cop told you?"

"He said that there was a fight. And then you chased her."

"I don't know if I was chasing her exactly. I was just trying to get some answers." Steve looked around the room as if searching for someone. "Look, that's really pretty much all the sh–, uh, the stuff that happened. I mean, then the rent-a-cop showed up and then the township cop showed up and, uh, here I am. But I'd kind of like to get going."

Cindy had more information than she had expected, especially since she had no legal authority to keep Steve. She was surprised that he'd said as much as he did.

"Steve, thank you very much," Cindy said, trying to catch his eye. He kept his eyes moving around the room. His thumbnail went to his mouth again.

"Yeah. Sure. Glad I could help."

Cindy stood and put out her hand and after a moment, Steve gave her his limp clasp. Cindy caught the eye of the officer, who understood immediately and started toward her.

"Steve, I have to ask you," Cindy said, standing and looking down on him. She felt like she was talking to a kindergartner. "Steve?"

"Huh? Yeah?" He finally looked up at her.

"I think it would be a really good idea if you stayed away from Bobbi. At least until things are straightened out legally between you two. If you don't," Cindy said, "you might cause problems for yourself down the road when you're in front of a judge again. You said that judges take a lot of things into account when they make custody decisions. So

I'm sure that any scenes like this one between you and Bobbi would not do you any good."

"Yeah," Steve said slowly, as if processing a complex thought. "I guess you're right." He paused as the officer approached. "Well, I waited this long. I guess I can wait a little longer to see Hunter."

"That sounds very reasonable to me, and I'm sure it would to a judge, too," Cindy said. She favored Steve with one last smile, then addressed the officer.

"Officer Bonner. Thank you for your time. I had a very helpful conversation with Steve. He provided me with some useful information. I think that the situation is under control now. Also, I think Steve understands the importance of staying away from Bobbi and Hunter until the courts make a decision." She looked at the officer as she spoke. Steve chewed on his fingernails and stared at his shoes. The officer winked at Cindy, then put his hands on his hips and gave Steve a look that was not quite a glare.

"If you're going to be reasonable, Mr. McCarr, then I think it's OK for you to go. But I'd advise you to follow this nice lady's advice. If I find out that you're harassing Bobbi or Hunter, I guarantee you that you're going to end up the one who is sorry."

Steve nodded rapidly without raising his head.

"I can't hear your head rattle, son. You giving me a yes that you're going to stay away from Bobbi and the kid?"

"Yes. Yes, sir," Steve mumbled.

"All right then. Get out of here," the officer said. Steve practically bolted for the door and didn't look back.

Bonner shook his head. "Twenty-two years of this crap. I can retire in three years. Jeez, am I looking forward to that." He caught Cindy's eye and she smiled. "Fish don't argue back," he said. "And they don't DUI either."

"Thank you for calling me," Cindy said. "It's always nice when we can get ahead of a case like this. Or try to," she said, sharing a bit of the officer's cynicism.

They discussed the case for a few minutes, with Cindy giving the officer her opinion that Bobbi's custody was legal and Steve had no rights to visit Hunter unless his legal situation changed.

When they were done, Bonner put out a hand. "Nice working with you, Mrs. Phillips. I hope you're on my next domestic. You're a pleasure to work with."

"Same here, officer," Cindy said, shaking his hand.

On her way back to her car, Cindy realized that she had a lot of work ahead of her on this case. It was obvious that Steve wouldn't be much of a father. But the important question was what kind of mother Bobbi was. Everything looked OK with Hunter, but Cindy had been in the child welfare business long enough to know that appearances could be extremely deceiving. In wealthy homes, for example, there were seldom signs of abuse. The veneer of wealth provided part of the cover; the parents conspired to do the rest. Terrible cases of child abuse had happened in such homes and left few outward signs. So although Cindy's instincts told her differently, she knew that Bobbi could just be covering well.

The next step, she knew, was to go see Bobbi. At work.

Chapter Forty-Five

Cindy pulled into the parking lot of Out of Bounds. It was full and dominated by pickup trucks, but she spotted a few BMWs, a Lexus and a new Cadillac. There were also two buses, a luxury charter and a school bus.

From the outside, Out of Bounds looked like an ugly but functional place of business. It had obviously started as one small building, now at the center, then sprawled outward and upward, probably as the owner piled up some profit. It had no windows, a cheap stucco exterior and a sign that read "Entrance around back." Cindy found a space, parked and turned the car off. Before getting out, she took a deep breath and gathered herself. The sign back at the main road had advertised "The area's finest exotic dancers," but Cindy knew that was a euphemism for nude dancers. It was a strip club. A booby bar. She wasn't sure what to expect inside. She feared that it might be a rough place, full of alpha males, rednecks and bikers. She didn't expect to be comfortable, but she hoped that she wouldn't be the only clothed female inside.

GIRL, 7

She found her resolve by thinking of Hunter. She needed to make sure that Hunter was safe in Bobbi's hands. Steve would clearly not be much of a father, so it was all up to Bobbi. Although Cindy didn't think that nude dancing was the best occupation for the mother of a young boy, she was willing to give Bobbi the benefit of her uncertainty. Perhaps she shielded Hunter well. Perhaps she was as good a mother as she had appeared to be at the mall.

Cindy exited her car and headed for the rear of the building. As she approached, she could hear and feel the music. It was a dancer's beat, steady and dependable. It thumped right through the walls of the building. Around back there was no line, just a glass-and-aluminum door that could be found on practically any business in America. To the right of the door, a sign read, "No Alcohol on Premisis," and another, spelled correctly, read, "You Must Be 21 or Older to Enter. We ID."

Cindy pulled the door open and the music got louder. There was a short hallway. At the end, right before the entrance to what must be the dance floor, was a man behind a cash register. The register rested on top of two glass display cabinets. The man's dark hair was spiked wildly and had streaks of blonde bleached into it. She feared the contents of the two display cabinets, but they turned out only to offer – at ridiculous prices – t-shirts, coffee mugs, key chains and other trinkets advertising the business. The man, bored, said, "Twenty." Cindy handed him a bill. He took it and without touching the cash register added it to an enormous wad of bills in his hand. "Need any ones?" he asked. Cindy could guess why he asked, but she said, "No, thank you."

The man picked up a rubber stamper. Cindy, familiar with the routine from her college days, held out a fist, offering the back of her hand. The man jabbed her with the rubber stamp. A purple circle with the date in its center appeared on the back of her hand.

"Thanks," she said. The man cracked his gum.

Cindy approached the two swinging doors that led to the dance floor. From inside, the music pounded. She pushed open the doors. The room inside was dark. Lights flashed wildly. She was immediately intercepted by a muscled man in a yellow t-shirt who stood up from a stool and beckoned her closer. She showed him the back of her hand. He shined a tiny flashlight on it, then nodded and settled back onto his stool. Cindy walked forward and began her assessment of the place.

The ceiling was high, far higher than she had thought. She had imagined a tight, closed, claustrophobic place. This place was more like a warehouse. Or a church. The walls, ceiling and practically everything else were painted black. Glittering disco balls and colored rock-concert lights flashed from the ceiling. The music, pounding from unseen speakers, was at a volume that made conversation nearly impossible. The huge dance floor was in the shape of a three-lobed club from a deck of cards. The dance floor was elevated about two feet from the walking floor. It was checkered black-and-white in a chessboard pattern. At the center of each lobe, a brass pole rose to the ceiling. Around the entire dance floor, with gaps of only inches in between, were chairs. Most of them were occupied by young men wearing jeans, t-shirts and baseball caps. They were cheering as naked or nearly naked women gyrated and posed on the raised dance floor. Crumpled dollar bills lay at the feet of the women.

To her surprise, Cindy noticed that there was a row of chairs around the perimeter of the room, set back several feet from the dance floor. These chairs had their backs to the room's walls and were occupied by a surprising variety of people. Cindy saw young and old, male and female, ripped t-shirts and designer clothes. The only thing that the sitters had in common was a dazed expression and an obsessive watching of the dance floor. In comparison to the rowdy boys at the edge of the dance floor, the back-sitters were still but attentive, like people watching a movie.

Cindy walked around the dance floor slowly and took mental notes. Those who wanted to be involved in the show and interact with the dancers sat at the edge of the stage and rewarded the dancers by throwing dollar bills at them or, in many cases, by tucking the bills into the straps and ties of what little the dancers wore. Those who just wanted to watch sat back against the walls and didn't pass out dollars.

Every fifteen minutes or so, the announcer's booming voice would announce a new group of dancers, who would slink onto the stage from a black-painted door at what would be the stem of the club-shaped dance floor. They sauntered out to applause and wolf whistles and took up positions that seemed determined by how popular they were. The more popular dancers got a lobe of the club-shaped floor to themselves and often used the brass pole in their routine. Other dancers, either less popular or too new to have fans, took up less advantageous positions on the dance floor. Cindy noticed that it was best to be close to the young males with dollar bills. The closer the dancer was to the men, the more dollars she was showered with.

The variety of the dancers surprised Cindy. She had expected a group of Playboy-style models, perfect specimens of male-imagined beauty. But some of the women were chubby, some were terribly skinny and some had faces and bodies that Cindy considered amazingly unremarkable. She had a pretty good idea of each dancer's physical attributes because no matter what costume they walked out in, each one ended up completely naked by the end of her routine. Then the announcer would announce a new crop. The dancers would crouch and unabashedly scoop up all the bills within reach, gather their discarded clothing and walk offstage as a new group strutted on.

Cindy found an open chair against the wall that afforded her a look at the dancers as they emerged. She settled back to wait for Bobbi to appear, hoping that she wouldn't run into anyone that she knew. "I'm researching a client" would seem to be a pretty lame excuse, she knew, and was unlikely to be convincing.

She didn't have long to wait. Apparently the dancers came out in cycles that repeated frequently. Bobbi soon strolled contemptuously to the dance floor dressed in a translucent pink baby-doll negligee, pink thong and gold stiletto heels. She was apparently a favorite, as she got a rousing cheer when she took up a position in the lobe across from Cindy's seat. Cindy tried to shrink into her chair. She didn't want Bobbi to see her.

As a new song with a hip hop beat began to pound from the speakers, Bobbi stood near her brass pole, legs apart, barely moving her hips. She held onto the brass pole with one hand. The other rested on her hip. The boys seated around her lobe yelled, waved bills and, apparently, shouted suggestions at her. Bobbi turned her head upward, rolling her eyes like a bored movie star. She kept up the minimalist hip swinging. The cries of the men turned more urgent, but Bobbi looked only more bored, her eyes on the ceiling.

Finally, oblivious to her audience, Bobbi reached between her breasts and pulled out a cigarette in a long white holder. The men cheered. Bobbi conceded to look at her audience. She took one step, and with one hand still on her hip, bent over at the waist toward the men. She held the cigarette near her lips with an expression that clearly indicated she didn't expect a single one of the louts to know how to respond. There was a brief flurry of activity and six young males held out lighters, flames flickering at the top.

Making her condescension obvious, Bobbi chose a dark-haired young man in a polo shirt and khakis. Still with hand on hip, bent at the waist, she shifted her pose just enough to indicate it was her weary wish that the khakied man light her cigarette. He did so with an expression of wide-eyed eagerness. As soon as the tip of the her cigarette began to glow, Bobbi stood back upright and strolled back to the brass pole, where she proceeded to ignore her audience again, eyeing the ceiling and taking slow puffs from her cigarette. Most of the dancers on Bobbi's shift were naked by now and Cindy wondered if she was going to bother to disrobe for her audience. The men seemed content to watch her as she was. Bills showered onto the floor around her feet even though she hadn't removed so much as a shoe.

Finally, her cigarette finished, Bobbi plucked the butt from her holder and flicked it into the audience. A man ran to retrieve it. She carefully replaced the holder between her breasts, tapping it down slowly until it disappeared. The men watched, enraptured. She raised her eyebrows and looked at her audience as if noticing them for the first time. She pushed one hip out and placed a finger on her cheek as if pondering. Her eyes gazed into the distance. The men roared and more bills hit the floor. Bobbi held the pose, then looked again at the men. She raised her eyebrows in an expression that asked, "Yes?" They nodded and cheered and high-fived each other until Cindy worried that someone would get hurt. As if bored, Bobbi shrugged and the right spaghetti strap of her baby doll fell from her shoulder. The men stared, transfixed. She began moving just slightly more to the beat, her hips and shoulders swaying. She closed her eyes. The other strap fell. Bobbi swayed to the beat and Cindy thought that the baby doll slipped almost imperceptibly lower. The top of the cigarette holder peeked from between her breasts. Yes, the flimsy pink garment was definitely sliding lower on Bobbi's body, although Cindy was at a loss to see how she was doing it. Bobbi now held her hands at her sides. She moved to the music, but with eyes closed and with an attitude of being all alone, dancing perhaps in her living room with the curtains drawn. Cindy admired Bobbi's disrobing skills. She had never found a way to make undressing graceful, especially with her hyper-awareness of the scars that laced her body. Bobbi obviously had no such hang-ups.

With most of the other dancers obviously nearing the end of the routines, Cindy wondered if Bobbi was perhaps running late. Cindy found herself worrying that Bobbi had lost track of time and would end up getting caught in a shift change, hurrying through her routine and disappointing her audience. Cindy realized the silliness of her concern, but that didn't lessen its intensity.

Bobbi was slowly increasing the pace of her gyrations. Her eyes were still closed and the baby doll slipped ever lower. The lacy top of the garment was now most of the way down Bobbi's breasts, but still without revealing what the men were paying for. The men watched Bobbi as if hypnotized. Slowly, slowly the pink baby doll slid lower and lower as Bobbi danced. Then, abruptly, Bobbi opened her eyes wide. Cindy found it frightening. Bobbi pulled the cigarette holder from between her breasts and tossed it to the man in khakis. He caught it clumsily. Bobbi grasped the top of the baby doll over her left breast and pulled it down an inch. Her expression now was sultry, as if she were disrobing for a lover. Her tongue crept out of her mouth and just touched her upper lip. It wasn't quite vulgar.

The pink garment slid down another inch and a nipple was exposed. The men broke into wild cheers and Cindy felt an odd envy. Not only were Bobbi's breasts obviously large, but if Playboy photo spreads were any evidence, they were shaped in a way that men preferred, jutting and perky. Cindy thought of her own small breasts. Frank's frequent admiration of them suddenly seemed inconsequential.

Cindy watched as Bobbi eased the baby doll down and down, past her breasts and her erect nipples, down her flat stomach with just a hint of muscle, past her perfect oval of a belly button and down. Bobbi stopped with the pink garment a ring around her hips. She gazed at her audience. One hand held up the flimsy ring of cloth that threatened to fall to her ankles. With the other hand, Bobbi made a palm-up "Well?" gesture. A shower of bills hit the floor around her glittering gold shoes. Bobbi tilted her head slightly and opened her mouth in an expression that asked, "Oh, surely you can't mean that?" She rolled her eyes and looked disappointed. She looked at the ceiling. She pulled the baby doll an inch higher on her belly. The men roared disappointment and more dollars hit the dance floor. All around Bobbi, the other dancers were crouching, clutching their costumes, gathering up their money, ready to exit.

Bobbi looked at her audience and let the pink fabric slide back down a fraction. The men stared. She suddenly shook her head and tugged the baby doll back up to cover her breasts. She turned her back as if to exit. The men howled and more dollars hit the stage. Bobbi stopped and looked back over her shoulder at her audience. They shouted. Her hips began to sway again and the baby doll slipped and fell. Bobbi stopped it at her knees. Her rear was exposed to her audience and they could not take their eyes off of her. She gyrated and held her over-the-shoulder pout at them. Then, just as the booming voice announced the next round of dancers, the baby doll slid to Bobbi's ankles. She stepped slowly out of it, then turned and faced the men. Cindy could see their eyes crawl over her body. She put a thumb under the waistband of her thong, tilted her head and raised her eyebrows again. The men threw bills at her feet in a frenzy. Bobbi began moving the music, easing the thong down and down until it too fell around her ankles. She stepped out of it, hooked it on painted toes of one foot and tossed it into the air. It landed behind her. The men clapped and cheered.

Bobbi, naked except for her high heels, strutted back toward her audience and struck a pose before them, one hand on her hip, the other in the air as if to say, "Behold me!" The men did.

Then Bobbi bent over, grasped the polo-and-khakis man by the chin and gave him a sultry look. He was frozen as she turned her expression into dejection and glanced at all the bills littering the floor. She put her lips to the man's ear and whispered something. Her tongue flickered. With an eager expression, he jumped onto the dance floor. On his knees, he gathered up Bobbi's dollar bills while she stood over him, naked.

As the other dancers exited the floor, the man gathered Bobbi's money. Once it was in a stack, still on his knees, he offered it to her. She gave him a lover's smile, took the stack and put a finger to her mouth. She kissed her finger, touched her left nipple, then pressed her finger to the khaki man's lips. He appeared to be stunned. She favored him with a brief smile, then began a hip-swinging stroll from her dance floor.

The man stood and climbed back over the rail to his seat. Bobbi stopped, turned, and put a finger to her lips as if struck by a thought. She smiled at the khaki man. She bent at the waist, picked up her discarded baby doll and thong from the floor and tossed the thong to him. The men roared their approval and Bobbi, naked, walked off the stage as if she had just accepted an Oscar. Behind her, the khaki man held the flimsy pink garment as if it was a holy robe thrown to him by the pope.

Cindy got up and left the building.

Chapter Forty-Six

The house was a well-kept brick two-story in an orderly but not wealthy section of the city. Bobbi answered the door at Cindy's knock. Cindy was startled at her appearance. Although the same basic outlines of her face were there, Bobbi today could easily have passed for a person completely different from the one who had owned the dance floor Saturday night.

She was dressed in grey sweatpants and a large flannel shirt over a t-shirt. Her hair was tied back into a practical ponytail. She recognized Cindy instantly and her eyes went cold.

"Yes?" she asked from the other side of the screen door.

"Hello, Miss Grable," Cindy said. "I wonder if I might have a few minutes of your time."

"For what?" Bobbi asked, her eyes locked on Cindy's.

"To talk about Hunter," Cindy said.

"Hunter's fine. He's at school," Bobbi said.

"I'm sure that's true," Cindy said. "But given the incident at the mall the other day, it's my responsibility to make sure that everything is OK with Hunter."

Bobbi turned her head slightly but kept her eyes locked on Cindy's. "What happened at the mall is over," she said. "That person has no legal claim to Hunter. I'm his mother and he's just fine. There's nothing to check on."

"I understand that," Cindy said. "But county Children and Youth has certain follow-up standards concerning an incident like the one that happened at the mall. Miss Grable, I don't want to be difficult. But the police were called and the policeman thought it was important to have Children and Youth involved. Now, I have to tell you that Children and Youth's standard procedure is that if you won't talk to me, then I have to get a warrant and subpoena and instead of talking here in your own home, where you're comfortable, we do it in a courtroom, in front of a judge."

Bobbi's eyes didn't waver. She seemed unafraid of the prospect of being hauled before a judge to talk about how she cared for her child.

"Miss Grable. Bobbi. Please," Cindy said, trying another tack. "I know you hate these intrusions. I don't blame you. I'd hate it too if some stranger came around and accused me of not taking care of my kid. But that's not what this has to be. I just need to talk to you for a few minutes. It's entirely possible that I can close this case right here. But I need your cooperation."

Bobbi eyed Cindy hard for another fifteen seconds. Then she said, "OK. For Hunter." She pushed open the door and Cindy entered.

"Thank you," she said.

"You want anything to drink?" Bobbi asked, walking down the hall to the kitchen. Cindy noticed that she was barefoot and looked for the walk that drove Steve nuts, the strut from the strip club dance floor. It wasn't there.

"A diet something would be nice," she said, following Bobbi.

"Diet Coke?" Bobbi asked, pulling open the door of a gleaming white refrigerator. Cindy noticed that it was devoid of fingerprints, something rare in a household with a child. She also noticed that the kitchen was clean and orderly. Dishes were stacked neatly in a drying rack. Small appliances, wiped clean, lined the back of the counter. There was a vase of fresh flowers on a small table under a window.

"Fine. Thank you," Cindy said.

As Bobbi unscrewed the cap of the soda bottle, she said, "You won't find anything here to write me up on. Me and my sister keep a neat house. We're not trash."

As Bobbi turned and offered a glass of dark cola and ice, Cindy said, "Bobbi. I never thought that you were. Part of the job is assessing the conditions that the child lives in. I'm sorry if that offends you."

Bobbi said nothing. She led the way down a short hallway to the living room. The room was sunlight-filled. The floors were polished wood with throw rugs. The furniture was modern, with a Scandinavian simplicity but an American attention to comfort. Everything seemed practical, rounded, comfortable, padded. A brick fireplace on one wall was filled with a large bouquet of flowers. Pictures of Hunter were everywhere, on walls and tables. In one corner was a collection of boy's toys, brightly colored trucks, cars and plastic building blocks arranged neatly. The entire home was organized, colorful, comfortable.

Bobbi, still watching Cindy observing her home, motioned for Cindy to sit down. She did, then Bobbi did. Bobbi crossed her legs and looked at Cindy. Bobbi's toenails were painted bright red. Her feet looked like they got a lot of care.

"OK, Miss Caseworker. Ask your questions."

Cindy put her drink down on a blonde-wood-and-glass coffee table, being sure to put it on a coaster. She pulled a notepad and pen from her purse and then placed the purse on the floor beside her chair.

"First, thank you for your cooperation," Cindy said. "As I said at the door, I understand your resentment of this process. However, it must be done. So –" Bobbi raised a cynical eyebrow and Cindy couldn't help but think of her dance floor expressions and how she had used them to neatly manipulate the men. "My name is Cindy Phillips. I work for Family Services. We're under contract with county Children and Youth to perform certain functions for them, such as interviews like this. Do you want to see my ID?"

Bobbi waved a hand. "No, I believe you." Cindy noticed that her fingernails were short and unpainted.

"OK," Cindy said. "Then maybe we could start with your real name."

"My name is Bernadette Wagner but everyone calls me Bobbi. That's Bee-oh-bee-bee-eye-eye."

"Are you married?"

"No."

"Age?"

"I'm twenty-nine."

"Is this your residence?"

"Yes. I own it jointly with my sister. She's at work right now."

"How long have you lived here?"

"About eight years."

"Do you work outside the home?"

"I'm an exotic dancer."

Bobbi's honesty surprised Cindy. She had been expecting the "waitress" answer that she had given the policeman at the mall. Cindy couldn't help but raise an eyebrow.

"At what establishment?"

"I have a regular gig at Out of Bounds. I hit a few other places if they call and ask nicely or if I get tired of Bounds."

"That's …." Cindy began.

"Cut the bullshit," Bobbi said. "I saw you there Saturday night. You know what I do. I know that you have to pretend you don't, but let's not pretend too much. I have to pick Hunter up from school soon."

"I'm sorry," Cindy said, ashamed of her deception. She put down her notepad. "I know that you work at Out of Bounds. I shouldn't have asked it that way. I promise. No more pretending."

"I make about seventy thousand a year," Bobbi said, her eyes locked on Cindy's. "I spend my money mostly on two things: Hunter and this house. I sock away more than fifteen thousand dollars a year. I've got nearly a million in an IRA. That's what I've saved and what I've earned on my money since I started dancing at fifteen. So, yes, I've been doing this since before I was legal. In the early years, I didn't make much. But I saw the potential. I've gotten good at what I do. You saw me up there. That was a pretty typical Saturday night. I made about eight hundred after the club took its cut. That's about average. I take ten weeks off a year, which means that I work about forty-two. From my take-home, I pay my taxes. Yes, I do. I'm legal. I'm an independent contractor. I also pay for a health care plan for me and Hunter. I bought this house with my own money, so my sister pays me a little to live here. It's pretty much a token amount, but it allows me to cover maintenance costs and heat and electricity, that kind of stuff."

She paused, although her eyes never left Cindy's.

"I know you came in here thinking that because I'm a dancer, I must be some kind of trash and Hunter is in danger. You're dead wrong. I love my little boy with everything I have and there's nothing that he wants or needs that he doesn't have. My job allows me not only to be here in the morning to wake him up and cook him breakfast – which I do every single day – but also to pick him up from school, spend all evening with him and then tuck him into bed at night. I lay down beside him and we talk about his day. I read him a book. We talk about what we're going to do in the upcoming weekend. Then I kiss him goodnight. Nights I have to work, I make sure that he's asleep before I leave. If he happens to wake up while I'm gone, my sister is here. I generally work an eleven-to-two shift, so I'm cleaned up and back home by three. I sleep till seven, when it's time to get Hunter up. When he's off to school, I grab a few more hours. Then I take care of all the usual stuff that a mother does. You know – I go shopping. I clean the house. I mow the yard. I watch a little TV. I do some laundry. Sometimes I have lunch with a friend. Three times a week, I hit the gym. Every school day at two-thirty, I drive over to the school and pick up Hunter. We spend the rest of the day together. Sometimes he helps me cook dinner. He's pretty good at mac-and-cheese, not so good at lasagna.

"Now, Miss Caseworker, if you're here to try to take Hunter away from me, I want you to look me right in the eye and tell me that what I just told you sounds like the life of a kid at risk. If you don't believe me that that's my life, you can ask my sister. Or my neighbors. Or you can follow me around for a week. I don't care. Hunter is the light of my life and I'm going to raise him the best that I can. I even have a retirement plan that I bet beats yours all to shit. I know that I can't dance forever. In fact, twenty-nine is pushing it a bit. I know that. You might have heard of a little bar across town called Blarney's. I have an arrangement with the current owner. When I decide to quit dancing, he retires and sells me the place. He clears about 80 K a year, but he's sloppy. I can tighten things up and market the place better. I bet I can clear a hundred a year. I've already got enough saved up to pay for Hunter's college education. I can pay for him to go to Harvard without breaking a sweat. And don't think that he won't – he's very bright. He's doing great in school. You can ask his teacher, Miss Marquet. He's sociable, he's good in math and great in English. He's creative, too. That fish is his." Bobbi pointed to a framed picture on the wall. It was a multi-colored fish, mostly in blue. It looked like a Chagall. Cindy was impressed.

"Now, I'm taking care of Hunter right now. If something happens to me, my sister Beatrice – we call her Bea – gets it all. And Hunter." Bobbi stopped and for the first time, Cindy noticed an uncertainty in Bobbi. "Bea's not … she's not as … outgoing as I am. She had some problems earlier in life – actually, we both did – and she responded differently. But she's a wonderful woman with a warm heart. She knows Hunter inside and out and he loves her dearly. If something happens to me, she gets the house and everything, plus a big, fat check from a life insurance policy that I have on myself. It's enough so that she will never have to work again and can stay home with Hunter all day. I trust her to raise him just as I would. Now, you tell me that Hunter's at risk in any way. You tell me that I'm a lousy mother. You tell me that my life doesn't revolve around raising him to be a happy, healthy, self-confident young man. You tell me where I've gone wrong, where I've screwed up." Bobbi curled her legs under her on the couch and looked at Cindy defiantly.

Cindy was at a loss for words. She looked around the house – neat, cozy, cared-for. She could find no evidence that there was the slightest reason to be worried about Hunter's well being.

"Bobbi. I'm sorry. I meant no offense. I believe what you've told me because I saw you with Hunter. I could see how the two of you related to each other, and believe me, that's something that is very hard to fake. Given this house and what you've told me, I feel pretty confident that I can get approval to close this case. I can't do that on my own. I have to get approval from the C and Y supervisor, but I don't think that there will be any trouble. The only possible problem will be with your occupation. But –" Cindy hurried on when she saw sparks snap from Bobbi's eyes, "But I'm sure that when I explain what you've told me here today, I'm sure that there won't be any problem. With closing the case, I mean."

Bobbi gave Cindy a smile that was just short of nasty. "How much do you make, Miss Caseworker? How is your retirement plan doing?"

Cindy sighed. "Bobbi, I'm really trying hard not to make this personal. My only concern is Hunter and it certainly seems that he's doing OK. I will ask around and I will check at school, but as I said, I believe you. You don't need to attack me. I will –"

"Oh, this isn't an attack, honey," Bobbi interrupted. "I'm being nice. You want nasty, you visit the dressing room at Out of Bounds and go a few rounds with the girls there. Your definition of 'bitch' will change, I guarantee it."

Bobbi was smiling a smile that Cindy didn't like at all. It spoke of experience and hard-won knowledge of things that Cindy didn't know about at all. She suspected that Bobbi was tough and streetwise. Cindy knew that she wasn't. The only thing propping Cindy up was her official status and her determination to be sure that Hunter was being cared for. Under other circumstances, Cindy would have found Bobbi intimidating and would have carefully avoided contact with her.

"I don't see a ring on your finger. So you haven't managed to find a prize among the assholes, either?" Bobbi said. Cindy couldn't tell if it was another jab or an attempt to find common ground. She decided to assume the latter.

"There is someone special. We're living together. But I don't know if it's going to end up in a ring," Cindy said, surprised at her own revelation to a stranger, and a scary one at that.

"He's got the commitment flu?" Bobbi asked.

"No. Actually, it's me," Cindy said, again surprising herself. Somehow, despite her meanness, Bobbi seemed safe to talk to. The remark Bobbi had made about something going wrong in her young life had struck a chord in Cindy. For once, someone might truly be able to understand how much work it was to carry the baggage around.

"I have plans. Dreams. Things I want to do," Cindy said. "Things I've been thinking about for a long time. It's not that I don't see him there when I think about my plans. It's just that he doesn't seem to share my ambition. I don't see him moving forward with me," Cindy said.

Bobbi's smile was knowing.

"I know what you're talking about. Hunter's sperm donor – Steve – I got to the point where I just couldn't imagine him sharing my life any more. He was just dull. Uninteresting. He had no plans. He just moved through the day. He had, like, three trains of thought – beer, sex and that damn motorcycle. He was great in the sack, but geez. At some point you have to grow up, right?" Bobbi looked at Cindy. "You might not be quite where I got to yet, but when – if – you get there, believe me, the shacking up will end in a hurry. When we girls have somewhere to go, we don't need an anchor," she said.

Cindy smiled. "I know all about that. I've got enough anchors."

"When you get right down to it, it's just us, isn't it?" Bobbi asked. "I mean us girls. We really can't trust anybody else, especially not a male. If we've got a goal, we're going to have to make it happen ourselves. We have to fight the battles, again and again, day after day." She paused. "It sure is hard to keep your eyes on that prize, isn't it? All that extra shit we have to wade through. Don't you start to wonder if it's all worth it?"

Cindy nodded. "I wonder every single day," she said. "Especially when it comes to trying to save – ah, help the kids. It's never easy. There's always some complication. I had this one client family with a little girl. She was only five. Her father –" Cindy's voice faded as she recalled Brittany and her promise.

I'm not keeping my promise to you, she thought. *I'm betraying you, Brittany, just like everyone else did.*

Everyone failed you, all the way down the line. I'm just the next adult who should have saved you but didn't.

"I – well, you have your failures," Cindy said. "I thought that I had fixed things between this little girl and her father, but he ended up hitting her on the head and killing her. I could have removed her and that wouldn't have happened, but I didn't. I take responsibility for that. That little girl's death was my fault. I carry that every day. I always will."

Bobbi was watching Cindy as she spoke and something changed in her eyes. It might have been a softening. She tilted her head and looked at Cindy without the usual near-contempt.

"I knew you were carrying something," Bobbi said. "Something really heavy. I know. It's there every day and it weighs you down, but you get up every morning and pretend it's not there. You get through the day. But sometimes when you're alone – or maybe in the middle of the night when he's snoring and a universe away – sometimes it just presses down on you, doesn't it? And you wonder how the hell you're going to get up and carry it around another day. You wonder how you find the strength each day. Your greatest fear is that one day, it's going to be too much, isn't it? That one day the bill is going to come due and you can't pay it. Am I right?"

Cindy's breath left her. She was appalled to feel a tear well up.

"I just – I don't –"

"Your big plan – your dream," Bobbi said. "It has something to do with trying to unload that burden, am I right? You have something that you think you can do so that little girl doesn't keep visiting you in your dreams. You think that if you do this thing, if you carry out this plan, then maybe you'll get a little peace. Am I right?"

Cindy gave in and tears slid down her cheeks, her professional front collapsing.

Bobbi rose from the couch quickly and walked to Cindy. She stood at her side and put her arms around Cindy's shoulders.

"It's OK to cry," Bobbi said. "You don't get to cry enough, do you? Got to keep the game face on. Can't let your guard down even for a second, or those doubts start clawing at you. Am I right? Let me guess. This is how you think – you're not good enough. You're confused. You don't really know what to do in most situations, but you just bull through as best you can. You find a way. Everyone else seems more confident, more accomplished, more certain, more sure than you are. Their mean comments cut you. You're so easily wounded. You go home at night and worry about things you did and didn't do because you're never confident that you're doing or saying the right thing. Even when you're feeling good about something you've accomplished, it takes just one negative comment for those feelings to collapse and wash away. Am I on to something here?"

"Oh, god," Cindy said. More tears slid down her cheeks. Bobbi hugged her tighter.

"Shh. You can cry. It's OK here. That's what I tell Hunter. This house is a 'crying is fine' zone."

Bobbi was silent a minute and Cindy let her tears slide. She was appalled at her unprofessional display of emotion, but Bobbi's incisive comments had cut to her heart. She was amazed at Bobbi's powers of perception.

"I was twelve the first time my father raped me," Bobbi finally said, holding Cindy and swaying slightly. "After the first time, he left me alone for about a month. Then it became pretty much a nightly thing. It lasted until I was fifteen and I ran away from home. Actually, I tried to run away at fourteen. The first time, when I was sneaking out of the house, Bea stopped me. She asked me what I was doing. I snarled something at her and she broke down. She was twelve then. She was younger than me, but she'd been suffering longer. He started on her when she was nine. It wasn't intercourse at that age, but he made her blow him and stuff. Then it progressed. He penetrated her for the first time when she was ten. We sat there on the floor that morning under the kitchen table in the dark and talked it all out, said all the things that we had always suspected about each other but had never been able to say. The next thing I knew, it was dawn and my plans were in serious jeopardy. Bea decided that she was going with me, but I couldn't get her to pack a bag. She didn't seem to understand that she couldn't just walk out the door with nothing.

"I'd been stealing from mom and dad for years, snatching a few bucks from their wallets and purses when they weren't looking. I had a paper route. I mowed lawns. I'd built up a nest egg. Bea didn't have one; she just wanted to walk out the door in her pajamas. I tried to explain to her how tough it was going to be. My plan had been to go to New York and disappear into the big city. I had a bus ticket and everything. Bea had shit. But I just couldn't leave her, especially not after hearing that she was being tortured, too. So I put all my stuff back and put my plans on hold. I knew that I had a project – I had to get Bea ready to leave with me. It was going to take some doing. She was so passive – still is. I had to keep her spirits up constantly, keep telling her that we'd have this great life together, try to play it up, keep her interested. She was so willing to just slide back into her life of passive acceptance. But I knew where that would end. One day she'd take too many pills, or get one of dad's handguns and jettison her baggage the permanent way. I couldn't let her do that. Not only was she my sister, but she was my fellow sufferer. She'd been through that same hell of seeing dad's dark form in the doorway as he stood there in his boxers, scratching his nuts – and you knew damn well what was coming next."

Bobbi pulled back from Cindy, reached to a nearby end table and found a box of tissues. She held it out to Cindy, who pulled out several and smiled a teary smile. She dabbed at her eyes and cheeks.

"That's awful," she said. "What did you do?"

"I finally got us to the point where we were ready to cut out," Bobbi said, sitting on the couch near Cindy. "Ten months and fourteen days after we sat on that kitchen floor and shared our worst secrets, we bolted together. I drew a picture of a hand with its middle finger raised. I left it on the table for Dad. That was the only note we left. We took a bus to Philly and tried to start over. That urban life turned out to be too tough on us. We needed a place where life was a little slower. I was actually fine, but Bea is – Bea takes a lot of things hard. She needs a place where things are slower, where they come at you at a pace that you can think them through. So we put a map up on the wall and threw darts at it. Hits on Philly and Pittsburgh didn't count. Bea's third dart hit Altoona. I found a place to dance – that's all I've ever done – and Bea eventually found a job as a bookkeeper at a dentist's office. So here we are." Bobbi smiled.

"I don't know what to say," Cindy said. "But running away like that. My, that was brave. And staying an extra year for your sister when you knew –" Cindy paused. "That's beyond remarkable."

"You could tell me your story," Bobbi said, going back to the couch, but staying on the end near Cindy. She retrieved the tissue box from the end table and put it where Cindy could reach it.

"I never – it wasn't sexual with me," Cindy said. "It was just what we call routine child abuse by my stepfather. Up until one night, when my stepfather and my mother put me to bed early so they could drink. I came back downstairs to get a doll. My favorite doll. Mom was gone to get beer. My stepfather was there and he was pretty well looped already. All I remember is coming down the steps and seeing him scowl at me. The next thing I knew, I was in the hospital and I couldn't move most of my body."

"He –" Bobby began.

"He beat the living shit out of me," Cindy said. "Thank god some neighbor heard me screaming and called the cops. Thank god for the cop who responded. They told me that he stopped the bleeding until the ambulance got there. They said that he – my stepfather – knocked me out, then started hitting me with anything he could find – a whiskey bottle, his fist, a bowling ball. I guess he stomped on my arm a few times."

Bobbi winced.

"I had to learn how to walk again," Cindy said. "I spent almost a year in hospitals. I guess that at one point, they had pretty much given up on me. Except for one doctor. He kept encouraging me. Then there were these books. I don't remember them really well. It's kind of strange, because at the time, I lived for them. But somebody must have found out about me. He – or she – had these fairy-tale books written about this princess. She was – well, it sounds silly now. But the story was that a black witch put a spell on this princess so that nothing was easy for her. She was always bumping into things and losing things and falling into rivers and nearly being swept away. All her best-laid plans always went wrong. Her earrings fell off and were lost and she could never find her favorite shoes and her pets always wandered away. But she kept – oh, this sounds stupid."

"No, please!" Bobbi said. "I really want to hear this."

"Well," Cindy said reluctantly. "She – this princess in these books, I mean – she never quit being a nice, helpful person. She would put on common clothes and go down to the village and help the poor children. She recognized that as bad as she had it, the poor kids had it worse. And by helping them – oh, this really is silly!"

"It is not," said Bobbi with a firmness that encouraged Cindy.

"This princess was just the most kind and gentle soul, but she was also very determined. She did what she could to help other people and ignore her own troubles. I remember at the time – I didn't make the connection between the princess's situation and my own until later – that I found something revitalizing about those princess tales. It gave me courage to deal with my own problems, to try to look beyond them and hope that one day everything would be normal again. It helped me think about other people, and how we all have our own tragedies, our own struggles. That we shouldn't ever get so caught up in our own problems that we forget that others have them, too. Some people have it a lot worse than we do." Cindy paused. "There are a lot of kids who were beaten as badly as I was who never walk again. Or who fall into comas and never come out. Or never wake up at all."

"That's amazing," Bobbi said. "And I would love to sit here and talk to you all day. But – I'm sorry – I have to go get Hunter."

Cindy jumped up, suddenly aware of how far she had drifted from her professional mission. "Oh, I'm being rude. I'm so sorry. I'll just –"

"How about if you come with me?" Bobbi said. "You can observe first-hand how I – what's the caseworker word? – *interact* with Hunter. You'll be able to write a first-class report."

Cindy smiled. "And maybe then I can leave you alone."

Bobbi smiled back. Cindy detected sincerity.

"You, lady, are always welcome in this house. No questions asked. We tough girls have to stick together."

"You're so kind," Cindy said.

Bobbi jumped off the couch. "So will you come with me?"

"Sure," Cindy said.

"Now if I can just find my shoes," Bobbi said.

Chapter Forty-Eight

Cindy again chastised herself for stereotyping. As they walked to the small wooden garage beside the house, Cindy had imagined that Bobbi would drive a gold Cadillac or something similarly ostentatious. Instead, Cindy was delighted to see that Bobbi had a white Honda four-door.

"I love my Honda!" Cindy said as she buckled into the passenger seat. She noticed that the interior of the car, like Bobbi's house, was neat, clean and dust-free.

Bobbi backed the car carefully out of the garage.

"Cars are tools," she said. "I want one that does what it's supposed to. I couldn't stand to have a car that wouldn't start." She backed the car onto the street, stopped and put it into drive. "It doesn't help that I don't know shit about fixing cars," Bobbi said. "And I am not about to bring some lunk into the house just to keep my wheels running."

Cindy noted that Bobbi drove carefully, keeping to the speed limit. She parked two blocks from the elementary school and they walked to the small plaza at the front of the school where the students would be released. Cindy and Bobbi stood outside and chatted a few minutes. Bobbi seemed to know most of the other mothers waiting. After a few minutes, a buzzer sounded and the empty hallways were suddenly filled with chattering, laughing, shrieking students. They burst through the doors and flowed onto the buses that had lined up at the curb. Cindy noticed as Bobbi scanned the crowd, apparently watching the door where Hunter usually emerged. Soon, a young female teacher swung the door open. Several dozen children spilled out and headed for the buses.

"That's Mrs. Marquet, Hunter's teacher," Bobbi said. Cindy followed her to the doorway.

"Good afternoon!" Mrs. Marquet called cheerfully. Cindy was amazed that she still had the energy to be perky after an entire day with first-grade children. Mrs. Marquet released Hunter with a pat on the head. He rushed out the door. Bobbi crouched down to catch his flying hug and Cindy thought of the hugs she got from Brittany. She closed her eyes tightly and banished the memory.

Hunter, in a white polo shirt, khaki pants and a camouflage-pattern backpack, hugged his mother, then bounced back.

"Mom! It was so cool! We had a fireman in our class today! He put on his facemask and stuff. He was showing us how to get out of the house when it's on fire. You crawl! It was so cool!"

Bobbi waved a thank-you to Mrs. Marquet, then put a hand on Hunter's shoulder and turned him toward Cindy. "Hunter, I want you to meet one of Mommy's friends. This is Miss Phillips."

Cindy crouched. "You can call me Cindy," she said.

Hunter gave her a cautious look, apparently recalling her from the mall scene.

"It's OK, Hunter," Bobbi said. "Cindy is a friend."

Cindy put out her hand. Hunter extended his reluctantly. Cindy figured that he was probably baffled at the ways of adults, where a person can be an enemy one week and a friend the next.

Bobbi put a hand on Hunter's shoulder as he shook Cindy's hand.

"The first time we met, I didn't know what Cindy was like," she said. "But now I know that she's a wonderful person."

"Like Aunt Bea?" Hunter asked, twisting his head back and up to look at Bobbi.

Bobbi laughed. "Yes. Just like Aunt Bea. Except Cindy isn't related to us. She's a friend of the family."

Hunter returned his gaze to Cindy, who was still crouching. "Well, OK," he said.

Bobbi looked at Cindy. "Any chance you could stay for dinner?" she asked. "Hunter makes a mean mac and cheese."

"Oh, cool! Could we? That would be great!" Hunter said. His eyes lit up and he bounced up and down. "I love to make mac and cheese! It's the best!"

"I would love to eat your macaroni and cheese," Cindy said, mentally revising her evening's plans. "I've heard that you make the best mac and cheese in the whole world."

Hunter eyed her carefully, but Cindy could see that she was winning him over. "Who told you that?" he asked with suspicion.

"Oh, Hunter, everyone knows about your mac and cheese," Cindy said. "I wouldn't miss it for the world." Out of the corner of her eye, Cindy could see Bobbi smiling widely.

"Then that's what we'll do," Bobbi said.

Later, Cindy sat quietly in the living room while Bobbi put Hunter to bed. She could hear her murmuring and singing to him but couldn't make out the words. A part of her was still astonished at how her day had turned out. She had arrived at Bobbi's house determined to make a professional assessment of Hunter's circumstances, then leave. She had expected Bobbi to be hostile and non-cooperative. She had expected the entire process to be unpleasant. It had turned out to be completely different. She felt like she had discovered a kindred soul. Bobbi understood things that no one else ever had; she seemed to know what Cindy was feeling.

True, Bobbi was odd. She was younger than Cindy by a few years, but she seemed much older. Cindy chalked that up to the time she'd spent in Philly. Bobbi hadn't elaborated on those years, but Cindy guessed that they hadn't been easy or fun. As a 15-year-old runaway in the big city, Bobbi had probably learned a lot of lessons the hard way. Cindy shivered. She didn't want to imagine what kind of awful things might have happened.

But somehow, Bobbi had found her way out of it and even turned her life in a positive direction. Except for being single and an exotic dancer,

Bobbi was pretty much a typical soccer mom. Her life revolved around her child. She drove a sensible car. Her life was neat and tidy; her yard was mowed; her house was painted and swept. She had her finances in order. Cindy grimaced inwardly. Bobbi's finances were certainly a lot better than her own. Even with Frank in the house, she was always bouncing checks and running out of money. She just couldn't get the hang of how money and time interrelated. She forgot how long it took checks to clear and how quickly debit cards debited. She was always either wondering how much money she had in her bank account or feeling stress because she knew it was low or negative. But Bobbi – Bobbi popped hundreds of dollars into a retirement account every month, yet still had this cute little house, a decent car and money to spend on Hunter. Cindy had noticed that Hunter's clothes were all new and clean; his toys were shiny and unbroken. The only scruffy toy she'd seen was the obviously much-loved stuffed turtle that he had carried when he came out to say a polite "good night" to Cindy.

Maybe I should take up dancing, Cindy thought with an internal chuckle that almost became an audible snort. She could just imagine herself up there on that stage. Actually, she thought, that was the problem. She couldn't begin to imagine herself up there. There was no way she could take off her clothes in front of a roomful of rowdy men, let alone in a sultry, provocative manner as Bobbi did.

Maybe if I – Cindy's thoughts were interrupted by the pad of Bobbi's bare feet down the hardwood floor hallway. Bobbi smiled.

"They're so cute when they're asleep," Bobbi said.

"Asleep already?" Cindy asked.

"Doesn't take him long when he's had a full day."

"That's good," Cindy said.

"Oh, and I'm so sorry about the mac and cheese," Bobbi said. "He likes it cheesy. He always puts those extra slices in. I'm used to it – I didn't even think about another adult eating it until it was too late."

"Oh, it was fine. Really," Cindy said. "I was amazed, actually. He really does know how to make it."

"Simple repetition," Bobbi said, rolling her eyes. "We have it at least once a week." She paused. "Well," she said. "Can I make it up to you with something a little more adult?"

"What do you have in mind?"

"How about a little wine?" Bobbi asked. "You don't have to be home anytime soon, do you?"

Cindy looked at her watch but she had already made up her mind. "Sure," she said. "I can stay. I should probably call Frank, though."

"Then come on out to the kitchen with me," Bobbi said. "You can use the phone out there."

Shoes off, legs curled under her on the couch and on her second glass of wine, Cindy realized that she had probably told Bobbi more of her secrets than anyone except Ev.

Haven't seen Ev in a while – probably need to get all this off my chest, she thought.

"One of those storybooks was called 'The Princess Runs for President' or something like that," Cindy told Bobbi. "And something about it just stuck with me. The premise was silly – I mean, how can you run for president in a kingdom? But the idea of being chosen to be a leader of your people – instead of being born to it – appealed to me. It stuck with me. Later, the same idea popped up when I started reading about all these famous women, especially ones who were really good speakers. Because it occurred to me – if you can communicate well, that is, speak well, you can get a message out to people … you can maybe get them not just to pay attention to you, but to listen to you." Cindy paused. "Then I had a really great speech prof in college. He was really encouraging. He kept telling me that I could speak in public, but I didn't believe him. Then one day he finally got through my thick head a simple idea: speak about something you really care about and it's all so much easier. He had been telling me that for a long time, but it took a while to sink in.

"So I picked child abuse. I wrote a speech on it and delivered it in class. At the end, the whole class stood up and clapped." Cindy, ever vigilant for vanity, flushed. "I mean, it probably wasn't that good, but they were nice enough to encourage me."

Bobbi looked at Cindy over her wineglass. "You got a standing ovation and you think they were just being nice?" Bobbi made a dismissive noise. "You're not giving yourself enough credit, Cindy. I bet it was a great speech. And you must have really gotten to them. I don't hear about too many standing ovations in college classes."

"Well, anyway," said Cindy, embarrassed, "I learned that if I wanted to, if I cared enough, I could speak well. But ... I haven't done any of that in a long time. Not really much call for it in my day job. Oh, I'm doing all the talking here. Let's talk about you."

Bobbi sipped her wine. "There's really not very much exciting about me," she said. "My life revolves around that little bundle of joy in there. He's the reason for everything."

"He's a great kid," Cindy said.

"Thank you," Bobbi said. "It might be a cliché, but my sun rises and sets with him. He's...." She paused. "He's the ... one thing that keeps me from thinking that my life's been a complete disaster. As you might have guessed, I haven't had such a great life –"

"That wasn't your fault," Cindy said.

"No, true, I got a shitty start," Bobbi said. "But I did some things ... I'm not much of a role model – never have been. I ... had some wild years. And I was stupid, selfish and careless. I've aborted ... I've had more than one abortion. And I reached a point where I realized that I didn't want to do that any more. I started to...." Bobbi closed her eyes and stopped. Cindy waited.

"This sounds ... odd," Bobbi said. "But for a while, I was ... haunted. I was haunted by the kids that I never had. Did you ever see that TV ad on abortion where they show a kid swinging on a swing set and then the kid disappears and there's just the swing, going back and forth? That's what happened to me. I started to have … visions. Nightmares. Sometimes I even saw things during the day, like some kind of a horror movie." Seeing the look on Cindy's face, Bobbi spoke quickly. "Oh, no, I don't mean like … bloody things. Nothing like that. But I'd be looking at a picture of a kid at someone else's house and all of a sudden the face would change and it would be this little blonde girl who I just knew was my little girl … one that I…." For the first time, Bobbi's voice broke and Cindy could see tears.

"One that you didn't have," Cindy said gently, putting a hand on Bobbi's foot.

Bobbi sniffed. "Yeah. That's a nice way to put it. 'One that I didn't have.' You have a way with words." Cindy smiled.

"So Hunter is my salvation. He's my last chance. It's like God handed him to me and said, 'If you treat this one right, I'll forgive everything else.' I really do feel like that. By the time I had Hunter, I was ready for a kid. I was ready to really love someone else. I was really ready to care for someone. So it worked out. I got a second – well, more like a fifth chance, maybe."

They both laughed but Bobbi sobered quickly. "So I know … I just know in my heart that if I blow it with Hunter, it's the last chance I'll have. My life is already shot to shit. The best I can do now is make sure that his isn't, too. So I'll always be here for him, to make sure that he has warm clothes and good food and a place to sleep. And to tell him every day that he's the greatest kid who ever lived.

Unlike my parents, who when they weren't screaming at us were ignoring us. It really does have an effect on you."

"It does," Cindy said. "People just don't get it. They think that their kid is born with all these flaws when really they install most of them. Neglect is bad enough. But when there's actual physical and mental abuse...." She shrugged. "We make our own monsters. I sometimes wonder how any of us turn out normal."

"So you're not going to be taking Hunter from me?" Bobbi asked.

Cindy blinked, stunned by the question. "Take Hunter from you? Good grief, no, Bobbi! You're a great mom. Whatever gave you that idea?"

"That's what you came here for, wasn't it?" Bobbi asked.

Cindy thought back to knocking on Bobbi's door. It seemed a lifetime ago.

"I came to assess. To observe," she said. "There was never any intent on my part to remove Hunter. And there never could be now, not knowing what I know."

"I had to be sure," Bobbi said. "Otherwise, I'll have to ask for that wine back." She smirked and Cindy laughed.

"Whew! You should probably be taking it from me. I think I've had enough."

"Are you OK to drive?"

"Yes. I've been going slow. I'll be fine," Cindy said. "And I probably should get going." She stood up. Bobbi stood, wineglass in hand. She eyed Cindy, deliberately placed her wineglass on the coffee table and went to Cindy for a hug. Cindy accepted and returned it.

"I'm very glad I met you," Bobbi said when they broke apart.

"Me too. This has been a really remarkable day," Cindy said.

"OK. Now that we know so much about each other, let's not be strangers," Bobbi said.

"I'm so glad I found you," Cindy said. "I think I really needed to talk."

Bobbi walked Cindy to her car, which was parked across the street. The night air was cool and smelled of summer and water on warm concrete. Crickets chirped. Warm golden light spilled from Bobbi's neat brick house.

Cindy opened her Honda's door and got in. Bobbi stood barefoot on the street.

"Beautiful night," she said.

"It is," Cindy agreed. "It's one of those nights that makes you wish you had something exciting to do." Cindy closed her door and rolled down the window. Bobbi was looking up at the stars. The sky was clear and they glittered and shimmered.

"You know, when I was seven years old, my grandmother took me to the ballet," Bobbi said, still looking up. "I had never been to a ballet and I was just ... enraptured. I watched those beautiful ladies move across that stage like butterflies. I couldn't believe how weightless they seemed. The ballet was two hours long but it seemed to me to be five minutes. When my grandmother saw how I responded, she took me backstage. She knew the artistic director. When I got backstage and met some of the ballerinas, I was amazed to realize that they weren't just graceful, they were strong. Really strong. They had to be to sustain all those movements and poses. I thought that was just remarkable – their strength made them graceful. They were all so gracious to me.

"My grandmother was always trying to make up for my miserable home life, so after that show, she paid for me to take ballet. I went for about a year to this local dance school run out of an old church. The instructor was this skinny, dark-skinned old guy – he seemed to me to be a hundred – and he was just ruthless. He would tell us to try a position or movement and when we got it wrong, he would stop the music and say, "No, no, that is not correct." And he would grab our arms and legs and move us into the right positions. Then he'd go sit down again, start the music and start barking orders again. He always wore his ballet slippers when he taught us. I can still see his lumpy feet in those worn black slippers. Every once in a while, he'd stand up and demonstrate something and you could tell that he must have been really graceful once.

"I was terrified of him but I wanted to be one of those graceful, beautiful ballerinas so badly that I kept at it. I practiced at home in front of the mirror. I dreamed of being a ballerina. I wanted to be strong and graceful and beautiful. One day after I was sure I had botched my entire session, the old man came up to me at the end of class when I was taking off my shoes. He looked at me with these old watery blue eyes and said, 'Most of these girls, they are here because their parents tell them to be here. But you. You are here because you love the dance. Am I right?' I nodded because I was too scared to speak. He put his hand on my head – the first gentle gesture I'd ever felt from him – and he said, 'You keep loving, you keep dancing, and one day you will be a ballerina.' Then he walked away and I just floated home."

Cindy sat quietly. Bobbi was now looking down the street.

"My grandmother died the next week and that was the end of my ballet lessons," Bobbi said. "Mom and dad sure weren't going to pay for them, although there was enough for three cases of Old Milwaukee every week. And at eight years old, I couldn't get a job or anything. So that was the end of my ballet career. And then of course, a couple years later, my father started his little thing. That wiped out whatever confidence I had left in myself."

Bobbi looked at Cindy. Bobbi's face was wet with tears. She sniffed and wiped each eye with a thumb.

"I'm 29 now. That's the age when ballerinas retire, not when they start," Bobbi said. "Some nights I lay awake and I ask my grandmother to forgive me because I'm dancing, yes, but not the kind that she wanted me to be doing. I'm sure that she would be ashamed of me."

Cindy reached out of the window and took Bobbi's hand.

"No she wouldn't," she said. "She would be proud of you. For Hunter. And your beautiful home. And for taking care of your sister."

Bobbi sniffed, turned and gripped Cindy's hand so tightly that it hurt. With tearful eyes, she said fiercely, "You've got a dream tucked away inside you. I know you do. I can feel it. Whatever it is, whatever you dream about doing, I'm telling you right now, Cindy – don't waste another day. Don't waste another minute. If you have a dream, go get it. Don't let anyone stop you, not even the Mr. Wonderful you're living with. Because you know as well as I do that the only thing that's going to lift that weight you're carrying is for you to make that dream come true ... or die trying. You don't know what you're capable of. You have no idea. Not until you try."

Bobbi released her grip and rubbed Cindy's arm. "Go be a ballerina," Bobbi said. "Don't wait. Go do it now. Don't end up like me."

Then Bobbi was walking back across the asphalt, still warm from the day's sun. Cindy watched until Bobbi was on her porch. Bobbi turned and waved; Cindy waved back, then put her car in gear and drove home.

Partway home, with no warning, Cindy shut off the radio while it was playing an old Paul Simon tune.

It's time to start, she thought. *It's time to start.*

And she knew that it was.

Chapter Forty-Eight

She knew it wouldn't be easy, but it had to be done. She braced herself in front of the bathroom mirror. *Go be a ballerina,* she said to herself, over and over. Then she opened the door and walked into the living room where Frank was watching a football game. He looked up and smiled as she entered the room.

"Frank," she said. "We have to talk."

His smile faded. She sat down and took a deep breath.

"Remember when I told you that I wanted to do something about child abuse on a bigger scale?"

Later, she stood alone on the balcony, a warm breeze caressing her, drying her face. She looked up at the stars. It hadn't been easy. But it was done. And strangely, she felt free.

Part Three

Chapter Forty-Nine

There is a lot to do. It is time to start.

She pulls up her list of contacts on her computer, finds a number that she looked up on the Internet a few weeks ago. She punches in the number.

"Hello, office of the Green Party of Pennsylvania," she is greeted.

"Hello. I'd like to talk to someone about being a Green Party candidate," Cindy says.

"OK," says the pleasant voice. "I think you need to speak with our state director. That's Scott Rivers. Please hold."

There is a pause, then a click. "This is Scott Rivers, how can I help you?"

"Mr. Rivers, my name is Cindy Phillips. I'm a social services caseworker in Altoona. I want to run for office and I'd like to run under the Green Party banner."

"Well, we're always delighted to have candidates run on our ticket," Rivers says. "I think it would be a good idea if we met and talked a little. How much do you know about the Green Party?"

"I've scoped out your website. I was a poli sci major. I'm familiar."

"I guess the main question is to what extent you agree with our stances," Rivers says. "From what you've read about us, do we click?"

"I'm on board," Cindy says firmly, her fingers crossed.

"Well, that's great," Rivers says. "Let's get together."

She makes plans to meet him in Harrisburg in two weeks. It will be a two-and-a-half-hour drive one way, but nothing is going to stop her now.

Before they hang up, Rivers asks, "Oh, and may I ask what office you intend to run for? We've been very successful with city council and township supervisor candidates. School boards have been good. We've had a little more trouble at the county commissioner level."

"Senator," Cindy says firmly.

"State senator?" Rivers pauses. "That's ... aiming high."

"Not state senator, Mr. Rivers," Cindy says. "United States senator."

She can feel Dr. Jacobi's hand on her shoulder. *You go get them, girl. Show them what you can do.*

"Well, this is going to be a very interesting meeting," Rivers says.

Chapter Fifty

Suddenly it all seems pointless. Useless. Trivial. Abruptly, Steele stands up, pushing back his big black chair.

The men across the table from him are huddled around a laptop computer. They stop muttering to each other and look at him. He glances down at the boardroom table before him. It is covered with three-ring binders, photos, papers, pens and abandoned coffee cups. His Rolex rests next to his laptop computer. As usual, he took it off to impress upon his opponents that he would stay as long as it took to hammer out a deal. As usual, Steele is alone. As usual, he has backed his opponents into a corner and they are trying frantically to catch up.

Everyone's shirtsleeves are rolled up; ties are loose. The room smells of sweat and male cologne. His opponents apparently all wear the same scent. Steele wears none.

"Screw it," Steele says, sliding the Rolex over his hand and onto his wrist. He reaches out and tells his laptop to shut down.

The leader of the opposition, a man with glasses, pale skin and receding hair, glances at his partners, then stands up straight.

"Jim. I'm sure that we can come to terms if –"

"Your terms are fine. You can have the god-damned place," Steele says.

His laptop has shut down. He closes it and stuffs it into his soft leather briefcase.

"Jim, I don't ... I ...." the man stutters to a halt.

"Look. I'll sell you the place for fifteen-six. Your price. Fine. It's worth eighteen, but I'm sick of arguing about it. It doesn't matter. Take it. You're right that it's going to need a new roof, but not in the next five years. The occupancy will hold. I talked to the tenants personally. The only one that's questionable is the financial firm on the third floor. I talked to a guy named Paul Smithmeyer. He likes expensive cigars and Triumphs. British roadsters. Take him a box of Cubans and talk to him about his cars. Make him feel like a big shot. He'll stay."

He grabs his jacket from the back of a chair and slides it on.

The men watch him.

"You do know where to get Cubans, right?"

The pale man nods. He has no idea.

"All right. Call my lawyers. They'll draw up the sale papers," Steele says.

He walks around the table, hand extended. One by one, the men shake. They seem stunned.

"Take it easy," Steele says, and he's out the door and down the hall.

In the boardroom, the three men turn their gazes on each other.

"What the fuck just happened?" asks one.

"I'm not sure," says the man with glasses. "But I think we just got the best of Jim Steele on a real estate deal."

"Maybe he had to piss really bad," the third man says.

They all laugh. Then, shaking their heads, they turn to dividing up the tasks involved in closing the deal.

Outside, Steele waits for traffic until he can cross the street to the lot where he parked his car. A man in dark shabby clothes approaches him.

"Hey, buddy, got a quarter?" the man asks.

Steele glances at him, puts his briefcase down and pulls out his wallet. He pulls the bills out and hands them to the man. He picks up his briefcase and strides across the street, leaving the man standing, staring at the sheaf of 100-dollar bills in his hand.

Minutes later, Steele is in the Porsche, the needle pegged on 80, speeding north. He's already forgotten about the deal.

Chapter Fifty-One

Cindy sits at a big table in the pleasant, bright meeting room of the Green Party's headquarters in Harrisburg, Pennsylvania's capital. With her in the room are two men and a woman who have been elected to local offices running as Green Party candidates. They also hold management positions in the Green Party.

Cindy has already survived three intense interviews designed to test her knowledge of the Green Party's stands on the issues, on her knowledge of the state's main issues and her ability to stand up to scrutiny. She passed the interviews and the State Police background check easily. At this, her sixth meeting in Harrisburg in four months, talk has turned to the viability of running Cindy as a candidate for U.S. senator. When she first proposed the idea, she was met with polite skepticism. But the more that Rivers and other Green Party officials listen to Cindy, the more they believe that they need to take her seriously.

"Walker is vulnerable," Cindy says for the hundredth time. "He's out of touch. He hasn't even been in the state in three years. He spends all his time in D.C., talking to lobbyists and eating at expensive restaurants. He wears a Rolex and travels in limousines."

"I won't argue with you," Rivers says. "I've told you I agree. But he's vulnerable to who? The Democrats are running Pacifico. He's been a popular Philadelphia mayor and he's already started touring the state. The Democrats are going to throw everything they have behind him. He's going to pound on Walker for being out of touch, too. If people are going to vote against Walker, they're going to vote for Pacifico, not you."

Cindy raises her eyebrows to say "And?"

After the hours Rivers has spent with her, he knows the look.

"And, Cindy, there's no way we can compete with that. The Democrats already have a $15 million war chest. Walker will raise probably double that from special interest groups. We have –" he pauses and looks at the other people in the room. The woman snorts a laugh; the men smile and shake their heads. "– exactly nothing, zero, to spend on a senatorial campaign," Rivers says. "We can't buy any ads. We can't afford a bus. We can't –"

"Scott, I keep hearing the word can't," Cindy says.

Scott closes his eyes to keep his temper. Cindy can be very frustrating on this issue. She refuses to budge. She refuses to acknowledge the reality that she cannot possibly win against two senatorial candidates with decades of years in politics, thousands of connections and millions of dollars to spend.

"How the hell are we going to get the word out? How will people know who you are?" Rivers says after a deep breath.

"I'll barnstorm the state," Cindy says. "I'll stop in every town. I'll personally ask as many people as humanly possible to vote for me. I'll launch a blog and take donations over the Internet. I'll get out the Green Party message. I'll be a voice for change from the usual Republican-Democrat lies."

"We can't afford a bus."

"You said that. I'll drive my Honda."

"What about your job?"

Cindy takes a deep breath.

"OK, Scott. Here's the best I can do. I'll quit my job. I'm not making that much there. I've learned to live on very little. If you pledge to me that you'll organize some fundraisers and raise the amount of salary I'm living on now, plus a little money to travel, I'll worry about the rest. I'll sleep in my car. I'll stay in Motel 6. I'll live on bread and water."

Scott has a pencil between his fingers. He bounces the eraser end on the table and watches it. He has never heard such determination from a candidate. And she's clearly thought it through. She has an answer for every one of his objections.

Rivers glances up at the other three officials in the room. He gets non-committal looks. Cindy has her eyes on him. She has a certain unrelenting look that he finds disconcerting. It's not hostile, but there is definite pressure behind it. *Do something*, it says. *Make a decision.*

"We have to present your candidacy to the executive board," he says at last. "Officially, we can't pay you to run. But we can reimburse you for costs and expenses. How much are you making? What kind of salary ... uh, reimbursement are we talking about?"

"I'm making twenty-one thousand," Cindy says.

"Benefits?"

"Buy me a major medical plan. I'm going to be doing a lot of driving. If I get injured, I need to be covered for big bills. But I don't need a prescription plan or regular office visit coverage or any of that stuff."

"That's probably another two or three grand," Rivers says.

"So hold a fundraiser. Raise twenty-five thousand and you have a candidate for U.S. senator," Cindy says.

There is a long pause.

"You really want to be a senator," Scott says.

"No, I really want to get some things to change," Cindy says. "And this is the best way."

Chapter Fifty-Two

Cindy was in the small drug store in a small town pushing a shopping cart when she saw the mother and the little girl at the register. The mother, thin, wearing new jeans and a leather jacket, was waiting in line, looking bored. Her little girl, five or six, in a dirty pink jacket and too-small stretch pants, was quickly eating a candy bar she had snatched from the rack near the register. She was glancing furtively at her mother as she stuffed the candy into her mouth. The mother began stacking change on the counter. A shiver went through Cindy. She pushed her cart closer, opened her purse, got out a $20 bill, folded it and palmed it.

The mother got to the front of the line. She asked for cigarettes. The clerk retrieved them, ran them past the scanner, glanced at the little girl and held out her hand for the candy bar. The little girl, cheeks bulging, tried to hide the candy bar wrapper. The mother glanced down and understood in an instant what had happened. Her face instantly distorted, her eye-linered eyes snapping with rage.

"You little shit!" she screamed. "Now I don't have enough for my goddamned cigarettes!"

The girl burst into tears. Chocolate-colored saliva ran down her chin.

"Mommy, I'm so hungry!"

The woman raised her hand and Cindy pretended to trip and shoved her cart hard. The metal cart shot from Cindy's grasp and crashed into a rack of magazines behind the little girl. The effect was satisfying, but more than Cindy had intended. When the cart struck the magazine rack, the rack skidded, then tipped, then with a tremendous crash, fell, scattering newspapers and magazines. The cart rebounded, narrowly missing the little girl. The girl stepped backward to avoid it, bumped into the candy rack and fell, still crying. The mother's eyes went to Cindy, who was on one knee.

Cindy started to rise; she winced and went back to her knee. The mother started toward Cindy as the clerk came around the counter. They helped Cindy to her feet.

"Jeez, what happened?" the mother asked, her breath smelling of cigarettes.

"Are you OK, ma'am?" the clerk asked.

Cindy gave them a brave smile. "I ... I just slipped. I'll be OK, I think. I'm so clumsy."

The little girl had stopped crying. She sat on the floor, chocolate on her chin, watching the show. Cindy limped in the little girl's direction. When she got close, she winced again and said, "Oh, my." She sat on the floor near the girl, holding her knee.

"I'll get the manager," the clerk said and left.

The mother looked at Cindy with concern.

"Jeez," she said.

Cindy put out the hand with the $20, still palming it. "Can you help me up? I think I'll be OK."

The woman grasped Cindy's hand to help her up. Instead of rising, Cindy transferred the bill to the woman's hand. The woman, aware that something was being slid into her hand, tried to pull it back. Cindy held on, keeping the woman bent over.

Cindy looked directly into the woman's eyes.

"That's a twenty," she said. "Buy your cigarettes, but get the girl something to eat."

The mother's eyes showed confusion, then understanding.

"Shit," she said.

Cindy kept her hand and her eyes.

"Please. I know it's tough raising a kid, but she's a precious little girl. She needs your love and protection."

The mother jerked her hand out of Cindy's, taking the twenty.

Cindy turned to face the little girl.

"Honey, your mommy is going to get you something to eat." Cindy turned her eyes back to the mother's. "Aren't you, Mommy?"

The woman's eyes were dark. Her lip twitched as she eyed Cindy.

"Yeah," she said. "We'll go get something to eat."

Cindy stood, brushing herself off.

"If you can't afford food, there are programs to help," she said. "One day, you might be relying on this little girl the way she relies on you now. That might be something to keep in mind."

The woman grabbed her daughter's hand and turned to the register, showing her back to Cindy.

Behind Cindy, the manager said, "Ma'am, are you OK?"

The little girl, standing beside her mother, turned and looked at Cindy. Cindy gave her a smile. She turned to the manager.

"Yes, I think I'll be OK. I'm so sorry for the mess."

The manager glanced at the rumpled piles of paper.

"Well, as long as you're OK," he said unconvincingly.

"Here's my name and phone number," Cindy said, handing him her business card. "If you have any trouble getting reimbursement for your damaged magazines, please have them call me."

She gave the small man with the cheesy mustache a smile and left the store.

"Too bad she hurt herself," said the mother as she handed over the $20 for the cigarettes and the already-consumed candy bar, "She's still limping."

"She didn't finish her shopping," said the puzzled manager. He glanced down at the card. "And it says here that she's running for senator."

Chapter Fifty-Three

When he arrived at work on Monday, Pannington's mail, as usual, was placed neatly in his in-box. The envelopes were all slit open, but because of confidentiality concerns, none of the letters was removed. In his usual careful manner, Pannington examined each of them, making notes, filing some letters and occasionally turning to his computer. Near the bottom of the stack was one with a hand-written address and no return address.

Pannington felt a pang of unease when he recognized Steele's handwriting. With a feeling of dread, he opened the envelope and pulled out a single sheet of paper, folded carelessly. The top half of the paper was covered with Steele's all-capitals handwriting.

PETE,
    THERE'S NO EASY WAY TO DO THIS, BUT YOU'RE THE ONLY ONE I TRUST TO HANDLE IT RIGHT. SO PLEASE PICK UP THE PHONE AND CALL THE ALLEGANY COUNTY SHERIFF'S

DEPARTMENT IN MARYLAND. JUST OUTSIDE OF CUMBERLAND, THERE'S A STORAGE PLACE CALLED GREEN RIDGE STORAGE. SEND THE DEPUTIES TO UNIT 12. YOU CAN WARN THEM IF YOU WANT.

THANK YOU FOR EVERYTHING YOU'VE DONE FOR ME. I'M SORRY IT HAD TO END THIS WAY. BUT AFTER MOM DIED, THERE JUST WASN'T MUCH LEFT.

I KNOW THAT YOU'LL MAKE SURE ALL THAT STUFF IN MY WILL GETS HANDLED RIGHT. THE MOST IMPORTANT REQUESTS ARE FOR CINDY PHILLIPS. IT IS REALLY IMPORTANT TO ME THAT SHE CATCHES A COUPLE BREAKS. HER LIFE DIDN'T START OFF BEING MUCH FUN. SHE DESERVES A BREAK.

AGAIN, THANKS, PETE. FOR EVERYTHING.

–JIM

Pannington rose slowly from his desk, walked across his office and closed and locked his door. He returned to his desk, read the note one more time. He put his head down on his desk for a few minutes. Then he picked up the phone and started doing the things he had to do.

Chapter Fifty-Four

Cindy was weaving through Pittsburgh traffic, trying to find a certain off-ramp when her cell phone rang.

"Cindy Phillips, Green Party candidate for U.S. Senator," she answered automatically. "How can I help you?"

"Girl! What's this I hear about you running for senator?"

Cindy was thrilled to hear Evelyn's voice. She directed her car to the berm and stopped.

"Evelyn! How are you? What are *you* doing?"

"What am I doing? What are you doing? Girl, you're crazy!"

"I guess so."

"Didn't anyone ever tell you that poli sci majors aren't supposed to run for office? We just talk about people who do."

"Well you know me. I'm crazy that way. Always a rebel."

Evelyn snorted.

"So tell me," Cindy said. "What are *you* doing? Where are you? How are you?"

"I'm an aide to Rutherford Brown. He's a U.S. representative from Virginia. My home state, you know. I pretty much run his Washington office."

"That sounds great. Do you like it?"

"There's never a slow day," Evelyn said. "But it's nothing compared to you! Running for senator! How exciting is that?"

"I don't have a snowball's chance in hell of winning," Cindy said. "But I just couldn't sit there in my office in Altoona any more, just imagining all the kids being abused all across the state. Do you know, I set Google to search for news stories on child abuse and it emailed me, oh, like three hundred stories a day. Every day. It just got to be too much to take. I had to do something."

"So how is getting your ass whipped while running for senator going to make it better?" Evelyn asked. "If you don't mind my asking."

"Well, I cut a deal with the Green Party in Pennsylvania," Cindy said. "I tour the state for the next year or so. I talk about child abuse and then I talk about Green Party stuff. I'm at a lot of fire halls and church picnics. I've got a blog going. It's actually turning out to be a lot of fun, but it is a lot of work. Long days. And most nights, I'm sleeping in a cheap motel somewhere."

"But how exciting!" Evelyn said. "You're actually doing all that shit that we talked about with our profs. How is it all working out in real life?"

"The key is talking to people," Cindy said. "You talk and talk and talk. You just try to make connections. The Green Party stuff – well, that gets me some hard looks. You know Pennsylvania

- what did James Carville call the state? Philly and Pittsburgh with Alabama in the middle. So sometimes people yell something at me. That's OK. I can handle it. Now, child abuse, there's a topic that no one disagrees with. Everyone agrees that there should be less of it. But no one has any idea what to actually do about it. Because I have an idea, people listen. You'd be amazed at how many people come up to me after my talk and tell me that either they were abused or they knew someone who was. And they all agree that something needs to be done, something more than what we're doing now – which is this crazy patchwork of laws and enforcement."

"So you're doing what, just driving all over?" Evelyn asked.

"All over," Cindy said. "I drive and drive. I started in Altoona. I'm over in the Pittsburgh area now. That's going to take a while. At least there are Democrats here. Then I'll head north to Erie, then across the northern counties, over to the east, down the east side, hit Philly, then over to Harrisburg. Then back to Altoona. And then if I have the time, I start it all over."

"That is just so exciting!" Evelyn said. "I wish I could do it with you. It would be so much better than dealing with all these assholes who haven't told the truth since they were elected."

"Come join me," Cindy said. "I guarantee long hours, no pay and a really bitchy boss, especially when she doesn't have time for lunch."

"Oh, I would kill to be with you. We'd have a blast."

"I bet we'd go over real well in the northern counties," Cindy said. "I already got some death threats through my blog. So a white chick talking about progressive government and a black chick with an attitude – Ha! Those rednecks wouldn't know what to say."

They chatted a few more minutes, then Evelyn said that she had to sign off.

Cindy pulled back into the busy highway traffic, feeling very anonymous and very nostalgic for her undergraduate days. She missed Evelyn. It would be really pleasant to have her along.

Chapter Fifty-Five

The two Allegany County Maryland deputies were having lunch at the downtown Cumberland McDonald's. They went through the drive-through, then backed the car into a space underneath the trees that lined the parking lot.

Deputy Rod Hansen placed his coffee cup carefully onto the cruiser's big dashboard, placed his fries between his legs, then unboxed and bit into his Big Mac.

"You hear about that guy out at the storage rentals?" he asked.

"Nope. Wasn't on it," said Maureen Malzi, his partner for the week.

Rod snorted. "Some rich D.C. real estate salesman offed himself. Rented one of those units out at Green Ridge storage. Backed his Porsche in, sealed the door with duct tape and turned the engine on. He put the roof down, popped "Who's Next" into the CD player and just sat there."

"Oh, god," Maureen said. She opened a clear plastic container holding a salad.

"Yeah. He turned a real nice shade of pink and the damn car ran out of gas. Jeez. He knew what he was doing. He disconnected the oxygen sensor in the engine so he got a bigger dose of carbon monoxide."

"That's awful. He leave a note?"

"Mailed it to his lawyer on Friday. Guy opened it Monday. We got sent over about oh-eight-hundred."

"Kids? Family?"

"None that anybody knows of," Rod said.

"Why'd he do it?"

"Nobody knows. Maybe he was in money trouble. You know those guys – sometimes they look rich, but you know – debt up to their eyeballs." He sipped his coffee. "Man, that was a nice car, though."

"If he wasn't local, why'd he do it here?"

"That was what threw Timmerman," Rod said, referring to the county sheriff. "He thought it might be narcotics. You know, with the car and all. But there was no sign of the stuff. The door was sealed from inside. And I guess the guy's lawyer cleared some of that up. Turns out he owns some land outside of town – over east a bit. Big farm, I guess. The guy grew up near Frederick, but some relative had the farm here and he used to visit it all the time."

"That's really sad," Maureen said. "Like he came home to ...."

"Yeah," Rod said, chewing. "Guess when the time comes, you want to be near home – and all your money doesn't mean shit."

"Can't believe that," Maureen said. "If you've got money, wouldn't you pay for therapy or something?"

"Well, like I said, maybe it was money trouble. Or woman trouble. You women can run a man right into the ground. You know what they say about why women live longer than men – you wear us out early."

Maureen punched Rod on his shoulder, square on his brown sergeant's stripes.

"Ow!" he said, pretending that it hurt.

Maureen laughed. "The truth is that you guys kill yourselves eating crap like that Big Mac. You ought to try something green now and then."

"I want something green, I can just look in the back of my fridge," Rod grumbled.

Chapter Fifty-Six

Her cell phone beeped.

"Cindy Phillips, Green Party candidate for U.S. Senate, how can I help you?"

"Cindy, it's Rick."

"Hi, Rick."

"There's some lawyer trying to get a hold of you. Says it's important and it's an estate matter."

"A what?"

"An estate matter."

She was puzzled. There was no one who was going to die and leave her anything.

"He probably has the wrong person."

"He says not. And he's been very persistent. Do you want his number?"

"I guess," Cindy said.

Rick gave her the lawyer's name and read the number to her. It was a 202 area code – Washington, D.C. She knew that from her days at Maryland.

"Thanks, Rick," she said and signed off.

Later that day, she had a chance to call the number.

"Beckham Rogers Crawford and Callan," an efficient female voice said after two rings.

"This is Cindy Phillips," she said. "I am returning a call from a Mr. Pannington."

"Mrs. Phillips, please hold."

There was a click and a brief silence.

"Miss Phillips, thank you for returning my call," said a male voice. "I have some information for you here regarding the estate of James Frederick Steele. You are named as a beneficiary."

"I'm sorry," she said. "You must have the wrong person. I don't know a James Frederick Steele."

"Are you Miss Cynthia Aretha Phillips, candidate for the United States Senate, of 1017 8th Avenue, Altoona, Pennsylvania?"

"Well, yes."

"Then you are the beneficiary named in Mr. Steele's will. He was very specific and very precise. He has left to you a 75-acre property in northwest Maryland, improved with a residential structure and a barn. There is also an amount of money involved."

She was sure that he had the wrong person and told him so.

"No, ma'am, I'm very certain that I have the right person. Mr. Steele was very specific."

A thought occurred to her.

"May I ask who Mr. Steele was and what happened to him?"

"Mr. Steele was a real estate developer in the Washington, D.C., area. He was quite successful and a long-time client of this firm." He paused. "Mr. Steele chose to end his life recently. We are charged with wrapping up his affairs. You are detailed quite specifically in his will as a beneficiary and are specifically named to inherit this property."

"I'm at a loss," Cindy said. "I didn't know this Mr. Steele and I don't know why he would leave me anything."

"Miss Phillips, I don't mean to intrude into your personal life. But I understand that as a child, you were a victim of a rather severe case of child abuse. Am I correct?"

Then it clicked. She pulled to the side of the road and stopped her car.

"He's the one who paid for my medical care, isn't he? And sent me those books."

Pannington was silent for a few seconds, then said, "Yes, ma'am, those were the arrangements that Mr. Steele made through this law firm. In his will, he made it very clear that he wished to provide you with some means to ensure your continued success. Thus the farm and the ... cash asset."

Cindy rested her head against the steering wheel. It was too much to take all at once. Her head was spinning.

"I'm sorry ... I'm sorry. This is just kind of overwhelming," she said.

"I understand. Please take your time," Pannington said.

"I ... I don't know what to say. Do we need to meet? What ... do I have to do anything?"

"Well, there needs to be a formal acceptance of the bequest," Pannington said. "I understand that you are in the midst of a campaign for senator and are on the road quite a bit."

"I'm pretty much constantly on the road at this point," Cindy said. "I haven't been home in weeks."

"We don't wish for the transfer of these assets to be any sort of inconvenience to you," Pannington said. "But we do need some signatures. The farm that you will receive is in northwest Maryland, near Cumberland, not too far south of Pennsylvania. Is it possible that we could arrange to meet there? I will be prepared with all the paperwork and a witness to make everything official. It would require just an hour or so of your time. And of course, you would get to view the property."

"I ... I guess. That sounds reasonable," Cindy said, her head still whirling. "When?"

"I will mail some materials to your office along with some proposed times and dates for a meeting. You can choose the one that meets your schedule best."

Chapter Fifty-Seven

Cindy's cell phone rang. "Cindy Phillips, Green Party candidate for U.S. senator, how may I help you?"

"Cindy, Rick here."

"Hi, Rick. How are things back at the office?"

"Actually, pretty good," he said. "We got a nice donation toward your campaign."

"You're kidding!" Cindy said, her mind running through her last few speeches. Who would have been moved enough to contribute?

"McCain Feingold applies, but the contribution is right at the maximum – two grand," Rick said.

"That's great!" Cindy said. "Who is it from?"

"That's the weird part," he said. "It's listed as being from the estate of a James F. Steele."

Cindy smiled.

"Good old James Steele," she said.

"You know him?" Rick asked.

"Never met him," Cindy said. "But he's been looking out for me for a long time."

"Well, with the other donations that are coming in from the website, I have some very good news for you," Rick said.

"Yes?"

"How would you like some company out there on the road?"

"Rick! You're not telling me that we can afford to send someone out here with me?"

"Not only that, but the exec board is so happy with you that I think they'll actually approve it. We can't pay much, but enough maybe to get someone to travel with you and take care of some of the logistics."

"What kind of money are we talking about here?"

"Well, with the way that the donations are coming in through your blog, it looks like we can cover expenses plus a sal—I mean, reimbursement of about twenty-four thousand."

"Rick! That's more than I'm making!"

"Well, the candidate has to make sacrifices. You want a companion or not?"

"Well, duh!" Cindy said. "Do you really have to ask?"

"All right. Well, you got anyone in mind?"

"Yes, I do, but I doubt that she'll bite."

"Shoot."

Cindy told him about Evelyn.

"Just ask her. Tell her no pressure and we completely understand if she wants to stay where she's at. But I talked with her a few weeks ago and I just feel that she should be given first shot. If she says no, then get back to me. I have a few other ideas."

"You're always full of them," Rick said. "Ideas, that is."

"Thanks for clarifying that, Rick," she said, smiling.

"All right. I'll call this Evelyn and get back to you."

Chapter Fifty-Eight

In Frederick, Maryland, the director of the public library had just returned to her office at the end of the day. She was on the phone trying to figure out a cryptic voice mail message when there was a gentle rap on the doorframe. She looked up. It was her intern with an armful of mail.

"Oh, thank you, Annette. I got distracted today and completely forgot about the mail."

The director hung up and accepted the bundle. Annette didn't turn and leave immediately. She stood awkwardly at the desk.

"Miss Carson, uh, could I talk with you?"

"Why, of course, sweetie," the director said. "Do you want to close the door?"

When Annette hesitated, Mrs. Carson said, "Go ahead and close it." Annette did. She took the seat in front of Carson's desk. She looked nervous.

"Annette. What's the matter?"

"Mrs. Carson ... you know I like working here. And the people are really great. And I'm learning a lot."

"We like you, too, Annette," Carson said carefully, giving Annette her full attention.

"But ... I know this is an unpaid internship ... but my dad got laid off at work and my parents said they can't send me as much money ... and I ... well, I hate to ask this, I really do, but is there any way that ... you could pay me? Even a little bit?"

Carson looked at Annette's flushed face, her body language betraying exquisite discomfort. Well, we don't pick librarians for their bold salesmanship, Carson thought.

"Annette .... I'm sorry," she said. "I would love to pay you. You do the work of two people around here. And you do great work. Wonderful work. But ... oh, Annette, my budget is so tight. I've had to cut back the hours of the regular staff. You know we had to cut our hours earlier this year. I'm working the checkout desk for the first time in six years. And the word from the state is that they're going to cut our appropriation again. I'm already down almost forty percent in our new book purchases. The board is very unhappy."

She paused and looked at Annette. "I would love to pay you, Annette, but I just can't. There is simply no money, and it looks like there's going to be even less next year." She paused and looked at the ceiling. "Maybe ... could you find another internship, one that pays? I hate to lose you, but I'll give you an absolute gold-plated recommendation."

Annette sighed. "It's too late. All the internships are filled. Especially the ones that pay. Well ... I'm sorry I bothered you, Mrs. Carson. I figured that you probably couldn't pay me but ... well, I had to ask ... so I knew." She stood up.

Mrs. Carson stood too. "Annette, I'm so sorry. If there were any way ...."

"I know. Thank you, Mrs. Carson. I understand. I ... I have just a little more at the end of the 600s to tidy up and then I'll go."

"Thank you, Annette," Carson said helplessly.

As Annette left, her shoulders slumped.

Mrs. Carson closed her eyes, then sat down at her desk. It just isn't fair, she thought. Libraries are so important to a community. They literally offer a universe of ideas, entertainment and information. Thousands of years of human wisdom are right here, right in this community, she thought. Why, when times get hard, the community turns to the library. Workers line up to use the library's internet connection and computers. Books on finding jobs and writing resumes fly off the shelves. Reference requests boom as people come in to look up information on companies that they'd like to work for and areas of the country where they might have to move. And what happens when the state budget gets a little tight? Libraries are the first thing to get cut.

Mrs. Carson thought about how hard she had to fight just to get the state to pay for directional signs on nearby roads to help people find their way to the library. She sighed as she remembered the man from the state highway department who finally showed up to put up the three – three! – signs that the state had grudgingly agreed to pay for.

"We like these library signs," the highway man had told her, showing her one of the blue-and-white aluminum rectangles.

Delighted, Mrs. Carson had asked, "And why is that?" He, too, must admire their simplicity and handsome use of color, she thought.

"Cause when the Saturday night drunks drive around shooting at signs, they usually hit these first. Saves us having to replace the important ones," he said, chuckling.

"Oh," Mrs. Carson had said, her enthusiasm gone. "Wonderful."

Back to reality. She turned her attention to the mail. As she automatically opened envelopes – something that a long-gone secretary used to do for her – Mrs. Carson thought hard for a way to pay Annette. She knew every crevice of the budget and she could think of no line item that wasn't already set at an absolute minimum.

She opened an envelope with a bill inside. "PENDING RATE INCREASE" was stamped across the top in red ink. She scanned it. The city was raising water and sewer rates by 6 percent. Great, she thought. There's no money for this unexpected increase. Maybe we could shut off the hot water taps in the bathrooms, she thought. Maybe we should just shut down the bathrooms entirely and send people to the convenience store across the street. This is insane.

She sighed as she picked up another envelope. Its stiffness and texture caused her thoughts to break. She looked at the envelope. Expensive paper. Return receipt. The return address was a law firm in Washington, D.C. Oh great, she thought. Now we're being sued.

She slit the envelope and pulled out a stiff piece of paper. As she unfolded it, a blue rectangle of paper fell out. She read the letter:

Dear Director Carson,

My name is Peter Pannington and I am a partner in the law firm of Beckham Rogers Crawford and Callan, Washington, D.C. This firm represents the estate of Mr. James F. Steele, recently deceased. Mr. Steele was a longtime member of your library. In accordance with the execution of his last will and testament, Mr. Steele asked that I complete the following:

Ensure your receipt of the enclosed check. The funds provided by this check are completely unrestricted. Mr. Steele's specific request was that you "use these funds as you see fit to improve the library."

Convey to you the following statement from Mr. Steele: "I got my start in commercial real estate by reading and doing research in your library. It provided a wonderful refuge when I needed to think and work. I also enjoyed the wide range of fiction available as I know that life is not all about work. You and your staff were always pleasant and helpful. I know that you are facing some funding challenges and I hope this helps."

Mrs. Carson, it might help for you to know that Mr. Steele owned a farm outside Cumberland, which he very much enjoyed visiting. If you have any questions, please do not hesitate to contact me.

The letter was signed by Pannington in neat blue cursive letters.

Mrs. Carson picked up the blue rectangle of paper and gasped. It was a check. She closed her eyes a moment, then opened them again. Very deliberately, she focused on the box holding the amount of the check. Yes, she confirmed, there were five zeros after the initial 5. She counted them just to be absolutely sure.

"Oh my," she said aloud.

Then she jumped to her feet and opened her door. Annette emerged from the nonfiction stacks at the same moment, her coat and backpack on.

"Goodnight, Mrs. Carson," Annette called cheerfully. "I finished the 600s. See you Wednesday."

"Annette?" Mrs. Carson said, her voice cracking.

Annette stopped. Something in Mrs. Carson's voice worried her.

"Mrs. Carson? Are you OK?" Annette took a tentative step toward the director, thinking that maybe she was ill.

Mrs. Carson's hand fluttered to her chest. She blinked and swallowed. "No, no, Annette, I'm fine. I ... well, I just think that maybe we will be able to pay you a little something after all. I just received ... some good news about our budget."

Annette broke into a wide smile. "Oh, that is so great, Mrs. Carson. You don't know ... I mean, that will really, really help."

"Go on home," Mrs. Carson said. "As usual, you've done more than your share today. We can talk a little more on Wednesday. But I think we'll be able to work something out."

Annette left with a big smile and a little wave. After Mrs. Carson locked the door behind the departing intern, she slumped against the doorframe.

I'm sorry I don't remember you, Mr. Steele, but God bless you, she thought. Then she hurried back to her office to make sure that the check was still there.

It was.

Chapter Fifty-Nine

Her cell phone rang. "Cindy Phillips, Green Party candidate for U.S. senator, how may I help you?"

"Rick here. Cindy, how would you like a lawyer? Legal counsel?"

"Hi, Rick. Doesn't the party have someone on retainer?"

"No, I mean someone committed to your campaign. I don't think he can travel with you, but he can meet you at some events and can be on call if you need him for something specific."

"Well, can we afford it?"

"Pro bono," Rick said.

"Who is it?"

"A Harold Kaufmann, esquire. Heard you talk in Pittsburgh a few weeks ago. He said he came up to you afterwards."

She remembered a small but broad, balding, disheveled man with intense eyes. He had come out of the crowd when she had finished a lunch-hour speech at Point Park in Pittsburgh. She remembered a nice suit worn at the creases and a floppy leather briefcase. He had gripped her hand

and said, "You make more sense than any political candidate I've ever listened to. And I completely agree with you about child abuse. When are the feds going to get off their asses and realize that it's the future of this country that we're talking about?"

They held a brief conversation, she remembered, and he asked for her card. She gave it to him. He looked at it, then handed it back to her.

"Got it," he said.

"Don't you want to keep it?" she asked, confused.

He tapped his head. "All stored up here," he said. "I'd just lose the card."

She thanked him and then it was time to turn her attention to another person. "Thank you for coming," she said, stepping forward with a smile and her hand extended. Out of the corner of her eye, she saw the rumpled man bark at a cab, which immediately pulled to the curb. He got in and the cab drove off. She had forgotten about him after that.

"What's he want?" she asked Rick.

"He said you're on the right track and he wants to be a part of it. He said he'll hook up with you when you're in the western part of the state. Otherwise, he'll be on call twenty-four-seven. And all services are completely pro bono."

"Don't we have to count the value of his services as donations?" she asked.

"You let me worry about that stuff," Rick said. "You just keep doing what you're doing. I can tell you that the exec board is thrilled. You're generating phone calls and internet donations like we've never seen. You're striking a nerve out there."

SENATE RACE TIGHTENS
AS PACIFICO GAINS ON WALKER

HARRISBURG (AP) – Democratic Philadelphia Mayor Donato Pacifico is gaining on incumbent U.S. Senator Robert Walker, R-PA, in the race for a U.S. Senate seat, according to the latest Associated Press poll.

The latest AP poll, conducted by DecisionFinders Inc. of Alexandria, Va., shows Pacifico at 42 percent to Walker's 47 percent in a poll of likely voters. The poll, conducted last week, has an error margin of plus or minus three percentage points.

"Pacifico is within striking distance," said Dr. Roger Stephens, a political science professor at Penn State University. "More importantly, he [Pacifico] is gaining."

The previous AP poll, conducted three weeks ago, showed Walker at 48 percent and Pacifico at 39 percent.

Stephens credited Pacifico's gains to increasing voter interest in the race as election day nears and allegations that Walker has fallen out of touch with Pennsylvania.

"The Democrats have been hammering on Walker about not being back to the state in nearly three years," Stephens said. "Pennsylvanians are beginning to take a second look at Walker and apparently not liking what they see."

Walker's campaign manager George Simon dismissed the poll results as "meaningless."

"Sen. Walker is the best man to represent Pennsylvania and the voters of the state know that," Simon said. "Over his three terms in the senate,

Sen. Walker has brought jobs and business to the state of Pennsylvania. People know that and respect it and they will choose Sen. Walker to represent them again on election day."

Pacifico campaign spokesman Alphonse DiMalzoni said that the poll results show that "Pennsylvanians are choosing an active, engaged leader over a wealthy, out-of-touch lifelong politician."

Democrats have leveled charges that Walker is too involved in the politics of Washington, D.C. and not concerned enough about the residents of Pennsylvania. Walker is chairman of the powerful Appropriations Committee and active in national GOP politics.

Walker's campaign has fired back that under Pacifico, the city of Philadelphia has suffered a net loss of jobs and that Pacifico lacks the experience to be a U.S. senator.

"My guess is that this one will come down to the wire," Stephens said. "There are two strong candidates who have raised tens of millions of dollars and who are willing to spend every dime to get elected."

Stephens noted that there is a third candidate for office, Cynthia Phillips of Altoona, who is running on the Green Party ticket. Stephens said that although the Green Party has "no chance" of winning the election, it can play a role in the outcome.

"Democrats and the Green Party have some cross-pollination," he said. "The Green Party will likely pull votes from Pacifico. Like Nader in the Bush vs. Gore presidential race, the Green Party could pull just enough votes from the Democrats to allow Walker to win."

In the AP poll, Phillips showed at less than one percent.

Chapter Sixty

Her cell phone rang. "Cindy Phillips, Green Party candidate for U.S. senate, how may I help you?"

"Heard you need a manager," Evelyn said.

"Evelyn! Hi!" Cindy said.

"Count me in," Evelyn said. "I'm cleaning out my desk as we speak."

Cindy was stunned into silence.

"Girl, you still there?"

"Ev ... I ... I can't ... I ..."

"You can't what?"

"I can't believe that you're coming on board. I thought that – "

"All you need to think about is that I'm not going to miss an opportunity like this," Evelyn said. "This is once-in-a-lifetime stuff."

"But your job with Rutherford ... "

"It's a job. I can get another one. I have lots of D.C. contacts. Besides, girl, you're going need a chief of staff when you're senator, right?"

"Ev, I don't ... I just ..."

"All you need to do right now is tell me where you want to meet," Evelyn said. "I gave them two weeks. So where are you going to be two weeks from today? We need to hook up. And don't even tell me that you'd think of hiring someone else to be your chief of staff."

Chapter Sixty-One

Following the directions that the lawyer had given her, Cindy turned her Honda off the highway and onto the winding two-lane road. Still following directions, she drove through countryside with pleasant rolling hills. After eighteen miles, she saw the large barn and a row of pine trees on her right. She turned there, as directed. The road that she turned onto was compressed dirt. The Honda bucked over the potholes and Cindy slowed down, worried about her tires. She saw a billow of brown dust swirl behind the car. The road bent gently to the right, weathered wooden fences and farmland on either side of her.

As she rounded the bend, she saw the house. It was a stately, well-kept wood-frame farmhouse with a huge porch wrapping around it. A gigantic oak tree dominated the front yard. Behind the house was a barn, several small outbuildings, more trees. Even further behind were rolling hills dotted with clumps of trees.

As she approached, she noticed that a small white fence separated the yard from the lane. A blue sedan and an old red pickup truck were nosed up to the fence. She parked beside the blue car and got out. Her poor Honda was coated with dust; but then, so was the blue car. A Volvo, she noticed. Expensive looking.

The Honda's engine ticked as it cooled. The small sound seemed very loud in the country quiet.

There was a charming little gate in the white fence. She swung it open. An ancient sidewalk led to the house's porch. Grass growing over the walk's slabs had turned them into a series of ovals and rounded squares. As she stepped on them, she thought of crossing a stream by stepping on rocks.

She looked up and noticed a man sitting on the porch. He had removed his jacket. His crisp white dress shirt, tie and dark pants seemed out of place on the house's porch. He should be wearing overalls, she thought. He was gazing off to the side, out over the fields. As she watched, an older man in overalls and a baseball cap pushed open the screen door, two glasses in his hands. He offered one to the man in the suit; thanks were exchanged.

The older man raised his glass in Cindy's direction.

"Gonna need a third," he said.

The suited man said, "What?" then turned and noticed Cindy. He stood immediately, came down the porch steps and offered his hand. The rest of him was as neat and crisp as his suit, Cindy noticed. Glasses with very small lenses covered dark, intense eyes. He had a neatly trimmed goatee.

"Miss Phillips," he said as they shook. His hand was smooth and dry. He didn't try to crush her hand as many men did.

"Call me Cindy, please," she said. "You must be Mr. Pannington."

He smiled.

"Call me Peter, please. This is Charlie," he said, indicating the man on the porch. Charlie stood, raised his glass to her again and said, "Miss Cindy."

"Charlie is the caretaker," Pannington said. "He's been taking care of this place for ... what?" Pannington turned to Charlie. "How many years?"

"Good two dozen," Charlie said.

Cindy followed Pannington onto the porch. It was a relief to step into the shade of the porch, leaving the pounding sun. Charlie disappeared inside the house. As the screen door slammed, Cindy felt a cool draft from inside the home.

"Please," Pannington said, "sit down."

She selected an Adirondack chair and lowered herself into it. She noticed that Peter waited to sit until she did.

Charlie emerged with a tall glass of lemonade. Ice clinked as he offered it to her.

"Ma'am," he said. She saw that his fingers were wrinkled but thick and powerful. His nails were broken but clean. She took the glass.

"Thank you."

"Not at all, ma'am," Charlie said. He selected a rocking chair, sat down with a "whuff," placed his drink on a small table, took off his hat and fanned himself with it. Under the hat, his hair was white and sparse.

"Well," Pannington said. "I'm delighted to finally meet you. I wish it were under other circumstances, but ...."

"Isn't funny how a ... passing sometimes brings people together," Cindy said.

Pannington nodded.

They exchanged pleasantries about the weather and the beauty of the drive to the farm for a few minutes, then Pannington drew a leather briefcase onto his lap.

"We can take care of all this in just a few minutes," he said, one hand resting on the briefcase. "I think it's perhaps more important that you get to see the property. Is it OK with you if we do the paperwork first and get it out of the way?"

"Sure," Cindy said. "You're the expert."

Pannington smiled as he began pulling papers out of the briefcase. He placed them neatly on a clipboard, each marked with a red arrow showing her where to sign. Pannington pulled a fat green pen from his pocket, uncapped it and handed it to her.

When she took it, it was heavy.

"Nice pen," she said.

Pannington closed his eyes and for a second Cindy thought that she had somehow offended him.

"I'm sorry," he said opening his eyes. Cindy was startled to see pain in them. "When Jim ... Mr. Steele ... was wrapping up his affairs, he used that pen. I ... it was a silly, sentimental thought ... I just ... I'm sorry. Please continue." He offered a brave smile.

"Would you rather that I didn't use this pen?" Cindy asked.

"No, no, absolutely not," Pannington said. "It's actually very appropriate. I was simply caught off guard by the realization – you know how those little reminders come back at you when you've lost someone."

To cover the awkwardness, Cindy said, "Can you tell me more about James Steele? He's been so nice to me and I never even met him."

"I was honored to call Jim Steele a friend since the sixth grade," Pannington said. "Our lives were quite different, but we found common ground."

Cindy nodded. "I understand. Thank you for letting me use this pen. It is appropriate. And it's not silly at all. I'm glad to know that you and Mr. Steele were friends." She began signing.

"In grade school," Pannington began as Cindy started working her way through the stack, "I was ... not a physical child. I was the kid with the glasses and the pale skin. I can't tell you how many times my books were pushed out of my arms, my papers scattered."

Cindy stopped signing and looked up. "Why are children that age so cruel?" she asked, remembering.

"I don't know," Pannington said. "I wish I did."

"My theory is that it's parents, at least partially," Cindy said. "I don't think enough parents impress upon their children how wrong it is to be cruel to those who are ... powerless. Childhood and adolescence are difficult enough without getting grief from other kids."

Pannington nodded.

"Schools are getting a lot tougher on bullies," Cindy said. "But when I went to school, it was just considered to be part of growing up. If you were the victim, and you complained, you were likely told, 'oh, just deal with it.'"

"It was the rare parent who admitted that his son or daughter was a bully and acted to prevent it," Pannington said. "But bullying was actually how I met Jim."

"What happened?" Cindy asked. "I hope that Jim wasn't the bully."

"To be honest, Jim was known in school for being tough and ready for a fight. But even then he had a personal code of honor. To my knowledge, he never bullied, although he did fight," Pannington said.

"So what brought you two into each others' circles?" Cindy asked.

"It wasn't under the most auspicious of circumstances," Pannington said. "There was some violence involved, I'm afraid."

"Oh, my," Cindy said. "Would you mind telling me about it?"

"Well," Pannington said, "At the risk of boring you ...."

"No, please tell me," Cindy said. "Really. Truly. I'm very interested. I'd like to know a lot more about Jim Steele."

Pannington gazed at Cindy a moment, holding her eyes. He placed the briefcase on the floor beside his chair. He picked up his lemonade and looked past Cindy, into the fields.

"It was actually one very pleasant spring day," he began. "It was near the end of the school year – this would be near the end of fifth grade. On that day, I intentionally missed the bus, something that I would never do. I was always a rule follower, not a rule breaker. I knew that my mother would be upset if she found out, but I had a plan. All throughout the previous week, I had been working on a special gift for her. In art class, we had been working on creating these very ornate eggs, laying down layers and layers of colors. I'm not sure of the genesis of the project, and looking back, it seems a bit of an odd one for me to have devoted so much time to. I excelled in English and science, but my artistic efforts were always a bit ... pedestrian. And I knew it. So when my art teacher remarked how beautiful my egg was becoming, I responded. She even held it up to the class as an example. I remember looking at it with new eyes after she had praised it. I began to take even greater care as I put down layer after layer of color.

"When it was done, it looked – to me – nearly magical. It was just an egg, but I had transformed it into a crimson, gold and purple beauty. My art teacher compared it to a Faberge egg."

Pannington chuckled. Cindy smiled.

"Anyway, I was quite proud of my effort. And I couldn't wait to show it to my mother. And to present it to her. So on the day that my egg was complete, I intentionally missed the bus, knowing that the roughhousing that went on would have crushed my egg. It was quite colorful, but it was an egg just the same."

Cindy had stopped signing and was giving her whole attention to Pannington. Behind him, Charlie fanned himself slowly and listened.

"I could hardly wait to show it to my mother. So I hatched a plan."

Cindy smiled.

"Not only would I miss the bus to avoid the egg's destruction, but I would also spare my mother the difficulty of picking me up from school. I would walk from the school to her workplace. My school was on the outskirts of our small town and my mother worked at a downtown law firm. So I figured that I would doubly delight her: I would show up unexpectedly at her workplace and I would present her with my beautiful egg.

"My art teacher helped me pack the egg carefully in small box, then into a paper bag. I cradled it as if it were a precious thing."

"It was," Cindy said.

"Yes, I guess it was," Pannington said. "Well, I set off from the school. All the other students had departed, the buses were gone, and most of the teachers were gone. I began my journey in the springtime sun, imagining the look of joy and wonder that would cross my mother's face when I unveiled the egg. I walked in a sort of automatic pilot, lost in my daydreams. I knew the town well. There was no chance of getting lost. But I had forgotten that the most direct route from the school to downtown involved a trip through a few blocks where there lived boys that I usually avoided. Unfortunately, my automatic pilot sent me on that most direct route.

"I 'came to,' you might say, about in the middle of this section of town. It wasn't a slum by any means – there was no such thing in that town – but it was a section of town where the sidewalks were broken, lawns were unkempt and most of the beautiful brick homes had been cut up into apartments. It was a part of town where windows were more likely to be open than to be filled with an air conditioner. Cars likely lacked hubcaps and chained dogs barked from many yards.

"I decided that my best bet was to keep walking. I had yet only one hill to climb, then to descend the other side, and I would be at the center of downtown. Mother's law office was only a block from the center of downtown. It would have made no sense, I calculated, to attempt to detour out of the bad neighborhood at this point. I would have to walk just as far to get out of the neighborhood as I would to arrive at downtown. So, with my daydreams banished and my senses sharpened, I walked onward.

"Just as I had dared to think that I was safe, I heard loud voices and laughter. From ahead, emanating from one of the porches of the houses that had been built for one family, but which now housed three. The voices were rough and so was the language. As the rabbit knows the hound, I knew that these were my tormentors. I froze. I knew that I could not walk past the porch unnoticed. And there could be only one outcome from being spotted.

"I'm afraid that I have never been a man of action. As I stood, desperately seeking an escape route, a head popped up above the porch banister.

The head bore a backwards baseball cap and as soon as I saw it, dread gripped me. There was a delighted shout, an arm pointed, a name was shouted. Then came the sound of what sounded like hundreds of boys scrambling to their feet, and suddenly they were pounding down the walk toward me. I knew that I was on their turf. I knew that there were no teachers to save me. Analytical as I was, I was no fool. I turned and ran.

"There were whoops behind me. I risked a glance backwards and was terrified to see that like a wolf pack, they were spreading out, aiming to box me in.

"As I said, I was not a physical specimen by any means. There was no doubt of the outcome. I had run only because it was a better choice than standing and waiting. In a very short time, I found myself panting, sweating and surrounded. Still clutching my bagged egg, I decided that my demise would be like that of Nathan Hale. I would go to the noose, but my head would be held high. I would retain my dignity to the end.

"And then it began. One boy would dart in and I would be clouted or kicked. My glasses spun off my face. A fat boy picked them up in his no doubt greasy hands and put them on his face, intentionally placing them crookedly. 'Look at me,' he said, walking with little sissy steps, 'I'm Peter Faggot Pannington.' I was enraged but I was also mortified. I wondered if that was truly the appearance that I presented to the world: crooked glasses, a mincing walk, slumped shoulders, darting eyes."

Cindy's face showed pain. The pen was still in her hand, but the documents were forgotten. Pannington continued.

"I tried as best I could to protect the egg, but of course, by protecting it, I drew attention to it. I was shoved and the bag was snatched from my hands. My Nathan Hale emulation collapsed and I begged, 'Please. Please. That's for my mother.'

"That, of course, was exactly the wrong thing to say. The leader, a redheaded boy built like a tank – broad and muscular – pulled the box from the bag and grinned at me as he held it up. 'Well, what do you think fag boy has in here for his mommy?' he asked.

"There was another shove, then another, and I fell. Someone sat on me. I was unable to move; I could barely breathe. 'Hey,' the redhead said to the fat boy. 'Give fag boy back his glasses so he can watch this.'

"I have never felt such an absolute despair as that moment. Not only was my week of painstaking, delicate work about to be destroyed, but I would never get to present it to my mother. I would never see her face light up with radiant joy. I would never hear her delighted praise that I had achieved something of artistic value. I was absolutely, completely powerless.

"My glasses, smeared and bent, were shoved back on my face. I'm afraid then that I began to cry. The redhead removed the egg from the box and raised it high for the others to see.

"'What the fuck is this?' he asked."

Pannington paused. "Please excuse my vulgarity."

"No, no, you're describing what happened," Cindy said. Charlie snorted.

"'It's a decorated egg,' I said, I'm afraid a little plaintively. The redhead looked at me and I have never seen such contempt. 'I know that, asshole,' he said. 'What, now you're going to get smart?' He approached me holding the egg. I can still remember his red high-top basketball sneakers approaching me through the dust. Red Converse Chuck Taylors. The laces were filthy, black and knotted, giving the shoes a lumpy and evil appearance. The sneakers stopped a few inches from my face. I struggled, but the boy sitting on me probably had twice my weight. The redhead bent down.

"'You're just a little twit,' he said, and smashed the egg on my forehead. It was hardboiled, so most of it then fell before my eyes into the dust. Its beauty was gone; fractured like that, it was just a lump of white and yellow gunk with some dark flecks in it."

Cindy closed her eyes.

"The redhead grabbed me by the hair and lifted my head. He made some comment about my tears and ripped my glasses off my face. I knew then that as bad as the egg smashing was, things were about to get worse. I was about to get hurt. Perhaps badly. I imagined broken teeth, a punctured eye. I was absolutely terrified. Broken limbs were not out of the question. My shining triumph of a day had turned into a nightmare.

"And then there was a yell. The redhead's head snapped up and for just an instant, I had hope that it was his parents – or someone's parents. I twisted my head to see, but even without my glasses I could see that it was not a parent who had entered my circle of torment. It was another boy, and a large, husky one. My hope shattered like my egg. One more abuser had arrived.

"But then I noticed a strange thing. The other boys were backing away, looking down. The redhead had taken on a pouty look as if he had been denied a toy. I heard magic words: 'Get off him.' The mountainous weight that had been crushing me lifted. I rose to my knees, gasping a bit. When I had my breath back, I noticed that the new boy, the large stranger, was standing alone in the midst of the ring of outlaws. But his attitude was that of Clint Eastwood – surrounded he was, but the advantage was still his. He bent and picked up my glasses. To my astonishment, he wiped them off on his shirt and handed them to me.

"I put them on, blinking. 'You OK?' he asked me. I'm afraid that I nodded, although I was far from OK. As I now had my vision back, I couldn't help but glance down at my egg. Not much was left of it. The stranger's eyes followed mine down, then went up to the redhead's. I had no doubt that in an instant the stranger had divined the entire series of events, from my walking through the neighborhood with a treasured art project to the dusty humiliation that had just ended.

"The stranger looked at the redhead, with an Eastwood squint, I'd like to think. And he said,

'You're such an asshole, Eric.' As if that were some kind of signal, the rest of the boys all backed up a few steps. Eric, still looking sulky, said, 'I don't want to fight you.'

"The stranger smiled, an even, sunny smile. 'Damn right you don't,' he said. 'But you're gonna.' Then, acting on some signal invisible to me, the two boys locked into a wrestling hold and the other boys were cheering and shouting. I backed out of the field of battle and knew that I should just run. But I stayed. Along with the desire to see the red-head beaten was the feeling that the stranger had cast some kind of shield over me. As long as he was near, none of the other boys would dare touch me. So, whether it was vindictive or not, I stayed."

Pannington paused.

"And?" Cindy said, smiling. "The stranger was Jim."

Pannington smiled back. "Yes. My paladin was young James Steele, who because of his own experiences, hated to see the weak and defenseless picked on. I had never said so much as a word to him as we passed in the school hallways. In fact, at that point, I didn't even know his name. But I stood and watched that fight with a relish for violence that I didn't know I had.

"Jim, who was used to pretty heavy punishment at home, was simply relentless. It's quite possible that the redhead was stronger, but Jim was more determined. After a few minutes of scuffling, Jim had Eric down. Jim placed his knees on either side of Eric's chest, pinning his arms. Jim balled up what seemed to be a huge bloody fist and cracked it across Eric's jaw. The redhead's head snapped to one side and I saw blood splatter into the dust. 'That's for picking on the kid,' Jim said. Another blow snapped Eric's head the other way. There was more blood. 'That's for busting his egg,' Jim said. And then he grabbed Eric's hair, lifted, and completely without mercy slammed his head back on the ground. 'And that's just for being a general asshole,' he said.

"Then he stood. Eric lay still, coughing and oozing blood. I remember being completely amazed at Jim's composure. He had just been in a fight that would have exhausted me both physically and emotionally. I would have been barely able to stand. But he seemed only mildly winded, as if he had sprinted up a flight of stairs. He brushed his hands off, dusted off his jeans, and turned his gaze one by one on the ring of boys. None would meet his eye. They backed up, heads down, and began to drift away.

"I wish I could say that I thanked him, or that he touched a cowboy hat and rode off into the sunset. But what really happened was that he walked back to wherever it was that he had been coming from and I walked on to downtown, trying to compose a cover story for my unkempt appearance and broken glasses that would not upset my mother."

"My," Cindy said.

Pannington blinked, then flushed. "I'm sorry," he said. "That was ... a bit of a personal digression. I didn't mean to–"

Cindy put out a hand and touched Pannington's knee.

"No, no, it's OK. It's a wonderful story. I really know Jim Steele a lot better now," she said. "I'm glad you told it."

Charlie grunted and stood up.

"Great story," he said. "Anyone else want more lemonade?"

Both Pannington and Cindy nodded. Charlie took their glasses and went inside.

"I ... sometimes have that effect on people," Cindy said. "They just seem comfortable talking to me."

"I didn't intend to go off like that," Pannington said. "But I know something of your history, and ... that pen. It just got to me, like Jim was here or about to pull up in his Porsche."

"So how did you and Jim become friends?" Cindy asked.

"Well, my personal code of honor dictated that I thank him. As school was winding down, I had only a few days. So I found out where his locker was, straightened my backbone and approached him. 'I'd like to thank you,' I said to him, I'm sure rather stiffly. He was shoving books into his locker. He glanced at me without recognition. 'No problem,' he said. 'That wasn't a fair fight that you were in.' I didn't know what else to say, so I started to turn away, feeling that I had accomplished my goal, although in a rather minimal fashion. Jim said, 'Hey.' I turned back. 'You any good at English?' he asked. I'm sure there was a brief pause while my brain scrambled to make the connection between being in a fight and English class. 'I got my final paper due next week and it's just not coming out right,' Jim said and I realized that he was asking for my help. I was thrilled to offer payment to him. 'I'm not bad,' I said, knowing that I was going to get an A+ in the course. 'Well, if you could help me, that would be great,' Jim said. I agreed and we planned to meet at the library that weekend. And ... well, that was the start of it.

"That year and into high school, I helped him with English composition. He was a terrible speller – always was – as some people just are. I think it might be genetic. But he learned how to narrow a topic down, conduct research and write a coherent, organized essay. It came easily to me, just like dominating a ring of tough boys came naturally to him. I'm sure we made an odd pair – I was thin and small and bookish; he was husky and outgoing."

"That's a wonderful story," Cindy said. "And so you were friends for the rest ... the rest of his life?"

"Yes," Pannington said. "We drifted in and out of touch, of course, but when we both ended up in Washington, D.C., we would get together monthly for drinks and dinner."

"And you're his lawyer," Cindy said.

"Actually, my specialty is corporate law. Monstrously boring, but it pays well," Pannington said with a smile. "Jim's interest was commercial real estate, which is of course an element of corporate law. So I was able to handle his transactions and give him advice."

Pannington looked up at the ceiling of the porch. "Although I must say that Mr. James Steele led me into some interesting areas of commercial real estate law. He was ... adventurous by nature and some of his deals were ... well, I remember on several occasions telling him that I would have a hard time justifying to a judge the path that we had taken."

"My guess is that he didn't mind," Cindy said.

"No, he didn't. In fact, he seemed to relish those. He would always tell me that if it came down to a courtroom, I should tell the judge that I made him do it. My complaints that my actions would not be acceptable under the bar's code of ethics under any circumstances went unheeded. He would just smile and tell me that I spent too much time in the office surrounded by books. 'There's a way you get things done on paper and there's the way things get done in the real world,' he would say."

Cindy shook her head. "I wish I could have met him."

"Jim Steele was a good guy," Charlie said, startling Cindy. "He was one-of-a-kind."

"Well, why don't you finish signing those and we'll take a little tour?" Pannington said.

Cindy resumed signing. Some of the pages required a witness. In those cases, Pannington asked politely and Charlie took the pen in his thick fingers and signed his name.

At Charlie's first signature, Cindy was seized by an unreasonable fear that he would mark a big X, but he signed his name in a neat, precise cursive that was almost feminine.

"You have very nice handwriting," she said.

Charlie grunted. "Back when I went to school, they taught penmanship," he said. "You learned to write nice or you got your knuckles cracked."

Cindy laughed. "That's another thing that has changed in schools," she said. "I'm not even sure if they teach cursive any more."

"Damn shame if they don't," Charlie said.

After a few minutes and some guidance from Pannington, all the signatures were complete. Pannington took the clipboard of paper from Cindy and placed it in his briefcase. Cindy extended the pen to Pannington. He pulled the cap from his shirt pocket, then hesitated.

"Would you like to keep it?" he asked her.

"That's very kind of you. But I think it means a lot more to you than to me," Cindy said. She looked around the porch. "Besides, I get a house. You get a pen. Doesn't seem fair."

Pannington laughed.

"Yes, you're quite right. Thank you." He took the pen, capped it and placed it inside his brief-case. He stood.

"Well. Shall we stroll?" He offered his elbow. Cindy placed her arm through his. As they left the porch, the sun struck them and Cindy wished that she had a broad white sun hat.

As they walked across the grounds, Charlie trailed behind, plucking at plants, poking at bushes, shaking his head and peering at sections of grass that appeared quite ordinary to Cindy. He occasionally took off his hat and rubbed his head.

"You are now the owner of this structure, the outbuildings and seventy-four acres of land," Pannington said. "There is a trust fund set up at a bank in Cumberland. Even in poor economic conditions, it should generate enough interest to pay

the taxes with some left over for maintenance."
He glanced back at Charlie, who was standing with
one hand at the small of his back, peering at one
of the outbuildings. "Charlie's salary is covered,
along with a medical plan and a retirement plan.
There will be money for supplies, tools, materials, all that the property needs to be kept in fine
shape."

"My," Cindy said, becoming overwhelmed at
the gift she had been given. The grounds were not
landscaped in the professional sense, but everything was neat and trimmed. Bright flowers lined
the front and sides of the house. At the corner of
a small wooden shed, a rabbit munched grass, eyeing them warily. She was pleased to see that it did
not dart as they walked past it.

"The taxes are paid automatically by the trust,"
Pannington said. "Weekly, an amount of money is
transferred to an account that Charlie has access
to. He uses that to purchase tools and materials.
Should there be a large capital expense required,
Charlie is to contact you. The trust will release
any reasonable amount that you request. Say, for
example, that the house needs a roof. The trust
will release sufficient funds. Charlie usually does
the job himself, or, if it is beyond his abilities, he
contacts a contractor whom he trusts.

"Monthly, he is issued a paycheck and an amount
is placed into his retirement fund. If there are ever
any concerns about money relating to the upkeep
of the property or Charlie, please contact me,"
Pannington said. "Jim left a reserve account with my
firm that is to be used for unforeseen events. I have

been given authority over that account and I will gladly use it to maintain this property."

Cindy stopped walking and Pannington stopped with her. He pulled out a bright white handkerchief and dabbed at his neck and brow. She was pleased when he pulled out a second and offered it to her.

"Peter, just how much money did Jim Steele have?"

"By the standards of today's Bill Gates and other mega-billionaires, Jim's fortune was quite modest," Pannington said. "But Jim accumulated substantial assets and lived relatively simply. He did spend money on a residence – a condominium – and on a car. He spent money on this property because it was a refuge for him. And he liked to eat at fine restaurants. But he was single. He never married, never had children. He had no one to spend money on but himself, and his income far outstripped his expenses."

Pannington turned to Cindy.

"This was a man who might work for two years without a single dime coming in. But then he would close a real estate deal that would bring him two or three million dollars after expenses. That was far more than he needed to live. He also, under my guidance, invested wisely. His revenues in excess of expenditures were not only substantial, but his money began to compound."

"I'm an idiot about money, Peter," she said. "So just tell me. How much money did Jim have when he died?"

"When we deducted outstanding expenses, Jim was worth about 19 million when he died,"

Pannington said. "Not a huge fortune, but more than enough for one man. And more than enough to do the things that he wanted to do."

"I know that he gave money to my campaign, but that was apparently chickenfeed," Cindy said. "He set up the trust for this farm. What else did he do with it?"

Pannington sighed, took Cindy's arm and they resumed strolling.

"He tried to pay back everyone and everything that had ever helped him," Pannington said. "He left money to libraries, to shelters for abused women and children, to various foundations that work on behalf of children – mostly abused children. He left money to certain individuals who had befriended him. A certain bar owner in Washington was quite startled to receive a check."

"A bar owner?"

"Jim was eclectic in his choice of friends. He had few of them, but they covered the economic and social spectrum. He had a favorite bar, one that he considered a refuge. He apparently was very good friends with the owner. He left the man a considerable sum, no strings attached."

"Wow," Cindy said. "This feels kind of dreamlike. Like I'm going to wake up and find that I'm back where I started, with just my old Honda and a few bucks in the bank."

"Cindy, in addition to this property, there is a cash amount associated with Jim's bequest to you. It won't make you wealthy, but it will make it easier for you to run for senator full-time. I understand that you resigned from your job to campaign full time."

"Yes, but I'm OK. Really. The Green Party is covering my expenses and paying me a stipend," she said. "It's enough, really."

"Well, then you should be even more OK," Pannington said with a chuckle. "In addition to this property, Jim left you a hundred thousand dollars."

"I ... I don't know what to say," Cindy said. She watched as a small flock of birds launched themselves from the big oak in the front yard and swooped in perfect unison over the hills beyond the house. She wondered where they were going.

"Jim felt very strongly that you should be compensated for the terrible start you got in life," Pannington said. "He believed that victims of child abuse are penalized from the start of their lives – due to the lingering effects of the abuse – and often are unable to catch up to the rest of the world, so to speak. He thought that money was a poor substitute for a good family life, but that it was better than nothing. He might have even have used those exact words."

"I have to ask ... why me? Why not one of the thousands of other victims of child abuse?"

"Well," Pannington said, "Jim read of your ... terrible incident of abuse in the newspaper. His heart went out to you. He felt quite strongly that since he had the assets, he should do something to try to put your life right."

"And so he paid for my medical treatment."

"Exactly. He placed Dr. Jacobi in the position of directing your treatment. I met with Dr. Jacobi and arranged that any medical treatment that he considered necessary for your full recovery should be undertaken at any cost. Jim knew that he had the resources to make that happen ... and that your care would have been substantially degraded if you were left to rely on the charity of the United States medical system."

Cindy felt tears well up. "He didn't even know me."

"No, he did not. But Jim was never one to restrain his generosity when he felt so moved. That was what motivated him to pay for your medical treatment. And then when he found out that you were running for senator and talking about child abuse, he wanted to ensure that you would be able to run a good campaign. He was restricted by campaign finance law from giving you large sums, but he felt that his donation to your campaign, this property and the cash sum should be enough to cushion you ... should you be unsuccessful."

Cindy smiled. "He knew that I don't have the slightest chance of winning," she said.

"Yes, Jim followed politics. He was a realist; he knew that some real estate deals could be made or broken by the support of politicians. So he followed politics and he made strategic donations to various power brokers. He knew how the system works. So, yes, he knew that the odds are against your success. And he wanted to be sure that – since you gave up everything to run – that you would have somewhere to go when the campaign was over."

"I ... I really wish that I had met him," Cindy said. "I know I keep saying that."

"I will miss him every day of my life," Pannington said. He was silent a moment, then said, "So. Shall we view the interior?"

Cindy nodded, afraid to trust her voice, and they turned back toward the welcoming farmhouse.

Chapter Sixty-Two

Walker, his tie loosened, suit jacket off, leaned back in his leather chair and glared at the gray-suited man in front of him.

"I want to know what the fuck is happening out there and I want to know now," he said. "I want to know why the voters are picking some goddamned dago over me. I want to know why the fuck he isn't sinking in the polls like a rock. And I want to know what we have to do to turn it around."

The young man in the expensive suit and the very white shirt did not fear Walker.

"You're nose-diving because no one has seen you inside the state's borders in three years. People forget what you look like. So they're buying into the idea that you're out of touch. If you remember, I told you two years ago that you had to start making visits back to your state."

"Shit," snarled Walker. "Voters have the memories of retarded slugs. I could show up in their goddamned living room and they'd forget about me in a week."

"That's not true and you know it," the young man said. "You need to be on TV and in the news-papers. It's not hard to do. You show up and we'll do the rest. But you told me –"

"I remember what I told you," Walker said. "And it's as true today as it was then. There's too much going on in this town. Jesus, if I leave town for ten minutes, Rogers runs to the press and bitches about my leadership."

"So let him go," the young man said. "You can take the hit, especially if you're back in your state. The people of Pennsylvania elect you, not the Democrats on your committee."

"And the floor votes." Walker said. "I have a ninety-nine percent voting record to think about."

The young man rolled his eyes. "Yeah, it's real important to be there to approve National Pork Week. Look, you can definitely afford to miss a few votes if you're back home. When Kerry ran for president, he missed sixty percent of the votes that year. People understand that. They're not going to hold it against you if you miss votes because you're back home presenting checks and kissing babies."

Walker shook his head slowly from side to side, glaring.

"Fuck!" he yelled abruptly. "Shit!" He muttered under his breath.

The young man waited. Eventually, Walker's attention swung back to him.

"All right. I should have listened to you and Carberry. But that's history now. Water under the goddamned bridge. What the fuck do I do now?"

"The oppo guys aren't coming up with much on Pacifico. He's pretty clean. The best we got was that stat about lost jobs. It doesn't look like there's going to be much else there."

"Come on!" Walker bellowed. "No unregistered nanny? You mean to tell me that this guy has never cheated on his wife? I've seen her! She looks like a goddamned Aunt Nelly! He's never banged a secretary, never grabbed an intern? Come on! He's from fucking Philly!"

"He's clean," the young man said. "No sign that he's ever been anything except faithful."

"Then make something up!" Walker yelled. "Jesus! I don't pay you guys to be pussies!"

The young man put up a hand. "There's a cleaner angle. The Green Party is running a candidate."

Walker snorted, then laughed. "Green Party? The fucking Green Party? The Wingnut Brigade? Who are they running, some fag from the ACLU?"

"No, they're running a social services caseworker from Altoona," the young man said.

Walker laughed again. "A what? Oh, that's great." He waved his meaty hands in small circles in front of his face. "Oh, yeah. We're afraid of him! A goddamned caseworker from Altoona! Christ, I can't believe there's even anybody left in that rathole of a town. What is he, the last non-senile resident?"

"He's a her. And that rathole of a town is actually doing OK," the young man said. "Norfolk Southern is hiring at the locomotive rebuilding shop. They've stabilized the tax base by taking on the slum landlords. They're not rolling in cash, but they're doing OK."

Walker's grin disappeared. "That's what I hate about you eager young bastards. You're always so up on shit like that. Jesus, what do you do, subscribe to the goddamned local paper?"

"If you knew stuff like that about Altoona, we wouldn't be sitting here trying to figure out what to do about Pacifico gaining on you," the young man said.

Walker's big silver-haired head turned slightly to the side, but his eyes stayed on the young man. The rest of his big body remained perfectly still.

"You're not getting smart with me are you?" he asked.

The young man picked up the undercurrent of menace but wasn't worried by it.

"I solve problems," he said. "That's what you pay me to do. If I can't be honest with you, then we can't solve problems. Now, do you want to be sworn in as a senator again next year or should I just issue a press release about your retirement?"

Walker's left eye narrowed as he kept his gaze on the young man.

"We were talking about the Green Party," Walker said.

"The Greens pull votes from Democrats, not Republicans," the young man said. "You and Pacifico are going to end up neck and neck, barring any ... unforeseen negatives popping up on one of you. Pacifico, as I said, looks clean. We can't count on getting anything. And you've covered your tracks pretty well –"

"Watch it," Walker said. "I don't have anything to hide."

The young man gave Walker a skeptical look and rubbed the thumb and pointer finger of one hand in a circular motion.

"Shit," Walker said. "That's buried."

"We hope."

"Yeah. Whatever. It's dead. Move on," he said.

"So, assuming that it really is a race on issues –"

"You can say that without a smirk," Walker interrupted.

"– then you two are going to end up tied," the young man said. "On money, you're even. We can't count on a war chest advantage. As for votes, Pacifico gets almost all of Philly and core Pittsburgh, the Democratic strongholds. You get the Philly suburbs and everything else in the state. You'll do OK in greater Pittsburgh because the economy is stagnant and voters think you live there. You have the power of incumbency but Pacifico is running a good race. You're getting hurt on the out-of-touch issue but the gun nuts in the middle and north of the state would vote for Hitler before they'd vote for Pacifico."

Walker snorted.

"So, if we can get the Greens to siphon off some votes from the Democrats, that could be just the edge that you need. Just enough. Just like Nader in 2000. He killed Gore by just snipping a few percent off."

"So what do we do? Give them money?"

"As a matter of fact, yes. Their candidate is working the state hard. She's meeting and greeting and getting some press attention. It's like she doesn't know that she doesn't stand a chance."

"Get to the point."

"I see it like this: You and Pacifico are each going to pull 48 percent. The remaining four percent usually vote for Mickey Mouse or someone about as likely to win. But say the Greens take three percent. That would mean, say, taking two percent from the Dems and one from the Mickey Mouse vote. Pacifico ends up with forty-eight minus two, which is forty-six percent. And you stay at forty-eight, because, as I said, Republicans don't ever vote for Greens."

"Can the Greens pull three, with two for sure coming from Pacifico?"

"Good question. In every election where they actually try, the Greens usually pull about one percent. That's consistent across the country, in election after election. But that's without an organized attempt to siphon off Democrat votes."

"Nice to know that only one percent of the country is tree-loving wackos," Walker said.

"The Green candidate is working hard. With some money, she should be able to pull two percent. We should push her hard in Pittsburgh. The economy's bad. With some media money, some voters over there will decide that a new party is the answer. Philly's tough for you – Pacifico is a popular mayor. Philly itself always goes Democratic, but you've got the suburbs. She'll get a few votes from the Altoona area, because she's from there. But most of the gun nuts aren't going to vote for a chick."

"So, like I said, what do we do, give the Greens money?"

The young man shrugged. "Sure. We'll set up a front group. Call it 'Citizens for a Fresh Start' or something like that. Make it look like it's grassroots. We'll shovel it some money and have it back the Greens. We can also set up a 527 organization to run TV and radio ads in support of the Greens. 527 orgs don't have the funding restrictions that the parties do. We can run a lot of pro-Green ads under that umbrella and no one will know who's actually paying for it."

"Don't overdo it. Jesus. What if she actually gets serious votes?"

"Won't happen. And if she does pull votes, she'll pull from the liberal Democrats. Believe me, Republicans and conservative Democrats are not going to vote for some skinny little girl talking about child abuse."

"Child abuse? Is that her issue? I thought the Greens talked about trees and gay rights."

"They usually do. But she's got a pretty good spiel on child abuse. It gets some people. It's getting her some attention from the media. The news media always feel guilty that they don't cover issues like that enough. So they write it up in connection with her campaign and feel like they've done their piece to stop child abuse for the year. She's got a blog, too."

"A what?"

"A blog. Web log. She posts ... stories, thoughts ... ideas. On the internet. People read it. It's kind of like keeping a diary, but on the net where everyone can read it."

Walker looked puzzled.

"What's the fucking point?"

"Well, if you don't have a lot of money, it's a good way to get the word out about your campaign. Encourage donations. Web logs cost a lot less than traditional advertisements and you can change the content every day if you want. Every minute, if you want."

Walker snorted. "Whatever. Can't see how that's as good as billboard and TV."

The young man shrugged. "It's a new world. Blogging is the next big thing in politics."

Walker waved a hand. "Whatever. I just want to win this next election. Then I'm good for another six."

"Right," the young man said. "In any case, we can leverage her hard work with a little money and some apparent grassroots support. It should pull just enough from Pacifico to get you back into office."

"Sounds good. I just —"

"I warn you," the young man interrupted. "It's not going to be a cakewalk. You're going to have to get out there and campaign. And it's going to be a squeaker. You'll win by one, two points. Three would be a landslide. But what can you expect when you haven't set foot in the state in three years?"

"You keep bringing that up," Walker growled.

The young man shrugged. "If you want a fourth term, then spend part of your third at least pretending that you give a shit about your home state."

Walker rolled his eyes. "You mean go home and suck up to the locals."

"Yup. Kiss babies. Present checks. Show up at Lions Club meetings. Get seen talking to guys in hard hats."

"Back to reality," Walker said. "How much money are we talking about here?"

"Oh, maybe a million or so."

Walker flinched. "Jesus. I could use that."

"Believe me, it's better spent boosting the Greens. They can't win anyway."

"And you'll get this money where?"

"You leave that to me. Get me a list of people to call for a 'special victory fund' or something like that. Separate account from your re-election campaign. Think about people who owe you or need something from you. I'll handle the arrangements. You just call 'em and stroke 'em and you'll be fine. You might have to give them a little extra time next year."

Walker grumbled something inaudible, then sat up straight. "Well, all right. OK. Is that all you have for tonight? I need a steak and a whiskey."

The young man stood up. "We're done."

Walker put out his hand. "OK. Thanks. Talk to you soon." They shook.

"Senator, I'll be in touch," the young man said. "Get me that list."

Walker nodded, then watched as the young man walked across his office and out the door. He pondered a moment, rubbing a chin grown rough with stubble from a long day. Then he pushed a button on his phone.

"Bring the car around. I feel like The Palm."

He pulled on his jacket and left his office.

Chapter Sixty-Four

Heading back to Altoona for a brief respite, she got a message that a "Dr. Jacobi" had called. He was in town for only a few days and wanted to speak with her. She got directions to his house.

She freed up an afternoon and drove out to see him. His house was nothing like she expected. She had imagined a McMansion with a faux brick exterior, lots of windows and cathedral ceilings on a cul-de-sac in an upscale development. Instead, when she found the address, it was a nondescript white split-level, vinyl-sided, with Penn State-blue shutters. The lawn was neat suburban typical. A few kids rode their bikes in the street. They wore helmets. The cars parked on the concrete driveways of the nearby clones of Dr. Jacobi's house were Chevys and Fords, not Jaguars and Cadillacs.

She parked her Honda in the driveway, walked to the door and rang the bell. She heard footsteps and then the door was swept open. He stood on the other side in his stocking feet, jeans and a t-shirt. He was nearly bald. On his face was a huge and genuine smile.

"Cindy! What a thrill! I am so glad that you could make time to see me. Please, come in."

He held open the door with one hand and made a sweeping gesture with the other. She entered, noting standard beige carpeting. He led her up a short flight of steps into a big-windowed living room right out of a studio set designed to say "middle America." The TV was new and the stereo equipment on the racks under the TV looked serious and intimidating, but the room itself was typical. Country-style couch and matching lounge chair. A wooden rocking chair. Plain end tables. A stack of magazines on one. Photos of a much-younger Dr. Jacobi and what must have been his wife on another. Everything was in its place; the house had the feel of being occupied by a fussy bachelor.

"Please have a seat," he said, turning toward her. Then he stopped. "No. Wait. Let me look at you." She withstood his scrutiny for a minute as he scanned her with his bright eyes. "You look good," he said at last.

"Thank you," she said. "You do too. Where'd you get that nice tan?"

Dr. Jacobi laughed. "A little South American sun. I'll tell you all about it. But can I get you something to drink first?"

She asked for a soda and he entered the kitchen as she sat down carefully on the sofa.

"I was truly stunned when I heard about the senate campaign," he said from the kitchen. She heard a hiss as he opened a bottle. "But then I thought about it and I realized that it made perfect sense." She heard the refrigerator door close, then an ice rack cracked and popped. He emerged from the kitchen, glasses of dark cola in each hand.

"Thank you," she said has he handed her the cool glass. He sat on the couch with her, but gave her a respectful yard of space.

"Well," he said, still smiling. "I'm sorry if I'm grinning like a fool. But you just can't believe how truly happy I am to see you. And how proud I am of you. Running for senator!" He took a sip.

She looked down shyly and took a sip. "The senate thing – I'm a pretty long shot," she said.

"Yes, but the point is that you're out there talking about child abuse, getting the message out. Am I right?"

She nodded.

"That's how things get started. That's how things get improved," he said. "Someone starts talking about it. Other people get interested. It snowballs. Things begin to happen. It reaches a critical mass. The news media begin to report on it. And suddenly it's a national consensus and – well, that's when things really start to pop."

"Dr. Jacobi, you seem ... I don't know," Cindy said. "The last time I saw you, you were much more...."

"Bummed out," he said. "Unhappy. Grumpy. Yes, that was me. You asked about the tan. Well. I really want to talk about you, but if you're wondering what this old man is up to, I'll be happy to tell you."

"Please do," she said.

"I'll keep it brief because I really want to talk about you," he said. "And please call me Ron."

She smiled an OK.

"Well, about the time that you came under my care, my life wasn't going too well. My marriage was in the dumps. In fact, not too long after you left the hospital, Brenda left me. Brenda, my wife. One of the thing she said to me as she packed her stuff, right in that bedroom down the corridor, was that I had a heart for everyone but her."

He paused and took a drink.

"We were never able to have children. That might have been part of the problem, but ... oh, well. I can speculate endlessly. The point is that Brenda thought that I could love medicine but not her. She thought that I was dedicated to my patients and my colleagues, but not to her. She might well have been right. At that point in my life, I was ... baffled. I didn't know what was important. I couldn't seem to find a focus. And unfortunately, Brenda appeared – at that time – to be just another obstacle to figuring it out. She was a ... a complicating factor."

He sighed. "Maybe I could have turned it around with her, but I didn't really want to try. I didn't know what was going on with me, but I did know that everything in my life seemed to be dust in my hands. And then," he said, turning his eyes to Cindy, "you came barging into my emergency room.

"I watched you. Observed you. Of course, it was all clinical at first. But then I began to see more in your fight to survive and then your fight to walk again. It took a while, but I gradually realized that if I wanted my life to mean something, then it was up to me to make that happen. It wasn't going to fall out of the sky onto me. Meaning, I mean. You have to give your own life meaning. No one can do that for you. And you pointed the way."

"What on earth did I have to do with it?" Cindy asked. "I was a seven-year-old who had to re-learn how to walk."

"That was exactly it," he said. "I never saw anyone respond to a serious, life-changing injury like you did. You didn't go through the usual stages of despair and hopelessness. You just starting fighting and fought every step of the way. Something in you fought to bring you back to consciousness. Then you fought to sit up in bed. Then you fought to walk. And then...." He closed his eyes and Cindy was alarmed to see tears well up. He put his drink down on an end table and took quick wipes at each eye.

"I'm sorry," he said, his eyes red but his smile bright. "You fought every step of the way. You were never bitter, even though you had every right to be. You never blamed anyone. Every single day, you grabbed those damn crutches and clanked up and down the hallway."

He began to laugh. "You never knew, but those poor rehab hospital nurses had to listen to more complaints...."

"About me?" Cindy asked.

"Yes, about you. One old lady asked if I could ask you not to make so much noise as you walked up and down the hallway. I told her that you had been the victim of a terrible accident and that you were re-learning how to walk. I thought that she'd cut you a little slack. But the old bird just pursed her lips and said, 'Well, if I were learning how to walk again, I'd show a little more consideration for the other patients. All that clacking and squeaking.' "

He laughed again and she joined him.

"I'm glad that I was so inspirational," Cindy said. "But I honestly don't remember much of it. No details, anyway. Most of that time is just a blur of being in the hospital. Several hospitals."

"Well, something inside of you wouldn't say die," Dr. Jacobi said. "And you were just this innocent little kid who had been beaten within an inch of your life, but there you were, so proud of every step."

He stopped and she let there be silence.

"I can't tell you how inspirational you were," he said. "Many people on the staff talked about how they admired you."

"I had a lot of help," she said. "As I remember, the staff was great. And my fairy godfather, who paid for all that care. And I remember those books."

"One of the most remarkable things I've ever seen," Dr. Jacobi said. "A complete stranger shelling out thousands for the care of someone he never met." He found his glass again and took a drink.

"Did you ever find out who it was?" he asked.

"James Frederick Steele," she said. "A real estate developer in Washington, D.C. He had apparently been abused as a child, but shook it off and made a ton of money as an adult. Well, maybe he didn't shake it off. He ... I guess he ran out of hope earlier this year," she said. "He committed suicide."

Dr. Jacobi closed his eyes.

"That's absolutely too damn bad," he said. "I can't believe that a man like that would have nothing to live for, after overcoming abuse in childhood."

"I don't know the details," Cindy said, "but his lawyer – I met him because Steele left me a farm in Maryland – said that Steele was a great guy but was always troubled. He said that money didn't mean much to him. It was just kind of his way of keeping score. You know, like James Steele, nineteen million; all the other rotten bastards, zero."

"He paid almost a half-million in care for you," Dr. Jacobi said. "I don't know if you knew that."

"No, I didn't, but thank you for telling me," Cindy said. "In addition to the farm in Maryland, he gave two grand to my campaign."

"Remarkable," Dr. Jacobi said.

"So, anyway," Cindy said, trying for a clean break. "You were telling me about you. About a big change in your life."

"Yes. Right," he said. "I was ... anyway, I was ... very inspired by you and your fight. I thought that if a little girl can come in here and fight like that after what was done to her, then I have no right to allow myself to turn into a sorry mess. So I started doing some serious thinking about what I wanted to do with my life. It took a while. Years, actually. Remember when you came to see me about your college choice? I was so proud of you. It just inspired me. You had this whole new life.

That's what I wanted. A new life, a new chance. A chance to do something completely different.

"I took six months off from the hospital – you should have seen the look on the administrator's face when I asked for that – and I got in this little red Toyota I had bought and I just started driving. For some reason, I drove north. I drove all the way through New England and found myself in Manitoba. Absolutely glorious up there. The silence. The trees. The lakes."

He shook his head.

"It was just me and my thoughts and a bunch of old cassette tapes of music that I hadn't listened to in years. Decades. But the drive and the solitude had the effect I was looking for. I decided that Brenda was right. I loved medicine more than anything else. And if that was what I loved, then damn, I was going to practice medicine."

"And?"

"And at first I had these ridiculous notions of finding a little town somewhere out west with no doctor and becoming the town sawbones. You know, handling everything from flu to births to surgery. Telling dads to go boil water. Carrying a little black bag and going on house calls. Well, it didn't take too much thinking to realize that medicine has changed from that. You can't really do that any more in America. But if you leave this country, you can."

He turned his gaze on Cindy and she could feel his excitement.

"So I did a little internet research and talked to a few colleagues. There is a huge, crying need for decent medical care in many countries outside the U.S. We bitch about our medical system, but at least we have one. There are kids in many countries who never see a doctor unless they're near death and maybe not even then. There are many countries where the most prenatal care a mother gets is advice from her mother. There are a lot of countries where hand washing and sterilization are – god help us – still newfangled concepts."

"Doctors Without Borders," Cindy said.

"Yes, something every much like that," Dr. Jacobi said. "It started at my church." He finished his soda and put it aside. "One of our missionaries from Brazil returned and spent a week living with one of our church families. He gave the sermon one day. He talked about working with Médecins Sans Frontiéres" – she smiled at his French – "and sitting there in that pew, it just clicked. I wanted to get up and yell, tell the congregation that I had finally figured it out. But I managed to keep my seat. Afterwards, I went up to the missionary – Dan Shepard was his name, if you can believe that, and the next thing you know, I had signed up to go Brazil with him."

"Wow," said Cindy, impressed.

"It took a while to get organized – there's more than you would think. I had to get a visa, immunizations. I had to hit the books and study the Brazilian culture. I even went back and reviewed some medical procedures that I hadn't handled in a while, like normal births. Working the emergency department, I always got the ones where mom had already delivered or where the kid was stuck halfway."

"And so you went down?" Cindy asked.

"Initially, I went down with Dan for about six weeks. It just cemented that it was what I wanted to do. Those people. Well, I worked in rural areas outside Sao Paulo. These are the most honest people I've ever met. There is no subterfuge, nothing fake like we've gotten used to here in the U.S. Do you know how ... how artificial this country seems when you spend six weeks sleeping on a straw mattress and providing medical care in a clinic that has exactly six scalpels and no x-ray machine?"

Cindy smiled and shook her head.

"It's just remarkable," Dr. Jacobi said. "And the gratitude...." He paused. "I have never, ever seen people so completely and honestly grateful for the simplest of procedures. There was this one little boy, four, had a nasty ear infection. Inflamed, swollen, he was just crying from the pain. I put him on a simple antibiotic and it cleared up in three days. You'd have thought that I had pulled him from the brink of death. His entire extended family showed up to thank me. They insisted on feeding me."

Dr. Simons made an exaggerated look of caution around the room. "Don't tell anyone about that," he said. "Those antis weren't exactly ... cleared for export," he said.

Cindy laughed. "I promise not to tell anyone," she said. "So, you're going back."

"Yes. Indefinitely," Dr. Jacobi said. "I leave in two weeks. I can hardly wait."

"Did you quit at Altoona Hospital?"

"I have never had more satisfaction in my life than telling Calvin Simons that I was resigning to go treat rural Brazilians for free. It's something that is simply not in Calvin's frame of reference. Everything with him is tied to money, so something done for free just doesn't compute." Dr. Jacobi smiled at the memory.

"He kept asking me if I was sure. I think he thought I was going through some sort of mid-life crisis. I told him – several times – that this was not a mid-life crisis. It was an actual mid-life change. He just couldn't grasp the concept."

"Well, you seem so happy ... I'm very happy for you," Cindy said. "It's always nice to see someone who has gotten on the right track."

"I can't tell you how it has freed me," he said. "I feel that my life has been leading up to this. I'm doing something that means something. I'm going to be useful." He paused. "Hell, maybe one of these Brazilian kids that I treat will grow up and cure cancer or something."

"Or maybe they'll just grow up healthy and have a happy family and after a long life, die a natural death surrounded by family and friends," Cindy said.

Dr. Jacobi looked at her. "Or that, too," he said. "And that would be just fine with me."

There was a silence. Cindy could hear the kids outside whooping as they rode their bikes down the street.

"But enough about me," Dr. Jacobi said. "You're on to something pretty exciting, too."

"It was exciting in the beginning," Cindy said. "Now it's just work."

"So what prompted this?"

"I can't seem to get in front of child abuse," Cindy said. "I thought that as a caseworker, I could get out in front of it, prevent it, educate people." She sighed. "But it was the same old. Reactive, not proactive. I was responding to situations where things had already gone bad. Kids were already being abused and it was already part of the family's standard operating procedure."

"I remember you telling me that you didn't want to go into medicine for that reason," Dr. Jacobi said. "You didn't want to treat them after the damage was done."

"Same deal," she said. "Oh, in social work you get to do a little education. I spoke in front of parent's groups and teachers and so on. But the parents who bother to go to those things are the ones who are least likely to abuse anyway. It's the parents who don't get it who abuse, mostly. They aren't likely to go to a seminar on how to prevent abuse because they don't even think of it that way. They just think that it's OK to beat your kid bloody because he talks back."

"I just don't understand it," Dr. Jacobi said. "Child abuse cases were some of the toughest ones to take. They come in to the ER, these frail little kids, sometimes infants or kids two or three years old..... ." He stopped.

Cindy sighed. "Yes, it just never ends. Oh, there were some talks where I thought I'd done some good. Like to new parents. You can really educate them about shaking a baby. About not shaking a baby, I mean."

Dr. Jacobi nodded his understanding. "I saw a few of those over the years. Kid, infant, comes in to the ER, usually very sluggish, pupil responses slow, none of the usual infant behaviors. Kid just lays there. The hell of it is that there's usually no immediate exterior sign of the shaking. You have to hit them with a CT scan and look for signs of sub-dural hematoma or cerebral edema...." He paused because Cindy was giving him a look.

"What and what?" Cindy said, laughing. "You lost me with the sub-enema or whatever that was."

They both laughed.

"Sorry," Dr. Jacobi said. "Bleeding or swelling inside and outside the brain, basically. The parents always try to tell you that the kid fell out of his crib or down the stairs. I'd just look at them. As soon as I heard that excuse, I knew they were lying. Ninety percent of the time, anyway."

"Well, I lost one little girl who I shouldn't have," Cindy said. "She was being hit a lot, but nothing really horrendous. Her dad would lock her in a closet. He broke her arm once, not badly. She spent a lot of time hiding under the bed. It was just ... routine abuse. She just always had bruises. Isn't that sad? A little girl who was always bruised, always in one kind of pain or another.

"I worked with the father, trying to get him to see the beauty of his little girl. I thought I was getting through to him. I thought that when he went back to work, his temper would level out and maybe he'd quit drinking, but something went wrong. One day, he flipped out and hit her. Right over her right eye. Crushed her skull, snapped her head back. She...."

Cindy stopped and put her head down. Dr. Jacobi wordlessly held out a box of tissues. She snatched one and sniffed into it, then wiped her eyes. She looked back up.

"We lose too many," he said. "But some hurt more than others. Some never quite leave us."

"Exactly," Cindy said, smiling her gratitude for his understanding. "I ... I really thought that I had finally been proactive, that I had finally had an intervention that worked. And then ... I found her," Cindy said. "Too late. Hours too late."

"I'm very sorry," Dr. Jacobi said.

Cindy sniffed again. "Well, yes, anyway. I lost Brittany. And it was my fault. And I just couldn't let it go. I kept working it over and over in my head. I had to figure out how best to get in front of it, how to educate people, how to make them think twice before the raise their hand to a child."

"And you came up with...?"

"Two things," Cindy said. "Education and a big old hammer."

"A hammer?"

"Child abuse laws across this country are fragmented," Cindy said. "Local law enforcement handles them. Expertise varies with investigations and in medical treatment. Penalties vary. Many people don't think you can even get arrested for beating your own kid. I guess they think it's like your car – you bought it, so you can abuse it if you want to. They don't get it that kids don't belong entirely to them – they belong to the future of this nation."

She stopped. "Well, that sounded really inane. But it's true. And that train of thought led me to this: When you rob a bank, who investigates?"

"The FBI," Dr. Jacobi said.

"Exactly. But why?"

Dr. Jacobi shrugged. "Deposits are federally insured," he said. "The federal government has a stake in getting its money back."

"Exactly," Cindy said. "And don't you think that this nation has a stake in having its kids grow up happy and healthy?"

"You know that I agree with you on that," Dr. Jacobi said. "But you're proposing that the FBI investigate child abuse?"

"Yes, when it rises to a certain level," Cindy said. "Just like all the movies. When the big crime goes down, the guys in dark suits and sunglasses show up and say, 'Thanks, sheriff, we'll take it from here.' "

"Hmm. Interesting thought," Dr. Jacobi said.

"The FBI will bring the resources of professional evidence-gathering, lab work and investigative technique. They'll stop the squabbling that sometimes happens between county agencies. And it will impress upon people that beating your kid on a regular basis is wrong. Being arrested by the FBI is going to get your name into the newspaper. And it's not just your business. Kids belong to the future."

"So you want to ... what? Pass a law to that effect?"

"Yes, in some form. Make the FBI responsible for investigating child abuse crimes that rise to a certain level – in cases of death, certainly, but also where there is a horrendous crime, or a pattern of consistent, long-term abuse. I haven't worked out the language yet, but I've started."

"It's my turn to say wow," Dr. Jacobi said. "I'm very impressed."

Cindy sighed. "So, that's why I'm on the road, touring the state, begging people to vote for me for senator. I know that probably only about fifty of them will. But I get to talk about child abuse and how serious it is and that something needs to be done about it. Something coordinated and serious. That's part of the education aspect, too."

"Speaking of being on the road," Dr. Jacobi said. "How are things going?"

"Being on the road is OK," Cindy said. "My biggest problem is my car. It's wearing out, plain and simple," Cindy said. "It's been a great car. But I've had it since college and now this tour of the state … well, I've got, like 230-thousand miles on it. Really," she said to Dr. Jacobi's raised eyebrow. "And I'm afraid that I haven't been as nice to it as I should have."

"Meaning?"

"Well, I sort of forget about oil changes."

Dr. Jacobi laughed. "I'm amazed you've gotten it as far as you have, then. That's the main thing that keeps a car running – fresh oil every three or four thousand miles."

"Well, it's just wearing out. It's losing power and burning oil. I'm embarrassed. I have to try not to accelerate too hard, because I look like I'm dusting crops."

Dr. Jacobi laughed. "Not very senatorial," he said.

"No, it's not," Cindy said, laughing.

"Well, I was hoping I might be able to help you with your campaign for senator," he said. "And I think now I know just what to do." He stood up. "Come with me a second."

She followed him downstairs, noting a well-appointed lower-level family room as they walked. He led her out to the garage and flipped on the light. In garage were two cars. In the near bay was a small red sports car that looked like it belonged in a science fiction movie. In the far bay was a big silver four-door.

"What's that?" Cindy asked, pointing to the red car.

Dr. Jacobi smiled widely. "Nissan 390 Z. One of the most ass-kicking road-legal cars on the planet. Brazil and that car right there are the answers to my mid-life crisis."

"And what," Cindy said, pointing to the big sedan, "is that?"

"Ford Crown Victoria," Dr. Jacobi said. "Good old American iron. Rear-wheel drive. V-eight engine, forty-two thousand miles, power every-thing, air conditioning that will turn her interior into a meat locker. They built them for decades. Just recently stopped. Police departments across the nation are in mourning. You won't find a more solid, reliable car."

He reached up and pulled a set of keys off a hook near the door. He held them out to Cindy. "She's yours."

"Dr. Jacobi ... I can't," Cindy said. But she was thinking of the presence that the car offered, the smooth ride, the huge trunk for boxes and boxes of campaign flyers. A back seat big enough to sleep in when the motels were few and far between.

He caught her hand and pressed the keys into her palm.

"Please," he said. "Take her and give her a good home. I never drive her any more since I got my Nissan. She needs to be driven. And I'm definitely not going to need her in Brazil."

She turned toward him. "I ... no, I can't," she said. "This probably counts as a campaign donation and that car is definitely worth a lot more than two thousand dollars."

"Well then, it's not a gift, it's a loan," Dr. Jacobi said, smiling. "And let's say that I loaned her to you before I ever heard about anyone running for the senate. I'll need her back, oh, say sometime before the turn of the century. I'll be out of the country for a while, so when I get back, if I need her, I'll call."

"Oh, Dr. Jacobi...."

"Ron. Please."

"Ron. I don't know what to say. It's such a nice car. And...."

"And you need a car. So take it. When I'm back in the U.S., I'll stop by Capitol Hill and ask for Senator Phillips. Maybe we can do lunch."

Then there was nothing for her to do but hug him, which he accepted with delight.

"I told you before," he said, one hand resting gently on the back of her head. "You go get them, girl. Go show them what you can do."

When she told Kaufmann about the car, he didn't miss a beat.

"Thank god," he said. "I don't know how much more my kidneys could take of that Honda. I mean, it's a nice enough car, but your struts are shot and that thing takes bumps like a barge running aground."

"I'll have you know that my Honda has been a perfectly fine car for most of my adult life," she said in a tone of mock indignation. "I even rescued a turtle once with it."

"Well, you can rescue a lot more turtles with a Crown Vic," Kaufmann said. "And it's a lot more like the kind of car that a candidate for senator should be driving."

"OK, but what about McCain-Feingold?" she asked, turning serious.

"You said he loaned it to you."

"Well, technically, yes."

"Technically, what? Do you have the owner's papers in your name or not?"

"Uh, no."

"Are you paying the insurance on it?"

"No. He paid something like five years in advance."

"And he said he wants it back some day, right?"

"Well, yes. He said that. But –"

"And he mentioned it to you before he ever knew you were running for the Senate, right?"

"Well, actually –"

"OK, let me phrase the question differently, Miz Phillips. Did Dr. Jacobi, fine upstanding citizen that he is, mention in any way that he was giving you the use of this automobile for your campaign for senator? Or is it reasonable to assume that he loaned it to you for your personal use and, is it further reasonable to assume, that he assumed that you would continue to use the Honda for your campaign?"

"Well, I...."

"And further, Miz Phillips, did you at any point intend to use this car for personal purposes, such as trips to the grocery store, or did you intend to use it solely for the campaign, with no personal usage whatsoever?"

"Harold, I've completely lost track of your question."

"Then I'm doing my job. Quit worrying about the damn car. You're fine. Your opponents are accepting the equivalent of suitcases filled with unmarked bills. You're accepting the loan of a used automobile from an old friend who is leaving the country on a charitable mission. Trust me, you'll be fine. This isn't even going to appear on the FEC's radar screen."

"Thank you, Harold. I always feel much better after I talk to you."

"Thanks. I like it when my clients clear their conscience by dumping it on my karma. Thank god I charge by the hour."

"Not me you don't, Harold."

"Oh, yeah. I forgot about that. Must have been a rare lapse into congeniality."

Chapter Sixty-Six

Green Party State Director Scott Rivers, Cindy's liaison Rick and Cindy were sitting in the conference room of the Green Party's headquarters for a rare in-person visit by Cindy. She was catching up on paperwork and discussing the progress of her campaign.

They were discussing Walker, when she suddenly asked, "You do have an oppo unit," she said to Rick. "Right?"

He suddenly looked uneasy.

"Well, we're not like the two big parties," he said. "We don't dig up dirt on the other guy."

"No, but you do have ... operatives ... who keep track of the other guy, right? Track his movements, report back about the size of his rallies, who attends, that kind of thing?"

Rick glanced at Scott.

Cindy glared at them both. "We're on the same side here, guys."

Scott pursed his lips. "Well, yes, we do some of that. We have people. Not operatives – you make it sound like a John LeCarre novel."

"Well, get one of your 'people' to shadow Walker in the evenings for a week or so. Find out what restaurants he goes to and when he goes. I guarantee you he's not eating at McDonald's."

"And we will do what with this info?" Scott asked.

"See what you find out, then we'll figure out what to do with it," Cindy said.

It was Scott's turn to glare.

"Cindy. We're on the same side here. I'm not going to send our guy out to spend hours and hours following Walker from restaurant to restaurant if I don't know what you're going to do with the info. We don't mudsling. We're not like that."

Cindy sighed. "Just see what your … man can find out. Then we'll decide what to do with it."

Scott eyed her warily. "You're not going off the deep end here are you, Cindy?" Scott asked. "Because if you lose the focus of this race, which is to promote the Green Party, then this becomes a useless exercise."

"I thought this was about grassroots democracy and equal opportunity," Cindy shot back. "This is bigger than the Green Party getting a certain percentage of votes."

"Without the Green Party, you're going to have a hard time getting any votes at all," Scott said, leaning across the table.

"Scott, that's about the –" Cindy began, but was interrupted by Rick, who stood up abruptly.

"Uh, look, people … Cindy … Scott," Rick said, eyeing each of them in turn. "A few minutes ago, I heard both of you agree that we're all on the same side here. Am I right? Motivations vary but our goals are the same – get Cindy into office. Right?"

Scott sat back into his chair slowly and nodded his head. Cindy nodded and sighed. Rick raised one eyebrow.

"I've been out there with Cindy," Rick said. "She works hard. She gets the message out – the Green Party message. And with a little work and support, she's going to do very well at the polls. I'm certain of that."

"I get it, Rick," Scott said, waving his hand in the air. "OK. I get it."

"I'm sorry," Cindy said. "I'm kind of tired and it makes me jumpy."

"It's OK," Scott said. "I didn't mean to jump on you there. I know you're doing good work out there."

Cindy managed a smile and put out her hand. Scott took it. Rick put his over theirs.

"OK," Rick said. "Now how about a kiss?"

They all laughed.

Later, they were eating pizza at the table in the meeting room.

"...and he has this house in Squirrel Hill in Pittsburgh," Cindy was saying. "Very nice house. Very nice neighborhood. A nice, sturdy, brown-brick with a big front porch and a two-car garage," Cindy said. "And he hasn't been in the place in more than three years. Three years! That house sits cold and dark. He doesn't even pretend to live there any more. He lives outside D.C. in a really nice house, near some of his other rich buddies in the Senate."

Rick shook his head.

"Do you know that in his second term, in the winter, a pipe broke in the place and it wasn't discovered for two weeks. A neighbor finally noticed that the windows were all steamed up from the inside. Did a ton of damage. But no one knew because no one lives there."

"Did he fix it?" Rick asked.

"He didn't. He doesn't live there. And he doesn't even technically own the place. Not by himself, anyway. He owns it jointly with a company called Mortgage Investors Inc. or something like that. I'm sure that the company is something cobbled together by some of his rich Republican friends. They just look at the mortgage payments as the price of doing business with Senator Walker. I'm sure he didn't pay a dime for the cleanup – the Mortgage Investors company did that."

"How do you know all this?" Scott asked. He had been quiet up to now and he used the tone that Cindy knew would lead to more questions if she didn't have a good answer.

"In school, at Maryland, we did a unit on incumbents who have lost touch. One of my classmates wrote a whole paper on him. I proofread it for her. It was full of stuff about Walker. And you know what's sad?"

Scott and Rick both shook their heads no.

"All the stuff that my classmate found for this report was all public record. She got almost all of it from newspapers and Senate records. Some info was pulled together by citizen groups that hate the power of incumbency. Isn't that sad? All that info is right out there for the voters to find, but they ignore it."

She leaned forward and Scott knew that she was about to make her point.

"So, if someone were to bring this out about Walker, and make it very public, like front-pages-of-newspapers public, don't you think that some people here in Pennsylvania will have a hard time voting for Walker again? People like that woman I talked to up in Erie who was selling her dresses so her kids could eat?"

"Well, yes," Scott said. "I'm sure it would hurt him. But we don't sling mud, Cindy. We stay focused on the issues. That's not negotiable at the Green Party."

"Oh, Scott," Cindy said, smiling. "I'm not talking about the Green Party releasing such information. Don't you think the Democrats would love to know all that? Have it handed to them?"

And then Scott could see the steel behind the smile.

They sat down for what Scott called a "Reality Session" before Cindy left to hit the road again. The purpose of the meeting was to review the poll numbers.

"As I've been telling you, Cindy is wowing them out there," Scott said from the front of the room, in front of a screen. He had cobbled together a quick presentation. A small gray projector attached to a laptop computer beamed colored slides onto the screen behind Scott. The lights were dimmed. Evelyn and Carl, an assistant provided to Cindy, sat along the wall behind Cindy, who had a seat at the table. Rick was running the projector. There were a dozen senior members of the Green Party's state hierarchy around the table. Cindy had been introduced to them all at various times since her campaign began, but she couldn't begin to remember their names.

Although Scott often found Cindy frustrating (and the feeling was mutual), he was genuinely impressed by the results she was getting. People were listening to her and she was motivating them to donate to the campaign or volunteer.

"Poll numbers are very preliminary at this point," Scott cautioned, "but we have reason to hope for a good showing if we continue on the track we're on."

Rick pushed a button on the laptop and a slide popped up. It was a chart of numbers.

"As you know, the Green Party usually pulls about one percent in national and statewide races," Scott said. "That has held true through the last six elections."

He beamed a tiny but bright red laser point on the chart.

"This is a real election poll," Scott said. "This one was done according to professional standards. We asked people who are likely to vote in the next general election if they were considering a vote for a Green Party candidate. Normally, we can grab about two percent on these polls. But you can see here that we are approaching five percent." His red dot circled a number from the chart. "If this holds – well, I don't have to tell anyone in this room what it would mean if we pulled five or six percent in a general election for a national-office race."

He paused and grinned at his audience. "We pretty consistently come in with one percent of the vote total. If we can pull five percent, people will really sit up and take notice. For one thing," he said, looking at Cindy, "they will have to invite us to the next debate."

There were several chuckles in the room from people who knew about Cindy's recent exclusion from the Pittsburgh debates between Pacifico and Walker. Since the Green Party had not won three percent of the vote in the previous election, they had been barred from the debate. Cindy and Scott had protested, but to no avail.

"This, folks, is an astounding poll," Scott said. "If I can ask you to imagine –" He stopped speaking as someone at the back of the room started clapping. A few more joined in. Scott stuck his laser pointer in his shirt pocket and joined in. Rick clapped enthusiastically and gave Cindy a thumbs-up. Evelyn grinned widely. Cindy gave a little wave and looked down.

"Cindy is talking to – what, about four hundred people a week?" Scott asked.

Evelyn and Carl nodded.

"And let me tell you that she's doing it the hard way," Scott said. "She's standing outside factories when the whistle blows at the end of the day. She's talking to people going in and out of convenience stories. She's stopping people going into the library. She even buttonholes smokers who step outside for a minute."

"No one is safe," Evelyn said, and the group chuckled.

Scott wrapped up with a prediction that the Green Party would pull a strong third place, winning three to four percent of the total vote, turning the Green Party into a player in the state of Pennsylvania and earning attention from the national press.

"Cindy is our ticket to respectability," Scott said.

He kept his smile as the meeting broke up. He approached Cindy as she finished accepting congratulations from the various Green Party movers and shakers.

"Cindy. You know how important this race is," he said.

"Scott. You don't have to tell me," Cindy said.

"Can you hang in there? You must be getting tired." He put a hand on her shoulder.

Cindy could feel Evelyn hovering protectively near, ready to move in if Scott overstepped.

"Five percent for a Green Party candidate in a race for U.S. senator would be remarkable," Scott said. "It would be beyond all expectations – beyond anything that any Green Party candidate has pulled in for a national office. Five percent would be something to take to bank. I know it doesn't sound like much, but boy would it open doors," he said.

Cindy looked into his eyes. "Scott, I told you, I know how this game is played. I know that we're not going to win. I just hope to do a little better than every other loser. And maybe get people to think about a few issues along the way."

Scott smiled and his hand on her shoulder turned into a massaging grip.

"Great. Great." Scott said, smiling. "If you need anything out there, you just call."

"I'm good, Scott," Cindy said.

"You know that's all bullshit, right?" Evelyn asked Cindy as they headed out of town the next morning, back on the road. The Crown Vic purred down the four-lane road, discreetly sucking up expansion-joint bumps and muffling the noise from the highway.

"All Scott's nice little charts and graphs?" Cindy asked. She was shuffling through some papers that Scott had given her, but she was paying attention to Evelyn.

"Yeah. All that stuff. Means nothing," Evelyn said.

"I know," Cindy said, looking up at the road and sighing. "I know that it doesn't mean anything. Just because people say they've heard of the Green Party and say that they might possibly consider voting for a Green Party candidate in the next election – well, yes, I know. Means nothing." She went back to her pile of papers. "But it is nice to see those numbers going up, even if it's just a little bit. I guess."

"Well, I have a feeling that Mr. Scott might be off a bit," Evelyn said.

"Yeah, we'll be lucky if we even show up on the returns on election day," Cindy said. "I'll be that candidate with the zero after my name because I won't get enough votes to even register."

When Evelyn was silent, Cindy looked up. Evelyn was giving Cindy her patented "Don't mess with me" look.

"What?" Cindy said. "Now what did I say?"

Evelyn snorted and turned her attention back to the highway. "I'm saying that it's going to go the other way," she said. "Come election day, you're going to rack up a lot more than that five percent that has Mr. Scott's undies all in a bundle."

"Oh, Ev," said Cindy, patting Evelyn's leg. "Where do you find this unending optimism? I'm going to get my ass kicked and you know it."

Evelyn kept her eyes on the road. "You keep thinking that way, and that's exactly what you will get," she said. "But your field campaign manager has a feeling about things like this, and she thinks you're going to kick ass – not get yours kicked. I don't know how it's going to happen, exactly … but I feel pretty sure that you're going to surprise everyone."

In the back seat, Carl woke up. "What? What are you two arguing about now?"

"I told you, Carl, we don't argue," Evelyn said. "We discuss. We're discussing making you pay for lunch. Now go back to sleep."

She got a grunt in response.

"Thank you for your optimism," Cindy said quietly. "And for coming along and putting your life on hold while I tilt at windmills."

Evelyn just shook her head and kept driving.

Chapter Sixty-Seven

ON THE CAMPAIGN TRAIL – The blog of Cindy Phillips, Green Party candidate for U.S. Senator from Pennsylvania –

I was in Erie a few weeks ago. I spoke at a park near the lake. I stood up on a picnic table. I got a pretty good crowd for a lunchtime speech – maybe 20 people. When I was done, this woman came up to me. She had her hair pulled back in a bun and she was wearing a way-too-big flannel shirt and jeans. She was one of those women who are probably forty but look sixty because of the care lines on her face. She came right up to me and told me that she was out of money to feed her kids. Her husband lost his job and she has three mouths to feed: His and two kids. She said that they were OK for a while with her husband's unemployment. But then it ran out. She got a job at the local dollar store working the cash register. 38 hours a week, just enough that she's not full time and can't get benefits. She told me that she had sat down to pay the bills just a few days earlier and the family was out of money. Flat out. And she could see that for the foreseeable future, the family's expenses were going to outstrip their income. Way outstrip. I mean, like two dollars coming in and four being owed.

She told me that she had already sold all of her jewelry. She had started selling her dress shoes and her dresses, figuring she would never need to wear them again. She sold her wedding dress. She wears her husband's clothes. She was even sneaking and selling her husband's tools, a few at a time, and hoping he wouldn't notice. She buys stale bread from the factory outlet store and buys rice in 20-pound bags. The family has long since stopped eating meat. She was worried that once the mortgage and the utilities and the car payment were made, that there would be zero left. Nothing. Not a dime. She was terrified of the day that she opens the cabinets in the kitchen and there's nothing there and there's not a dime in the bank.

I wonder where the incumbent PA senator ate last night? I wonder what the bill was? I wonder how long that woman from Erie could feed her family on what he paid for one meal?

Chapter Sixty-Eight

The doorman opened the gleaming back door of the black Lincoln Town Car for Senator Walker. Walker grunted as he stepped out of the car, a heavy black coat thrown over his shoulders and a red silk scarf falling from his neck. A heavy gold watch wrapped his left wrist and peeked out from under his dark suit jacket sleeve.

"Enjoy your evening, senator," the doorman said as Walker passed.

Walker pressed folded bills into the man's hand and leaned in close.

"Sir?"

"See that I'm not ... bothered," Walker said. "I don't want any press in here."

"Certainly, sir," the doorman said.

The Town Car pulled away smoothly and Walker strode down the red carpet under the restaurant's canopy. A second doorman waited to sweep open the door for him.

"Senator!" someone yelled from Walker's left. He looked – and something bright exploded in his eyes. "Christ!" he yelled, raising an arm.

"Thanks, senator," said the man with the camera who had popped out from behind a low brick wall beside the restaurant. "Just a fan who wanted a candid."

The man turned and walked quickly away. Walker, lowering his arm, noted through spots that the man was dressed in a long, dark coat and heavy shoes. He wore an old-fashioned snap-brim fedora.

Walker turned on the doorman. "That," he said pointing to the rapidly departing photographer, "is exactly the kind of shit I don't want to deal with tonight."

The tipped doorman stepped closer. "I'm very sorry, sir. I didn't know he was there. I apologize –"

"Just keep those assholes out. Jesus. That type couldn't afford a meal here anyway," Walker said.

He turned and the door was swept open for him. The maitre 'd behind the tiny desk smiled in immediate and genuine recognition.

"Senator. Welcome. Your usual table, sir?"

Chapter Sixty-Nine

Don Pacifico stood behind a curtain at the back of an unused stage in the VFW hall. The aide responsible for his wardrobe was fussing with Pacifico's lapels.

"Am I going to have to have words with my dry cleaner?" he asked her, smiling. His amusement was lost on her.

"With your tailor, maybe," she said seriously. "Who do you use?"

"Rispoli. Just like daddy did," Pacifico said. "And his daddy before that."

She gave a final pat to his left lapel and stepped back.

"Well."

She looked uncertain and reached for the lapel again, but Pacifico said, "It's fine, I'm sure. It's all fine. I'm going to take it off in a minute anyway. Where's Al?"

Pacifico's spokesman and media handler pushed aside the curtain and stepped through the slit. Pacifico caught a glimpse of the long rows of tables and old men milling around.

"Looks good?" Pacifico asked.

"Looks real good," Alphonse DiMalzoni said. "Good turnout. Media's showing up, too."

"Let me see that photo again," Pacifico asked. Al pulled a large black-and-white photo out of one of the twelve identical press packets that he was carrying.

The photo was a glossy black-and-white eight by ten. It showed Walker, eyes wide, mouth open, on the carpet outside a clearly very expensive Washington, D.C. restaurant. His left arm was raised in a defensive gesture.

Pacifico grinned. Behind Walker in the photo was a worried-looking man in doorman's garb. Even better, there was a line of gleaming and expensive cars at the curb. Pacifico knew that the scene was not one familiar to the average Pennsylvania voter.

Walker's long heavy coat and scarf were flung over his shoulders like a cape, giving him a regal look. With his silver hair and the chunky watch on his raised left arm, he looked like a very wealthy man of privilege, and a startled and angry one. Not the sort of man who attended VFW barbecue lunches.

"Where did we get this again?" he asked Al.

Al shrugged.

"It came in the mail. A negative and prints."

"And we're sure that this is Walker?"

Al snorted.

"No question. The focus is razor-sharp. Anybody who knows the guy would recognize him."

"Any chance that it's a made-up photo? I know they can do amazing stuff with digital photos these days."

Al pulled out a photo for himself and peered at it.

"That's The Palm." He shrugged. "Walker is known to frequent the place. He dresses like that. Even if it is a fake, it's an accurate reflection of reality."

"And DNC cleared this?"

"Cleared it, hell," Al said. "They made it pretty clear that if you don't use it, they're going to be pissed."

"All right," Pacifico said, glancing at his watch. He handed the photo back to Al. "Let's do this."

Al pulled the curtain aside and Pacifico stepped through. He walked across the stage, past the podium and onto the floor, scanning the crowd. He found what he was looking for in a senior citizen in a windbreaker with U.S. Navy patches, a flannel shirt and stiff blue jeans.

"Hello!" Pacifico said, extending a hand. The man, looking startled, grasped Pacifico's hand. "Pleased to be here," Pacifico said. "I'm Don Pacifico."

"I'm Paul Rogers," the man said.

"Paul, I'm pleased to meet you. How are things going? You ready to dig into a good old fashioned barbecue?"

"Well, yes, sir," the man said, looking star-struck.

Pacifico turned his full attention to the man. Watery blue eyes. Yellow teeth. A little stubble. Late 60s, he judged.

Keeping the man's hand in a firm grip, Pacifico asked, "Paul, are you a veteran?"

The man drew himself up a little.

"Yessir," he said. "United States Navy. Saw duty in Korea, the forgotten war."

Pacifico removed his hand from the clasp and placed it on the man's shoulder. He looked into his eyes.

"Paul, this is one American who didn't forget Korea and never will," Pacifico said. "Thank you for your service. You've done your part to keep America strong and free. I hope our country's done right by you since then."

"Can't complain," the man said.

"Paul, you might not know that I served my country. I was honored to serve in the U.S. Navy too. And you know what?"

"No, sir," Paul said, his attention riveted on Pacifico.

"For some reason, they saw fit to commission me as a staff corps officer. I served as the Navy's version of a lawyer, what they call a judge advocate general."

"Jag," Paul said.

"Don't hold that against me," Pacifico said, smiling.

Paul smiled back.

"So I know what kind of sacrifice you made to serve your country," Pacifico said. "Paul, I bet you had some buddies who didn't come back, didn't you?"

Paul looked down, then back up.

"Yessir," he said. "That happened a couple times. It's ... it's not something that you talk about a lot."

Pacifico sensed without looking that some of the other people in the hall had noticed the conversation and were drifting closer.

"Paul, you might not know that I'm running for senator. I pledge to you right here, right now, that veterans are going to be one of my priorities when I'm elected. I'll fight for veterans every damn step of the way, just like you did in Korea."

The man looked embarrassed.

"Well, I never actually saw any action," he said. "I was a cook. Never fired a shot."

Pacifico slightly increased the pressure of his grip on Paul's shoulder.

"Paul, it doesn't matter if you spent the war slinging hash or firing a machine gun. Or writing legal briefs," Pacifico said with a smile. "War means that every man has to pull his weight. And you pulled yours, didn't you? And I bet you'd do it again today if your country asked, wouldn't you, Paul?"

Paul looked at Pacifico.

"You're damn right I would, sir," he said.

"Call me Don," Pacifico said. "And I knew you'd say that, Paul. Because I would, too. In a second."

He looked into the veteran's eyes again.

"Paul, can I count on you to support me in the election?"

Paul took a half-step back from Pacifico. He snapped to attention, his body straight and stiff and his gaze elevated.

"Petty Officer Second Class Rogers reporting for duty, sir!" he said and saluted Pacifico.

Pacifico straightened and saluted back crisply.

"Petty Officer Rogers," he said, "At ease. Thank you for everything you've done for your country."

Pacifico stepped forward and extended his hand again. Paul grasped it firmly. Pacifico made it a two-handed grip.

"Paul, if you ever need anything – anything at all – you call my office. I'll get the job done for you."

Knowing his cue, Al produced a stiff white business card and handed it to Paul, who took it and looked at it.

Pacifico gave him a second. The man looked up from the card.

"Why, I sure will, mayor," he said.

"Thank you, Paul. Thank you," Pacifico said.

A crowd had gathered around the two men. Pacifico noted approvingly that three television news camera crews and a gaggle of photographers had witnessed his exchange with Paul.

Pacifico removed his jacket and threw it onto a nearby table. He rolled up the sleeves of his white dress shirt as the crowd of men watched him. He loosened his tie. The men waited.

"Well, gentlemen, are we ready for a good old fashioned barbecue?" He smiled broadly.

Behind him, Paul Rogers looked at the business card again. It was very white and stiff and had a gold seal embossed on it. Then he turned his attention to Pacifico, who was saying something about a senator who apparently had been photographed doing something improper.

There was no question in Paul's mind who had his vote. Later, looking at the photograph of Walker that he had been handed, he knew that he had chosen the right man.

Disdaining the podium, Pacifico strode between the tables after the men had a chance to eat.

"I can't thank you all enough for coming out today," Pacifico said. "I am always comfortable in a group of men who have served their country and who know what it means to sacrifice. Men who know what the term American really means. Men who know how important strong leadership is to this country."

Around the room, men nodded.

"I'm going to keep this real short," Pacifico said. "There's an election coming up. You, veterans and voters, will get to pick Pennsylvania's next senator. The choices are pretty simple. You can elect a wealthy power broker who hasn't bothered to return to Pennsylvania in three years. Or you can elect a man who understands that America starts right here, in Legion halls, fire halls and union halls. A man who understands that Americans want a safe, secure place to raise their children ... or to spoil their grandchildren."

A chuckle ran through the room.

"Gentlemen, it's up to you. It's your choice. I'm simply asking you to consider voting for me, Don Pacifico, on November second. If you decide to cast your vote for me, I can tell you that I will consider it an honor – a great honor – to represent you in Washington, D.C."

"How'd we do?" Pacifico asked Al as he got into the passenger seat and slammed the door.

Al glanced in his rear view mirror, got the thumbs-up from the driver of the security van. The van pulled out into the street, moving slowly, and Al pulled out in front of it.

"Kicked ass," Al said as he directed the car out of town. "Those vets ate it up. And they really –"

"No pun intended," Pacifico said.

Al gave him a quick smile.

"Yeah. Ate it up. Ha. Anyway, they liked you. You were right on message: solid performer, vet, known quantity versus rich power-hungry asshole."

"Any negatives?"

"None. You had them. The only wandering eyes in there were guys wondering if a third trip to the buffet table was too many."

"Nice," Pacifico said. "You did good prep work on that one. What's next?"

"Soccer moms," Al said. "AYSO field out in the burbs. We'll be there in about twenty minutes if I hit a few green lights."

"Core message?"

"Essentially the same," Al said. "Security. Keeping kids and country safe. But play down the military connection. These women don't want to think that you solve problems by shooting, like some gunfighter."

"And they don't want to think about little Billy being drafted and sent to Afghanistan," Pacifico said.

"Right," Al said. "Talk about kids. Your kid. Talk about safety. And play up the 'rich and disconnected' angle on Walker. These women aren't doing too badly – you're going to see a lot of Lexus SUVs in the parking lot – but they don't think of themselves as wealthy. They think that they're comfortable. Seventy percent volunteer time to help people who aren't as ... blessed as they are."

"Gotcha," Pacifico said. "And the don'ts?"

"Stay on message. Don't go too negative on Walker, numbers show that they hate that. Talk about Walker being out of touch, but don't get personal. And don't be condescending. These women aren't stupid. Fifty-five percent have four-year degrees. They subscribe to Newsweek and Atlantic Monthly. Talk to them like they're stupid or ignorant and you'll lose them fast."

"Good," Pacifico said, settling back in his seat and closing his eyes. "I'm going to –"

He winced and leaned forward, his face in a grimace.

"You OK?" Al asked.

"Ahh. Heartburn. Too much barbecue sauce."

"That stuff was wicked," Al agreed. "You sure you're OK? Need a Tums?" Pacifico shook his head wiped his eyes.

"No ... I'll be OK. Just ... jumped up and grabbed me there. Ahh." He settled back in his seat and closed his eyes. "I'm going to grab a minute. Wake me when we're close."

"You got it," Al said, checking the side-view mirror to make sure that the security van was still behind them.

Chapter Seventy

Cindy is walking down a dark alley. The street under her feet is slippery with something that she can't see. The windows of the buildings that loom left and right are broken and lightless. She is searching for something. She strains her eyes to see, but she can't penetrate the gloom more than a few feet. She can't even tell where the light is coming from. It is silvery like moonlight, but when she looks up, she sees nothing but blackness. She strains her ears, but hears nothing but a steady drip, drip, drip of water. Or something liquid enough to drip.

A squeak, no ... a squeal. Ahead of her. A definite sound! She tries to speed up, but she's afraid of falling. Now she hears it again and this time, it's a definite scream, then words: "No, daddy, no, daddy, no daddy! Please!"

Cindy breaks into a run, desperate to help, desperate to arrive before it's too late. Even as she thinks about falling, her right leg slides out from under her as she brings it down. Her left knee hits the street with a crack, but she feels no pain.

Cindy scrambles to her feet, something dark and slippery on her hands.

"I'm coming, Brittany!" she yells. "I'm coming! Be nice to your daddy and he won't hit you! Hold on! I'm coming!"

Somewhere ahead, a phone rings. The screams and the ringing grow louder as Cindy stumbles down the alley at a half-run. *I'm not going to make it,* she thinks. *I'm going to be too late again.* Despair runs with her. The scream sounds again, louder, merging with the ringing, both growing louder and louder until Cindy herself screams, falling, skidding on her knees, her hands over her ears to block out the ringing that rattles her skull ... and then she is sitting up in a strange bed.

The dark room whirls, then settles with a bump. The window is over there – that vertical slit of light. The phone rings and a square red light on it blinks. Cindy looks at the clock. Its red digital numbers tell her that it is 3:57. A.M., she realizes. The phone shrills again. Cindy reaches for it.

"Hello?"

"Girlfriend! What is with you? It rang forever!"

"Ev ... I was sleeping." Cindy yawns. "It's four in the morning, woman!"

"Politics never sleeps," Evelyn says. Cindy can detect joy in her voice.

"OK, what wonderful idea did you come up with now? I tell you, it better be a pretty good one to wake me up like this."

"Do you get CNN in that fleabag motel you're in?"

"Yeah, I was watching some last night."

"Well, flick it on, sister. They're about to do their top-of-the-hour roundup and you don't want to miss this one."

Cindy found the remote control on the bedside table. She turned on the TV and CNN came on. The channel was showing a commercial for some device that did all sorts of apparently useful things to eggs.

"Ev, you can't do this to me," Cindy said. "What's going on?"

"Just wait," Evelyn said. "Come on. Please. Give me thirty more seconds. Let me be a drama queen."

"OK," said Cindy. She could hear over the phone that Evelyn had her television on.

The commercial ended and a flashy CNN graphic galloped across the screen.

"OK, here it comes," Evelyn said.

The scene changed to a woman with long dark hair sitting behind a desk. A head-and-shoulders shot of a silver-haired man appeared over the woman's left shoulder.

That's Pacifico, Cindy thought. As the woman's mouth began to move, Cindy realized that she had muted the TV. She grabbed the remote and punched up the volume.

"... -didate Donato Pacifico, mayor of Philadelphia, has been rushed to the hospital following an apparent heart attack. An emergency room doctor at the hospital confirmed that Pacifico was brought to the hospital by ambulance in what was described as a critical state. The doctor, who wished to remain anonymous, said that Pacifico was unconscious upon arrival. The doctor characterized Pacifico's heart attack as very serious and added that, quote, I can't see him doing much of anything anytime soon, and that includes campaigning, unquote.

"Pacifico's campaign would confirm only that the candidate has been taken to Liberty Memorial Health Center in Philadelphia. Alphonse DiMalzoni, spokesman for the campaign, said that a statement would be issued in the morning. Pacifico, a Democrat, is locked in a tight race with Republican incumbent Bob Walker."

Cindy found herself short of breath. She realized that she had stopped breathing.

The TV woman turned a page in front of her and without looking down, began, "Computer giant Microsoft today responded to charges that –"

Cindy muted the television. She realized that she still had the phone pressed to her ear.

"Oh my god," she said.

Evelyn made a noise like someone had squeezed her. "Oh my god is right," she said. "Someone up there loves you, girl!"

"He's out. He's out." Cindy said. Her head whirled with the implications. "If Pacifico is out .... what ... it's only three days till the election! There's no way that the Democrats can get someone else on the ballot. Oh my."

"And guess who stands to inherit Pacifico's votes?" said Evelyn, glee in her voice. "The Green Party stands on main issues really aren't that far from the Democrat's," she said. "People who were going to vote for Pacifico because he's a Democrat are sure as hell not going to vote for Walker. They'll vote for you. And those people who just want Walker out are going to vote for you. And don't forget about those people that you won over the hard way – by meeting and greeting them. Now, when you add all that up...." Evelyn said.

"Oh my," Cindy said. "We could win."

"You better get started on your acceptance speech," Evelyn said.

"I need Scott's home number," Cindy said. Evelyn, ever hyper-organized, had it memorized. Cindy snapped on the light and wrote it down on a tiny pad of paper provided by her budget motel.

"I'll call you back as soon as I talk to Scott," Cindy said. "Oh, my god. I can't believe this. Ev, can you stay awake? We're going to have to have a conference call. We need to map out a strategy for the next three days. We'll have to ... oh, just stay up until I can get ahold of Scott."

"Girl, I couldn't go to sleep now if you hit me with a sledgehammer."

"OK, I'll talk to you soon."

Cindy hung up and sat with the phone in her hand, trying to assimilate the news. Pacifico's heart attack was a terrible thing for him and his family. From the sounds of the news report, he might die or be disabled. Cindy's heart went out to his family. He had been doing well in the polls. They were probably trying not to get too excited, but it had to have been on their minds lately – Senator Pacifico. But now.... Cindy reined in her emotions. This was pure politics now. If someone was going to win this race to represent Pennsylvanians in Washington, it sure wasn't going to be Walker.

She dialed the number that Evelyn gave her. The phone rang, rang, rang, rang, rang. She hung up and dialed again. It rang and rang and then there was a loud clattering and a sleepy voice said, "Yeah?"

"Scott, it's Cindy."

"Jesus, Cindy, it's ... four in the morning."

"Scott, wake up a second. Listen to me. This is important."

She heard a yawn and a muttering as someone asked Scott a question.

"Cindy – a candidate. It's OK," he said. Another yawn. A breathing into the phone as Scott apparently moved to another room. A "whuff" as Scott apparently sat down in a chair.

"OK, Cindy. I'm awake. At four twenty-four in the morning. What do you need? Don't tell me you're pulling out."

"Exactly the opposite," she said. "Pacifico had a serious heart attack. CNN is reporting that he's in a Philly hospital. They quoted a doctor who said his condition is critical and he won't be able to campaign or anything. He's out, Scott."

A long silence.

"Cindy. You would not, absolutely not, bullshit me about something like this, would you?"

"Oh my god, Scott. You know me by now! Would I call you at four in the morning and kid around about something like this?"

"Is the report reliable?"

"It was on CNN. Lead story at the top of the hour. Ev called me."

Long silence.

"OK," Scott said. "Hold with me here a minute. If Pacifico's out, then ... then we're in pretty damn good shape."

"Exactly," Cindy said. "Scott, I know there isn't much money. But if we ever needed to pour it on with TV and radio, this is it."

"Cindy, we can't afford TV. And in three days? We don't have time to –"

"Scott, do you want to have a Green Party senator in Washington or not? This is decision time. If you're serious, then it's time to call in all your gold coins, every favor you're owed. It's time to make some promises if you have to. It's time to put every dime we can scrounge up into this campaign. This is ... this is the kind of thing that happens once in a hundred years in American politics. Scott, this is the kind of event that can change everything."

"Cindy, I ...."

"Scott, I have about a hundred grand in the bank. I was going to live on it when I lost, but it's yours. I'll close the account. It won't carry us through a full media blitz, but it's a start. If you can round up another fifty, that can get us on the Philly and Pittsburgh TV and radio stations. They'll tape the ads in a hurry if we hand them a hundred and fifty grand over the next three days. We need to saturate those markets with ads that point out how close the Green Party's stands are to the Democrats'. The ads need to be tasteful – we need to be careful not to cast any aspersions on Pacifico, but we need to tell people that if they can't vote for Pacifico and they sure as hell aren't going to vote for Walker, then we – me – I – am the logical choice. We need to –"

"Cindy, you said 'hell.'" Scott said.

"Scott! This is no time to worry about my language!"

"Cindy, calm down. I'm sorry. I'm just kidding. I'm still trying to wake up." He yawned. "I agree that this is a once-in-a-lifetime shot. I'll get on the phones first thing in the morning and round up some support. There are some people who owe us. And –"

"Scott, no, call them now. As soon as you hang up with me. Wake them up. Impress on them how important this is. How we can't afford to waste a minute. This is history textbook stuff. Tell them – if they want a Green Party senator, then they need to cough up cash now. Nothing else will do. It's that simple and that bold – right now, we need money. No promises. Nothing else will do. Cash. Now. Today."

"Cindy, you amaze me," Scott said.

"And we need to have a strategy session. As soon as possible. In a few hours, if we can pull it together. On your end, you need to pull in Willard, or whatever his name is, the chairman, and Rick, and a couple of your big rainmakers. And your volunteer coordinator. We need to fire up the grassroots. We're going to need someone at every polling place in the state handing out my pamphlets. I'll get my staff together. We should conference call on this no later than six a.m."

"In two hours?"

"Scott!"

"OK, OK, I get it. I'm with you," Scott said. "I can see where this is going."

"Where this is going is right to Capitol Hill, if we can get ourselves organized and get some ads on the air."

"Cindy, we first need to confirm Pacifico's condition. As soon as I can do that, I promise, I'll put the machine in motion. Where are you?"

"I'm at a motel in Allentown. I'm headed down to Philly tomorrow. Rick knows where I am. So does Ev. She's over in the 'burgh. Carl is with her."

"OK, Cindy, let me make some calls and I'll get back to you as soon as I can. Then we'll get this moving. Keep your cell phone charged."

"Thanks, Scott. I'll talk to you soon."

"OK, Cindy, goodbye."

He moved to hang up the phone but heard her say, "Scott?" He put the phone back to his ear.

"Cindy?"

"This is it, Scott. We can win this now. Win, not just show. You believe that, don't you?"

Scott was silent for a few moments.

"Cindy, I believe that if anyone on the planet can pull this off, it's you."

"I need you one-hundred percent behind me."

"I know you do. And I'm there. I promise."

"OK. Thank you."

After Scott hung up with Cindy, he sat for a moment, thinking. Then he shook his head and chuckled. He dialed a number from memory.

The rough voice that answered after two rings did not sound at all sleepy.

"It's true," the voice said before Scott could introduce himself. "I'm at the hospital now. Pacifico is in critical condition and is hooked to every machine they've got. The entire family and campaign staff is here. There are Cadillacs filling the parking garage and dark suits clogging the whole floor. Everyone's either crying or pissed off. It doesn't look good. He's not going anywhere any time soon unless it's up to see St. Peter."

"Anything else I should know?" Scott asked.

"Nothing dirty about it. He was at home, in bed, sleeping, with his wife when it happened. She called 911."

"And there's no question – he's out of the picture?"

"He's out. You can assume that he's either disabled or dead."

"OK. Thanks."

"You're welcome."

"Before you go, one quick question. You told me once that a fifty will get you a lot of info. But how the hell do you get your info when you're talking to doctors? A fifty is pocket change to them."

The cigarette-rough voice on the other end of the line chuckled. "You should know by now. You never go for the guys at the top. They never know what the hell is going on. They just think they do. At a business, you talk to secretaries. At a hospital, you talk to orderlies. Janitors. Bedpan changers. Those people are invisible, but they're at the scene and they've got eyes."

"And, I assume, they know a critical patient when they see one," Scott said.

Another chuckle. "You get the right person, they've seen it all. They might be invisible, but they're not stupid."

"As usual, your services have been ... indispensable. Thank you. Oh, and nice work on that photo. I hear that the Democrats loved it."

"No problem."

Scott hung up and took a deep breath. After years of eking out the smallest gains, celebrating city council and school board elections, he was finally presented with a huge prize: The election of a Green Party candidate to the United States Senate. No Green Party organization in any state had yet managed to accomplish that. Scott knew that if Cindy got into office, he would be a national hero. There would be plenty of praise to go around. There would be invitations to speak, there would be phone calls from people he respected and admired ... there would be new opportunities. He took a deep breath. If Cindy gets in ... the whole world would be different. Brighter. Bigger.

So it was time to get busy. He began looking up names in his phone. Cindy was right. It was time to get this ball rolling, even if it was nearly five a.m.

Chapter Seventy-One

Walker was wrestling with his tie when the phone rang.

He glanced at his wife, who was still snoring.

"Frieda, get that," he yelled.

The tie refused to cooperate. The knot was all crooked.

The phone rang again.

"Frieda, get the goddamn phone!" he yelled as he unknotted the tie and started again. The phone rang.

"For chrissakes, Frieda, will you get the goddamned phone!" he yelled.

He was just about to fling the tie and go find Frieda when she appeared in the doorway.

"For you, senator. Very important."

"Next time, answer the goddamn phone before it rings off the hook," he said.

"Yessir," she said, lowering her eyes. "I am sorry, sir."

Walker waved her away. He walked to the bedside table and snatched up the receiver.

"What?"

"Pacifico had a heart attack at two a.m. He's a vegetable. He's out."

"What?"

"He's done. He's out. He's everything but dead."

Walker was silent a moment, thinking.

"Then we're in."

"Some people will vote for a dead guy. So some will vote for him regardless. But, yeah, I'd say you're in."

"What happens if people turn stupid and elect a dead guy?"

"Well, he's not dead yet from what I understand. But if the voters elect someone who cannot serve, then the governor appoints someone until a special election is called."

A broad smile spread across Walker's face.

"So, old Briggs will get to appoint someone? Huh. Good goddamn thing I gave him all that money and talked to his fat-assed wife."

"Yes, that turned out to be a good move."

"So, let me get this straight. If I win, I win. If Pacifico wins, I get appointed."

"Well, there might be some fuss about appointing a Republican if a Democrat won."

"Oh, come on! We've got more pull than that with a Republican governor!"

"True. It would be hard not to appoint a three-term incumbent from the governor's own party. I'll make some calls, but I think we're in good shape. Congratulations, senator. Welcome to your fourth term."

"Nice way to start my day. Thanks for the call."

"Don't stop campaigning. And for god's sake don't say anything remotely derogatory about Pacifico."

"All right. Thanks for the info. Talk to you."

Walker hung up and began whistling.

"What was that all about?" asked his sleepy wife from the rumpled bed.

"Oh, just the sweet sound of victory," Walker said, selecting a new tie. "The sound of Senator Walker's fourth term gearing up."

"That's nice," his wife said, turning back to her pillow. "Then we won't have to move. I would hate to have to find another caterer."

Chapter Seventy-Two

Cindy was navigating through Philadelphia, looking for a senior center where she was supposed to deliver a last-minute speech, when she found herself in the midst of a medical complex of gleaming white-and-glass buildings.

"Liberty Memorial Medical Services Complex" read a tasteful and professional blue-on-white sign.

Oh my, she thought. *This is where Pacifico is.*

Spotting a parking garage, she pulled inside. She had to drive four levels deep before she found a spot. Without knowing why, she exited her car and found her way to the elevator.

She rode it up to the main floor, stepped out into a lobby and located what must be the main reception desk. A ceiling of blue glass and white struts soared above her in the huge and brightly lit lobby. She approached the round desk. A woman in a blue suit and very professional looking hair bun said, "May I help you, ma'am?"

"I ... I was wondering if I could talk to someone from Mayor Pacifico's family," Cindy said, feeling stupid even as she spoke the words. *They're not going to be here. It's three o'clock in the afternoon.*

"Are you a family member, ma'am?" the woman asked with a professional minimalist smile and tilt of her well-formed head.

"No. But I'm ... I'm running against ...." *That sounds stupid.* "I'm a candidate for the U.S. Senate like Mr. Pacifico was. Is." She winced. "I just ... I'd just like to ... it would be nice if I ....." She shuddered to a halt, the woman's clear gaze on her.

"You're running against Mr. Pacifico, is that right?" the woman asked. "To be a senator?"

Cindy nodded, unwilling to trust her voice again.

"You must be Cynthia Phillips," the woman said.

Cindy was stunned.

"I, well, yes," she said.

The woman smiled and put out her hand. Campaign mode took over and Cindy took it and shook professionally.

"I've heard a lot about you," the woman said. "I think it would be great if you won and that nasty Walker had to retire."

"Why thank you," Cindy said. "That's ... very nice to hear here in Philadelphia."

"You have a lot more support than you think," the woman said, "especially with women."

She picked up a white phone.

"Let me buzz the room, Miss Phillips. I'll see what I can do."

"Thank you so much."

"Not at all." The woman turned her attention to the phone for a few seconds, then said, "May I speak with Mrs. Pacifico, please? This is the reception desk."

She looked up at Cindy and smiled, then looked down.

"Mrs. Pacifico? This is Melissa at the reception desk. I have a Miss Cindy Phillips here who wishes to meet with you. Yes, that Cindy Phillips. Would you be able to give her a minute? Yes? OK. Shall I send her up or...? OK.... OK.... OK. Thank you, Mrs. Pacifico."

The woman hung up and looked at Cindy.

"They'd like you to go up." She stood and pointed to a brushed-aluminum bank of elevators across the gleaming, white-tiled lobby. "Over there. Take an elevator to the sixteenth floor. There's security, but I'll buzz them and let them know you're on your way."

"I can't thank you enough," Cindy said. "You've been so helpful."

"You know," the woman said, "up till right now, I was kind of thinking about not voting at all. Or voting for Mr. Pacifico anyway. But seeing you show up here like this, well ...." she looked into Cindy's eyes. "You coming to pay your respects to your opponent like this is really impressive. Miss Phillips, you've got my vote."

"Thank you very much," Cindy said automatically. "Thank you for your support."

"Not at all," the woman said. "And you can be sure I'll tell everyone I know how you showed up here."

Then Cindy was walking across the lobby toward the elevators, her thoughts trying desperately to catch up with events.

The elevator reached the sixteenth floor and gave a self-satisfied ping. She stepped out and was immediately met by a large blonde man in a dark-blue security uniform. He had a walkie-talkie out and was speaking into it. He held up his free hand to stop Cindy.

"Yeah. Got it. Right. She's here," he said. He hung the walkie-talkie on his belt and gestured to Cindy. She followed him through a set of wide beige double doors, down a long hallway and to a large patient room. The security guard stood aside and gestured for her to enter.

In the room, the wall opposite the door was a huge pane of glass with a spectacular view of the city. The room was furnished like a hotel room, with muted earth tones. The only jarring note was the white linoleum floor.

On a hospital bed was a figure barely recognizable as the energetic Mayor Pacifico. His silver hair was flattened and oily looking. He looked terribly thin. He was surrounded by and hooked to a variety of machines with blinking lights, subdued beeps and hissing noises. His eyes were closed and the only movement he made was a slow rising and falling of his chest.

At the foot of the bed were two chairs. In one slouched a young man with a Sicilian's olive skin tone. The other chair was immediately vacated by a surprisingly short woman with dark hair and bright red lipstick. The woman rushed to Cindy, her arms spread. Cindy accepted the embrace and the one-cheek, other-cheek Italian-style greeting. The woman smelled of expensive perfume.

She was dressed in a sensible dark blue dress with a knitted shawl over her shoulders. As she pulled back, Cindy could see that the woman's eyes were bloodshot, but her face was welcoming.

"Oh, thank you dear, thank you so much for coming. You don't know how much it means to me that you would stop and see us," the woman said.

The woman stepped back, but kept hold of Cindy's hands.

"So this is the famous Cindy Phillips," the woman said. "I must get a good look at you."

The young man had shoved himself to his feet and stood behind the woman.

"Miss Phillips, oh, my manners!" The woman let go of Cindy and moved aside so that she could introduce the young man.

"Miss Phillips, this is my son Donato junior. He's as delighted that you are here as I am."

Cindy put out her hand. "Mr. Pacifico," she said.

The young man's lips twisted into a wry smile. "Mr. Pacifico is over there. I'm Donny," he said.

"Donny. Pleased to meet you," Cindy said. His grip was firm and cool. His eyes went to his mother, then back to Cindy.

"Likewise," he said.

Introductions over, Mrs. Pacifico grabbed Cindy's elbow and directed her to the bedside. Donny returned to his chair. At the bedside, Mrs. Pacifico's manner became subdued.

"He rests so peacefully," she said, grasping Cindy's hand. Cindy returned her clasp.

Mrs. Pacifico gazed at her still and silent husband.

"You know, he really is a wonderful man," she said.

"I have heard nothing but good things about him," Cindy said, groping for the right words. "I wish I had been able to meet him." As soon as she spoke in the past tense, she was terrified that she had said exactly the wrong thing. But Mrs. Pacifico grasped her hand more tightly and sighed.

"Yes, you two would have had much to talk about, wouldn't you have?"

She looked up at Cindy. Cindy could see tears welling in her eyes.

"They say that he's ... gone," Mrs. Pacifico said. "Thirty-three years of marriage. Three-and-a-third decades of married happiness. All I ever wanted in a man, a husband and a partner. And now ...." she turned and looked back at the man on the bed. "In one night, with no chance to say goodbye, he's gone. Taken from me."

It seemed very natural for Cindy to turn and hug Mrs. Pacifico. The older woman sobbed once, then detached herself from Cindy and pulled out a lacy handkerchief to dab at her eyes.

"Oh, yes, those we love can be taken from us so suddenly," she said. "So suddenly."

She gazed another moment at her fallen husband, then turned to Cindy and said, "Well! We mustn't dwell on what we cannot change. Please, come sit and talk with me. I am dying to hear all about you. How interesting you must be! I understand you've been working very hard to get elected."

Mrs. Pacifico and Cindy walked to the foot of the bed, where Donny pulled up chairs for them both. Cindy sat down, smiling her gratitude at Donny. He gave her another of his wry smiles. He scooted his chair nearer to his father, removing himself from the conversation.

"So," Mrs. Pacifico said when they were both seated, "You simply must tell me all about yourself. I have been so impressed by your campaign. You've been working very hard, I know. And your message on child abuse – well. It's about time that someone started that conversation." She tucked her hankie into a sleeve and turned her attention to Cindy.

"Well," Cindy said, "I don't know how much there is to say."

"Oh, do tell me, please," Mrs. Pacifico said. "What made you decide to run for office? It's such a terribly difficult thing to do. So disruptive to one's life. You must have a goal. Do tell me!"

"Well, to be honest, there was this little girl," began Cindy.

Two hours later, she left the hospital nearly too stunned to find her car. It seemed like a lifetime since she had impulsively pulled into the parking garage, thinking that she would make a quick courtesy visit to the Pacifico bedside. Instead, she found a composed and intelligent woman who was handling in a very graceful manner one of the worst things that could happen to her.

As she started the Crown Vic, she thought about Mrs. Pacifico's loss. And just like when she thought about the children, the tears came. She put the car back in park and sat quietly, sobbing, for two minutes. Then she wiped her eyes, put her car in gear and called Scott to apologize for missing the planned speech.

PACIFICO WIFE URGES VOTE FOR PHILLIPS
PHILADELPHIA (AP) – Lucinda Pacifico, wife of stricken Mayor Donato Pacifico, is urging voters to elect Green Party candidate Cynthia Phillips in tomorrow's general election.

"I have met and talked with Miss Phillips," Mrs. Pacifico said in a press conference called late yesterday. "She is a fine woman, a fine candidate and she shares the sensibility and ethics of my brave and wonderful husband."

Mrs. Pacifico made the remarks following Phillips' visit to the hospital room where the mayor remains unconscious and in critical condition following his heart attack two days ago.

"Miss Phillips was kind enough to drive all the way over here from Altoona just to pay her respects and offer her best wishes to my husband and our family," said Mrs. Pacifico. "I think that alone entitles Miss Phillips to the respect of her fellow Pennsylvanians."

Mrs. Pacifico went on to say that she had a "pleasant conversation" with Phillips during the three-hour visit and that she found Phillips to be an "intelligent, lively and well-informed young lady."

"Pennsylvania could certainly do much worse than having a senator with Miss Phillips' energy and character," Mrs. Pacifico said.

The mayor remains unconscious in a critical state and doctors are not sure when, if ever, he will emerge. His heart attack three days before the election sent Pennsylvania's politics into a spin. Democrat Pacifico had pulled neck-and-neck with three-term incumbent Robert Walker, a Republican who sits as the chairman of the Senate's powerful Appropriations Committee in Washington, D.C.

During his campaign, Pacifico had portrayed Walker as an out-of-touch power-hungry politician who has neglected his home state. Pacifico had presented evidence that Walker's alleged home in Pennsylvania, a house in an upscale Pittsburgh neighborhood, had flooded two years ago but Walker hadn't known about the incident for weeks because he no longer lived there.

"My opponent lives in Washington D.C.'s fanciest restaurants and on the corporate jets and limos of the richest lobbyists," Pacifico had charged shortly before his illness.

Walker's campaign responded that the incumbent's power and prestige in Washington were put to good use for Pennsylvania, bringing in jobs and government contracts for businesses.

In recent weeks, Pacifico's charges seemed to grab the attention of Pennsylvanians. Pacifico rose rapidly in the polls to tie Walker, each at 48 percent in a poll just a day before Pacifico's heart attack.

Chapter Seventy-Three

Evelyn came up behind Cindy, who was sitting in front of one of the three huge television sets provided by the Harrisburg-area hotel where the Green Party's hastily arranged victory party was being held.

Cindy still couldn't bring herself to trust the numbers. The polls had closed at 8 p.m. Right now, at 11:17 p.m., the news channel was showing a picture of her over a picture of Walker, and beneath him, a photo of Pacifico. The numbers to the right of the pictures were:

Cynthia Phillips – G: 43%

Robert Walker – R (I): 40%

Donato Pacifico – D: 17%

87% of precincts reporting.

Surely they have the numbers screwed up, Cindy thought. *Any minute now, they're going to come on the air and correct their mistake.*

Behind Cindy, the hotel's ballroom was filled with chattering Green Party members and hangers-on. People, drinks in hand, stood around round tables covered with white tablecloths and sprinkled with green-and-white glittering stars. Green and white "Phillips for Senator" banners had been stuck on the walls.

Around Cindy, who was sitting in a padded metal-frame chair before the televisions, was a semi-circle of space. No one approached her until Evelyn did.

"Cindy," Evelyn said, putting her hand on Cindy's shoulder.

"Ev," Cindy said.

"Cindy," Evelyn said gently. "They want you to make a speech."

Cindy didn't move.

"Cindy," Evelyn said again. "The war room just reported in with the latest exit polls. You've won. He's going to get a few more precincts in the hinterlands, but you took Philly by storm. You almost took Pittsburgh. Cindy. You won."

Cindy turned to look at Evelyn. Her eyes were unfocused.

"Cindy," Evelyn said, putting her hands on Cindy's shoulders. "You won. You did it."

"But ... results are still coming in ... it's still early," Cindy protested.

"Come on, girl!" Evelyn said. "You know how this stuff works. Remember Polls and Election Stats? It's impossible for Walker to win now. Even if he wins every uncounted vote from here on out, he can't beat you. There just aren't enough votes left for him to catch up to you. You did it. You kicked his ass."

Cindy closed her eyes. "Then it's over."

"Actually, it's just beginning," Evelyn said. "And I have to ask...."

"Yes, Ev?"

Evelyn took a deep breath.

"Have you given any thought to your choice of chief of staff, Senator Phillips?"

GREEN PARTY WINS STUNNING VICTORY

HARRISBURG (AP) – In an unpredictable turn of events, Green Party candidate for U.S. senator Cynthia Phillips defeated three-term incumbent Robert Walker for one of Pennsylvania's U.S. Senate seats.

The Phillips victory follows Democratic candidate and Philadelphia Mayor Donato Pacifico's massive heart attack three days before the election.

Political analysts across the state attributed the Phillips victory to requests from the Pacifico family that Pennsylvanians vote for Phillips. Pacifico's wife Lucinda held a press conference the day before the election and urged Pennsylvanians to cast their votes for Phillips.

"Phillips was in a lot better shape once Pacifico was out of the picture," said University of Pennsylvania political science professor Terry Sinese. "But the endorsement of Mrs. Pacifico put her over the top."

In polls a week before the election, and before Pacifico's heart attack, Phillips had registered just over two percent in the polls. Pacifico and Walker had tied at 48 percent each in the same poll.

Tuesday, Phillips defeated Walker 43 percent to 40 percent, which analysts described as a "solid" margin. Pacifico, although still in critical condition in a hospital bed, won 17 percent.

Phillips' victory is the first time in United States history that a Green Party candidate has been elected to a federal-level office.

Phillips' campaign staff and Green Party officials described themselves as "elated" with the victory.

"Senator-elect Cindy Phillips represents the absolute best of the Green Party," said Phillips Campaign Manager Scott Rivers. "Miss Phillips and the Green Party believe that people, not corporations, should control the political process. Miss Phillips will prove to be an outstanding senator for the people of Pennsylvania and a voice of sanity in Washington, D.C."

The candidate, who Rivers said has spent more than a year on the road meeting "ordinary Pennsylvanians," was unavailable for comment.

The Walker campaign did not return calls asking for comment.

Chapter Seventy-Four

"Well, fuck me," Walker said. "It looks like this might work."

He leaned back in his black leather chair and put his hands behind his head. His tie was loose and his white dress shirt was wrinkled. In front of him, scattered across his senator's desk, were papers with columns of numbers, scribblings, assorted pencils, coffee mugs and a bag spilling Doritos. On the other side of his desk, the young man had removed his jacket, rolled up his sleeves and loosened his tie. In front of him was a laptop computer displaying columns of numbers.

"It'll work," the young man said. "We'll have to make a few phone calls this week."

"So, what should we call ourselves?" Walker asked. "Political Consultants and Lobbyists, Inc.?"

"Too literal," the young man said, leaning back. "How about we name it like a law firm. Walker, Dewey, Cheatem and Howe, that kind of thing."

"Speaking of lawyers," Walker said, "we're going to need a good one. Any ideas? How about Meyers, the committee's counsel?"

"He won't budge," the young man said. "He's set where he is. Besides, I'm not sure that he has the ... uh, aggressiveness that we'll need."

Walker looked at the ceiling and pondered.

"What about Mullen, the hatchet man for what's-his-name, the asshole who wrote that ag bill that gave Montana farmers two hundred million bucks to treat their cow manure?"

The young man laughed. "No way. Mullen knows he's on the way up with Senator DeMasters. He's thinking about being attorney general one day. On good nights, he dreams about the Supreme Court. He's not going to leave that possibility behind."

"Shit," Walker said, bringing his gaze back to the young man. "President DeMasters. Ha! Oh well. Doesn't matter. We'll find someone."

"If we can find the right guy, all we have to do is dangle this payday in front of him," the young man said, tapping the laptop.

"Damn straight," Walker said. "The lobbyist business pays a hell of a lot better than being a senator. And without all the hassles about goddamn rules of order."

"And those annoying elections."

Walker snorted. "Yeah. No more baby-kissing. Thank god."

"From here on out, it's just ass-kissing," the young man said, grinning.

Chapter Seventy-Five

"I know this building!" Cindy said as the cab she was riding in approached the office building she had been assigned to.

"Russell Senate Office Building," Evelyn said. "You recognize it from Mr. Smith Goes to Washington."

"I didn't realize ... I didn't make the connection," Cindy said, staring at the building in amazement.

"Which entrance you want?" the cabbie asked.

"Constitution, Northeast," Evelyn said before Cindy could open her mouth.

"You got it," the cabbie said and began nosing a lane closer to the building.

"It's a very ... handsome building," Cindy said.

"First stone was laid in 1906," Ev said. As usual, she had done her homework. "Named for Senator Richard Russell Junior, a Democrat from Georgia who served almost 40 years in the Senate. There's a statue of him in the rotunda. And wait till you see the Caucus Room. McCarthy and Watergate hearings were held there."

"No way!" Cindy said, amazed.

"You've never been down here to see this?" Ev asked.

"Never," Cindy said. "Not this building, any-way. When I came down here, it was always for the usual suspects: The White House, Washington Monument, Lincoln Memorial."

"Southwest entrance, closest to the Capitol," the cabbie said as he stopped, double-parked. "Eighteen-fifty, ladies."

Evelyn paid and tipped the driver as Cindy exited the cab, still staring at the huge building. It wasn't tall, but seemed as massive and permanent as a mountain. From where Cindy stood on the sidewalk, the white walls of the building stretched away from her at an obtuse angle, almost running to their vanishing points. Greek-style columns ran the entire length of each wall. Between the pillars were tall, round-top, deep-set windows. Broad, shallow steps led to the entrance, a door that looked tiny in comparison to the scale of the rest of the building. On the roof, directly over the entrance, an American flag snapped in the winter wind. On the sidewalk, Cindy and Evelyn pulled their heavy coats tighter.

"Capitol is right behind us, back there," Evelyn said, jerking her thumb over her shoulder.

Cindy squinted. "Ahh. Yes. The capitol." She could see the famous dome.

Although she had been to Washington many times as a student, she couldn't imagine looking at the buildings as her workplace, where she would be reporting for work every day, walking the huge echoing hallways, answering the phone, eating lunch, spending most of her waking hours. The scale of the buildings in this part of town did not lend themselves to easy assimilation for one who had not grown up in a city. In Altoona, she had shared a tiny office with another caseworker in a fading 80-year-old building that had once been a rich merchant's house. The hallways had been narrow; the floors had squeaked under worn carpeting. This building, with its marble and pillars and grand scale and within sight of the Capitol, was in another universe.

It just doesn't seem real, Cindy thought. *Any moment now, some guy in a dark suit and sunglasses is going to jump out of a nondescript Ford four-door and tell me that there's been a terrible mistake and Walker won after all.*

"Brr. Awfully damn cold for Washington," Evelyn said, hinting.

"Well, it is January," Cindy said, pulling her gaze from the capitol and her thoughts from the strangeness of it all. "Although this is nothing compared to winter in Erie. The wind comes right off that lake and – whoo!"

"Well, let's get inside," Evelyn said.

"You have my room assignment?" Cindy asked.

Evelyn narrowed her eyes and pulled an envelope from inside her coat. "Right here, girl! You think I'd forget that?"

"Ev, thank god for you. Because you know that I'm perfectly capable of getting all the way down here and having no clue which room is mine."

"Well, I'm sure someone would be willing to help you, senator." Evelyn said.

"Stop it!" Cindy said. "I haven't been sworn in yet."

Evelyn shook her head. "When's it going to become real for you?" she asked as they walked up the broad, shallow white steps of the Russell building.

"At this rate, never," Cindy said. "What have I ever done to prepare me for this?"

A man bundled in a trenchcoat and plaid scarf held the door for them. Both smiled their thanks as they stepped inside. Cindy was immediately lost again, staring up at the vast echoing space above her. The domed roof soared three stories above them. The huge round space was surrounded by layers of Greek-style columns with archways in between.

"It's like a ... wedding cake," she said to herself. "Or the Coliseum."

Across from her, twin broad marble staircases rose toward what Cindy abruptly recognized as the Caucus Room. Cindy, fascinated with the sights, almost walked past the series of desks and metal detector frames that restricted entrance into the rotunda. A polite young man in a Capitol police uniform stepped not quite in front of her and said, "Ma'am?"

"This is Senator-elect Phillips," Ev said, stepping forward. Hearing that title applied to her still made Cindy shiver. Even more than the buildings, it was unreal.

"I'm her chief of staff," Ev said and pulled out her ID badge. Ev's was on a chain around her neck. Understanding the situation now, Cindy fumbled for her badge, finally finding it in an inside pocket of her dress jacket. She didn't remember putting it there.

"My apologies," said the young officer after a glance at the badge. "I didn't recognize you, Senator Phillips." There was that spine tingle again.

"That's perfectly OK," Cindy said with a smile. "I'm new."

"Welcome," the young man said with a smile that seemed genuine.

"This is a … remarkable building," Cindy said. The officer took a moment to look up and around.

"It is," he agreed. "When you're here six hours a day, though, you kind of get used to it."

"Thank you, officer," Ev said and prodded Cindy forward. Cindy stopped, unsure if she had to go through the metal detector.

"Senators, staff and accredited journalists don't have to go through the detectors, Senator," the officer said. "Just show us your badge or your pin and we'll get you right through."

Cindy smiled a thank you as Evelyn skirted the detector and walked confidently toward a bank of elevators. Cindy followed, glancing back. The officer gave Cindy a small salute, then turned his attention to other people coming through the doors.

"I just can't get used to … to …"

"To what?" Ev asked as they walked, heels clicking, across the cavernous space. "To privilege?"

"That's the word!" Cindy said. Then, quietly, "I don't deserve any of this. This is crazy. I'm just Cindy Phillips. What the hell am I doing here?"

Evelyn stopped walking and turned on Cindy. Cindy stopped and noticed off to the side the statue of what must be the late Senator Russell. He looked like someone's grandfather in a suit and vest. One hand was in his pocket; the other was extended, palm out, at waist level. He looked like he was either asking for a handout or calmly explaining something. His ordinariness made her feel a tiny bit better.

"You do deserve to be here and don't you ever forget that," Evelyn said sternly, drawing Cindy's attention. Evelyn's eyes flashed. "You worked hard to get here. You won an election that no one thought you could. You have a mission. You have a reason to be here. All this ... fancy stuff like buildings with big domes and marble and polite security guards is just icing and fluff. It's just the way the game is played here. There's money here. Big deal. The real reason you're here is going to mean a lot of work. You should be grateful for little things like jumping right through security because you're going to need all your extra time to get the people here to pay attention to you. There's a lot going in this town and not everyone cares about abused children."

Evelyn looked at Cindy's face and detected anxiety. She softened her tone.

"Come on, Cindy! This is just the like the first day in high school. New building, you don't know where anything is, everyone's a stranger. It just takes some getting used to."

Ev smiled but Cindy sighed deeply. A tall man in a suit strode by, deep in conversation with what was apparently an aide. The aide was holding a piece of paper and stabbing at it with his finger. The tall man was shaking his head. Their voices were lost in the huge space.

"Ev, I just don't know if I can handle all this," Cindy said. "I mean, I don't know what I'm doing. I don't know the first thing about ... anything!"

"You think any first-term senator does?" Evelyn asked. "You're just feeling small because you're standing under that damn dome. Come on!" She pulled Cindy to the elevators and pushed the up button.

"Now, we're going to introduce you to your homeroom teacher. And we'll get you some nice, stiff jeans, some shiny white sneakers and a shirt with the tag still scratchy and you're going to feel right at home," Evelyn said.

Cindy cracked a smile. Evelyn laughed.

"Look. This is the greatest adventure that the two of us are ever going to have. We're in D.C.! We're going to meet famous and interesting people. We're going to make history here, girl!"

Cindy smiled as the elevator dinged and its doors rumbled open, disgorging a pack of people all in suits, all talking. They poured out of the elevator, still talking, separated to go around Cindy and Evelyn and kept walking, splitting off in pairs and threes, going in different directions.

Cindy and Evelyn stepped on the elevator and were joined by two gray-haired men in dark suits, white shirts and striped ties. They were talking low and seriously and didn't even seem to notice that they had company. One of the men pushed the elevator button for the third floor without look-ing. They muttered. Cindy tried to hear, but they seemed expert at talking just low enough that oth-ers couldn't understand them.

The elevator dinged twice, the doors slid open and Evelyn pulled Cindy out of the elevator. They stood in a long, broad hallway lined with wooden doors and marble panels.

"All the way at the end, on the right," Evelyn said. They began walking. Cindy saw that each door had a window of old-fashioned translucent glass. Light came through but the pane wasn't transparent. On the pane was, in gold leaf, "The Honorable," then the name of a senator and his home state and an office number. Some of the doors were open; most were closed. The few peeks she could sneak looked like the interior of any older office build-ing, although with fancy wood trim and big win-dows looking into a courtyard.

"And here we are!" Evelyn said. She unfolded an envelope and two brass keys fell out. Cindy looked at the door. The room on the other side was dark. The office was the next-to-the-last one in the row. A nearby door lead to a staircase.

There was no lettering on her door. Evelyn unlocked it and pushed it open. The door opened into a rectangular room furnished with a wooden desk, three sturdy wooden chairs with leather seats, floor-to-ceiling bookshelves on one wall and a window overlooking the street. The carpet was a royal red. The walls were off-white and showed fine cracks in some locations. In two corners of the room, flanking the window, stood flagpoles.

One bore the United States flag; the other was bare. There were two doors, one on each side of the room.

"Cozy!" Evelyn said and flipped two light switches near the door. The lights hummed, buzzed, then snapped on.

"I could have had a bigger office," Cindy said. "But it would have been about a hundred miles from the Capitol. Everyone told me to take the smaller office that's closer."

"Good choice," Evelyn said. "We like older stuff anyway, right? Tradition."

The desk in the room had a blotter and a complicated looking telephone on it.

"Receptionist sits here," Ev said, walking behind the desk. He shoes tapped over a large piece of heavy plastic laid over the carpet. The room had a furniture-polish smell, not unpleasant. Evelyn walked to one of the doors at the side of the room. It swung open to reveal a small office with two desks and two chairs but no window. Three filing cabinets stood in row along one wall.

"Aides in there," Evelyn said. She walked across the main office to the other door. It opened into a larger room, paneled in dark wood. A large window overlooked the same street as the main room. There was a huge desk with a shiny top. Two naked flagpoles behind the desk flanked a credenza that matched the desk. A marble fireplace with an ornate mantel dominated the far wall. "And you're in here," Ev said.

"And so are you," Cindy said, pointing to the other side of the room where a smaller but still ornate desk shared a corner with a bookshelf. Tellingly, the big desk had one simple phone on top. The smaller desk across the room had two phones.

Evelyn pulled out the big leather chair behind the large desk.

"Come on!" she said. "Have a seat!"

"I feel like I'm sneaking into an uncle's private library," Cindy said, walking cautiously across the room.

"Get used to it," Evelyn said. "We're going to be spending a lot of time in here."

Cindy hesitated, then sat carefully in the big black leather chair. It was remarkably comfortable.

"How's it feel?" Ev asked.

"Good," Cindy said. "Well padded."

"See?" Evelyn said. "You're right where you belong."

Chapter Seventy-Six

"**R**eady?" the senior senator from Pennsylvania asked her. He was a tall man with short, dark, neatly combed hair who seemed too young to be a senator. His suit was immaculate; his shirt was blindingly white and his power tie was deep blue with crimson diagonal stripes. Cindy was pretty sure that the suit-and-tie combo cost as much as the weekly wages of a lot of people in Altoona.

She knew the young senator's record. He was a rock-solid conservative in his second term. Cindy thought of all the terms she had heard applied to him. Fast-riser in the party. Friend of the current administration. Up-and-comer. Mover and shaker. A conservative's conservative. Presidential material, it had even been whispered. Some terms were less than complimentary; those were from liberals and Democrats. Wingnut. Religious whacko. Obsessed. Power-hungry. Inflexible. Puritanical.

But he had been a perfect gentleman to her. In fact, the first congratulatory call that she received the night of the election was from him. He had been courteous and had wished her well and said that he was looking forward to working with her. Given the very different agendas of the Green Party and the Republicans, she doubted that was true. But right now, in the Senate chamber, he was treating her as a complete equal. His smile seemed genuine.

"Ready," Cindy said as firmly as she could, although she detected a waver in her voice. She hoped he didn't notice.

The senator put out an elbow clad in deep blue fabric. Cindy hooked her arm through his and they began the slow walk down the royal blue carpet of the majestic Senate chamber, past row after row of absurdly small wooden desks. Cindy had never seen so much polished wood, not even in church. She felt like she was walking down a wedding aisle. That made her think of Frank, which gave her a pang, so she quickly dropped the thought and focused on the here-and-now.

At the end of the carpet, at the front of the room, the vice president of the United States stood in front of what looked like a large and very ornate judge's bench. Cindy had never seen him except in photos and on TV. *He looks shorter and chubbier in person,* she thought. He watched them as they approached. A few feet from the vice president, the senior senator gracefully released her. Cindy took three steps and stood before the vice president. He looked at her with calm and watery blue eyes. He gave her just the hint of a nod.

"Senator-elect Phillips. Greetings." He smiled. "Are you ready to make it official?"

She smiled. "Yes, sir, I am."

"Then raise your right hand, please," he asked and his smile vanished. His aura became serious. He raised his right hand.

Cindy raised her right hand and put her left onto the fat black Bible resting on a skinny dark wood pedestal between them. The vice president put his left hand on top of hers. His hand was warm and dry. She wondered what would have happened if she had insisted on swearing on the Book of Wicca or something. Could they refuse to swear her in?

"Repeat after me, please," the vice president said. She noticed, now that she was close, that his teeth were yellowish and his tie actually looked a little frayed at the knot. Maybe it's his favorite and he wears it all the time, she thought. But surely the vice president can afford a closet full of ties. She was worried about her own wardrobe, worn thin and thready from more than a year on the road. The pantyhose that she had on were her only pair without conspicuous holes.

"I do solemnly swear that I will support and defend the Constitution of the United States against all enemies, foreign and domestic ...." The vice president said, speaking slowly and carefully.

"I, Cynthia A. Phillips, do solemnly swear that I will support and defend the Constitution of the United States against all enemies, foreign and domestic," Cindy repeated. She had memorized the oath but let the vice president do it his way.

This can't be real, a part of her brain whispered. *Who are you? You're a caseworker from Altoona. You can't really be just about to be sworn in as a United States senator. Something is wrong. A giant fraud has occurred.*

She ignored the voice. She did not want to screw up the oath.

"...That I will bear true faith and allegiance to the same...."

"That I will bear true faith and allegiance to the same."

Senators have to know so much, she thought. *My god, they have to know about foreign policy. What do I know about foreign policy? Exactly zip. I couldn't find Afghanistan on a map.*

"...That I take this obligation freely, without any mental reservation or purpose of evasion...."

"That I take this obligation freely, without any mental reservation or purpose of evasion."

Does doubting that you can do the job amount to "mental reservation"?

"...And that I will well and faithfully discharge the duties of the office on which I am about to enter, so help me God."

"And that I will well and faithfully discharge the duties of the office of which I am about to enter. So help me God."

And then it was over. The vice president smiled, lowered and offered his hand. She shook it, feeling dazed but keeping her smile intact. *Thank heaven for campaign mode,* she thought.

"Welcome, Senator Phillips," he said.

"Thank you, sir," she said.

Dear god, she thought. *Now it's official. Now I really am Senator Phillips.* She suddenly felt as if she had undertaken a huge obligation, signed for a loan far beyond her ability to repay.

She turned and the senior senator was waiting for her. He smiled again. They again hooked arms and he walked her slowly back up the carpet. "Congratulations and welcome," he whispered just as they broke apart upon reaching the cluster of other senators waiting to take the oath. Two more lined up, a senior and a newbie, ready to take the long walk that transformed a citizen into a legislator.

Cindy looked up to the balcony where visitors could watch the ceremony. Evelyn and Cindy's foster parents were there. Her foster father's arm was around her foster mother, who was dabbing at her eyes with a handkerchief. She gave a sideways wiggle of the cloth for a wave. Her foster father gave her the usual grinning thumbs-up. Ev was smiling her hundred-watt smile. Cindy's natural mother was not in the audience. Cindy had not seen her for years. She had no idea where her stepfather was.

Cindy smiled up at her foster parents, grateful that they were there, grateful that someone cared, that someone was willing to drive five hours to watch her in a 30-second ceremony. The other new senators all had family members watching from the balcony. Cindy was glad that she too had people to share the moment. She only wished that Dr. Jacobi could have been there. But as always when she took a big step, she could feel his arm around her shoulders and the whisper in her ear: *Go get them, girl. Show them what you can do.*

Go be a ballerina, she told herself.

Chapter Seventy-Seven

"**O**pen it!" Ev said. Cindy looked at the heavy rectangular package, wrapped in what looked like pages from the Washington Post but which was actually genuine wrapping paper, designed to look like the Washington Post. *How odd,* she thought. *If you wanted to wrap something in the Post, just use the actual paper. How like D.C. to make the simple complicated, to substitute the copy for the original.*

She smiled at Ev and tore the package open. It was, as she had suspected, a book. The book was called "The Congressional Deskbook." It was dense, heavy and thick.

"All the basics are in there," Evelyn said. "Committee structure, rules of order, budget processes, everything."

"Great," said Cindy, rolling her eyes. "That all sounds so thrilling."

Ev kept her smile. "You're going to master that stuff just like you mastered meet-and-greet," she said. "Believe me, there are senators whose IQs aren't much higher than a room temperature. You can handle it."

"It's a great book," Cindy said, slumping into her desk chair. "I'm sure it will be useful. It's just … There's so much to learn. And I have no idea where even to start."

"Best advice I heard was this," Evelyn said. "Spend your first year watching, observing and learning. Keep your mouth shut. Second time through, it'll all make more sense. Third year, you're comfortable. Fourth year, you're a pro. Fifth and sixth years … well, that's when you really get shit done."

"That sounds like a lot of waiting and watching," Cindy said.

"It is. But it's a big job. As you said, a lot to learn. And when you pounce, you want to have everything ready to go, right?"

"I guess."

"I wouldn't even think about making your maiden speech until your second year," Ev said. "In fact, that's kind of the standing tradition. Although it has been broken."

"Maiden speech?" Cindy asked. There was so much she didn't know. She was grateful for Evelyn's expertise, but knew that she couldn't rely on it forever. She was going to have to master this job or she would never accomplish her goal.

"Your first speech from the Senate chamber floor," Ev said. "It's a big event. Most people try to make sure that it's a meaningful speech on an important topic." She eyed Cindy. "My guess is that yours should be on child abuse."

"Well, yes, that would make sense," Cindy said. "And to be honest, it would be nice to not have to worry about making a speech that important for at least a year."

"Just don't think that you can blow it off until the last minute," Ev said. "Not that you're the sort of person to do that. You were quite a pain in the ass about preparation in college, if I remember. That study-nerd attitude will serve you well here."

Cindy smiled. "It's not that I like studying. I'm just not that smart. I needed a lot of prep time. You steel-trap-brain types can wait until the last minute to study. You and what was that guy's name – the big partier who said he never studied until the night before and then did so drunk?"

Evelyn snorted. "Skip. Yeah. Asshole. Anyway, the point is that even though there's going to be a lot of stuff to distract you, you're going to have to start planning that speech like tomorrow."

"Ev, please," Cindy said. "I can't even find this building by myself from our apartment yet. Can I have a few weeks before I need to start thinking about the most important speech of my political career?"

"Well, OK," Ev said, her eyes sparkling. "But in the meantime, we've got to staff this place up."

"Bring Carl on board. We already discussed that."

"OK. But you have a budget for a four-person staff. Besides me and Carl, you have room for a receptionist and one other aide."

"Any ideas?" Cindy asked.

"I've got plenty of those," Evelyn said. "Should I … reach out, as they say in this town?"

"Oh, by all means," said Cindy, rolling her eyes. "Reach out and touch anybody you want."

"I'll have a list ready for you tomorrow," Ev said. With a barely restrained grin, she added, "Senator."

Cindy opened her mouth to protest, then realized that she couldn't. "Oh, I'm not going to get used to that anytime soon," she said. She sat up and put her hand on Evelyn's, which was resting on the desk. "Promise me. Please. When it's just you and me, Ev, it's still just Cindy and Ev. Always. Just like in the dorm room at two a.m. with a six-pack and a pack of Skittles and a cheesy romance movie. Just Cindy and Ev."

Ev smiled and clasped Cindy's hand. "I promise. I'll quit teasing you. I'm really, really proud of you. But I promise – it's Cindy and Ev. Forever."

Cindy smiled her thanks. She felt grateful. She was glad for Evelyn's company and knowledge. But she still felt the weight on her shoulders that had descended as soon as she completed the oath. Twelve million people in her state and three hundred million across the country were counting on her to make their lives better and she had absolutely no idea how to do so or even where to begin.

Ev, who seemed to be able to read Cindy's mind, was looking at her intently.

"We'll do this our way, girl," she said. "Just like you got me through stats. One step at a time."

"One step at a time," Cindy agreed. "Our way."

Chapter Seventy-Eight

Grace VanHolden was stumped. The planned speaker for the annual dinner of the Kalamazoo County Women's Club, a local author of mystery novels, had just called and begged off. Claiming an unexpected demand from her publisher that required her presence in California, she apologized profusely and promised to speak at a future event.

Grace had been true to her name in dealing with the disappointment, but she was still stuck with an annual dinner and no interesting speaker to encourage people to buy $40 tickets to the event. The annual dinner was one of the club's primary fund-raisers. The club could not afford to call it off, and without an intriguing speaker, members couldn't be expected to sell enough tickets to make money, let alone break even.

Grace sighed as she reviewed the list of speakers available from the bureau she had contacted in desperation. Many of the speakers would be fascinating and a sure draw – but their fees put them far beyond the club's ability to pay. What the club needed, Grace knew, was someone who would speak for little or no fee on a topic that would draw people – especially women.

A prominent and flamboyant civil rights lawyer was available – for $25,000. An aging movie star with a reputation for wild flings was available – for $15,000. A famous female author would speak – for $10,000 and a stay in a four-star hotel. *Kalamazoo doesn't even have a four-star hotel*, Grace thought. She'd have to stay in Grand Rapids. *And then we'd have to drive her around … and she'd probably want a limo, not my Buick.*

Grace scrolled down the web page of the speaker's bureau. Toward the bottom of the list, the prices declined, but so did the fame and fascination factor of the speaker. Lots of academics: A professor would speak on string theory, whatever that was. Not worth $2,500. That was pushing the limits of what the club could pay and still make a profit. There were rehabilitated criminals: A Wall Street broker who found Jesus after he was caught bilking customers out of $200 million would speak on "What your broker isn't telling you, but God is." *Probably all the stuff you didn't tell your customers*, Grace thought. And there was just the bizarre: A former postal worker was willing to speak on "the confluence of government secret operations, the military-industrial complex and the control of America by the moneyed elite." *Snoozefest for sure*, Grace thought. And there was Theodore Roosevelt. Yes, back from the dead, apparently, he offered a combination of "motivational speaker and environmental enthusiast."

For $950. Even the postal guy wanted $250 and travel expenses.

With a feeling of despair, Grace clicked on a link to go to the "Budget-friendly speakers" section of the web site. She had no hopes for finding anything useful, but she wanted to exhaust the list before she complained to the speaker's bureau that none of its clients met her needs.

She scrolled through lists of unknown experts, obscure stars and washed-out clingers to fame. A title caught her eye: U.S. Senator. Senator? Grace stopped and examined the entry. As she read, her hopes rose that the speaker might just be a perfect match. A female U.S. senator, actively serving, would speak on "Child Abuse: Why it won't go away, why you should care and what you can do to help." *Well, that sounds perfect*, thought Grace. But surely the speaker was in the wrong place. A senator surely wouldn't speak for – Grace examined the speaker's compensation requirements – for travel and lodging fees alone? And she was willing to stay in a private home? Grace couldn't believe what she was reading. She knew that the women in her club and many of those in her community would be very interested in hearing a female senator speak, especially on such a relevant topic.

She scribbled down the speaker's name and picked up the telephone to call the speaker's bureau. Yes, they confirmed, Cynthia Phillips was a sitting senator from Pennsylvania. Yes, she would speak on child abuse. And yes, she requested only travel and lodging fees. And finally, crucially, yes, she was available on the night of the annual dinner.

Feeling as if she had found a Rembrandt in a thrift shop, Grace happily booked the senator. As she waited on the phone for confirmation from the bureau's customer service rep, she allowed herself to be proud of her discovery. She knew that her fellow club members would be thrilled. She imagined them asking her, Oh, how did you ever find such a perfect speaker? And she would smile and shrug.

"Oh, just a little Internet research," she would respond, modestly.

Chapter Seventy-Nine

"I'm going to break the cardinal rule of speech-making," Cindy said from the podium at the Kalamazoo County Women's Club. "I'm going to throw some statistics at you right off the bat."

She paused and smiled.

"My college speech prof would kill me," she said, "but these are a few numbers that might help put child abuse into perspective."

Her audience, about two hundred well-dressed women and a smattering of men, listened politely. On round tables before them were the remains of dessert and cups of coffee. The lights had been lowered. Cindy knew that the post-meal lassitude would soon set in so she had to make her point quickly.

"For credibility's sake, these figures come from The U.S. Department of Health and Human Services," Cindy said. "The department releases new child abuse statistics every April. The numbers are compiled from state reports." She gave a small smile. "Unfortunately, I'm not making these numbers up. Each day in the United States, more than four children die as a result of child abuse in the home. Last year, that meant that an estimated fifteen hundred children died of abuse and neglect. Let me repeat: one thousand, five hundred children died from abuse and neglect last year.

"More than three-quarters of the children who die are younger than four. Almost 90 percent were under the age of eight. That's deaths from abuse and neglect," Cindy said. "The number for kids who are abused but aren't killed is much higher. An estimated 906,000 children were victims of abuse and neglect last year. Yes, nine hundred and six thousand kids."

Cindy paused to let the numbers sink in.

"Bear with me for a few more seconds," she said. "Homicide is the leading cause of injury-related deaths of children under one year old. Overall, it is ranked 15th as the cause of infant deaths. The killer is typically the mother, father or stepfather. Infants are most likely to be killed by their mother during the first week of life. After that, the killer is more likely to be a father or stepfather.

"Last year, more than 2.9 million reports of possible child abuse were made to child protective services across the U.S. To put that number in perspective, on average, a case of potential child abuse is reported every 10 seconds. That's a lot," Cindy said. Heads around the room nodded.

"However, the actual incidence of abuse and neglect is estimated to be three times greater than the reported numbers." Cindy smiled. "That's because people don't always pick up the phone and make the call that they should. Now, I know everyone's feeling a little sleepy, so I'll do the math for you." There were chuckles around the room.

"Two-point-nine million actual reports times three is eight-point-seven million." She paused. "That means that there were probably nearly nine million incidents of abuse last year. Nearly nine million incidents."

Cindy surveyed the room which was silent except for the occasional clink of a stirring spoon.

"My managers at the speaker's bureau are always after me to be concise, precise and interesting," Cindy said. "Fortunately, given my subject matter, they don't expect me to be humorous." There were a few smiles. "So you'll be happy to know that the most boring part of my speech is over. I apologize for hitting you with all those numbers, but it is important that you have some perspective on the scope of the problem before I move on to the next section.

"Now, I must apologize in advance. For part two of my speech, I'm not going to play fair. I know that you are all responsible and respected members of the community here in Kalamazoo County. I'm sure that you all have your favorite charities and those organizations that you give money and time to."

Cindy smiled at Grace VanHolden.

"I know that this women's club does good works. But my message is simple: You aren't doing enough about child abuse. No one in this country is. The bad news is that the problem is not going to go away, ever. All we can do is hope to make it better; that is, have less child abuse going on. One good way to accomplish that is to have more severe punishments for the offenders. We also need to have more awareness by the general public of the problem, because there is a real cost to child abuse. That's part three of my speech and I'll get there in just a few minutes.

"Groups like this one are absolutely vital in the fight against child abuse because no one else is going to do anything about it. The children themselves cannot. By definition, they are victims. And obviously, children are not going to form action committees and hold fund-raising events. Your elected leaders are not going to do anything about child abuse without prodding. Why? Children can't vote. Worse, child abuse is not something that you can throw money at and then point to progress. It's not like building a bridge or a new highway or buying the military a thousand new tanks. All you have are numbers. Numbers like the ones I just gave you. And, unfortunately, most people have the same reactions to those numbers that you did. A few numbers, and your eyes start to glaze over. It becomes meaningless very quickly. There's just too much there to absorb. The numbers are meaningless. They're abstract. What does it mean that eight-point-seven million incidents of abuse happened last year? Really, it means nothing. What means something is that when you hear a kid next door repeatedly scream in pain, you pick up the phone to call nine-one-one but hesitate. You wonder: Is it really my business? Do I really want to get involved? What if I'm wrong?

"So let me throw one more statistic at you: Nine in 10 Americans polled regard child abuse as a serious problem, yet only one in three reported abuse when confronted with an actual situation."

Cindy paused.

"The only way that child abuse is going to get the attention that it needs is if you do three things. One: Make fighting child abuse one of the priorities of your organization. Raise awareness of the abuse that is going on right here in southwest Michigan. Two: Pressure your state and federal legislators to take action to make child abuse a more serious crime. Three: When you hear that scream of pain, pick up the phone and dial nine-one-one and tell the dispatcher what you heard. And forget about whether you're being nosy. Your call might save a life. Your failure to call might cost a life.

"I'm going to be unfair to you one more time. I know that you came here expecting a delicious dinner, a little socialization and a nice speech with a little humor. So I apologize because what I'm going to say next is not nice and there is absolutely nothing funny about it.

"Let me tell you the story of a little girl, just two years old, who will never get any older. She won't be opening any presents from Santa this Christmas. She will never have a chance to go to the prom. She will never get to find a loving husband and raise her own children. She will never even get to take another breath. This happened right here in Michigan. And this is the really terrible part: Little Lacy was killed by her parents even though they never laid a finger on her. They simply let her lie in her crib until she starved to death."

Cindy scanned the room. There was not a sound. All eyes were riveted on her.

"Some of you might already be familiar with this case. If so, I congratulate you, because you are paying attention to child abuse cases," Cindy said. "But I'll bet that not everyone in this room has heard about Lacy Trueman. So please allow me to fill you in. About a month ago, a warrant was issued for the arrest of Lacy's parents. Police and social workers say that they deliberately starved their little girl to death. When found, she was in a broken crib in a filthy house. The police report describes Lacy's home as full of lice, feces and old food.

"Lacy weighed only 11 pounds when she was found. The average weight of a healthy two-year-old child is 22 to 34 pounds. So Lacy weighed half of the lowest normal weight of a child her age. Half."

Cindy rattled her papers.

"Allow me to read from the police report: Lacy was suffering from extensive insect infestation on various parts of her body and hair. She was also suffering from a condition known as hair tourniquet, meaning that hair was wrapped tightly around three of her fingers of her right hand. Once the hair was untangled and removed from her fingers, it was observed that the skin underneath was deeply lacerated, exposing tendons. Lacy also suffered from severe diaper rash to the point of having open sores on her buttocks."

A woman stood abruptly, bumping her table as she stood. Glass tinkled. The woman dashed out of the room, her hand over her mouth. Around the room, Cindy saw expressions ranging from disgust to anger to sadness. Cindy knew that some of the anger and disgust was directed at her.

"That was brutal. And I'm sorry. But there's one more thing I want to point out. A pediatrician consulted in Lacy's case said that it would have taken two to three weeks of little or no nourishment for the little girl to starve to death. So let's be clear about what happened. For two to three weeks, helpless two-year-old Lacy lay in her filthy crib, bitten by bugs and suffering from festering wounds while she slowly starved to death.

"That," said Cindy, "is the true face of child abuse. And it is happening right here, in your backyard, whether you like it or not. That is what we must confront if we are to make a difference. Now, you might legitimately ask me why, when there are so many other needy causes, how I can stand here and ask you to spend your time and money fighting child abuse. Why not help war veterans or animals or cancer victims? I'm not asking you to drop support for those causes. Of course they are worthy. I'm asking you to find room in heart, in your wallet and in your schedule to help in the fight against child abuse. There are two reasons why I ask this, both very simple. One: Children are defenseless. They cannot protect themselves. Little Lacy Trueman must have felt that something was terribly wrong when she suffered a second and third and fourth day of hunger pangs. She must have cried. But what could she do? She was literally helpless.

"Second, children are the future of this country. A silly cliché. You've heard it before. But it's true. But I'm asking you to take a minute, just one minute here tonight, and actually think about what that means. The children of today are tomorrow's teachers, doctors, bus drivers, plumbers, nurses, presidents and CEOs. The effects of child abuse often keep adults from fulfilling their potential. What cost will we pay if so many of our future adults are burdened by the psychological problems that linger from a childhood of abuse? What cost are we paying right now?

"A few more numbers for you. Then I promise I'll quit. Men and women serving time in the nation's prisons and jails report a higher incidence of abuse as children than the general population. In fact, more than a third of women in the nation's prisons and jails reported abuse as children. That's 33 percent. In the non-prison female population, 12 percent to 17 percent reported child abuse. About 14 percent of male inmates reported abuse as children, compared to the 5 percent to 8 percent of men not in prison.

"Again, I'll do the math for you. Let's assume that one case of abuse can alter a child's life for the worse. If so, then those percentages, when applied to the eight-point-seven million children who were abused at least once last year, means that we've already permitted the creation of about two million people whose future involves a crime serious enough to land them in jail. When we allow children to be abused, we as a society make our own monsters.

"If you would, think for a moment about the effects on this nation of allowing millions of incidents of abuse every year. How many will grow up suffering from the odd psychological cocktail of rage, a lack of self-confidence and a feeling that they've been cheated? How many Einsteins will never think a single deep thought because they suffer brain damage at the hand of an abusive parent? How many Olympia Snowes will never have a chance to lead the U.S. Senate because they starve to death in a filthy, broken crib? How many Florence Nightingales will never help a single patient because they are killed by a drunken and enraged father? How many Rosa Parks will never get to glare at a rude white man, refuse to give up her seat and spark a revolution?

Cindy paused.

"I've been unfair to you this evening and I apologize for that. But allow me to leave you with one child abuse case with a happy ending. Relatively speaking, of course. There really is no happy ending to any child abuse case.

"Mary Ellen Wilson was a girl born a New York City slum. Her father died and her mother didn't want her. She was placed in a foster home. Her foster mother beat her, kept her chained to a bedpost and fed her only rarely. The girl spent the first nine years of her life in a hell that most of us can only imagine.

"Mary Ellen was treated worse than a slave. She was allowed to wear only one set of clothes and was rarely bathed. She slept on a piece of rug under a window in the living room and was locked in a closet when her foster mother left the house.

"Mary Ellen had no toys to play with and was never allowed outside to play with the other children. A New York policeman who lived in her building found her locked in a closet in her home one day. He said later that he gave Mary Ellen candy, which she had never tasted before. Though he treated her well, the policeman never took action to save Mary Ellen from her abuser. Eventually, Mary Ellen's plight came to the attention of concerned neighbors and a nurse who worked in neighborhood as part of a social program.

"The nurse managed to gain entry to Mary Ellen's house one September day and found the little girl covered in bruises and scars. Mary Ellen had a gash in her forehead made by her foster mother with a pair of scissors. Despite the clear signs of abuse, the nurse and neighbors couldn't get Mary Ellen removed from the custody of her caregiver."

Cindy paused.

"Any social worker will tell you that this is not an uncommon problem in child abuse cases. Courts are reluctant to disturb existing relationships, even when there are signs of abuse. The nurse made several return visits to check on Mary Ellen, each time finding fresh evidence of abuse.

"Now some of you are wondering why the nurse couldn't get the courts to help Mary Ellen after repeated, documented cases of abuse. Surely there must have been a judge willing to get involved, you're thinking. Well, you're right and wrong. I've been a little deceptive. Mary Ellen's case took place in 1874. At the time, there were no laws on the books to prevent the abuse of children or punish those who abused. No laws at all against child abuse. It was, technically and actually, legal.

"The nurse, Etta Wheeler, persuaded the local chapter of the American Society For The Prevention of Cruelty To Animals to go court on Mary Ellen's behalf. You can see the irony now," Cindy said. "There were laws to prevent the abuse of animals, but not children.

"Fortunately, the tactic worked. The courts could not deny that Mary Ellen was, by definition, an animal. Mary Ellen was removed from the home and the foster mother was put on trial. Mary Ellen's foster mother was convicted of assault and battery and sentenced to a year of hard labor in the city penitentiary. In court, Mary Ellen told the judge that she had been whipped nearly every day with a twisted length of rawhide. She could not remember ever having been held, touched or physically comforted by anyone, and particularly not by her foster mother. Think about that just for a second. This girl, nine years old, had never felt a mother's love. She had never been cuddled, hugged or just held when she cried.

"But I promised a happy ending, and here it is. Mary Ellen went to live with Nurse Etta Wheeler's sister. In 1888, at the age of 24, Mary Ellen was married. She had two daughters who both grew up to be teachers. Mary Ellen died in 1956, at the age of 92.

"More important for today's children, eight months after Mary Ellen's trial ended, the New York Society for the Prevention of Cruelty to Children was created. This prompted other states to create similar agencies for the protection of children. By 1900 there were 161 such groups in the U.S."

Cindy shuffled her notes into a pile. She hadn't needed them much during her talk, but they helped keep certain facts and figures in front of her.

"We are facing a similar situation today in terms of public attitude and a legal system unprepared to handle serious, long-term child abuse cases. Although there are laws against child abuse, they are fragmented and inconsistent. They vary from state to state. In many states, no single agency is charged with investigating, prosecuting and following up serious child abuse cases. It often falls to a patchwork effort of county caseworkers and state and local police departments. If you're are all familiar with bureaucracy, you know that not having one agency in charge means that some cases fall between the cracks.

"Investigative experience varies. Caseworkers, who are often key in proving cases of child abuse, are not trained investigators. They're case workers. And police forensic techniques vary widely. Proving a case of child abuse can require the same attention to detail and delicacy as a rape investigation. But too often, even if evidence is gathered, it is not enough to prove long-term child abuse. The result? Abused children end up right back at home, right back into the hell that we should be helping them escape.

"In addition, the penalties for child abuse vary from state to state and county to county. What is considered a dreadful case that shocks a rural community might be considered nearly routine in an urban environment.

"The solution that I propose, and which I am asking your organization to help with, is to work to raise awareness of child abuse here in your home state. Please tell your legislators that child abuse needs to be treated at least as seriously as bank robberies and illegal copying of DVD movies. Tell your legislators that the FBI needs to be placed in charge of investigating and prosecuting serious, long-term cases of child abuse. I believe that protecting our children is at least as important as protecting the latest hot DVD movie release.

"I'm going to close now," Cindy said. "First, I'd like to thank you for your attention. Again, I apologize for abusing your expectations. You've all been kind and generous, most particularly Grace VanHolden, who allowed me to stay at her beautiful home." Cindy gave Grace a smile.

"If you take anything at all away from my speech tonight, please remember just this one thing: Right now, as I stand here, thousands of children are being abused. They are crying in pain and desperation. Tomorrow, thousands more will be abused. None of them – not one of those children – can stand up and defend herself. They need you. The Mary Ellens and Lacy Truemans of the world have no one to help them. Except you. Please don't fail them.

"Thank you."

The applause was tepid.

As Cindy stepped down from the stage, Grace met her.

"That was ... interesting," Grace said.

"I'm very sorry if it was not what you hoped for," Cindy said. "I've tried to get the speaker's bureau to make the description of my talk a little grimmer, so people are better prepared. But ..."

"Oh no, no, it was fine," Grace said with a nervous smile. Cindy couldn't tell if she was being honest. "I think it's a very ... important topic. And I'm glad that you provided a new perspective on it."

"Thank you," Cindy said.

"We ... I guess we sometimes forget how ... horrible some things are. Maybe we get a little too comfortable," Grace said, looking at the diners as they stood in small groups, talking, putting on coats, laughing, hugging. She turned to look at Cindy. "Maybe it's a good thing that every now and then we get reminded of just how awful some things are. Like abused childrens' lives."

"I'm sorry if I was a little indelicate," Cindy said.

"Was that ... that story you told about Lacey Trueman ... that's true?" Grace asked. Cindy thought that she detected a slight watering in Grace's eyes.

"Unfortunately, yes, that's ripped right from the Detroit Free Press," Cindy said. "It's sad but true. No matter where in the country I speak, all I have to do is look through a week or so of newspapers from that area and I can find a terrible case of child abuse. It's rampant."

"Oh, my," Grace said. She looked away, then said in a bright tone, "Oh, look! Here come some members. I'm sure they will want to speak to you."

Cindy engaged campaign mode and turned to the approaching women, a smile on her face.

"Hello," she said, extending her hand. "Thank you for listening to me."

Chapter Eighty

"You know I love you, but this is never going to pass," Evelyn told Cindy. "You're not even going to get it to the floor for a vote. This just isn't on the leadership's agenda and you don't have a party structure to back you up."

They were sitting on the couch of the Cindy's apartment, the one that they used to share when they were in D.C. But Evelyn had found Devin, an analyst at a public policy think-tank, and much to Carl's disappointment, she had moved into Devin's place. Evelyn had worried about how Cindy would take the change, but Cindy had been positive and encouraging.

"If you think he might be the one, then you definitely need to spend some time living together," Cindy had said. "Nothing lets you figure someone out like arguing about whose turn it is to take out the trash or scrub the toilet."

"I think he might be the one," Ev had said. "Seriously."

So with that blessing, Evelyn moved out and in with Devin. But she still spent a lot of time in her old apartment, strategizing and socializing with Cindy. Tonight was a Skittles-and-beer session to talk about the child abuse bill Cindy wanted to introduce. Ev thought it was too soon to introduce the bill. Cindy was only in her second year as a senator. Cindy thought that it might take four years – the rest of her term – to get enough votes to turn the bill into law.

"So how do I get around not having a party structure?" Cindy asked.

"Have a power structure," Ev said. "A base of support that doesn't rely on the two big parties. Have a special interest group that really, really likes you."

Cindy sighed. "And just how does one go about getting such a power structure?"

"Well, girl, in your case, you have a big problem. Children don't vote. And every politician in this town has already given lip service to child abuse. One of the first things out of anyone's mouth when he's running for an office is that he supports the American family and that he loves kids. And his staff makes sure he kisses plenty of babies on TV to prove it."

"But that's the last anyone talks about it," Cindy said. "Whatever they said about kids and families, it gets left behind when they get down here and the high-priced oil and gun lobbyists start showing up."

"Right," Ev said. "But there's hope. I did a little research for you." She levered herself up and went to her leather attaché. She put aside the pantyhose she'd stripped off as soon as they were inside the door. From the attaché, she pulled a dark blue folder with a quarter-inch of paper inside it. She took it to Cindy and handed it to her.

Cindy noticed that the tab of the folder was, as always with Evelyn, labeled neatly. In this case, it read "Defendkids.org."

"Defendkids dot org? What is that?"

Ev smiled as she settled on the couch and tucked her legs under her. She popped a few Skittles in her mouth. "Remember how we had this same conversation about a year ago? About how it was funny that guns have a lobby and senior citizens have a lobby and dairy farmers have a lobby. Drugs have a lobby. Fish and deer and elk and spotted owls have a lobby. Hell, almost everything in this country has a lobby. Except children."

"And I told you that if there can be a lobby for guns, there can be a lobby for kids," Cindy said.

"Exactly," Ev said. "And that's it right there. Someone apparently figured out that the kids need a little help. Kids can't vote, but neither can guns. So Defendkids dot org lobbies for them. Kids, I mean."

Cindy opened the folder and scanned the pages. They were mostly press releases from Defendkids. org. There were a few photocopied newspaper articles, but Cindy noticed that the name of the group, highlighted in Ev's efficient hand, was usually deep in the story. There were a few printouts from what was apparently the group's website. It was a meager collection, but Cindy felt a rising hope. She looked up at Ev, who was grinning.

"They look like they mean it," Cindy said.

"Oh, they're very serious. They've even had some victories lately. They managed to keep Virginia from easing the penalties for incest and rape of a child. God knows where the legislature got the idea to reduce the punishment for that kind of stuff, but the bill was pretty far along by the time Defendkids dot org caught wind of it. To make up for their late start, they put on a really intense lobbying campaign, got people to write letters, put up billboards, all that stuff. The bill ended up dying in committee. Once word got out, no elected official was willing to say that he supported it."

"Oh, Ev," Cindy said. "That's just what we need! Someone to fight side-by-side with. Someone who can get the grassroots stirred up like that." Cindy got a faraway look in her eye. "Oh, how nice would it be to have a bunch of letters to the editor show up in Shipman's hometown newspaper? Oh, what I wouldn't give...."

"Well, before you have us taking over D.C. with letters to the editor in the hometown newspaper of the majority leader, here's a little reality check," Ev said. She fell into her briefing voice, crisp and no nonsense. "The group is growing but still small. Fewer than 10,000 paid memberships. It's not well funded. The fight in Virginia almost exhausted its coffers. I understand they've got less than a quarter-million on hand now. It doesn't have a big sugar daddy and it's working on a few people, but there's no big donor on the horizon. The website is a little primitive and might be a turn off. Worst, no one knows this group exists. No one. You stop 100 people outside the supermarket in Anytown, Middle

America, and 100 of them are going to tell you they never heard of this group and don't know what it does. Contrast that to the NRA."

"But … we can help," Cindy said. "A partnership. I've got the legislative angle covered, obviously. If they can work on awareness of my child abuse bill … I know people will support it if they hear about it. If I learned nothing else in a year of talking to Pennsylvanians, I know that there's a huge undercurrent of support for anti-child abuse laws. If they do that, stir up the grassroots, I can make speeches for them, mention them in press conferences … surely … there has to be a way to get more attention and money."

"Oh, there are ways. Many ways. But mostly what it takes is time," Ev said. "And although this group is a bunch of fighters – I mean, really. They're tough and determined. They've signed up some people who know how the game is played. Andrew Vachss is on their board. But they're no where near the NRA's league. I mean, right now, the dairy farmer's lobby has about a hundred times the influence of Defendkids dot org. They're a tool and a partner, yes, but they're going to need a lot of TLC and money before they can turn up the heat in D.C. Virginia's legislature is one thing. Capitol Hill is another." She threw a Skittle into the air and caught it in her mouth.

"One of those is going to stick in your throat and you're going to choke to death," Cindy said. Ev smirked.

"OK, it's a start," Cindy said. "It's better than no children's lobby, which is what I thought the situation was 10 minutes ago."

Ev smiled. "There's my eternal optimist!" she said, patting Cindy on the foot. "I'll get you a meeting next week with one of their people. I think you'll be impressed."

Chapter Eighty-One

Cindy still felt like a charlatan looking at people across the vast expanse of her polished oak desk. But she had learned that it conveyed power and prestige, which were the currency in Washington, D.C. As Evelyn said, you either played the game or you perished.

So she played the role.

"Thank you for coming," she said after the handshake to the young male lobbyist from Defendkids.org. He waited to sit until she did. He had thin straw-colored hair and crooked gold wire-frame glasses covering intense brown eyes. His big-knuckled hands gripped the briefcase on his lap.

"Thank you for seeing me, Senator. I know that your time is valuable."

"I have lots of time for organizations that are interested in fighting child abuse," Cindy said. "You might not know that child abuse was a central topic of mine during my campaign."

The man looked like he'd been jabbed with a needle. "No!" he blurted. "I did not know that. Senator, I apologize. It ... your campaign just didn't appear on our radar screens. Not that you weren't out there fighting the good fight, but –" Cindy held up a hand to stop him and he did.

"Don't worry about it," she said. "Seriously. No offense taken. Honestly. I ran under the Green Party banner and up until three days before the election, I didn't have even the slimmest hope of winning. If Mayor Pacifico hadn't had a heart attack, I think he'd be in this chair now and I'd be back in Altoona filing court papers on child abuse cases. I'm not surprised that you didn't know about my campaign until it was over."

"Your campaign strategy those last few days was brilliant," the young man said. "I can't imagine how difficult it must have been to visit that hospital room where –" Again, Cindy held up a hand to cut him off.

"It wasn't a strategy," she said. "I did what seemed right and decent at the time. It was truly incidental that it had an influence on the election. That's the truth. A lot of people in this town will try to take credit for serendipity. I'll tell you what really happened, and that was that I got lucky."

The young man was nodding rapidly. Cindy suspected that he was terrified that he'd said the wrong thing. She sighed.

"Look, Chris," she said, using the name he'd given her at their introduction. "I'm not like most of the people here in D.C. I'm not here to gather power or get rich or be a player on the national stage. I'm lucky to be in this seat and I'm pretty sure that I'm going to be a one-termer. I'm here, to be honest, for one reason. That reason is to do something about child abuse in this country. It's not being taken seriously enough. I'm hoping that before I get booted out of office in four years by some well-funded challenger that I've at least made this nation stop and take a second look at kids. At the value of kids. Maybe some people will start to realize that kids have more value than all the oil in the Gulf of Mexico and ANWAR combined. Maybe a few people will start to think about making sure that those who abuse children are punished accordingly. When I shut off the lights in this office for the last time, I want to know that I gave it everything I had – that everything I did, every breath I took, every step that I took during my years here in this office were dedicated to making that vision come true.

"I want people to think before they raise a hand to a child, before they lock a kid in a closet, before they decide to spend thirty bucks on a carton of cigarettes rather than feed their kids. I want fathers to think before they ramrod their kid into a high school athletic program and then spend the next three years telling him how badly he sucks at sports. I want parents to treasure their kids like a gift of immeasurable value from God, which is what they are. I know it's a huge task and that I quite likely might be a fool on a hopeless errand. But Chris," Cindy said and paused to spear him with her gaze, "I honestly don't care what anyone else thinks of my mission. While I'm in this chair and while I have one vote of the one hundred in the United States Senate, I'm going to do everything, absolutely everything, that I can to reach my goal.

I'm not going to stop even if I lose this office. I can make the most difference from here, but if I have to rent a bus and tour the country to get my message out, I will."

She stopped. Chris was looking at her with a wide-eyed intensity. She raised her eyebrows at him to ask, "Well?"

He swallowed and re-gripped his briefcase.

"Senator, pardon me if I seem … a little startled," he said. "But I feel like you've just handed me the Holy Grail. I … we, my group – Defendkids dot org – have been looking for a champion just like you. We've been looking for a federal-level legislator who shared our agenda and who was willing to fight with us. Up to now, no one was willing. Not really willing. Not willing to fight. Not willing to stand up against the leadership." He paused and shook his head. "I'm sorry … I don't mean to presume. But what you've just said is pretty much a restatement of our mission. We're completely and utterly dedicated to improving the plight of children in this country, primarily by fighting child abuse, neglect and child sexual assault. We – if I might use the term – are obsessed. We're possessed. We're beyond dedicated … we're downright fanatical." He swallowed again. "I'm sorry. That makes us sound crazy –"

Cindy cut him off. "No," she said. "It makes you sound committed. Which is what I need in a partner. I need a partner group that is absolutely, completely, one-hundred percent committed to raising the profile of children in this country — and nothing else. I need a group that is as single-minded about kids as the NRA is about guns. That's the only way that an interest group can have any influence here in D.C. You have to be oblivious to everything but the interests of your constituency … in this case, children. Nothing else matters. If the world is falling away, you have to keep fighting right up to the last minute. You don't care about terrorism or the budget or health care. You care only about one thing: children." She paused. "Do you think that describes Defendkids dot org, Chris?"

He swallowed hard. "It does. Absolutely. We're … well, I hope you'll understand if I tell you that we make jokes about ourselves. We're … we're nuts," he said and finally smiled. It was a genuine smile, one full of hope and Cindy realized how few of those smiles she had seen since she'd come to Washington.

She arranged her face into her best "serious senator" expression. "Then, Chris, it looks like we can do business. What do you bring to the table?"

He excitedly unlatched his briefcase and pulled out a sheaf of papers.

"We can do it all for you," he said. "We're a true grassroots organization … not one of those fake groups cobbled together for fundraising purposes. We're four-oh-one-c-three certified. We recruit only via word-of-mouth and our website. People pay twenty-five dollars to join for a year. But we're players. We've got a board of directors of people who can make things happen. They're influencers, the kind of people who can get an opinion piece published in the New York Times. Lots of professors and authors. A few CEOs. A couple of movie stars."

Cindy raised her eyebrows to indicate that she was interested and impressed.

"Also," he said, "We can do billboards and grassroots letter-writing campaigns to elected officials and newspapers. We've got people who will make phone calls and who will stand outside a poll on a rainy election day – all day – and hand out pamphlets. We've got people who will go door-to-door for you, people who will not quit. We're all … all obsessed a little bit," he said, faltering. After a moment, he rallied.

"But we're effective. We just had a big victory in Virginia. We halted an attempt to reduce the penalties for child sexual assault. And we're learning and growing. We might not be the AARP, but we're dedicated. We're serious. And we're growing. Who knows? One day, people might talk about the NRA and Defendkids dot org in the same breath." He stopped, almost breathless, and smiled at Cindy. "Call me crazy," he said. "But I think that's entirely possible."

"You know what, Chris?" Cindy said. "I do too. And I'd like to be a part of it."

Chris leaned across the desk and extended a hand. "Senator, I'd like to be the first to welcome you aboard … I'm sure that we will be good for each other."

"I'm sure we will," Cindy said, grasping his hand. "And we need to get started right now."

Chris nodded rapidly and dove back into his briefcase. He pulled out a yellow legal pad and a pen.

"You're from Pennsylvania and you're in your second year," he said. "So, senator, when would you like to start your re-election campaign?"

"Forget my re-election," Cindy said. "I have a bill."

Chris's eyes widened. "A child-related bill?"

For an answer, Cindy pulled open a desk drawer and pulled out a bound copy of her draft. She handed it across the polished desk.

"Have your people look this over," said Cindy, playing Senator to the hilt. "Then get back to me and tell me how you can help me get it into law. We have four years."

Chris took the fat file of paper with near reverence. Cindy watched as he skimmed it quickly, turning pages faster and faster. He whispered to himself as he read: "FBI ... serial child abuse ... effective national registry of convicted abusers ... FBI files federal charges ... coordination of local law enforcement ... mandatory sentencing ... withholding of federal funds..." He flipped through the final pages and looked up at Cindy. She could see a glow in his eyes, the same glow that she had seen in the eyes of hundreds of people who had come up to her after her campaign speeches, tears in their eyes. They had wrung her hand and practically pleaded with her to do something about child abuse.

"This ... this is...." Chris paused. He closed his eyes a moment, then opened them. "Pardon me, Senator, but I feel how Arthur must have felt when he pulled the sword from the stone." He grinned. "My apologies for all the stupid

Arthurian analogies. But this is ... this is what we've been looking for. This is it. This is the law that we want to have passed. This is what we're fighting for. Good lord. We didn't think this would be possible for years. Decades." He paused and his eyes wandered to the ceiling. Then he blinked and turned back to Cindy. "Do you really think this has a hope of passing?"

"Not without help," Cindy said. "That's why you're sitting right there in that chair."

Chapter Eighty-Two

Senator Walter Shipman, leader of the Republican majority in congress and a very powerful man in Washington, leaned back in his chair and eyed Cindy. She fought to keep her cool. To keep her courage up, she thought of the children. She sat perfectly still.

Shipman swung his big black chair slightly back and forth. He steepled his fingers in front of his mouth.

"Let me be perfectly clear, Cindy," he said. "It is OK if I call you Cindy? Well, there is no chance in hell of your bill seeing the light of day." He paused. "I'm sorry. You wanted my honest assessment and that's it. There it is."

"And may I ask why?"

Shipman ticked items off on his fingers. "One, your bill drastically expands the reach of the federal government into the personal lives of Americans via the FBI. Unacceptable. Two, your bill allows the federal government to threaten state's rights by withholding federal funding for important state-run programs. Unacceptable. Three, because your bill expands the duties of the FBI, it would require significant additional expenditures. Or reallocations of funding from other priorities. Distasteful. Four, I'm not sure that it will pass constitutional muster. Unlikely at best. So why bother? Five...."

He paused and looked at Cindy.

"Five, you have haven't exactly been helpful to the Republican majority. You've voted directly against our interests at least a dozen times since you took office. That's the twelve that leap to mind. I'm sure research would uncover some others."

He put his hands on his desk, palms down and stopped swinging.

"Your bill, should you introduce it, will die quietly in committee. If you try to make a fuss about it – run to the press or something similarly ill-advised, then it will not only die, but I will personally take an active role in criticizing it and making sure that no Republican senator will ever vote for it."

"That's really not fair," Cindy said.

Shipman shrugged. "Fair to whom? Fair to you? Fair to –"

"Fair to the children," Cindy interrupted. She thought of Brittany and kept her eyes on his.

Shipman was silent. His aura grew hostile. His hands went back to forming a steeple in front of his mouth.

"Oh. I see," he said after a minute of silence. "Now it's about children."

"With all due respect, sir, it has always been about the children. With me, anyway. What else would it be about? Why else would I introduce a bill to try to change the way this nation views child abuse?"

Shipman abruptly stood up and walked to the window behind his desk. He clasped his hands behind his back and talked to the window.

"I believe that I have finally pegged you," he said. "For a while, there were a lot of questions swirling around you, Miss Phillips. How will she vote? Which side is she on? A lot of people in the senate wondered. You voted with us a few times, and we appreciated that. But it was clear that you were not wholehearted in support of the Republican agenda. Well, I think that today you've shown me your true colors. And, I'm sorry to say, I don't think there's much common ground here."

He whirled and glared at Cindy. It took all her will not to flinch.

"You unseat a valuable incumbent through sheer luck. You come here to Washington where cooperation is paramount, yet you are not a team player. You are not willing to work with others. You are unwilling to assist my party with our agenda, yet you come hat in hand, asking me to allow an ill-advised bill to not only clear a committee but to actually get to the floor for a vote." He shook his head and chuckled, but there was no mirth in it. "And you actually want me to believe that this bill of yours is some sort of well-intentioned bill to help children instead of a blatant power-grab by you and the ... what is it? Oh yes, the Green Party. The Green Party. The Green Party. Funny. I don't recall child abuse being a priority of the Green

Party." He turned back to the window. Cindy was too stunned to speak.

"Miss Phillips, my advice to you is simple. Go back to your office. Stay in touch with your home state. Spend the next four years voting and supporting my party's interests. Find a way to get re-elected. Pray that my party doesn't target you for defeat. If – and it's a very large if – if you get re-elected, then, and only then – " he whirled to face her again – "then you may come to me and beg for a favor. Until that happens, I advise you to keep your bills in your desk drawers."

Shipman sat down at his desk and fixed Cindy with a look of intense disapproval. Cindy, stricken, fought back tears. Her defenses crumbled. She fought to keep her face blank, but she could feel a burn spreading upward from her neck and across her cheeks. *I really screwed up this time*, she thought. *He's never ever going to let my bill see the light of day. I just blew my only chance. I failed again. I thought he would be reasonable but this game is a lot tougher than I thought.*

Shipman put his hands flat on his desk and leaned toward Cindy, spearing her with his glare.

"Allow me to guarantee you two things, miss: One, your child abuse bill is DOA. Two, you may expect a professional and well-funded opponent when your seat comes up for election. I advise you to start campaigning now if you don't want to be humiliated."

He straightened up. "I think this meeting is over."

Cindy had no response. She only wanted to escape. She left Shipman's office without a word. She held her tears until she got back to her office, where she locked the door and sobbed.

Chapter Eighty-Three

"**A**sshole!" Evelyn said, stomping across the office. "Asshole! How dare he? You're a legally elected senator. How dare he treat you like a schoolgirl?"

"Well, he did," Cindy said. "And it worked. He scared me. It was all I could do to keep from crying right there in his office."

"Thank god you didn't," Ev said. "He would have taken that as evidence not only as weakness, but that he had beaten you."

"He did beat me," Cindy said. "We're screwed. He's the gatekeeper. He controls what gets to the floor for a vote. If he shuts me out, I'm stuck. There's nothing I can do."

Evelyn's eyes were blazing. Cindy had never seen her so furious.

"Oh yes there is," Ev said. "There are only a hundred votes in the Senate and the GOP's majority is razor-thin – three votes. Sooner or later, they're going to need your vote to get something passed." Ev showed a tiger's predatory grin. "And that's when you make a deal. On your terms."

"Ev," Cindy said, "that might take forever. They've only asked me to help them twice in the two years I've been here. And you know that now they're not going to come to me for help except as a last resort. Shipman isn't stupid. He knows that if I'm their only chance of getting something passed, I'm going to extract a promise. It might be three years before he comes to me for a vote ... and by then, I'll be out of time on my child abuse bill."

"You're going to extract more than a promise," Ev said. "You're going to demand a deal. A very specific deal. And don't worry. With only a three-vote majority out of a hundred votes, they're going to come to you sooner than you think. And when they do, you're going to lay it out. They want your vote, they're going to have to put your child abuse bill up for a vote. You're going to demand a yea or nay vote, not a voice vote. Every senator in the country is going to have to stand up and vote yes or no on the most important child protection bill in a hundred years."

Ev turned to Cindy. "In politics, patience is power. We'll bide our time. We'll spend the time working over a few of the wimps and the moderates, the ones who are most likely to vote for our bill. And when the time comes...."

Cindy shivered. "Ev, I'm glad you're on my side."

"Asshole!" Ev said. "Ooh, I'm going to love seeing the look on his face when you lay out your demands. And when your bill sails through the senate."

Cindy was quiet while Ev paced the office. Suddenly she whirled on Cindy.

"You've been collecting photos of abused children every time you go on one of those speeches, haven't you?" she demanded.

"Uh, yes. Yes," Cindy said. "I didn't know what good they would do, but every time I get asked to speak, I stop in a local police department and get an evidence photo from a child abuse trial. I was thinking of doing some kind of art gallery showing…."

"Forget art," Ev said. "How many do you have? I mean, from how many states do you have pictures?"

"I don't know. Maybe two dozen or so."

"OK, well, we need to get a photo from every state," Evelyn said. "Let's put a staffer on it. We need a nice crisp clear evidence photo from every state in the union. One that makes you want to cry just looking at it. Little girls with big eyes and bruises. The same type that you've been collecting."

"And we're going to do what with them, Ev?" Cindy asked. "Mail them to Shipman?"

Evelyn snorted. "He'd throw them in the trash. No. Much better. Listen."

Eyes gleaming, she explained her idea to Cindy. As she listened, Cindy's eyes grew wide.

"Oh my god, Ev. Do … do we dare?" she asked.

"Do we dare?" Ev asked with outrage in her voice. "Do we dare not to?"

Cindy grabbed Ev in a hug. "Oh my god. How did I get the best chief of staff in the whole country?"

Returning the hug, Ev said, "Because you're who you are, girl. Because you are who you are."

Chapter Eighty-Four

"Here's the list," Evelyn said, sliding it across the coffeehouse table to Cindy. "These are the moderate Republicans who are pissed at being ignored by the current leadership. These are also the Republicans who are known for being softies on bleeding-heart issues like family and kids. And the ones who are … well, just stupid enough to be talked into opposing the leadership. Our basic arguments are simple. We offer them either a chance to give the GOP leadership a kick in the ankles by voting for your bill, a chance to vote for a real kid's bill or … well, for the third group, we'll figure it out as we go. We should be able to stay ahead of them."

"Aren't they going to be afraid of retaliation?" Cindy asked.

"Certainly. Of course they will. They're not stupid," Ev said. "Well, except for the third group. But that's the beauty of your bill. Because of its very nature, it gives them cover. Who could criticize them for voting for a bill that protects kids from abuse? And even if the leadership does make an issue of it, they can always go back home to their voters and say –" Evelyn deepened her voice and drew herself up like a self-important politician – "Yes, my friends, I voted my conscience on this bill ... I bravely stood up when the leaders of the party wanted me to sit down and be quiet.... Or some such crap. And what voter is going to tell them that they shouldn't have supported a bill that protects kids? It's the perfect cover."

Cindy took a deep breath. "OK. Two questions. When do we start visiting these senators? And when do we bring Defendkids dot org into it?"

"First question – the answer is tomorrow. I've lined up a bunch of meetings. We'll go together, but you'll do most of the talking ... senator to senator, you know." She smiled. Cindy rolled her eyes.

"Sometimes I still have trouble with that," Cindy said. "Especially late at night. Who am I to be –"

"Enough of that talk!" Ev said sternly. "You're a senator, we're going to talk to senators, so you do the talking. I'm the ever-loyal aide brought along to make sure that you don't slide off message and to remind you when it's time for your next appointment."

"And what exactly do I say to these senators?" Cindy asked. "Please, please, please vote for my bill even though it's going to make Shipman – the guy who can take away your committee chairmanship – really angry. Now, that sounds like a powerful argument."

"Oh, ye of little faith," Ev said. She leaned over and pulled a fat sheaf of paper from her briefcase. "I've got briefs on every senator that we're going to talk to. All the angles ... all the approaches.

Exactly what tack to take. I've been working on this for months. Here." She handed the pile of paper to Cindy. "Skim these tonight. We'll refine it in the morning before we head out."

Cindy reluctantly took the pile. "What ever happened to evenings where I put up my feet, ate ice cream from the box and watched TV till bedtime?"

Ev snorted. "No time for that in D.C. No one here has a life outside of work. That's the price you pay for having influence," she said. "Even social events are work. Who's talking to who? Who has who cornered? Who isn't talking to who?"

Cindy sighed and leafed through the pages. "I can see where this can get old quick."

"You know the cycle, girl," Ev said. Remember American Politics 101?"

"I'm afraid all that has turned to mush at the back of my brain," Cindy said. "Refresh my memory."

Ev switched to her briefing tone of voice. "The arc of a career in Washington, D.C. has four parts, according to Michael Kinsley. Idealism, pragmatism, ambition, and corruption. When you first get here, you're all fired up with a cause. That's about all you have – a belief and a lot of energy. In case you're wondering, that's you two years ago," Ev said. "Second phase, you figure out the system and learn how to pull the levers to get what you want. That's what you're learning right now. Third, you realize that you can't get shit done without power and authority, so you start to play the game to win. Fourth, you get really tired of it all and begin to exploit the system to benefit yourself."

"Please shoot me before I get to phase four," Cindy said.

"But that's the fun part," Ev said. "That's when you get to end phone calls by saying things like, 'Look, I have to go. I'm late for golf with the president.'"

Cindy laughed. "OK. Fine. But we've got a long way to go before we start exploiting the system. So for now, can you answer part two of my question?"

"When to bring in Defendkids dot org?" Ev asked. "Tough question. If we launch them too soon, they'll peak too soon. If we wait too long, they won't have time to apply full force when we need it. Either way, their impact is dissipated. So there's no point in winding them up until we know that we have a deal with Shipman about getting your bill on the floor for a vote."

Cindy sighed again. "There's nothing on the horizon that he's going to need my vote for."

"That's fine for now," Ev said. "It gives us time to lay the groundwork. Then, when he does come us in his smarmy way, we'll be ready to shoot him between the eyes."

"You do have some vivid imagery," Cindy said.

Ev narrowed her eyes and looked mean. "After the way he treated you, there's nothing I'm looking forward to more than seeing that worm squirm."

"You're a hard case, woman," Cindy said.

"Live for revenge is my motto," Ev said.

"Get some sleep is mine," Cindy said. "Can we be done?"

"See you at seven sharp," Ev said. "And we'll go rope us some moderates."

Chapter Eighty-Five

Ev and Cindy sat in the bright, well-appointed office of the man known as Senator J. Preston Caldwell, a.k.a. Senator Blowdry, representing California. He was the first appointment but belonged to the third group on their list.

"Senator, think about the advantages," Cindy said, following the strategy that she and Ev had worked out. "You're a Republican senator in a state that is traditionally liberal and growing more so every year. More and more of your constituents are wondering if you really share their beliefs."

Senator J. Simpson Caldwell raised an imperious eyebrow at Cindy. "My polls indicate that the voters in my state are well pleased with my efforts," he said.

Cindy smiled her party smile. "Senator. I'm sure that much of your state is pleased with you. You're a very successful politician." Caldwell visibly swelled a bit with the praise. "But your state is changing. Your Hispanic population has increased what –?" she glanced at Ev, who mouthed a number

"—fourteen percent over the past three years. That's very rapid growth."

"Of course it is," Caldwell said. He reached up and patted his perfectly brushed blonde hairdo, frozen in place by who-knows-how-many spritzes of hairspray, Cindy thought.

"That's nearly ... nearly five percent a year." Caldwell smiled at his quick calculation.

"Right, senator," Cindy said. "Very perceptive. At that rate, your state will be more than fifty percent Hispanic in less than five years." She paused to let that sink in. To be sure, she repeated it. "In five years, your state will be composed of fifty percent Hispanic voters. Now," she said. "What have you done to reach out to those voters, senator?"

Caldwell stiffened in his black leather chair. He looked to his left and drummed his manicured nails on his desk.

"I'm well aware of that. I've reached out," he said.

"Do you speak Spanish?" Cindy ventured.

"No," Caldwell said. "But I'm taking classes. In the meantime, four of my staff are fluent. I've learned a few ... key phrases that I work into speeches. I am careful to appear at events that are important to Mex—ah, Hispanic voters. Constituents, I mean. I do not ignore them."

"Yes, senator. You've made great progress, no doubt. But I'm sure that you've also thought about the fact that Caldwell is not ... not exactly a Spanish name," Cindy said.

Caldwell's frown deepened. He patted his hair. "My great-grandfather ... my name goes far back in

California," he said. "Augustus P. Caldwell founded the San Francisco Times. Today, it is considered to be one of the greatest newspapers in the nation," he said. Cindy had the impression that he had used the line many times.

"It is a great newspaper," Cindy said. "In fact, I read it when I can." Ev quickly turned her automatic eye-roll into a non-committal glance at the ceiling. "But many Hispanics will not know your ... impressive family history," Cindy said. "They will be looking for a reason to vote for you. You have to provide them with a level of comfort ... something that will convince them that you understand their lives."

"I fully support welfare reform and the president's undocumented worker amnesty proposal," Caldwell said, looking stern. He glanced to his left again. "I mean, of course, the temporary work permit proposal." He patted his hair. "Saying 'amnesty program' was a slip of the tongue and I am sure that it will not be repeated outside this room." He fixed Cindy with a raised-eyebrow look.

"Of course, speaking senator to senator," Cindy said, "I wouldn't betray your confidence." Cindy resolved to read the San Francisco Times if only to see the kind of coverage that Caldwell got from the newspaper's political reporter.

"I am opposed to the building of a wall along the U.S.-Mexico border," Caldwell said. "It would stifle legal trade and hinder the free movement of legal immigrants in addition to being a significant expenditure of funds which could be better applied elsewhere such as the defense budget."

"A brave and principled stand, senator," Cindy said. Satisfaction emanated from Caldwell. Cindy wondered if he had memorized the statement.

"But it's somewhat in opposition to the Republican Party line, isn't it?" Cindy asked.

Caldwell looked uncomfortable.

"It is, uh, yes, and that has been brought to my attention by the leadership," he said. "However, we've been able … I've explained to them that my Mexican-American voters are strongly opposed to a border fence. So we've come to an agreement," he said, gaining confidence as he spoke.

"They allow you to be out of step on that issue and you agree to support them on every other issue," Cindy said.

"Yes," Caldwell said, drawing himself up. "We have an agreement. They were very reasonable."

"I'm sure they were," Cindy said. "But what I'm getting at is this, senator: Your state is becoming more and more Hispanic. In the near future, there are going to be more issues where the desires of your voters and the aims of the GOP leadership do not match." Caldwell watched Cindy, one eyebrow raised in a look of mild skepticism. "Sooner rather than later, there's going to be a lot of pressure on you to vote for something that your Hispanic voters strongly oppose. That's going to be a tough call, senator."

Caldwell nodded. Cindy hoped he was following her chain of reasoning.

"What you need, sir, is an issue that the leadership isn't too concerned about but which your Hispanic voters feel very strongly about. What you need is an issue that you can vote on and show your Hispanic voters that you really understand their needs."

Caldwell frowned and nodded, giving the impression that he was thinking deeply about Cindy's statements.

"When Hispanic voters are polled, there's one issue that comes up again and again as one of their top priorities. Do you know what that issue is, sir?"

"Immigration," Caldwell said immediately.

"Right. Yes. That's true," Cindy said. "But immigration is an issue where your voters and the leadership disagree. Right?"

Caldwell frowned more deeply and clasped his hands on his desk. Cindy noticed that his white paper blotter was spotless.

"Uh, yes. Right. There's that conflict...." Caldwell said.

"So how about this issue? Family."

"Family?" Caldwell repeated, frowning.

"Family," Cindy said firmly. "Hispanics value their family connections very highly. They believe that nurturing children is very important." Cindy gave him a moment to absorb that information. "There are two very good things about the family issue," Cindy said. "One, it appeals very strongly to Hispanics. In fact, some polls have shown that Hispanic voters think that not enough attention is paid to family issues here in the U.S. Second, I don't think you can find a single senator who will tell you that he is opposed to strengthening the American family. A vote in favor of the family is pretty well insulated against criticism." Cindy smiled. Caldwell looked up from his desk, caught her smile and returned it.

He really is very handsome, Cindy thought, looking at Caldwell's cheekbones, white teeth and smooth California tan. Too bad there's nobody home.

"Knowing those things, senator, how would you like the chance to vote for a bill that will both please your voters back home and which no one could ever criticize you for supporting?" Cindy asked.

"That sounds like the perfect bill!" Caldwell said and laughed heartily – rather too heartily for the degree of mirth in his comment, but Cindy and Ev gamely joined in.

"That's great, just great!" Caldwell said and chuckled again. Cindy smiled her best smile.

"I know that you value families, senator. It shows in your respect for your great-grandfather and his accomplishments."

"He founded one of this nation's greatest newspapers," Caldwell said. "And I happen to have a beautiful young daughter."

"Senator, I'm going to be introducing a family bill," Cindy said. "I'm not sure when exactly, because it depends upon some issues with the leadership. But when I introduce that bill, can I count on your support?"

Caldwell put on his 'I'm listening' frown again.

"Correct me if I'm wrong, senator, but you are with the Libertarian Party, am I correct?"

"Green," Cindy said.

"What?" Caldwell asked, looking confused.

"The Green Party, not the Libertarian," Cindy said. "I was elected under the Green Party banner."

Caldwell nodded, his expression serious. "And you're from Michigan, am I right?"

"Pennsylvania," Cindy said.

"Of course! Pennsylvania! Sorry," Caldwell said.

"No problem, senator," Cindy said. "I'm new and there's a lot of confusion out there about me."

There was a prolonged silence. Cindy waited, watching Caldwell's expression. Just as she feared that he had gone on a mental vacation, he smiled at her. He tilted his head and looked at her intently. He glanced at Evelyn, then back to Cindy.

"Senator, do you think we could … have a minute alone?" he asked.

Ev jumped up and put out her hand. As Caldwell stood and shook her hand, she said, "Thank you for your time, Senator Caldwell. I truly appreciate it. I'll be happy to wait outside." She gave him her best smile and walked out of the office, closing the door behind her. As soon as it clicked, Caldwell reached beneath his tailored dark-blue suit jacket and hitched up his pants.

"Well," he said. Cindy kept her smile on maximum wattage.

Caldwell glanced at the door, rubbed his lips, then sat down. His haughty, raised-eyebrow demeanor had vanished. He seemed almost humble.

"Uh, senator … may I call you Cindy?"

"Of course," Cindy said. "And…?"

"James will do fine," he said. "That's what the 'J' is for, you know."

"Another name with a great and long history," Cindy said.

Caldwell looked to his left.

"Cindy. I ... You know that I can't make any firm promises about your bill. I mean, if the leadership opposes it ... well, you know that could make it very difficult for me. You know that I'm in line for vice chairman of the Select Committee on Ethics," he said, straightening his back. "When I get re-elected, I stand a pretty good chance of getting that appointment." He paused. "Provided, of course, that I don't go against the leadership."

It astonished Cindy that a senator who was obviously frightened of his party's leadership was about to be appointed to the one committee that sometimes had to take on the power structure. But she knew that in D.C., such things not only made sense, they also happened with alarming regularity.

"I understand, James," Cindy said. "I wouldn't ask you to mess anything up. But I should tell you that the bill I'm going to introduce will be pretty groundbreaking. It's going to be one of the most important family-oriented bills ever introduced in the Senate. It might cause a little ... discomfort among people who don't like change. But can I ask you – if you had a chance to vote on a bill that might be compared to the civil rights bill, and one that would make your voters very happy – and one that no one could ever really criticize you for supporting, do you think it might be worth making the leadership just a little irritated?"

"I really try very hard not to irritate anyone," Caldwell said.

"I understand, senator. And I'm not asking for a firm commitment. Just a promise that you'll consider voting for my bill when it comes out of committee and makes it to the floor."

"And you said that this is going to happen when?"

"I'm not sure," Cindy said. "There are a few issues that have to be resolved first. It might not be for a while. But I'd like to know that you are one of the senators who will take the bill seriously."

Caldwell smiled. "Oh, I know how that goes with the committees. I'm on Agriculture, you know," he said. "Lots of work there."

"It's a very important committee," Cindy said.

There was another extended silence.

"Cindy," Caldwell said, seeming hesitant.

"James."

"Do you think … I … well, you're a very attractive young lady. Do you think that sometime, perhaps, we could … have dinner together?" He smiled at her and Cindy could feel him cranking up the charisma.

"I'd be delighted, senator," she said, crossing her fingers under her chair. "I'm pretty booked for the next several weeks, but when things slow down after the holidays…."

"Oh, yes, I'm very busy too," Caldwell said hastily. "I was just thinking that it might be a nice … change to talk to someone who's not quite so … so … much a part of Washington, D.C."

Cindy found herself using a gentle smile that she usually reserved for children. "I understand, James. It must be tough being this far from home for most of the year."

"Oh, you don't know," Caldwell said. "It's terrible, just terrible. And the weather." He shivered.

"Just give me a call sometime, James. I'm sure that we can work something out," Cindy said. Deciding that it was time to bring the meeting to a close, she stood and offered her hand. Caldwell jumped to his feet. He took her hand but instead of shaking it, he stunned Cindy by bowing and gently brushing his lips across her knuckles. She was further startled when his touch sent an electric charge through her.

He kept her hand as he raised his eyes to hers. "I am delighted to have met a fine young lady such as yourself," he said. Cindy retrieved her hand and could feel herself blushing.

"Thank you, senator … James." Cindy said. She tried not to run from his office.

Chapter Eighty-Six

"**G**irl! He did not!" Ev said over coffee at a small shop within sight of the capitol dome.

"He did," Cindy said. "He even put his other hand behind his back when he did it. But that's not all."

Ev widened her eyes. "Tell me you didn't…."

"Oh, my god, Ev, no!" Cindy said. "I was just going to tell you that I compared my child abuse bill to the civil rights bill. To Caldwell. It just kind of slipped out."

Ev closed her eyes a moment, then burst into laughter.

"I wanted to impress him … impress him about how important it is," Cindy said helplessly, but Ev's laughter was contagious.

"Kissed your hand, you princess!" Ev gasped.

Cindy chuckled, then laughed. She had to put her coffee down and soon the two of them were laughing uncontrollably. They laughed until both had to dab tears from their eyes with one of the shop's brown-and-clearly-unbleached-with-chemicals paper napkins.

"Oh my god," Ev said, recovering. "As soon as I saw those cheekbones, I knew I shouldn't have left you alone with him!" She reached out and took Cindy's hand. "Girl, you need to get some action. When J. Preston Caldwell gets your blood moving, you've been alone for way too long!"

"Or I've just been in this town too long," Cindy said.

"Oh, girl," Ev said, still laughing. "You poor thing. Now you're going to have to go on a date with Senator Blowdry. You'll be the talk of the town."

"You're right. I didn't think about that," Cindy said miserably. "The gossip pages will be calling us a couple. Is he married?"

"Divorced," Ev said and raised her coffee cup to her lips, but another snort of laughter made her put it back down. "Divorced but rich." She paused. "He really kissed your hand?"

"Well, not really kissed. He just kind of brushed," Cindy said.

"With his lips?"

"Of course with his lips!" Cindy said. She sat up straighter. "He was actually a perfect gentleman."

"Oh, I'm sure he was, girl," Ev said. "He'll be a perfect gentleman right up to the moment he leads you to his bedroom door."

"Ev!" Cindy said, looking around the shop.

"Don't tell me you haven't heard the stories," Ev said. "Why do you think he's divorced?"

"I'm not attracted to him!" Cindy protested. "I … he just asked me to dinner, and I said yes. It can be a business dinner. What's so funny about that?"

"What's funny is that this table has a higher IQ than he does," Ev said. "And he's not going to think that it's a business dinner. He's going to be all over you."

Cindy sighed. "Well, I told him that I'm busy for a few weeks. So I have a bit of a reprieve. Maybe I can put him off a few times and before we know it, my term will be up."

Ev looked at Cindy over her coffee cup. "You just wait until the flowers start showing up, girl," she said. "He's going to make it really hard to say no."

"I don't have to say no," Cindy said. "I just have to survive a dinner date. I think I can handle that. For the sake of a vote on my bill."

"You just be careful what you say yes to in this town," Ev said, smiling. "There are eighty-four male senators."

Chapter Eighty-Seven

"**S**enator," her receptionist Shirley said over the intercom. "Another flower delivery."

Cindy thanked her, sighed and stood up. Caldwell had sent flowers every day since their meeting.

She went into the outer office, where Shirley raised her eyebrows at the latest floral explosion. This one was even larger than usual and had a note attached. Cindy rolled her eyes and took it to her office. Shirley laughed.

Back in her office, she set the flowers on her desk and opened the small envelope attached to the vase. The handwritten note read: "Might I request the pleasure of your company this Friday at 8 p.m.? I shall be delighted to pick you up and return you to your home safely."

Cindy sighed again. She supposed that it was time to get it over with. She punched her intercom and said, "Shirley, please get me Senator Caldwell."

"Certainly," Shirley said. Cindy waited a minute. Her phone beeped. "Senator, Senator Caldwell is on line two."

"Thank you, Shirley," Cindy said and punched line two's button.

"Hello, James," she said.

"You may refuse," he said. "I will not be at all offended and will be content to admire you from a distance."

Cindy noticed that once he made his romantic interest in her clear, his mannerisms in her presence had changed from the supercilious senator to the gallant knight. Even his language had changed.

"James, I will be thrilled," Cindy said, glad that she had to put enthusiasm only into her voice, not her entire body.

"I shall see you then," he said. "Goodbye, my lady."

"Goodbye," Cindy said and hung up.

She wondered what kind of price she was going to pay to get Senator Caldwell to support her bill. One dinner date was certainly worth it, she thought. But what about the difficulty of putting him off if he wanted more? And if he did make a move, how could she put him off and avoid upsetting him, thus guaranteeing that he would vote against her bill, not for it?

She sighed and found that she was feeling something that she never thought she would: She was longing to be back in Altoona, a caseworker, where even the most complicated situations were simple compared to the many-tentacled problems that confronted her in D.C.

Chapter Eighty-Eight

His car was a deep olive-green Bentley. He had a uniformed driver, who called her "Ma'am" and opened the door for her. Inside, the car was startlingly quiet. The back seat was leather, spacious, and clearly designed to be used as a conversation and meeting space. Caldwell was wearing a suit so deeply blue that it was just short of black. It fit him perfectly and Cindy had no doubt that it was tailored exactly to his measurements. His shirt was excruciatingly white and his tie, obviously silk, was perfectly knotted. Cindy worried about her off-the-rack black dress. It was clearly not nearly in the same class as Caldwell's clothing but he complimented her on it.

He kept his hands to himself during the drive to the restaurant. He was calm and cordial. The conversation was shoptalk.

The restaurant had no sign out front. The maitre 'd knew Caldwell. The menu was a tiny scroll listing just four entrees and three appetizers. No prices were listed. Caldwell asked her preference, then ordered for her. The lighting was dim, their table was tiny and Cindy was sure that they had at least four waiters. Used dishes were whisked away. All she had to do was look up and a waiter appeared, eyebrow raised, ready to refill her wine glass or do her bidding. After the main course, the chef came to their table. He clearly knew Caldwell and sought his approval. Caldwell was gentlemanly and complimented the man on the meal. The chef bowed deeply to Cindy before he left their table.

Caldwell was obviously used to the level of service, but Cindy found herself constantly thanking the ever-present white-gloved staff who did everything from pulling out her chair to scraping crumbs from the tablecloth to giving a three-minute description of the entrees.

Despite Cindy's efforts to keep it businesslike, the conversation turned to family. Cindy decided to let Caldwell do most of the talking.

"My daughter's name is Marie," Caldwell said proudly over exquisite coffee served in tiny cups. "She's the most beautiful thing I've ever seen. She has these big eyes…. She's just … a beautiful little creature."

An idea leaped into Cindy's mind. She saw her opening. She put her hand on Caldwell's. He became still. His hand was warm. She hoped that the mild affection she had developed for him was genuine and not just the wine.

"James, I don't want to upset you. But I can see your love for your little girl. And that's what she is, isn't she? No matter how old she gets, she'll always be your little girl. Right?"

Caldwell nodded and Cindy thought that she detected the slightest gleam of tears in his eyes.

"And Marie is privileged. You have enough money to make sure that she has everything she wants and needs. And she has you for a father, a daddy who will always protect her and care for her. A father who will always stand between her and harm. A father who would give his life for her, if that's what it took."

"My god, I'd give her the heart from my body if she needed one," Caldwell said. With the hand not covered by Cindy's, he snatched up a napkin and dabbed at his eyes. He cleared his throat and looked around.

"I know you would," Cindy said. "I can sense that in you. You're a wonderful father. What makes you a wonderful father is the sacrifices that you would make for your daughter if you had to. Just imagine," she said, "If you weren't in the positive financial situation that you're in. What if things were … a little rougher? What if, somehow, you had barely enough money to get by?"

Caldwell frowned and replaced the napkin on the table in front of him.

"Well, I…." he began.

"Just pretend," Cindy said. "Now, imagine that you're both really hungry. And it's just you and your girl. And you have just a few dollars. If it came down to you getting something to eat or your little girl getting something to eat, what would you choose?"

"She would eat," Caldwell said without hesitation.

"See, I knew you would say that," Cindy said. "You made that choice because you love and cherish your little girl. You know that she's a gift from heaven."

Caldwell nodded. He moved his hand to clasp Cindy's. She let him.

"But James, you have to realize that there are parents out there who don't have much money. And they have children too, precious little children, little gifts from God. God gives children to us all, rich or poor." *That's not true,* a voice whispered to her but she ignored it.

"For some families, there isn't enough food to go around. But some parents decide to satisfy their own hunger before their children's. Some parents are even worse – they actively abuse their children. They beat them. The hurt them. They do nothing but yell at them. They don't … value them. They do nothing to help those children become happy, healthy adults. Or, they neglect them. They don't care about their kids and only take notice of them when they do something wrong.

"You might think that's rare, but it's not, James," Cindy said. "It's not. The news media picks up only on the most appalling cases, but child abuse is routine and common. You might not see it in your circle of friends. So you'll just have to believe me when I tell you that there are thousands and thousands of children out there who cry themselves to sleep every night. It might be from hunger, or from the pain of yet another beating. Or just the pain of being told by a parent that you're worthless and useless. Often, they're sad and lonely and wish that someone loved and cared for them."

Cindy was startled to see a huge tear escape from Caldwell's right eye and slide down his cheek. Just as she noticed it, he grabbed his napkin, turned away and dabbed at his face.

"I would never …," he began. "I could never hit Maria. Or refuse her food." He smiled. "I can hardly refuse her anything at all when I look at her pretty little face."

She held his hand tightly. "You wouldn't hurt a child. But others do. That's what my bill is about, James," she said. "We can't stop all child abuse – no law can. What can stop child abuse is if it becomes more socially unacceptable to abuse children. If more parents stop and think before they raise a hand to hit a child. My hope is that if we make child abuse a more serious crime – so serious that it is investigated by the FBI – then the entire nation will start to think about it more. And maybe when people think about it more, they'll do it less. Do you see what I mean?"

Caldwell sniffed. He looked around, then down at the table. Cindy waited. Finally, he raised his eyes to hers.

"I know … I know that I'm not the smartest man around," he said. Cindy opened her mouth to protest, but he held up a hand. "No, no, please. You're telling me the truth. Let me tell you the truth. I'm … lucky. I know that. I was born into money. I've never wanted for anything. In fact," he said and looked around the restaurant again, "To be honest, I've never worked a day in my life. I've never done so much as dig a hole. I know that I'm lucky. And some people in this country … look down on that. It's a negative, not a positive.

"The other bad thing is that being smart is not like being … muscular or being a good tennis player. If you want to be muscular, you can spend a lot of time lifting weights and you'll get big muscles. If you want to be a good tennis player, well, you can hire a coach and spend a lot of time and you'll become a decent tennis player. Maybe not a pro, but you'll become skilled. So even though people look at skills and things like that and admire the people who are muscular and who are great at tennis … deep down inside, there's a little bit of … a shrug. Because people always think, 'Well, he might be a really good tennis player, but if I really put my mind to it and really worked at it, I could be a decent tennis player too.' So I guess there's always a little bit of … disrespect deep down inside. But when you're talking about intelligence, it's different."

Caldwell closed his eyes, took a breath, then opened them and looked into Cindy's eyes again.

"Intelligence … you can't get better at that. No matter how much you try, you can't be smarter."

"You can –" Cindy began.

"I know what you're going to say," Caldwell said. "Yes, you can read a lot of books. And you can do word puzzles and stuff to make yourself a little sharper." He smiled. "Believe me, I have. But if you don't understand those books because they're … beyond your ability to understand, then you're not really making yourself smarter. Even knowing a lot of facts from books doesn't count as intelligence if you can't put them together, can't see the big picture. The truth is, we're pretty much stuck with the level of intelligence that we're born with. I know that I didn't win that lottery. I won the money lottery, sure. But I didn't win the brains lottery."

He was silent a moment and looked over Cindy's head as if gathering his thoughts.

"I know people who are so smart that they make me feel like … like a dumb dog. I know people who have thoughts and ideas every day that I will never have after a lifetime of thinking. I know people who have these … bright, shining ideas that I will never have. Like you do."

Cindy felt guilty for her early assessment of him. *There is somebody home,* she thought.

"But one thing that I do have," he said, "is that I can love. I can care. I can feel. No one can take that away from me. And maybe there are people, artists, who feel things more strongly than I do. But I still feel them, and they're real feelings. Maybe I can't turn them into poems or paintings, but they're still my feelings. No one can take that away from me. I love my little girl like no one else can."

He paused.

"And if that's what your bill is about … if it's about saying to kids that even though they're not that smart, and if maybe they watch the world and know that they're not the best at something, well, they can still grow up and do something useful," he said. "Maybe they can even … become a United States senator."

He smiled, a bright, wide smile of accomplishment. Cindy got the impression that for the first time, he had managed to express something very important to him. She smiled back.

"That's exactly what my bill is about," Cindy said. "All I ask is that kids get to have a childhood free of abuse, free of criticism that stops them before they ever get a chance."

He squeezed her hand. "Then you have my vote, I promise," he said. "Even if it will make Dan Shipman hate me."

Chapter Eighty-Nine

Caldwell's driver brought the car to a smooth stop exactly in front of Cindy's apartment door.

"I had a wonderful evening," she said. "Thank you so much."

They were holding hands. Caldwell had been silent for most of the drive from the restaurant.

"I ... I had the best evening of my life," Caldwell said. "I don't even know what to say. You're such a wonderful young woman. You have such ... life to you. You just ... sparkle." He sighed. "So many people in this city are just ... oh, the politics. Sports. And the gossip. They just talk, talk, talk. It's all so ... dreary. Like a rainy day."

Cindy heard herself asking, "Would you like to come up for a minute? For a drink? I think I have some wine that has probably aged quite nicely in the back of my fridge."

Caldwell stiffened and Cindy was afraid that she had offended him.

"I ... well, I ... of course," he said, finding his manners. "I would be delighted."

He leaned forward and murmured instructions to the driver, who got out and opened Cindy's door for her. As they walked to the door of Cindy's apartment building, Caldwell's Bentley purred away. Cindy wondered where the driver would go and what he would do.

Caldwell went to sweep the apartment door open for her, but it was locked and his tug only made it rattle. He recovered nicely.

"Your door, my lady, appears to be secured," he said. "Might I have the key?"

Cindy, smiling, pulled the plastic card from her tiny purse.

"Why yes, sir," she said. "You certainly may."

Caldwell took the card and turned to the door. When he hesitated, Cindy realized that he still had no idea how to open it. *He probably doesn't open many doors for himself*, she realized.

"The slot to the right of the door," she said. "Insert the card and pull it back out."

He did so and the door clicked. He swept it open and gestured for Cindy to enter first.

"Thank you, kind sir," she said.

"Not at all, my beautiful lady," he said.

Cindy couldn't deny it – it was a tremendous pleasure to be treated with respect and admiration. If Caldwell was faking it, he was doing a great job. But she felt that his gentlemanly gestures were genuine.

She smiled at him and they went upstairs.

Chapter Ninety

Cindy, Evelyn and Stan Petersen were in Cindy's office. Shipman had apparently declined to appear in person to negotiate a deal, instead sending his Petersen, his chief of staff.

Stan Petersen was nothing like Shipman. Petersen was courteous and pleasant. He was young, dark-haired and had intelligent eyes. He also had a soft voice and an infectious laugh. He completely lacked Shipman's "arrogant professor" aura. He acted more like a friendly neighbor who could be trusted with your mail and a house key when you went on vacation. Even his suit seemed to be cut from a more relaxed fabric, one that moved easily with him.

"Opening the Arctic National Wildlife Preserve – ANWR – for drilling has been kicked around Congress for about 20 years," he said with the deliberate casual imprecision of someone who knows the precise truth. He pronounced ANWR "An-whar."

"I'm sure that you're familiar with the arguments on both sides of the issue. The environmentalists are afraid that drilling for oil there will ruin a pristine Alaskan wildlife preserve. The other side thinks that it's time America developed its own sources of oil to reduce our reliance on mid-eastern countries." He smiled. "I can kind of guess where you come down." His broad, white, open smile reminded her of someone, but she couldn't pin it down.

"You don't have to frame it for me," Cindy said, smiling neutrally, remaining cautious but courteous. She viewed Shipman as an enemy and even though Petersen's demeanor was friendly and open, he worked for Shipman. She knew that she would have to keep that in mind during negotiations. She knew that if she forgot for even a second that Petersen worked for the enemy, it would work against her. If this was truly her only chance to get her child abuse bill to the floor for a vote – and she believed that it was – then she had to be vigilant about every detail and seize every advantage.

"My apologies, Senator, if I'm telling you things that you already know," Petersen said, giving her an apparently sincere smile. "In this business, it's sometimes hard to know who's holding back to gain an advantage and who truly doesn't understand."

"You can assume that I have a working knowl-edge of An-whar and the issues surrounding it," Cindy said.

"Good! Great! Then let me cut right to it," Petersen said. "We need your vote. We know that this is a tough one for you." He smiled again.

Tom Cruise, she thought. *That's who has that smile.*

"But we think it's a fair trade. You give us your support on a vote to expand America's domestic oil reserves. We give you the chance to bring your bill to the floor for a vote."

"No," Ev said sharply. She was sitting to Petersen's left. "That's not the deal. We don't get a chance to bring our bill to the floor for a vote. We get our bill onto the floor for a binding roll call vote."

Petersen smiled and spread his hands apart. "Of course. I'm sorry for my imprecision. Of course you get your bill to the floor. That's the deal. You back us on An-whar, your bill gets to the floor for a vote. Simple."

Cindy didn't smile back. She caught Ev's eye. Ev spoke up.

"Here's the deal, Mr. Petersen," Ev said, leaning forward, her voice as cold as the wind that was whipping across the Potomac. "We will support one effort to bring An-whar to the floor for a vote. One effort. Whether that's a parliamentary maneuver or whether that's a vote to avoid a filibuster. One effort. In return, you support one effort to get our bill onto the floor. Tit for tat. " She fixed her gaze on Petersen. "We're not offering a yes vote on your bill. Unless you're willing to offer a yes vote on our bill."

Petersen's smile faded a bit. He put a fist in front of his mouth as if he had to cough. He frowned and looked down at his shoes. After a few seconds, he looked up.

"I'm, ah, sure that it would be very difficult to get Senator Shipman to vote in favor of your bill," he said.

"And you can be sure that it would be very difficult for me to vote to open An-whar for drilling," Cindy said, taking the baton from Ev. "So let's agree to allow each other's bills to come to the floor for a vote. Once the bills are on the floor, each senator can vote his or her conscience. One bill will be on drilling for oil in a nature preserve and the other to protect the nation's children. What passes, passes. What fails, fails." She looked directly into Petersen's eyes.

"Senator Shipman was under the impression that you would be willing to support an An-whar drilling bill," Petersen said, his fist still in front of his mouth.

"Senator Shipman has not spoken to me in weeks," Cindy said, "Neither has anyone from his staff. So I'm not sure where he got that idea."

"I'm, ah, not sure how this will play with Senator Shipman," Petersen said, at last removing his hand from in front of his mouth. He tried on a medium smile. "But I will of course take this back and present it."

"It's a fair deal that allows us both to avoid problems with our respective power bases," Cindy said. "We can both say that all we did was allow the bills to come to the floor for a vote. The will of the senate will determine whether the bills become law. We're both free to vote our own consciences on the actual bills."

She smiled, but made it a cold one. She was a little alarmed at how easy it was to summon a cold smile these days. She stood and extended her hand. Petersen leaped to his feet and shook.

"OK then," he said. "Someone from our office will be in touch." He grabbed his briefcase, touched his brow in goodbye and let himself out of the office. After giving him time to clear the outer office, Cindy and Ev both collapsed back into their chairs.

"Whoa," Cindy said. "What do you think?"

Ev, slumped in her chair like a teenager watching television, shrugged.

"It all depends upon how important the leadership thinks the vote on An-whar is. If this is considered to be a do-or-die issue, one that they're not willing to lose, then they'll probably go for it. But if not...."

"They're going to tell us to stick it," Cindy said.

"Right," Ev said, sitting up in her chair. "But even if that happens, that's not the end of it, girl-friend. We just sit tight and wait for the next time that they need us. We're making some progress in getting pledges of support. It's moving along. Slowly, but it's moving."

"You're so patient," Cindy said. "I'd just like to get this over with."

Ev smiled her tiger's smile.

"I know, I know," Cindy said. "Patience is power. Patience is power."

"Just keep saying that," Ev said. "And before you know it, we'll get our chance. Just like Dorothy."

Chapter Ninety-One

"This is so completely unacceptable that I don't even know why we're discussing it," said Scott Rivers, executive director of the Pennsylvania Green Party. Cindy had to remind herself of his last name and title – it had been months since she had talked to him. When she was newly elected, he had called her every day with promises of support and seeking inside information about Congress. She had little to offer him in those days. Gradually, his calls had become weekly, then monthly, then quarterly. She began to lose track of the last time they had talked and what she had told him.

His promises of support never materialized and she heard that he had been turned down for a national-level job with the Green Party. Apparently stung, he had not talked to her for nearly six months.

Now in her third year as a senator, she was talking to him about the deal she was trying to cut with Shipman to get her child abuse bill on the floor of the Senate for a vote. Cindy was more than willing to trade votes, but Scott was furious.

"Cindy, when you decided to run under the Green Party banner, you said that you not only understood what we fight for, but that you would help us fight. An-whar is a … an absolutely key issue for the Green Party. It is simply not negotiable. We're not going to allow the oil companies to make a fat profit while they destroy twenty million acres of the last untouched wilderness in North America."

"Scott, I'm not going to be voting for the drilling. I'm just voting to allow the drilling bill to come to the floor for a vote. I can still vote no on the actual bill."

"Cindy, I know how politics works down there. A vote to allow the bill to come to the floor might as well be a vote to allow drilling. You might was well drive up to Alaska and shoot the elk yourself," he said.

"That's not true," Cindy said, but Scott charged on.

"Don't play dumb, Cindy!" Scott said, anger entering his voice. "By now you know how it works. There's no way those bastards running the Republican Party these days will even put the bill up for consideration unless they're sure they have enough votes to pass it. So voting to bring it to the floor for a vote is only a formality. Once it gets there, it's as good as passed. So our only real chance to stop it will be right at the beginning – to make sure that it never even gets a real vote. And that's right where you want to betray us!"

Cindy let there be silence on the line. "Scott, that's an awfully strong word," she said.

"But it's the right one!" Scott shouted. "Voting yes on anything even related to drilling is … nothing less than outright betrayal. Yes! There! I said it again."

"Scott…." Cindy put her head down and put her left hand on her forehead. "This is a crucial issue for me. If I can't get my child abuse bill onto the floor for a vote, then –"

"Then what?" Scott shouted. "What? What will happen? You can cut another deal to get your damn bill voted on! Wait for another opportunity. You don't have to screw the Green Party to get your bill voted on. And why are you even worrying about child abuse? That's not a Green Party priority."

"It's my priority," Cindy said quietly.

"Jesus!" Scott swore. "I can't believe we're even talking about this! If there are ten issues that the Green Party lives and dies on, drilling in ANWR is one of them. And now you want to sell us out so you can get a vote on a bill that's not even on our radar –"

"Scott, let me set you straight on a few things," Cindy said, using her rising anger to put steel into her voice. "When I agreed to run under the Green Party banner, I was agreeing to support your Ten Key Values – remember that? Those values are mostly about having government work for people, not corporations. And solving problems through democratic participation. And non-violence. I don't recall An-whar being one of those."

"Ecological Wisdom," Scott said acidly. "Number three."

"Yes," Cindy said. "Wisdom. Ecological wisdom. It doesn't say 'vote blindly against every single oil bill that comes up'!"

"Drilling in An-whar does not constitute wisdom by any stretch of the imagination," Scott said. "You can squirm however you want, but if you vote to allow a bill on An-whar drilling to get the Senate floor, you've betrayed us. It's that simple, Cindy. There's no nice way to put it."

Cindy took a deep breath to hold back her knee-jerk response.

"Well, then, all I can say, Scott, is that I'm sorry," Cindy said. "I'm going ahead with the deal because it might be my only chance to get my child abuse bill passed. You can be sure that I didn't spend a year walking around the streets of Pennsylvania towns in freezing weather to get to the Senate and sit on my hands."

"You can be sure of another thing," Scott said. "If you vote to allow that bill to get to the floor, you will get zero support from the Green Party in the future. Zero. Do you hear me?"

There was a loud clatter and then silence. *He hung up on me*, Cindy realized.

She hung up her phone and sat quietly, looking at it. She had never liked Scott that much and had always suspected that he was using her to support his own personal ladder-climbing within the Green Party. But there were many others in the party, smart, reasonable, unselfish people who had given her their time, energy and money. She thought of all the Green Party supporters who had stood for hours outside the polling places on Election Day, handing out pamphlets asking people to vote for Cindy Phillips. She thought of the volunteers working phone banks, making call after call after call urging voters to support her. All those people who had sent in checks – sometimes just five dollars. She remembered someone at a Green Party function telling her that an eight-year-old kid had mailed in the contents of his piggy bank, asking the party to "stop people from cutting down so many trees." It was eight dollars composed of about five pounds of change and a few wrinkled dollar bills. At the time, the story had almost made her cry. *Am I betraying those people?* she wondered. *Am I letting them down?*

She thought back to those ten values that the Green Party stood for. At one point, she had them memorized. What were they? She closed her eyes to remember. Grassroots democracy, that was the first one. One about social justice. One on non-violence. One on economic justice. One on feminism that she remembered because she had always been leery of it. That was how many, five? She could only recall five of ten. And the one about ecological wisdom that Scott had mentioned. Six. Was voting to allow the full senate to vote on oil drilling in the Arctic National Wildlife Preserve a betrayal of those values?

She sighed. Without the Green Party's statewide organization, she knew that she had no chance of winning re-election. Even though the Green Party was a small third party without great influence, it still had a structure. There were volunteers. There was a donor list. There was a system that could help her get the word out. Without that structure, getting re-elected would be impossible. And the two big parties weren't likely to welcome her with open arms. The Republicans were a lost cause – Shipman had national influence and would never allow the party to support her. And the Democrats were unlikely to forgive her for stepping into Pacifico's shoes. She had read angry letters to the editor after the election accusing her of stealing Pacifico's votes. No, the Pennsylvania Democrats would choose someone from their internal power structure, an experienced politician, before they would back her.

So, she realized, with the loss of Green Party support, any thoughts of a second term would have to be banished. She had to stay focused on the here-and-now and get her child abuse bill passed in the next three years. Or it would never pass.

Chapter Ninety-Two

Cindy watched as both the Democrats and Republicans ratcheted up the rhetoric on drilling in ANWR. Both sides sent forth warriors and mercenaries to do battle on television talk shows and place quotes in nationally read newspapers. Think tanks weighed in with comments, observations and white papers. Environmental groups held rallies.

The Republicans accused the Democrats of "turning over the nation's gas pumps to unstable mid-eastern nations." Democrats fired back that Republicans were "putting the interests of greedy oil companies ahead of people and the environment." Names were called. Scoffs were issued. Accusations were made. Positions solidified. Editorial page editors called for calm. ANWR became an us vs. them issue, transcending oil drilling. It came to be seen as wealth vs. working class, environment vs. business, animals vs. the economy. Shipman himself made the rounds of the political talk shows, accusing the Democrats of threatening national security by forcing the U.S. to remain dependent on foreign oil.

"This is it," Ev promised when Shipman began making TV appearances. "Just wait. It's getting too hot. The GOP can't back down now and they're struggling for votes on this one. Wilson from Wisconsin is opposing the bill and so are a few other moderate Republicans, so they've got to pick up a few votes from conservative Democrats. And from you."

Cindy saw Ev's tiger grin again. "Hold tight, girl. It's coming."

Ev, as usual, proved to be right.

Word finally came to Cindy via Petersen. She was crossing the floor of the Russell Senate Office Building, in a hurry because she was late for a conference call in her office, when Petersen rose from a bench under the rotunda. He had his long black overcoat slung over one arm. He intercepted her with a small smile.

"Senator. I know you're in a hurry."

Cindy halted. She took a quick look around.

"Mr. Petersen, if this is something –"

"Just one minute," he said. The serious look in his eyes stopped her. "If you will agree to vote to end the filibuster that the Democrats are threatening on An-whar, then you have your child abuse vote."

A few business-suited people swept past them, chattering, intent on their conversations, but for Cindy, time froze. Her head whirled. *This is it,* she thought. *This is it. This is it.* She felt as if she'd discovered a huge prize that she didn't deserve, like finding a Van Gogh at a yard sale.

"Senator?" Petersen asked.

"A binding roll-call vote," Cindy said, recovering.

"Binding roll call," Petersen agreed.

"How soon?"

"After the An-whar vote. Probably not for three weeks, but definitely within six."

"A roll-call vote within six weeks."

"Yes."

"On my bill, unchanged."

"It will be released by the Health and Education Committee as you introduced it," he said.

"No public opposition by the GOP," she said.

"The leadership will remain silent and the rank-and-file will be told to do so as well," Petersen said.

"No b.s."

"No bullshit," Petersen said solemnly.

Cindy deliberately looked into his eyes. They were dark and serious and she tried to stare right through them, to see the core of the man. He held her gaze. She decided to trust him.

Cindy offered her hand. "You may tell Senator Shipman that he has a deal," Cindy said.

Petersen shook. "Senator," he said, and strode away on the marble floor under the rotunda.

Here we go, Cindy thought.

Chapter Ninety-Three

It was long after hours. It was night outside and most of the offices on Cindy's hallway were dark. But every light burned in Cindy's office and all hands were on deck. Every aide and volunteer had been summoned to Cindy's office for a war party. The people were scattered around Cindy's office, sitting on chairs dragged in from the outside office, on desks, on the floor. Cindy was amazed. They had never before all been in one room. She counted thirty-two people, not counting herself and Ev. Everyone in this room had sworn loyalty to Cindy in one way or another. Some were paid, but most were volunteers. Cindy had been amazed at how many had come out of the woodwork once word got out that she was the "child abuse senator." They were mostly young, and they knew that this all-hands meeting was a big deal. Ties were loose, shoes were off, sleeves were rolled up, but all attention was on Evelyn.

Evelyn was a hurricane of action. Cindy had seen her show energy and drive before, but she had kicked it up a notch or two, if that was possible.

Cindy, sitting quietly in her big office chair, watched with amusement. An outsider would conclude that Evelyn was the one living and dying over the child abuse bill's prospects, not Cindy. Ev perched on the side of Cindy's desk, facing the group, one foot on the floor. Cindy could see her in profile.

"And we've got to make fresh visits to the moderates," Ev said, scribbling on a yellow legal pad. "I'll start scheduling those. We need to the remind them of their promises and keep the pressure on. Cindy, that's you and me." Ev looked over her shoulder to catch Cindy's nod. She returned to her yellow pad. "And who's coordinating the art show? Do we have all those photos in? Carl?"

Carl, sitting to one side of Cindy's desk, jacket off, tie loose, responded to Ev's energy with a deliberate calm. It was as if he thought that he could tame her with his slow steadiness, Cindy thought.

"We've got photos from forty-seven states," he said. "We're missing, uh, Washington state. And two others. I don't know what's up with them, but I'll run them down before the vote."

Ev fixed Carl with a raised-eyebrow look. Cindy knew that although Carl remained disappointed by Ev's lack of romantic interest in him, he remained professional. In the office, they worked well together, sometimes finishing each other's sentences.

In response to Ev's look, Carl lifted the hand holding his pen and put it over his heart. "Swear to god. We'll have 50 photos if I have to drive out to Seattle myself."

Ev gave him her "you-damn-well-better" look, glanced at her sheet and barked, "OK. Defendkids dot org liaison. Jamie?"

A red-haired, skirted girl at the back spoke up. "I already put them on notice. They're ready to gear up when we give the word."

"We need to get their officers into this office for a meeting," Ev said. "This week. We've got to map out a grassroots strategy, phone banks, ad strategy and any other bright ideas that they have. Can you handle that?"

"Meeting. This week," the girl said, typing into her phone. "Got it."

"Who's got the media?"

"Right here," said a voice unusual in the group. Cindy looked up to see an older but not elderly woman raise her hand. She had a sweater and librarian's glasses on, complete with a chain of beads holding them around her neck. "Johnson. Emily Johnson."

"Mrs. Johnson," Ev said, the bark gone from her voice. "I think you need no introduction. We're glad to see you here."

Cindy knew from Ev's stories that Johnson had covered the White House for more than 30 years for the Associated Press. She had retired recently, but her three decades of experience had given her more bylines than the entire newsroom of most newspapers. She was on dinner-invitation terms with four past presidents. Cabinet members, foreign presidents and diplomats called her by her first name and smiled when they saw her. Upon hearing of Cindy's child abuse fight, she had shown up at the office and offered her services. When Cindy thanked her, Johnson had said, "Oh, I need something to do, honey. It's getting a little boring reading the news instead of writing it."

In the war room that Cindy's office had become, Johnson waved a yellow pencil at Ev.

"Don't you worry about the media, honey," she said. "These young reporters may not know a story if it bites them on the ass, but they'll catch on fast if I have anything to do with it."

"Mrs. Johnson, I have every confidence in your ability to produce headlines," Ev said with a smile.

Johnson snorted. "Ability's got nothing to do with it. It's pure orneriness."

Those in the room chuckled.

"Thank you, Mrs. Johnson," Ev said. Then, her deference for Johnson put aside, she snapped, "Democratic liaison. Jim! Who's on our side?"

Jim, a sandy-haired young man in a blue shirt and khakis, stood up. "We've got thirty-five for sure, including Cain. Roberts is a maybe," he said. "I'm pretty sure that –"

"Which Roberts?" Ev interrupted. "North Carolina or Kansas?"

And so it went, with Cindy watching, bemused, as Ev marshaled the troops and planned the battle.

Chapter Ninety-Four

"**S**enator, a Peter Pannington for you on line one."

"Thank you, Shirley." Cindy picked up her phone and punched a button.

"Peter! How are you?"

"Cindy. Very good to hear your voice. I hear that you are doing quite well here in our nation's capital."

"I'm getting by. Things take a while down here."

"My dear, if you think that federal legislation moves slowly, try corporate law," Pannington said.

"Good thing you get paid by the hour," Cindy said.

"Touché!" Pannington said. "You've discovered my evil secret. How else would I be able to afford a Ferrari and my penthouse apartment?"

"To what do I owe the honor of this call?" Cindy asked.

"Well, senator," Pannington said, his tone of voice switching to business. "I'm certain that you are busy. However, I promised Mr. Steele that I would keep an eye on you. And I notice that you've put the Maryland farm property up for sale."

Cindy bowed her head. "Boy, you don't miss much, do you?"

"Not when it concerns your welfare, my dear."

"Peter…." Cindy began. "I don't … I hope this doesn't upset you."

"You can't upset me, Cindy," Pannington said. "Are you in need of resources?"

"Peter … I'm gearing up for a vote on my child abuse bill. I'm in my fourth year in the Senate. It's pretty clear that I'm not going to have a second term and I'm not sure that I have the stomach for it anyway. I just want to get this child abuse bill passed and get out alive."

"And…?"

"And I've teamed up with a non-profit organization that helps fight child abuse. They're great people. They're a key part of my effort. I need to put some pressure on the senators to get them to vote in favor of my bill. I can't afford lobbyists. So the only way to do that is to stir up the grassroots – telephone banks, TV ads, billboards. That kind of thing. But the group … well, they need money. They fought a big battle in Virginia a while ago, used up a lot of resources and they're stretched thin. But I really need them to drum up some grassroots support in the next few weeks."

"Defendkids dot org," Pannington said.

"My, my. You really are up on things," Cindy said. "Yes, that's the group. They're rock-solid behind my proposal, but…."

"But you need money to make some things happen," Pannington said. "And you thought that you could get enough by selling the farm in Maryland to kick-start the effort."

"Exactly," Cindy said. "I can't even pretend with you, Peter."

There was a silence on the line. Just as Cindy was about to speak, Pannington spoke.

"Jim left a reserve account with me," he said. "I am permitted to use it as I see fit."

Cindy pulled in a breath and held it.

"If … if you felt that this was … that your bill is … a sufficiently important event that it would earn Jim's support were he alive … then I can release funds in support of your chosen organization," Pannington said.

"Oh, Peter. You have no idea," Cindy said. "Anything would help. Ten thousand dollars would help. My god, we'll take five."

Pannington chuckled and Cindy knew that she had him.

"My dear lady, there is significantly more than ten thousand dollars in the account," Pannington said. Then his voice turned serious. "You sincerely believe that Jim would have supported this effort?"

"Peter – I'll fax you a copy of the bill! If it passes, it will change the way child abuse is treated in this nation. And with any luck, it'll change attitudes as well. It's … I don't want to go overboard, but nothing like this has been passed in decades. Maybe ever. It's a … radical bill, Peter."

"Then consider it done," Pannington said. "And I shall waste no more of your time, my dear."

"Oh, Peter, I can't thank you enough. If this bill passes…."

"If it passes, then I imagine that Mr. Jim Steele will be raising his beer glass to us in some heavenly tavern," Pannington said.

"Oh, he will," Cindy said. "He absolutely will."

"And you will remove the 'for sale' sign from the Maryland farm?"

"I'll call the real estate agent as soon as I hang up with you," Cindy said.

"Thank you, my dear," Pannington said.

Chapter Ninety-Five

"Senator Caldwell on line four," the receptionist told Cindy over the intercom.

"Thank you," Cindy said and punched a button on her phone to pick up the call.

"James, how are you?" she asked.

"Not good," he said. She could hear in his voice that he wasn't kidding. "Shipman's hit man just left."

"I'm sorry to hear that," Cindy said. "Are you OK?"

"My ethics committee vice chairmanship is apparently … not going to happen if I support your bill," he said. "Mr. Petersen made that pretty clear."

"Oh dear," Cindy said. "James, what can I do?"

There was a long pause.

"I … well, I don't know," he said. "This is getting to be really hard. I really don't like having Shipman mad at me."

"I know the feeling," Cindy said. "But you have to think of it this way. Think of all the children who will be able to sleep soundly at night because you support my bill. Think of all the children who won't be beaten, who won't be starved, who might just have a chance to grow up and –"

"I know, I know," he said somewhat testily. "It's for the children. But it's also about my career."

"James," Cindy said, putting a hand to her forehead, "think of it this way. You're going to make a lot of votes as a senator. In the long run, fifty or a hundred years from now, most of them aren't going to matter. But a few of them will. A few of your votes will change this country. You might or might not get to be chairman of the ethics committee. And what happens on that committee might or might not change this country for the better. But I guarantee you, James, I absolutely, positively promise you, that a vote for my bill is going to make this country a better place for children – a better place overall. It's not often that you get to cast such a vote. In fact, a lot of senators come and go and their votes on things like National Pork Week and budgets and tax cuts … well, James, a lot of those votes are never going to mean anything. The only reason that they'll even be remembered is because deep in the senate's records, there will be an aye or a nay recorded. And then buried in piles of paper and shipped off to the national archives, where information goes to die.

"But James … how often are you going to get to take a vote that will allow you to go home to your constituents and look every single one of them in the eye and say, 'I cast a vote that made this country re-evaluate the value of its children'? How many votes will allow you to look out the window of that Bentley and see children walking down the street and think to yourself, 'I made their lives safer and happier'? How many chances like that are you going to get, James?"

There was silence on the line.

"I do … I do wonder sometimes when we take these ag subsidy votes … I wonder if … I wonder what it means," he said. "My staff tells me that I'm protecting this and saving that … but I wonder."

More silence.

"I just … hmm. Cindy, I sure would like to be vice chairman of the select ethics committee. It would make my father very happy."

"James," Cindy said, "I bet you'd like more to be a great father to Marie. So how would you like to be a protective father to the kids of the entire nation? Not just Marie, but a couple million kids? Think of it this way: You would never hurt Marie. But there are a lot of other Maries out there, little girls with big eyes. And they fear their fathers. He hurts them, he makes them cry. Think about all those pretty and sad little Marias out there. What if you could help them? If it were just a matter of money, how much would you pay to keep them from being abused?"

"I … well," James said.

"Well, it won't cost you a dime. All you have to do is say 'aye' when they call your name," Cindy said. "And think that one day, you'll be able to tell Marie, 'I voted for that bill.' I bet she'll be proud of you."

Caldwell was silent for nearly a minute. Cindy waited. Then he said, "Thank you, my lady. It always helps to speak with you. You clarify issues for me."

He hung up and Cindy was left listening to a dead line.

Chapter Ninety-Six

Chris from Defendkids dot org had brought in samples of the billboards that the organization was going to put up around the country. They were printed in color on heavy paper, all of them looking exactly like a miniature billboard, frame and all. They ranged from the nerve rattling to the nearly subliminal.

Chris leaned forward, anxious, as Ev and Cindy scanned them.

He pushed his glasses up on his nose. "They ... any one of them can be changed if you don't like them," he said. "We have the contracts for the space but haven't yet sent the actual art. So ... you just let me know."

Cindy was sitting at her desk and Ev was standing beside her.

"Oh my," Cindy said, looking at one. It was in black and white, showing a man in a stained t-shirt, looking like he was leaning right out of the billboard. His face was contorted in anger and one hand was balled into a fist. Beside in him in bold type, the billboard read, "He's about to teach his kid a lesson. Again. Maybe it's time someone taught him a lesson." Then, at the bottom, in smaller letters: "Help stop child abuse. Visit defendkids.org."

"Wow," Ev said.

"Is it too much?" Chris asked. "We can –"

"No, no, Chris, it's fine. It's just … a little hard-hitting." Cindy put the sketch down.

"It's great!" Ev said. "That'll get attention. Maybe it'll make someone mad and we'll get some serious press coverage." Chris smiled and sat back, relaxing a fraction.

"Oh my," Cindy said again, closed her eyes and held one of the sketches up to Ev.

This sample, also in black and white, showed a young girl, no more than eight, in a coffin. Her head rested on a frilly pillow and a teddy bear was tucked under her arm. On her face were bruises. The text read, "Her father was her judge, jury and executioner. Her crime? Spilled milk." And then at the bottom, "Help stop child murder. Visit defend-kids.org."

"Jeez. That one will get some attention," Ev said.

"We've got different varieties for different demographics," Chris said. "We'll run different races and nationalities so no one thinks that we're focusing on any particular group as child abusers. But we did hold true to the national statistics – most children who die from abuse are killed by a male figure in the household."

"And what happens when someone goes to the website?" Ev asked. Cindy was still stunned by the image of the little girl in the coffin.

"We offer a variety of choices," Chris said. "The whole site is set up to be very user-friendly and keep people moving through it. We open with descriptions of a couple of cases of really ugly abuse to grab their attention, get them emotionally involved. The stories and photos that pop up are based upon where they access the site from – we can tell in general where they're from based on their ISP address. So we have a localized child abuse story pop up. We have a database of about fourteen thousand cases, covering the whole country."

"And once they're crying their eyes out?" Ev asked.

"Then we direct them to information about Cindy's bill and we list ways that they can help," Chris said. "There are a bunch of options. They can donate money, they can volunteer, they can join our organization. They can call or send a letter to their home senator. They have the choice of either using one of a selection of boilerplate letters that we provide or they can write their own. We email it and snail-mail it directly to their senators. No cost to them."

"And you track them?"

"We track by zip code," Chris said. "They have the opportunity to give us more specific information about themselves, sign up for our newsletter, all that kind of stuff. But we'll be able to get aggregate statistics on visits to the site, if that's what you're asking."

"I am," Ev said. "It might come in handy to be able to tell senators that X number of voters from their state visited the site and spent Y minutes there."

"We can do that," Chris said. "Our web people are great. We don't have state-of-the-art technology, but we've got some very dedicated people working overtime on the site."

"Great!" Ev said. She looked at Cindy. Cindy was sitting very still, head down, hand over her eyes. Ev knew what that posture meant.

"OK, Chris, these look great," Ev said, gathering up the sketches and handing them to him.

"They're OK?" he asked.

"They're great," Ev said. "Run them."

Chris smiled and put out a hand. Ev took it and shook. Cindy looked up and took his hand after Ev shook. Her eyes were bloodshot.

"They're great, Chris, very powerful. Get them up," she said. Then, in a tight, angry voice: "Maybe people will finally get really pissed off."

Chris, a little startled at the venom in her voice, nodded and started for the door.

"Chris," Cindy said, stopping him. He turned.

"Yes, Cindy?"

"Who designed those?" Cindy asked. "Who came up with those ideas?"

"We work with an ad agency out of New York," he said. "Rutherman, somebody, somebody. I forget the exact name. They give us a break on price because we're a non-profit."

"But your ... your people over there at Defendkids dot org. You guys had some input, right?"

Chris nodded. "Most of the basic ideas came from us," he said. "The ad agency just helped us refine them."

"The … anger comes through," Cindy said. She managed weak smile. "You people are nuts."

Chris smiled back. "Thank you, Cindy," he said. "We like to think so."

Chapter Ninety-Seven

"I can't do it," Caldwell said.

They were sitting on a bench near the FBI building on Pennsylvania Avenue. Cindy had always thought the building hideous, its jutting sections looking like an architect trying to cover up mistakes.

"James. Why?"

He was hunched over and did not meet her eyes. Expectant pigeons strutted around them.

"I … This is all I know how to do," he said. "I can't run a newspaper for Dad. I see the people that they hire to run them. They come from Harvard and Columbia and they've worked at the New York Times and the Chicago Tribune. They're smart. They're sharp."

"You graduated from UCLA," Cindy said gently. "What makes you think that you couldn't rise to the challenge?"

"You went to college, right?" he asked.

"University of Maryland," Cindy said.

"Good school," he said.

"Thank you."

"Did you … were you … did you spend any time socializing or did you just study?"

"I was a studier," Cindy said. "I had to be. The … material didn't come naturally to me like it did to some people in my class. I had to pound it into my head."

"But did you ever go out and have a few beers?"

"Of course. It wouldn't be college if you didn't."

"So then you're familiar with the concept of a mercy fuck."

Cindy was startled to hear Caldwell use such a vulgar word.

"I … yes," she said. "I've heard it before."

"Well, my graduation from UCLA was a mercy fuck," he said. "I got in as a legacy – dad – and they let me stumble through. My final GPA was two point three three. Two point three three."

"I think that's passing," Cindy said carefully. "A gentleman's C."

"Ha!" Caldwell said. "A gentleman's C. That's OK if you actually earn a gentleman's C."

Still hunched over, he turned to look at Cindy. He squinted in the early morning sunlight.

"What if you buy exams and have your father talk to professors in order to make sure that you don't wash out with a boatload of Fs?"

"James," Cindy said. She put a hand on his shoulder. "You're too hard on yourself."

He turned to watch the pigeons. "Maybe I deserve to be hard on myself," he said. "What the hell have I ever accomplished? My great-great granddaddy starts a newspaper that a million people read today. Forget that. Never mind what it was

– he started a business that made so much money that three generations later I can live like a king. And what have I done? Spend the interest that my family earns on that money.

"The only chance that I might have to actually do something … to actually get my name into the history books like my grandfather, will be to do something with myself here in D.C." He paused. "People think that rich kids have all these options open to them. Pretty funny. I have two options: run a newspaper or what my family calls public service. That means run for office. And I'm not talking about running for mayor. I have absolutely no idea how to run a newspaper. So you see what that leaves me."

"You're doing pretty well here in D.C.," Cindy ventured.

"If getting elected with daddy's money and then managing to find my way to my office every morning is an accomplishment, then yes, I'm quite a success."

"You're in your second term," Cindy said. "The voters in California must have liked something about you."

"They liked dad's TV commercials," Caldwell said.

"But two terms –" Cindy began.

"Two terms because of fifty-million-dollar ad budgets and the fact that I toe the Republican company line," he said. "I've never done anything to piss off the leadership." He sat up and looked at Cindy. "And I'm not sure that I can start now."

He sighed.

"Look," he said and Cindy detected urgency in his voice. "If I get the vice chairmanship of the ethics committee, I can maybe make a mark, have an effect. There are always ethics problems in the senate … it comes and goes, but if you wait long enough, someone's bound to step over the line."

"James. Don't tell me that you're planning to screw someone to make a name for yourself."

"Not an undeserved screw," he said. "But if there's a clear case of corruption, and I root it out … well, then I've done my part, right? I've cleaned up the senate … I can go home and –"

"And do what?" Cindy asked angrily. "Tell daddy that you did the bidding of your GOP masters until a chance came along to climb a little higher by breaking someone's back? Is that an accomplishment?"

He turned and looked at her. "Yes," he said quietly. "It is. It's something I can stand on. Something that I can always point to and say, 'I did that.' "

"James, with my child abuse bill, you can say that. You can –"

"I can what?" he said forcefully. "Say that once again, I let someone else come up with the idea and I went along? Say that once again, I let myself be told what to do and how to vote? Say that once again, it wasn't my idea, but by god, I liked it and supported it! I'm sick of that! I'm sick of … following."

He was silent for a minute.

"See, you people with ideas don't understand. You have all these great thoughts … these things that come into your heads. And you convince other people – people like me – to go along. And we do. And sure, if you're nice, you share the glory. But in the end, it was still your idea and people like me were just the supporting cast. I want – just once – to be able to say that I had a good idea, that I had a plan that people followed, that I did something as a leader, not a follower."

He turned and looked at Cindy. "And the ethics committee appointment means that I can do that – I can be a leader, I can make something happen, instead of being a follower."

He swallowed and looked at the pigeons. They eyed him back, tilting their heads.

"Cindy, your bill offers me the opportunity to once again stand in someone's shadow. The ethics committee offers me the opportunity to cast the shadow."

He wrung his hands, then stood up. He looked down at his shoes but managed to raise his eyes to Cindy's.

"Please understand," he said. "This is about … making something out of my life. This is about proving that I'm worth all the money I spend. This is about proving that I can do more than just getting along and going along. I'm sorry. I would love to support your child abuse bill. I know how important it is, but if it means that I'm not the ethics committee chairman, then that's just too high a price to pay."

He stood up and put his hand out. Cindy took it and they shook.

"I guess this ends our dates," he said. "I'm sorry about that. I'll miss them more than anything."

Then he put his hands into his coat and strode rapidly away in the morning sun. Cindy watched him go, wondering how much she had lost.

Chapter Ninety-Eight

The senator left his committee meeting satisfied. He'd made a good point, stymied an opponent and the meeting had taken under two hours. All in all, a good start to his day.

As he approached his office, he noticed that the door was open. A buzz of conversation came from the office. Curious, he turned the corner and was met by the sight of every staffer in his office on the phone.

"Yes, ma'am," said his receptionist into the phone. "I understand. I see your point. OK. OK."

Other staffers were scattered about the office at desks, each of them glued to a phone, nodding and talking. His receptionist, a competent and trusted aide who had been with him more than 15 years, caught his eye and held up a finger, asking "wait a minute."

He raised his eyebrows and pointed to his office to indicate that he would be at his desk. The receptionist said into the phone, "Yes, Ma'am. I will pass that along to the senator." Holding the senator's eye, she nodded, scribbled something on a slip of paper and handed it to the senator. He took it and read, "phones tied up all day – child abuse bill."

The senator rolled his eyes and pointed to his office again. The receptionist nodded. He escaped to his office. Once sitting, he noticed that every light on his phone was glowing, indicating that every line was in use. He heard his receptionist close her call professionally and hang up. Her chair squeaked as she stood and walked to his office. Behind her, the phone on her desk buzzed before she had taken three steps.

"Senator, it's been like this all day," she said. "Callers. Mostly from your district. All worried about the child abuse bill ... the one they named Brittany's Law."

"Good grief," the senator said. "What are they saying?"

"It's running at least ninety percent in favor. The other ten percent are worried that the FBI is going to start investigating everybody who spanks their kid."

"How many of those are the aluminum-foil-hat folks?" he asked.

She smiled. "Very few. They have legitimate concerns."

"And these calls are all about ... Brittany's Law?"

"Yessir."

"Funny. I didn't think it was going to be that big a deal," the senator said. "Leadership downplayed it."

"Well, it's got your constituents all worked up," the receptionist said.

"How the heck did they hear about it?"

"I guess there are billboards up. And TV ads. That's where most people are saying that they heard of it. The ads tell them to go to...." She consulted her notebook. "Defendkids dot org. Then the website apparently has info about the bill. And it tells them to contact their legislator ... and provides your phone number, email and mailing address."

"How nice of them," the senator said dryly. "Would you have Lisa check that website out and tell me what she thinks?"

"Certainly, senator."

The phone buzzed again.

"I guess you'd better get back to the phones," he said.

The receptionist smiled, turned to go, then paused. "Senator," she said, "would you like to take a few of the calls? It might help you understand where people are coming from."

The senator hesitated, then reminded himself that if it was something that voters from his district were concerned about, then it better be something that he was concerned about.

"Sure," he said with a smile. "Send a few of them my way. But please screen out the fruitcakes first. No tin-hatters."

"Will do," the receptionist said with a smile and returned to her desk.

Child abuse, the senator thought. *Never paid much attention to that issue. Is it even an issue? Seems to be more of a society problem like poverty. Not sure you can solve it with legislation. So I wonder what the big deal is. There are always a few psychos who do something awful to their kids ... Read about that in the paper now and then. But it seems pretty few and far between. And they always seem like parents who are kind of on the edge anyway ... very poor. Bad parenting skills. Not the brightest people. Or some foster parents who take on one too many kids. Or they're drug-addicted. Or they're your average psycho. If it wasn't their kids they were beating up, it would be their neighbors. Or somebody down at the local bus stop. Wonder why the leadership is putting this up for a vote now. Must have something to do with looking family-friendly.*

His thoughts were interrupted by his receptionist, who said sweetly over his intercom, "Senator, a constituent for you on line four."

"Thank you," he said and picked up the call.

"Senator," said the breathless female caller. "I've been trying your office all day. Your local office phone is busy, too."

"My apologies," the senator said, using his calmest, smoothest voice. "I'm glad you were able to get through."

"This is about those kids," the caller said. "That's just awful."

"Ma'am," the senator said, "I'm not familiar with the kids you're referring to. Can you give me some more information?"

"Those poor children on that website. Oh, that's just awful. I started crying just reading about them. It said that you have a plan to stop it."

"Well, it's not exactly my plan —" the senator began.

"Whoever's plan it is, oh, sir, you have to vote for that law. No kids should ever have to go through that. And those parents need to be punished. And if it takes the FBI to do that, well, then I guess that's what has to happen. The FBI investigates all kinds of other crimes, don't they? Like kidnapping? And bank robbery? Then why can't they investigate child abuse?"

"Well, ma'am, there's the question of jurisdiction –"

"Now that sounds like lawyer talk to me, young man. Lawyer talk should never get in the way of helping people, especially children. If the FBI can investigate people for kidnapping, why can't they investigate child abuse? Now, I voted for you the last three times and I'll vote for you again because I think you're a good Christian man. But I won't stand for that lawyer talk. Makes you sound like a politician."

The senator sighed.

Chapter Ninety-Nine

Carl backed the U-Haul van up to a door at the back of the Capitol building that senators seldom used. He put on the four-way flashers as Cindy and Ev got out.

"Let's move it," Ev said. "We don't have all night."

Cindy punched a number into her cell phone. While they waited, the trio unlocked and raised the back door of the rented truck.

After several minutes, the door opened and a man in the uniform of the U.S. Capitol Police opened the door, spilling yellow light. He spoke briefly into a walkie-talkie, then stepped outside. Cindy approached him.

"Bill, I don't know how to thank you," she said.

He gave her a wan smile in response. "Just promise you'll help me find a new job when they fire my ass," he said.

Cindy put a hand on Bill's arm. "Nobody's going to fire you, Bill," she said. "If you catch any flack over this, just tell them that I gave you orders. I'll take the heat."

The Capitol policeman shook his head. "I'm nuts to let you do this," he said. "But if it's for them kids...." He trailed off.

"There's going to be a vote in the Senate chamber tomorrow that will change everything for kids," Cindy said. "You giving us just a few minutes to set this up is really going to help."

Bill smiled, Cindy thanked him and he turned back toward the door that Carl had now propped open.

"Senator, I...." He trailed off again.

Cindy stopped and faced him. "Bill. What? You can say it."

"I ... you know ... there was this kid that lived next to me when I was a boy ... back home. You know, you never saw his dad much. But this kid ... his real name was Yancey but he hated that name so we called him Yank. You know, Yank and me used to walk to school every morning. Some mornings, he'd have a limp or he'd have a bruise on his face. He always told me that he fell out of bed or he was wrestling with his brothers or something. Me and Yank, we were real close. I never thought much about it until I got a little older. Then I started to think about those bruises and why he always had so many."

Cindy stood very still. Behind Bill, Ev and Carl froze.

"I guess ... I guess ... his dad used to smack him around a good bit," Bill said. "After a while, I realized that there wasn't a lot of love in his house. Kind of made sense then why he liked hanging out at my place so much and why he always wanted to stay over. One time, me and Yank were talking and he asked me, 'Do you think it hurts to die?' And I asked him what the hell he was talking about, but then he didn't want to talk about it any more."

Bill looked down at his feet and shook his head.

"I think about all those times I just brushed him off. Didn't want him to stay over. I wonder what I sent him home to. Sometimes, I think about...." Bill trailed off. "In high school, Yank kind of went nuts. Took to drinking. Stole a couple cars. Started to get into trouble, you know?" Bill looked up at Cindy. "But he wasn't a bad kid. I knew that ... you don't walk to school with a kid for eight years and not learn what kind of person he is. But by then it kind of seemed like Yank ... just didn't want to keep living. Like maybe he thought it would be better, easier, if he ... if he weren't around."

Bill sighed.

"We make our own monsters," Cindy said quietly. "We always have."

"So, I guess if this is for the kids ... to help kids like Yank ... well, I guess I can kind of stand here and not see what I'm seeing, if you know what I mean."

Bill gave Cindy a small smile and turned back toward the door.

"Bill," Cindy said. He stopped. "Bill, what happened to Yank?" Cindy asked.

She always has to know, Ev thought.

His back to Cindy, Bill closed his eyes briefly, then opened them. Looking toward Ev and Carl but past them, he said, "Ran his daddy's pickup into a bridge support at about a hundred miles an hour," he said. "Our senior year. About three weeks before graduation. They said he had a lot of alcohol in his system. I guess it was like he finally got to the end of his rope. Ran out of hope."

Bill swallowed, winced, and said, "He never said anything to me. Never told me. We had plans to go fishing that weekend. So I don't know … maybe it was an accident. But maybe it wasn't, either. I just hope … I just hope it didn't hurt."

"Bill, I'm sorry about Yank," Cindy said. "It wasn't your fault."

Bill turned and looked at Cindy, then up at the sky.

"Yeah. Thanks. Anyway. OK. I guess you guys need to get going," he said. "I need to stand here as long as this door is open, but I got the other security guys on the radio and you should have all the time you need."

"Thank you, Bill," Cindy said.

"Yeah, thanks," Carl said.

Bill nodded and took a post with his back to the door, deliberately looking away, out at the dark sky over the Library of Congress.

The three unloaded the big, flat cart from the truck. Once the cart was on the ground, they started loading it with the easels. Ev was checking on the large panels at the front of the truck's cargo space. Each was a yard square and wrapped in a plastic garbage bag.

"These are all labeled on the outside, right?" she asked.

"Yup," Carl responded.

"OK. You guys get the easels set up and I'll get these ready to unload," Ev said.

"Aye, Cap'n!" Carl said and saluted. He rolled the cart through the door and into the Capitol building.

Chapter One Hundred

It was the day of the vote on Cindy's bill. The first people to enter the Capital building that morning found fifty-two easels spaced evenly around the Rotunda, the space underneath the dome of the U.S. Capitol. On each easel rested a yard-square rectangle of white cardboard. Affixed to the top of each piece of cardboard, in bold black letters six inches high, was the name of a state. Each state and the District of Columbia were represented. Underneath the name of the state, to a viewer's left, was a large black-and-white photograph of an abused child. To the right of the photo was the name of the child, his or her age, date of death and cause of death. Beneath that information, in slightly smaller type, was more detailed information about the child and his or her cause of death. Each case was related to child abuse; each child was under 10 years of age and each child had died at the hands of a parent, stepparent or caregiver.

As word spread, more and more people from the Capitol complex went to the Rotunda to view the display. Aides mixed with clerks; custodians with furrowed brows stood next to secretaries; senators and representatives all stood in near-silence, looking that the display of the costs and effects of child abuse. Few words were spoken except for an occasional "My god" or "Jesus." A few people broke down and walked quickly from the Rotunda, eyes down, crying into hands or handkerchiefs.

The fifty-second easel was placed before the hallway that led to the Senate's chambers. It held a white board that concisely summarized the nation's child abuse statistics from the previous year:

The National Child Abuse and Neglect Data System (NCANDS) reported an estimated 1,400 child fatalities last year. This translates to a rate of 1.98 children per 100,000 children in the general population.

Recent studies have estimated as many as 50 to 60 percent of deaths resulting from abuse or neglect are not recorded.

Very young children (ages 3 and younger) are the most frequent victims of child fatalities. Children younger than 1 year accounted for 41 percent of fatalities.

Children younger than 4 years accounted for 76 percent of fatalities.

More than one-third (38 percent) of child maltreatment fatalities were associated with neglect alone.

Physical abuse alone was cited in more than one-quarter (30 percent) of reported fatalities.

Another 29 percent of fatalities were the result of multiple maltreatment types.

Perpetrators identified as one or both parents were involved in 79 percent of child abuse or neglect fatalities.

Of the other 21 percent of fatalities, 16 percent were the result of maltreatment by non-parent caretakers. Five percent were unknown or missing.

Cindy had not spared herself or her home state. The board representing Pennsylvania showed an autopsy photo of a pretty dark-haired girl with a large black bruise over her right eye. The information to the right of the photo read:

> Brittany Edinburger, age 5, Altoona, PA. Brittany was the victim of serial child abuse and neglect by her father, who inflicted a variety of injuries on her, including a broken arm and being locked in a closet. Brittany was killed by her natural father with a blow to the right-front of her head by a hard and unyielding rounded object. Evidence presented at the trial of her father indicated that the object was a partially filled whiskey bottle. The powerful blow knocked back five-year-old Brittany's head with such speed and force that the bones at the base of her skull snapped and severed her spinal cord. She died from the blow. Brittany wanted to be a nurse when she grew up

so she could help people. Her favorite toy was a cloth doll named "Dolly" and her favorite color was purple.

Ev held out a sheet of paper to Cindy as they hurried to the Senate chambers. The paper flapped in the breeze. It showed two columns. One was marked "Yes" and the other "No." The "Yes" column was shorter.

"As of noon-thirty today, you've got 42 votes," Ev said. "So … it's going to be close. Really close. You might want to …." Ev paused. "You only need 51 to win … but you might want to start thinking about round two."

"Right now, I'm thinking about getting those 51 votes. I'm only nine away," Cindy said. "And that's it. Did the photos help or hurt?" she asked, switching topics.

"Hard to say," Ev said. "I didn't ask that specifically when I was vote-counting this morning. But two weeks ago, you would have lost by thirty votes. So you picked up aye votes somewhere. Something had an effect."

"What about Caldwell?" Cindy asked.

Ev grimaced. "He's not returning calls," she said. "In fact, one of his staffers told me that he's been MIA for a week. He left town a week ago without a word and hasn't been seen since."

"OK," Cindy said, quickening her stride and tightening her coat around her. "Let's go do this."

Cindy was sitting at her desk in the chamber as the senate took care of routine business. In a little while, the regular session would begin and she would call for a vote on her bill. But now the senate was tidying up loose ends, re-arranging the record of past events in the chamber and planning for the near future. The attention required for such activity was so minimal that most senators stood around in clumps, socializing.

Cindy was working on the words that would introduce her bill when a woman dressed professionally in a cream-colored suit, pearls and with her black hair pulled back into a perfect bun approached. Cindy recognized her as a Republican senator from Florida. A moment's concentration brought Cindy the name Teresa Yanez. *Cuban, Cuban community support* popped up with the name.

Teresa stopped at Cindy's desk. Cindy started to stand but Teresa bent over, smiled and said, "Don't stand up. You're fine. I just wanted you to know –." She glanced around the chamber. "You have my support. I'll be voting yes. I'm so glad you have the courage to bring this up."

"Thank you, senator," Cindy said.

She received a smile and a shoulder-pat in answer.

Feeling just slightly less tense, she returned to work on her speech when a voice spoke unexpectedly close, startling her.

"Counting them, are you?"

Cindy looked up, then to her left to see Shipman standing with his hands behind his back. He was trim in a dark blue double-breasted suit with gold buttons and shined black shoes. His smile was of the predatory type that she had become familiar with in D.C. His smile completely lacked mirth or mercy. It was condescending and a little vulpine.

"Senator Shipman. I didn't notice you approach," Cindy said, standing.

"I can save you the effort," he said, nodding toward her work. "Your bill will fail."

"Thank you for your confidence, senator," Cindy said.

"I just saw Senator Yanez scurry away from here," he said. "I'm perfectly aware that she is planning to break party discipline and support you. It won't matter and she will pay the price."

Cindy said nothing.

"I also must inform you that I've asked the rules committee for an inquiry into the little art display that you set up out there in the Rotunda. There's no question that it was the obnoxious stunt of a neophyte. I'm fairly certain that it is also a violation of senate rules."

"If I offended you, I apologize," Cindy said. "That was not my intent."

"It has nothing to do with offending me," he said. "It has to do with understanding how things are done here. You might know, Senator Phillips, that the senate has certain traditions, hallowed procedures that have been passed down for more than two hundred years. Those who violate those traditions usually find that there is a price to pay. That price is often that they find themselves … ineffectual. It becomes difficult to get their bills out of committee. Phone calls are not returned. Am I being clear?"

Cindy controlled her rising anger. She remembered Ev's words: He has no right to talk to you like a schoolgirl.

"Senator Shipman, I have a lot of work to do before I call for a vote on my bill. If you have something of substance to discuss, I'll be happy to give you more of my time. But if you're going to continue making threats, then I –"

Shipman cut her off by taking two quick, aggressive steps toward her without removing his hands from behind his back. He leaned toward her and lowered his voice.

"I'm well aware of your pitiful attempts to garner support, including your dalliance with Senator Caldwell. Senator Caldwell might be a bit … susceptible. But I'm certain that Senator Caldwell has made it clear to you how he will vote today," Shipman said. "I find your methods of attempting to win his vote execrable."

Cindy had had enough. "Mr. Shipman! Your comments are improper and out of line. I have nothing further to discuss with you."

She sat down and found that her hands were shaking. She was sure that her face was flushed. She bent over her papers and tried to concentrate on them.

She felt Shipman step even closer.

"You are about to experience what the press calls a stinging defeat," he hissed from behind her. "You have my condolences on the death of your ill-conceived bill."

He turned and walked away. Cindy closed her eyes and took a deep breath. In that moment, she felt a pure and honest hate for Washington, D.C. and the nation's politics.

Chapter
One Hundred and One

"Mr. President, honorable colleagues, my fellow senators," Cindy said, standing and projecting her voice as she had learned in her long-ago college course. "I will not waste your time with a long-winded introduction to this bill. I'm sure that you are all familiar with its provisions. I'm sure that you have strong feelings about it. Perhaps you have already made up your mind about how you will vote. Perhaps you have been influenced to vote one way or another. I ask only one thing. I ask that today, you vote your conscience. I ask that today, you vote without regard for the transient politics of the day. I ask that today, you vote for our nation's future.

"Fellow senators, today, with my vote on this bill, I choose to stand between the children of this nation and harm. Without flinching, I choose to stand between our children and their abusers. With no doubts whatsoever, I stand firmly and steadfast in defense of children."

She paused.

"I ask … who will stand with me?"

She counted slowly to twenty, then said, "Mr. President, I call for the question and I yield the floor" and sat down.

"Voting on the question will proceed, aye or nay," said the vice president said to the clerk, then frowned at Cindy. He banged his gavel and looked as if he had just suffered an attack of indigestion. Although he was officially the president of the senate and was addressed as such, the vice president rarely sat as the chairman. Cindy assumed that today he was there to help enforce party discipline, which in this case meant voting against her bill. Shipman was also making his presence obvious, stalking around the chamber and fixing senators with his most ferocious glare. When he turned his scowl on Cindy, she returned her sweetest smile and sketched a curtsey.

Aides scurried to the sides of their senators. Whispered conversations were held. Fellow senators glanced at Cindy. Ev appeared at her side, back from a last-minute round of counting promised votes, and put a firm hand on Cindy's shoulder. Ev smiled but said nothing.

The clerk stood and began to call out the names of the senators.

"The Honorable Senator from Missouri, Ronald R. Abelman!" the clerk called.

"Nay!" Abelman yelled without rising.

"Big surprise," Ev whispered.

Cindy put a slash under the "No" column on the paper in front of her.

"The Honorable Senator from New York, Avram P. Abraham!" the clerk called.

Cindy had seen Abraham in the Rotunda, looking at the black-and-white photo of a six-year-old New York girl who had been beaten to death by her stepfather. He had stood with his left arm across his ribcage and his right hand in front of his mouth. He had held the pose unmoving for at least fifteen minutes, staring at the little girl's bruised face.

Abraham rose, glanced at Cindy and said, "Yea!" then sat down.

Cindy slashed a pencil mark under the "yes" column. Two down, ninety-eight to go.

"Is Caldwell here?" Cindy whispered to Ev.

Ev leaned over to speak into Cindy's ear.

"Still MIA," she said. "But after what he told you, you're better off without him."

The voting continued. Cindy had never felt such tension. The chamber was dead silent except for the calls of the clerk and the ringing voice votes of the senators. The slash marks on the page in front of her accumulated. They slid to this side, then that side. Cindy tried not to let her emotions slide with them, but at one point the "nay" votes were ahead by ten and she found it hard to breathe. She felt as if the entire world balanced on an edge and would be shoved one way or the other by the vote in this chamber. She wasn't sure what she would do with her life if she lost the vote.

"Hang tough, girl," Ev said.

Cindy looked up at the observation balcony. It was tougher to get a ticket to this show than any Superbowl, she knew. That would explain the heavy presence of many former senators, people who gave wads of money to politicians and lobbyists who were so influential that their names were spoken with near reverence. She realized that the presence of such people meant that her bill was deemed important. But none of that helped her win votes on the floor. The observers knew well that even speaking aloud would get them immediately ejected from the chamber.

When her name was called, Cindy stood up and as firmly as she could without causing her voice to waver, voiced a resonant "aye!" A few minutes later, her fellow senator from Pennsylvania stood up and said "nay" firmly. He did not look at her.

Ev squeezed Cindy's shoulder. Cindy looked up. Ev inclined her head and slid her eyes to the side. Cindy looked in the direction Ev indicated. Across the chamber, Shipman was crouched beside Teresa Yanez's desk. Their heads were tilted close together and Shipman's shoulders shook with the vehemence of the gestures he was making.

"He wouldn't be working so hard if he weren't worried," Ev whispered.

Finally, Cindy's tally showed a tie at 49-49 with two votes left. J. Preston Caldwell was still absent from the chamber and his aides were missing too, apparently out in search of him.

"The Honorable Senator from Florida, Teresa F. Yanez!" the clerk called out, the last vote of the senators present.

Shipman abruptly stood up and stepped back from Yanez's desk. He took two steps backwards and folded his arms. Yanez stood and turned to glance at Shipman. Then she looked across the chamber at Cindy. Cindy held her gaze.

Please please please, Cindy prayed.

"Yea!" Yanez said, then quickly sat down. She immediately went into consultation with three staff members. Cindy glanced at Shipman. He was glaring at Yanez, his mouth a thin, tight slash.

Cindy made a slash under the "Yea" column. She noticed that her hands were shaking and her slash marks had become wavy.

Now her tally stood at 50 "yes" and 49 "no." If Caldwell voted no, the vote would tie at 50-50. The vice president, a staunch Republican, would get to break the tie and he would surely vote no, killing her bill. Cindy closed her eyes. Ev glanced at her watch, then crouched to talk to Cindy.

"No one objected, so they have to hold to the twenty-minute rule," Ev said. "It's been 18 minutes since voting started. If Caldwell isn't here in two minutes, we win."

Cindy turned to Ev. Ev's eyes and face were serious.

"The vice president isn't going to cut off the vote now," Ev said. "Right now, you win, 50 to 49. He's counting on Caldwell to get here and vote no, tying the vote fifty-fifty. Then he gets to break the tie."

Ev didn't have to explain further. There was no way on Earth that the vice president would support Cindy's bill. It was far more likely, statistically, that a meteor would crash into the Senate chamber.

The seconds ticked by on the big old clock on the wall. Two minutes passed. Three passed.

"Bastards!" Ev hissed as the standard twenty-minute voting window passed without action by the vice president.

Five minutes passed. Then six. Cindy's hands were cramped. She found that they were clenched into fists. She tried to relax, but it seemed hard to breathe, as if the air had become thicker. Everyone was waiting for Caldwell.

A senator from Alabama stood up, one who had voted nay.

"Mr. President!"

"The chair recognizes the honorable senator from Alabama."

"Mr. President, I request an indefinite extension of the time period for voting to allow for all senators to cast their votes on this question."

"Granted!" the vice president said and banged his gavel.

Even as Ev squeezed her shoulder again, Cindy leaped to her feet.

"Objection, Mr. President!" she called. Every eye in the chamber went to her.

"The chair recognizes the senator from Pennsylvania," the vice president said with obvious reluctance.

"The twenty-minute rule must hold, sir!" Cindy called. "There was no announced consent by the leaders of both parties to extend the time for voting as required by Senate rules. I move that the vote on the question be called closed and final!"

"Motion denied!" snarled the vice president.

"He can't do that!" Ev whispered urgently in Cindy's ear. "Demand a —"

The main doors to the chamber slammed open and a harassed-looking J. Preston Caldwell suddenly stood between them. His hair was mussed and there was a wild look in his eye. His tie was askew. Apparently running just three seconds behind, two dark-suited aides skidded to a stop behind Caldwell. The doors closed behind them with a loud clack. One aide reached for Caldwell. Cindy could hear the aide say urgently, "Senator! Don't –" He caught up and began whispering to Caldwell, but Caldwell shook him off.

Cindy saw Shipman, looking angry, begin striding across the chamber floor toward Caldwell.

The clerk stood. The vice president made a sideways slashing motion with the gavel and started to say something, but the clerk called out, "The Honorable Senator from California, J. Preston Caldwell!"

Cindy summoned all of her feelings for the abused children of the country, her despair at losing Brittany, her anguish when she saw undernourished children, children with blackened eyes and bruises. She recalled children she had seen recently at a grocery store, children with thin pale skin and matted hair trailing silently behind plump parents, their heads down, all the joy and vibrancy beaten and starved out of them. She closed her eyes for an instant to focus, then with every molecule of her being, she turned her gaze into a searchlight and beamed at Caldwell: *Please. Please. Please.* He met her eyes and when for an instant there was a laser pulse of communication between them, Cindy mouthed, "For Maria."

Caldwell swallowed, blinked and opened his mouth. Cindy could feel the very air of the chamber freeze. There was not a sound; no one moved. Even Shipman halted.

"The senator from California votes aye!" Caldwell shouted, breathing heavily.

Evelyn squealed and wrapped Cindy in a powerful hug. Cindy, unable to move or believe what had just happened, heard a cheer go up.

"The measure passes on a vote of 51 to 49!" the clerk called out.

Shipman stood in the middle of an aisle, his head down, the fingers of his left hand on his temple. The vice president, looking sallow and sullen, banged his gavel repeatedly.

"Order in the chamber!" he growled. "The matter is concluded. The senate stands adjourned," although no one had made a motion to do so.

"Dear Lord God in Heaven," Cindy said. It was all she could think of to say. She abruptly went to one knee beside her desk and bowed her head.

That one was for you, Brittany, she whispered. *Whatever happens from here on out, that one was for you.*

HOUSE PASSES SWEEPING CHILD ABUSE BILL

WASHINGTON, D.C. (AP) – The United States House of Representatives today approved a bill that would radically change enforcement of child abuse laws across the nation.

Following the U.S. Senate's razor-thin 51-49 approval of the same measure two weeks ago, the House voted 212-202 in favor of the bill, sending it to the president's desk. The president's signature of the bill would make it the law of the nation. The White House has refused comment on the bill.

The bill was officially H.B. 1444, but became known as "Brittany's Law" after an abused Pennsylvania five-year-old girl who was struck and killed by her father. The bill appeared abruptly on the Senate's agenda last month after languishing in the Health, Education, Labor, and Pensions Committee for several months. The sole sponsor of the bill was freshman Sen. Cynthia A. Phillips, Green-PA.

Although the bill barely cleared the Senate, it entered the House with strong popular support, apparently clearing the way for its rapid passage. House GOP leaders denied that a grassroots lobbying campaign affected votes on the bill, but rank-and-file House members told a different tale. House members told of receiving "thousands" of calls, emails and letters in support of the measure, leading many to support the bill.

"There was just a tidal wave of support for this bill," said U.S. Rep. Martin Hushman, D-CA. "My office hasn't received this much mail on a single issue since Social Security reform. If the phone wasn't ringing, the mailman was dumping bags of mail on my desk."

Some House members attributed the groundswell of support to a national television, billboard and internet advertising campaign conducted by the organization "Defendkids.org," a non-profit group dedicated to stopping child abuse. But members said that support for the bill came from across the country and all walks of life.

"I had calls from business owners and from janitors and everybody in between," said U.S. Rep. Duke Eachem, D-AL. "I'll tell you, a lot of people from my district took the time to pick up the phone and call on this one."

The bill, if signed by the president, would radically change the enforcement of child abuse laws in the country, including giving the FBI jurisdiction over what is defined in the bill as "serial child abuse" cases. Such cases are defined as those in which children are abused consistently over a period of time. Local law enforcement officials would be required to report such child abuse cases to the FBI, which would then assume control of the investigation when the severity of the case reached a certain threshold level.

The bill also authorizes the U.S. Congress to withhold federal highway and medical program funding to states that fail to enact certain child abuse measures, including mandatory sentences for those convicted of serial child abuse crimes and establishing uniform definitions of child abuse and child sexual assault.

Additionally, the bill would create a true national registry of child abusers and child sex offenders, allowing law enforcement officials to more easily identify offenders who move from state to state to avoid detection. Currently, no true national database exists and an offender can avoid detection and capture by moving often from state to state.

The bill's swift passage by the House apparently left many special interest groups and Washington,

D.C. think tanks surprised. Reactions to the measure's passage varied, with some groups celebrating while others doubted that the measure will earn the president's signature.

Joan Colburn, a spokesman for Defendkids.org, said that the bill is "a triumph for those who truly value the most precious resource of this nation – our children."

But Samuel Oxborn, a senior fellow with the conservative American Research Institute, said that bill is likely unconstitutional and illegally expands the powers of the FBI.

"There's not the slightest chance that the president will sign this bill," Oxborn said. "And even if he does, the U.S. Supreme Court will overturn it."

The president announced that despite the bill's passage by the House and the Senate, and the groundswell of public support, he would not sign it into law.

"It's simple," he said in response to a reporter's shouted question as he prepared to board a plane for a Mideast trip. "It's an unwarranted intrusion into the lives of American citizens. The crime can be handled – and is best handled – at the local level. The federal government doesn't need to get involved. I believe that the government that governs best governs least."

Then he smiled and waved and disappeared inside the airplane.

"I need to get in to see the president," Cindy said. "And just how am I going to accomplish that?"

Ev paced the floor. "He hasn't vetoed it yet," she said. "So there's still hope."

"There's no hope if I don't get in there to see him," Cindy said. "He's going to veto it any day. I don't know why he hasn't already."

"Because he's got a finger to the political wind," Ev said. "He's been roughed up lately by the press, so he's waiting to see the reaction to this one. He got killed on that leak disclosure. So he's hesitating. There's a chance ... a chance that he might –"

"Ev! He's not going to sign it unless he's pushed. He needs ... he needs to hear from me. He didn't see the display in the rotunda. He hasn't heard me yapping about child abuse in front of all those Rotary groups and all those One Minutes on the floor of the Senate. He's immune ... he's been completely distant from all of our efforts. If we're going to convince him, we've got to get right up there in his face. Hit him with a message that makes sense to him. Give him a reason to sign it ... a reason beyond politics."

Ev spun to stare at Cindy.

"You're exactly right. Exactly right," she said. "You need to lay it out to him, put it in his terms, make him see the light...." She paused. "You just need to get in to see him."

She tapped her foot in thought for a few seconds, then pushed an intercom button on Cindy's phone and yelled, "Carl!"

In a few seconds, the door to Cindy's office clicked open and Carl stuck his head in.

"Yes?"

"Carl, are you still seeing that White House staffer?" Ev asked.

Carl swallowed. "I ... uh, do you mean –"

"Yes. That little cupcake that works for the president's chief of staff," Ev said. "You didn't scare her away or anything, did you?"

"Uh, no," said Carl, stepping into the room. "But I haven't called her in ... a few weeks."

"Well, she's going to hear from you," Ev said. "You're going to give her flowers tomorrow."

"I am?" Carl asked.

"You are. As a matter of fact, you're going to deliver them personally. And then you're going to take her to dinner. And then you're going to ask her for a little tiny favor. A scheduling favor." Ev was smiling her tiger smile.

"Uh, OK," Carl said.

"Flowers, dinner ... all expenses are on the office," Ev said. "Take her to The Palm. Show her what kind of pull you've got."

"I can't get a reservation at The Palm," Carl protested.

"Oh yes you can," Ev said, picking up Cindy's phone. "In fact, you've already got one. Tomorrow night, eight p.m." She punched buttons. "Let me speak to Tony, please," Ev said into the phone.

"Wow," Carl said.

"Carl," Cindy said, leaning over her desk while Ev worked the phone. "Believe me when I tell you that your expense account tomorrow night is unlimited. Un-lim-it-ed."

"OK," Carl said. "Now can I ask what this little favor is?"

"You just want ten minutes on the president's schedule. Ten little, tiny minutes. For a U.S. senator," Cindy said. "Ten tiny little minutes, any time of day or night. President's convenience. Just have your friend scribble it in the appointment book."

"Oh boy," Carl said.

Ev covered the mouthpiece of the phone and said to Carl, "Remember when we watched Brad Pitt in 'Spy Game'? Well, this is your chance. You're on the hotseat. Can you make it happen?"

Carl blinked, swallowed and looked at Ev, then Cindy, then back to Ev.

"Sure," he said. "I'll ... I'll find a way. To make it happen."

Ev smiled and turned back to the phone.

"Yes that's right, Tony, eight tomorrow. Table for two. Very special evening for two young folks in love … I know … Aww. Oh! Love you too! Thanks so much! Owe you one." Ev made a kissing noise and hung up the phone.

"Oh, wow," Carl said.

"Get your hair cut," Ev said. "And wear your blue suit."

Chapter
One Hundred and Four

The president said, "Well, I just don't see how I can see my way clear to signing this one." He paused. "I know this has been your life's work. But it's got a lot of problems, senator."

There was the briefest of pauses, then the entire atmosphere underwent a conversion. Suddenly, all the air was sucked out of the room and replaced with something thicker but crystal clear. Carl's ears rang.

"Well, Mr. President, I have to be honest. I expected that," Cindy said.

Cindy smiled, a genuine smile. Her hand gripped the back of a chair, rippling the leather.

The president smiled back, but his smile was mild.

"Yes, I expected that answer," Cindy said. "But to be honest – and we are being honest here, aren't we? – I think that you should reconsider."

The president opened his mouth to reply, but she didn't stop.

"Mr. President. Please give me ten minutes to make three points about why you should sign this bill into law and change the nation. At the end of that time, if I haven't convinced you, I'll leave quietly. I promise."

The president eyed Cindy for a long second, then said, "OK" and sat on his desk, one foot on the floor, one raised. He gestured for Cindy to sit but she remained standing.

"Thank you for this opportunity. Three reasons, Mr. President," Cindy said. "Reason One. You know, Mr. President, you've often said that you're a faithful Christian. I respect that. Truly, I do. It takes guts not only to admit such a thing openly in the sarcastic and cynical atmosphere here in Washington, but it takes guts to admit that you're going to base some of your decisions on something that a lot of people in this country think are a collection of myths."

Again, the president opened his mouth to speak, but she raised her hand and – amazingly – he stopped.

"I happen to agree with you," she said. "I agree that one day we're all going to stand before God and answer for our sins. That's what keeps me going when I hear about a father who beats his infant son to death, or a mother who starves her daughter to death. Or about parents who lock their kids in dog cages. Too often, those criminals are penalized with only the mildest of punishments. A few months in jail; probation; a fine is all they get while the child that they abused is going to be penalized for life. When I hear of those cases, and

I think about how easily the abusers got off, I think, well, one day they're going to stand before God and they're going to have to explain themselves. Here on earth they got off easy, but it's going to be a lot tougher when the stand before the throne of the Almighty.

"Now, it's not only bad people who have to answer to God. I think that leaders like yourself, Mr. President, and me, people who were chosen – elected – to lead, have an additional responsibility. Not only do we have to answer for our common, everyday sins, but I think that we will have to answer for the decisions we made when our decrees could affect the lives of others. Maybe God doesn't expect perfection, but he does expect that we be judicious and fair. Don't you think, Mr. President, that God will forgive a few lapses of judgment, a few concessions to the political winds? But at some point, all leaders reach a tipping point – a moment in time where the majority of their decisions will be either self-serving or wise and just.

"Mr. President, you've made some tough decisions. You've stood at life's crossroads, faced with choices. Did you choose the one that you knew in your heart was right, even though you knew that it would cause you trouble and heartache? How often did you choose the right path even though you knew that you would be misunderstood? How many times did you take the easy path?

"You know, Mr. President, many people have stood at such a crossroads. And many have failed. I prefer, as I'm sure you do, Mr. President, to focus on those who did the right thing, who chose the right road, even though it cost them dearly later. I'm thinking about people like Winston Churchill. Martin Luther King. Abraham Lincoln.

"You've said in the past, sir, that you consider Lincoln to be a personal hero of yours. So I'm sure that you're familiar with the fact that he agonized over signing the Emancipation Proclamation. He was afraid that it would destroy the Union. He turned to friends and to the Bible and consulted every source of wisdom he could find to come to his decision.

"And of course we know the result. With the fate of the nation hanging on his decision, Lincoln chose the toughest path. He chose that path that he knew – knew beyond a doubt – that could lead to the history books labeling him The President Who Destroyed The Union. But he chose nonetheless, and of course, the rest is the history of our nation."

She swallowed. The president listened.

"When Booth's bullet had done its work, and Lincoln went to stand before God, I bet there was only one question on God's mind, don't you think, Mr. President? Don't you think that God probably fixed Lincoln with a terrible glare and asked, 'Well, Mr. Lincoln? Was your decision about the Emancipation Proclamation right? Do you stand by it, now that you stand before me?'"

"Even without knowing that the Union ultimately held and was repaired, Lincoln could straighten his back and look God right back in that fierce eye and say, 'My Lord, I believe that what I did was right and best.'

"And I bet that God smiled on Lincoln, maybe even clapped him on the shoulder. And he said, 'Very good, Mr. Lincoln. You are a just and honest man. You may go in now.'

"Now, Mr. President, I think that you know in your heart that you're going to one day stand before God just as Lincoln did. Just as all of us do. And when you do, when that day comes, when you've left your bed for the last time, and the long, strong arm of God is pulling you toward Heaven, how will you go?

"As you stand before God knowing none of your earthly conceits matter in the slightest, will you hang your head in ultimate shame and say, 'No, my Lord, when it mattered most, I failed you, I failed myself and I failed those who loved me, trusted me and depended upon me'?"

She paused.

"Or, Mr. President, when you are speeding toward Heaven, are you going to know in your deepest soul, beyond a doubt, beyond the power of any promise you made here on Earth, that when you are asked that one question, you will be able to level your gaze to that of God Almighty Himself and say, 'My Lord, I did what I thought was right and best, though I knew the road I chose would not be easy'?

"What of you, Mr. President? Will you enter His palace with your head hanging, knowing that your conscience is tarnished for all eternity? Or will you dare to look upon our Lord with a clear and firm gaze and give him the answer that he longs to hear but so seldom does from us pitiful humans?"

She stopped. The room silent except for the ticks of a grandfather clock. Carl calculated that she had six minutes left. The president's eyes were narrowed in concentration as he watched Cindy.

"Point two. Mr. President, with this bill before you, you have the chance to write your name into the history books. I cannot promise you that it will turn out as it did for Lincoln. But I am telling you that I am certain beyond any doubt that this bill before you is a challenge such as that which faced Lincoln. I believe with all of my heart that the fate of our nation hangs in the balance, as surely as it did when Eisenhower gave the order to invade Normandy. If our nation's future is to be bright, we must learn to value our most precious resource – children. Your presidency will be judged by the decision you make right here, right now, in this room. The eyes of millions of children are upon you – not only those alive today, but those yet unborn for generations. They are begging you, Mr. President. They are begging you to value them more than all the oil in the ground, more than all the wealth on Wall Street. They are begging you to value them as much as this nation values its hard-won and precious freedom. They are begging you to sign this bill and make it the law of the land.

"Point three. Thank you for your patience so far.

"Mr. President, you are a pragmatic man. You understand politics. So let me be blunt. You are a second-term president. You cannot be re-elected. During a president's first term, it is understandable if he holds some bills up to the political wind and sees which way it is blowing and perhaps allows himself to be swayed. But in a second term, a president's thoughts turn to his legacy. He wonders how history will treat him. Will he be placed in the category of great? Will he be judged merely competent? Or worse, will he be judged to have missed an opportunity to be great?

"So, for a second-term president, it is understandable if he holds some bills up to the wind, and seeing which way the political wind is blowing, nonetheless stands firmly against it.

"Mr. President, your decision here today, right now, is momentous. It will determine your legacy. It will make history. I beg you, Mr. President. Make the right decision. By signing this bill, write your name in the history books. And then sleep well knowing that when God Almighty calls you home, you can meet his gaze confidently and say, 'My Lord, when the time came, when my nation's fate hung in the balance, when I had a choice between the politically expedient and what was right, I did what I knew was right, though I knew my path would not be easy.'

"Mr. President, this bill has been passed by both houses of congress. It has the support of the people of the United States.

"Mr. President, please act now to save our children, this nation's most valuable resource. Please. I am finished. Thank you."

She stopped. Carl watched her watching the president. Carl was pretty sure that she went two minutes over.

The president sat still for a hundred seconds. Then he stood and walked to a window. He gazed out. Carl dared not look at the clock. He saw that Cindy kept her eyes fixed steadily on the president. Her gaze was unhostile but unrelenting.

The president shifted his gaze to the floor. A hundred more seconds went by, then two hundred. He turned around and looked down at his desk. He moved his jaw back and forth. Somewhere outside the White House, a police siren sounded. Carl saw that Cindy's hands still gripped the chair leather tightly. The grandfather clock marked the seconds.

Finally, the president looked up. He met Cindy's eyes for a long minute. She swallowed but her gaze did not waver. Then he gave her a quick nod and drew a pen from his inside left jacket pocket. He walked to his desk phone and pushed a button. The men who witness a presidential signature came in, two of them. The atmosphere of the room was charged and they wore looks of concern. The president raised the pen for the two to see, then very deliberately bent over the bill and signed it. The instant he finished the signature, Carl glanced back at Cindy. She still gripped the chair, but the leather was unwrinkled. Her eyes were closed.

"Thank you, Mr. President," she said. "Generations thank you."

Chapter
One Hundred and Five

'**C**HILD ABUSE MADE A FEDERAL CRIME,' said the headlines.

In smaller print below were such lines as "FBI to investigate child abuse cases" and "Serial child abusers will face federal courts."

Conservatives complained about the cost and harrumphed that yet again the federal government had extended its reach into the lives of ordinary Americans. Liberals wrung their hands over the specter of FBI agents diving into private lives. Moderates were puzzled. District attorneys sighed and told their staff that the new law would mean more work, not less, and that another bit of their authority had been chipped away and that they would work just as hard on child abuse cases but get little or no credit for convictions.

But in under-air-conditioned and overcrowded child welfare offices across the country, there was jubilation. For so many years, the blame for failure to prevent child abuse had been laid on their backs, even as politicians paid them a pittance, cut their budgets, increased their caseloads to impossible levels and refused to help them fight when the courts made terrible, wrong decisions. Men and women in county courthouses with stacks of buff-color folders on their desks and not enough hours to get through them felt certain that something had shifted. Finally, the nation was valuing its most valuable resource: its children. Finally, they felt, someone had recognized that their pursuit was worthy of the most serious attention. And finally, finally, those who violated one of the most sacred of trusts, those who abused the children in their care, would face a grim and determined retribution.

There was a small rectangular box on Cindy's desk, five inches wide and 10 inches long. It was wrapped in plain heavy white paper. It was addressed to Cindy at her Washington, D.C. office. There was no return address. A bright yellow sticker attached to it told her that the Capitol mail service had checked and scanned the box and it did not contain anything dangerous.

She carefully tore the paper. Inside was a black box with a lid. She lifted the lid off. Inside, wrapped in pink paper, was a pair of ballet slippers. They were worn and pink and about the size that an eight-year-old girl would wear.

Cindy pulled them out, baffled. Tucked inside one of the shoes was a white card. Cindy pulled it out and read:

> *Congratulations! You're a ballerina.*
> *Never forget what you accomplished.*
> *Love, Bobbi.*
> *PS. Hunter says Hi. He's doing great.*

Part Four

Chapter
One Hundred and Seven

The man sat in the spare room of grey-painted cinder block walls, furnished with a table and three chairs and a buzzing florescent lamp above. Behind him, back against the wall, stood a policeman in blue. The policeman refused to talk to him and when their eyes met, the man saw only contempt. The officer had left his firearm outside the room. The snap-down strap that kept his pistol secure in its holster flapped loose.

The man knew that the thick panel of blue-tinted glass on the far wall was an observation window. He knew that he was being watched and that a video recorder was focused on him from the other side of that window. He was sure that there were microphones in the room too.

The detective who brought him in had taken off his handcuffs and left him his Marlboro reds and his lighter. There was an ashtray on the table, a flimsy thing of paper with a thin layer of silver foil. He assumed it wasn't the standard glass so that it couldn't be broken and used as a weapon. Not that he had any intentions of attacking anyone. What he had done wasn't a crime, pure and simple. Kids had to be disciplined, as his father had always said as he slammed the closet door and left him in darkness.

True, that brat of his might have needed a bit more than the usual discipline to get ideas into his thick head. But, hell, the kid was almost ten years old. He could take a little roughing up. Needed it, in fact. He was always a bit of whiner, a little weak. He needed toughened up. Just like his father had told him a long time ago: This is for your own good.

Nothing that he had done to the kid was out of line. He'd never locked his kid in a closet, for example, as he had been. He'd never hit his kid full in the face the way that his father had hit him. A good crack like that usually gave you a black eye or a sore jaw. Something to remind you, his old man had said.

A good kick in the ass was what most kids needed these days, the man thought. He reached for his cigarette pack, shook one out, lit it with his red plastic lighter. He blew a cloud of smoke toward the window. Let the bastards watch, he thought. Not a damn thing they can do to me. Hell, they hadn't even arrested him yet. If he got bored, he thought that he'd start shouting about seeing a lawyer and getting his phone call. That always pissed off the cops. They hated it when you lawyered up.

His thoughts snapped to the scene a few hours previous when the officers had shown up at his house. He'd been watching Monday Night Football, pulling on a beer, when he heard the crackle of car tires on the gravel of his driveway. At first, he thought it had to be his piece-of-shit brother-in-law, coming over to bum his beer and his TV for the game. Goddamn Randy, he had thought. *I really don't feel like putting up with your stupid bullshit. I just want to watch the game.* But then the tire-crackle was followed by another. And the bastards didn't shut their lights off. They kept them shining right through his living room window.

Just as he got up, there was a pounding at his door. He knew that pounding. Cops. Christ. Just what I need now, he thought. But he hadn't done anything wrong and there was no weed in the house. So he jerked open the door. On his narrow porch were three cops. The one at the front was a fat guy with a grey beard and a long coat. The man knew a detective when he saw one. The detective said, "Thomas Anthony?"

He had replied, "Who wants to know?"

"Don't give me that shit," the detective said, holding the door open with one hand and holding up his gold badge with the other. "You wanna talk or do we have to come in there and trash your Rent-a-Center furniture?"

"Jesus, what the fuck for?"

In answer, the cop put the badge back in his pocket, took his hand off the door and reached into one of the pockets of his long coat. He brought out a slim rectangular phone. The front of the device was nearly all glass. The detective tapped the glass screen a few times, then held the phone up. The man could see that a crisp photo was displayed on the screen, a head-and-shoulders picture of his son. Dark mop of hair. Dark, wary eyes. No smile.

"That your kid?" the detective asked.

"Yeah." *Whatever he's done now, I'm really going to kick his ass. Like I need this shit,* the man had thought. Behind him, he could hear the sounds of kickoff. He was missing the game.

The detective swiped an index finger across the phone's screen. Another photo slid into view, a close-up of a hand, the palm up, fingers slightly spread, a wide crater of red gleaming and blackened flesh in the middle of the palm.

"That your kid's hand?" the detective asked.

A chill had taken Anthony. He placed his beer can on the floor. He swallowed.

"Your kid or not, pal?" the detective asked.

The man looked into the detective's eyes. They were grey and quiet, but there was no mercy there.

"Kid's a goddamn firebug," Anthony said. "Had to teach him about fire."

The detective swiped again. He held up the phone, now displaying a photo of one naked skinny left shoulder blade with just a section of neck and dark hair in the upper right corner. The skinny shoulder was marked with welts. Some were red and raised; others had scabbed over. Under the fresh welts were similar marks, but faded and healed.

"Your kid?" the detective asked again.

"Shit. I –"

"Your goddamn kid or not?"

"I –"

"I'm going to ask you one more time and then your life is going get real unhappy real fast."

"Yeah. My kid. But he's –"

"Shut up." The detective swiped the phone's screen again. The next photo up was of skinny naked male torso, nipples-to-waist shot, arms raised out of the frame of the picture. The ribs and the stomach of the pale skin were marked with a collection of splotchy bruises, purple, blue and yellow. It looked like a colored map of the continents.

"Your kid?" the detective asked.

"Yeah, but I –"

The detective's arm shot out with alarming quickness and the man was suddenly pulled down off the stoop, onto the porch and into the arms of two unfriendly looking cops.

"Get this piece of shit out of my sight," the detective said. The two cops had grabbed the man very professionally, twisting his hands behind his back. He felt cold metal on his wrists, then something thin and hard clicked into place around them. One hand went numb almost immediately. The cops hustled him down the walk, past the front of his house, one on either side of him, hands on his arms just above the elbows. He saw a police car and an unmarked car in his driveway. The cops marched him to the trunk of the marked car, pushed his groin against the car and bent him over at the waist. He could feel the cold metal of the car through his jeans. He was frisked professionally. He felt his wallet slide out of his back pocket. His cigarettes and lighter were pulled from his front t-shirt pocket.

A rear door of the police car was opened and one of the cops grabbed him by the back of his head and pushed it down to make him bend over. As he bent, the cop banged the side of his head against the car's roof. It was just enough of a bounce to hurt. His ear began to burn.

"Lot more where that came from if you give us any trouble," the cop said.

Then he had been shoved inside the car and the door slammed. No locks and no handle, he saw. And a metal grille between him and the front seat.

Oh, well, he thought. Just like the time he was busted for DUI. He'd do a few hours in the tank, then get out and all would be fine. He'd get one of those lawyers who let you pay over time. He'd get off with a warning and some community service. Maybe he'd have to attend some bullshit class and sit there and pretend that he cared.

He almost felt sorry for the poor stupid cops for going through all of this. Showing up with two cars. Like he was fucking Al Capone or something. They were going to haul him in and try to scare him, but some district magistrate would toss out three-quarters of the charges against him.

Then he began to wonder just what they had busted him for. It couldn't be dope. Since he had started working that out-of-town construction job with the long drive, he had laid off the stuff. It made him too sleepy. He was off the stuff. For a while, anyway. From the pictures the detective had shown him, it must have something to do with his kid. But what the hell? A father was allowed to discipline his own child.

He gave a short laugh. If the cops thought that they could make a child abuse charge stick, they were even stupider than he thought. A guy he had worked a construction job with a few years ago had been arrested for beating the shit out of his kid. He never even had to pay a fine. He just had to go to classes on anger management for six months. The man remembered the guy laughing. "You talk about people being able to do time standing on their heads," the guy had said. "Well, these classes are even easier. You just show up, sit there, then go home. If they ask, you tell them some bullshit like you realize that you did bad shit and it was just your temper and it was because your dad did it to you." The guy had given him a big smile. "And then you go home and nothing is any different."

Anthony wished he could light a cigarette. Damn! Why did they have to take his cigarettes?

He watched as his wife appeared at the front door in a t-shirt and sweatpants. The detective stood on the porch talking to her. She kept shaking her head and glancing toward the police cars. He could tell by the way she looked that she couldn't see him. Eventually, she disappeared into the house. The detective waited on the porch. She reappeared with their son, his hair tousled from sleep, dressed like his mother in a t-shirt and sweats. He looked confused. Anthony wanted to yell to him, but he figured that would probably earn him worse than a burning ear. Besides, he was pretty sure that his family couldn't hear him from inside the car.

His wife was shaking her head rapidly from side to side. The detective started talking directly to his son. At one point, his son shrugged and then held out his right hand, palm up. The detective looked at it. His son put his hand back down. His wife looked out at the police cars again.

The detective handed her a piece of paper, touched his brow in a goodbye, and walked down the steps. His wife and son stood in the doorway. She put her arm around his son's shoulders as they watched the cops walk back to the cars.

The cops who climbed into the front seat had been pretty nasty.

"What's this all about?" he said, keeping his tone friendly.

"Shut the fuck up," the driver had said.

"Look," the man said, "You come down here and haul me out of my house and –"

The cop in the passenger seat had turned around and fixed him with a stare.

"Listen to me, asshole," he said. "One more word out of you, and we're going to pull over and you're going to try to escape. And god knows what might happen to you if that happens. Guys get hurt real bad trying to escape."

The cop turned back to face forward and Anthony decided that silence was his best choice.

And now he sat in this interrogation room. For what? Apparently for trying to keep his kid from being a firebug. He had caught the kid – what, three or four times – playing with matches. Once in the bathroom. He could have burned the house down. So holding the kid's hand over a candle for a good minute seemed a perfect way to point out the dangers of fire. And then he made the kid put the candle out with his hand. Anybody knew that all you had to do was wet your fingers and pinch the wick and the thing went right out. Wasn't his fault the kid didn't know that.

The marks on the kid's back – hell, his dad had given him worse than that. A couple of smacks with that old extension cord were what the kid needed, with the smart mouth that he had. A few good cracks and he'd learn to talk back to his father. His father had hit him with a leather belt, and that had hurt a hell of a lot more. Anthony figured that his kid must be a pussy if he couldn't take a few whacks from an extension cord.

And those bruises on the kid's chest and stomach. Well, the kid had earned those when he decided to turn and fight against the extension cord. He had to learn that his old man was still the boss of the house. If he wanted to fight, he'd get a fight. And he got one. The kid had ended up curled on the floor, puking. The man remembered standing over him, victorious, reminding the kid who was in charge. And then he made him clean up the puke. Served him right for turning on his father. Kids just don't do that shit.

Anthony crushed out his cigarette in the flimsy ashtray just as the door opened. The grey-eyed detective came in, followed by two men in dark suits and ties.

What the fuck, the man thought. *I didn't even have a chance to call my lawyer*. Then he noticed their short hair. And their eyes, which were even colder than the detective's, if that was possible.

"Mr. Anthony, these men are from the FBI," said the detective. "They'll be handling your case."

Suddenly the room seemed very cold.

"The what?" Anthony said, trying to cover his confusion.

One of the suited men leaned over and picked the cigarette pack and the lighter off the table.

"Federal Bureau of Investigation," the man said. "You might have heard of us."

To Anthony, the man looked like some of the guys he'd seen who came back from the wars in Iraq and Afghanistan. Young, but with very old eyes. Eyes that had already seen an entire life's worth of bad shit. Eyes that might not understand that a kid needs a good ass-kicking now and then.

Anthony thought that he might not see his cigarettes again for a while.

"What the hell is the FBI doing here?" he asked.

"Investigating," the detective said.

"Investigating what?" For a moment, Anthony thought that he was being set up. They'd ask him to do a dope buy to nail a big-time dealer.

"Child abuse," said the agent who had taken his cigarettes. The man hadn't seen what the agent had done with them, but they had disappeared.

"Child abuse? Since when does the FBI investigate child abuse?"

The agents and the detective exchanged glances.

The cigarette-stealing agent chuckled and pulled out a chair, shaking his head.

"Mr. Anthony, it looks like you're in for a long evening. You seem to have fallen out of touch with the latest trends in law enforcement."

The agent sat down, smiling. The man didn't like the smile at all.

"I'm Special Agent Kelly. My partner is Special Agent Carlson." Carlson nodded. "We're going to have a little chat and then you get to make a decision."

Carlson walked behind Andersen, pulled out the last chair and sat down.

"If you need me, just yell," said the detective.

Kelly turned to the detective. "Thank you for your assistance. You've done good work here."

The detective nodded and left. The door closed behind him with a click.

Anthony suddenly felt much less confident.

"I get my phone call, right?" he asked, wishing he had a cigarette to boost his bravado.

"For what?" Kelly asked. "You haven't been arrested yet." He leaned forward an inch and looked Anthony in the eyes. "Something you're feeling guilty about?"

Anthony sat back in his chair.

"Shit, no. But you can't hold me here forever. You have to let me go or let me make that call to my lawyer."

"Mr. Anthony, we have, oh …." Kelly glanced at his watch. "…another two hours or so before a judge would give us any grief about keeping you here. So we can have a good hour of conversation before we need to worry about getting lawyers involved."

"So what do we need to talk about?" Anthony asked warily.

Kelly sat back and centered his tie on his chest. "Mr. Anthony, are you a boxing fan?"

"No. I mean, I watch the big fights. Maybe once or twice a year," Anthony said, wondering where the line of questioning was going.

"But you know a little about boxing, right?"

"A little, yeah."

"So, let's say that you sat down to watch a 'big fight' as you said – a fight that had been hyped up. You get together with some of your buddies and you maybe get some beverages and some bags of chips and you're ready to watch a good fight, right?" Kelly smiled. "You're looking forward to what – a hour, maybe 90 minutes of a good fight, right? That's why you watch boxing. It's an athletic event. Two guys go at each other and the best man wins, right?"

Anthony, still wary, said, "Yeah. Like that, I guess."

Anthony looked at the other agent. What was his name? Colson? Carson? The agent sat quietly, his chair pushed back from the table about six inches further than Kelly's. He met Anthony's gaze without hostility but without wavering. Anthony realized that he was bracketed by the two agents.

"So, Mr. Anthony," Kelly said, "what if you sat down to watch this fight, and they announce the first fighter. He's a professional. He's got years of experience in the ring. And he weighs 200-some pounds. He's a big guy. He's got big arms and big chest muscles."

Kelly fixed Anthony with his eyes. "That's not unusual in big fights, right? A guy built like that."

"Uh, no. Most of the heavyweights are like that. They're big guys."

"Right," Kelly said. "People like to watch the heavyweights. Those guys hit the hardest and put up the best battles, right?"

"Some of the smaller guys do OK," Anthony said.

"But those matches are usually not on TV. Would you make a point of watching them?"

"Guess not," Anthony said with a shrug. "Wouldn't go out of my way or anything."

Kelly nodded. "And then say that they announce the second fighter. He weighs 120 pounds. And when they take off his robe, he's a lot smaller than the first guy. He's got muscles, sure, but nothing like his opponent. And let's say that it's clear that the second guy is a lot smaller than the first boxer. Like, say, the big guy has about eight inches of height on the smaller guy. And they announce that the little guy has only been boxing for six months."

Kelly paused.

"Now, Mr. Anthony, if that happened, would you be excited about the fight? Would you be looking forward to a good match, a knock-down, drag-out fight that would keep you entertained for an hour or so? Is that what you'd be thinking?"

"It wouldn't be a fair fight," Anthony said. Then an inkling of where the conversation was headed occurred to him.

"Exactly!" said Agent Kelly, slamming his hand down on the table. He looked into Anthony's eyes. "Now maybe you see where I'm going with this, Mr. Anthony."

"I got no idea," Anthony said with quiet defiance.

Kelly's eyes narrowed. He leaned forward. His voice dropped. "Listen to me, Mr. Anthony." Kelly's voice held menace. "You know exactly what I'm talking about. When you decide to punch out your son, is that a fair fight? You've got maybe a hundred, hundred and twenty pounds on the kid. You work construction. You lift stuff all day. Your kid carries his bookbag to school. You've been in fights before. You've kicked some ass in your day. Your kid, he's still trying to figure out whether he's the sort of man who stands up in a fight or runs to live another day. Am I right, Mr. Anthony?"

"Kid needs to learn to fight," Anthony said. "I'm not raising no pussy."

"But that's beside the point here, isn't it, Mr. Anthony? Because we're talking about you versus your son. Not your son versus some bully. Right?"

"To be honest, Mr. Kelly," Anthony said, putting emphasis on the "Mr. Kelly," "I have no fucking idea what we're talking about. And I think it's time that I got my lawyer on the phone. I don't like the way this is going."

Kelly sat back. He centered his tie on his chest again. He looked at his fellow agent. "Well, Mr. Carlson, it looks like Mr. Anthony has a mental block. He's able to see how it's not a fair fight when as heavyweight goes up against a featherweight, but he can't see how it's not fair when he decides –" Kelly abruptly leaned toward Anthony "– to beat the shit out of his son."

"I think I need to talk to my lawyer now," Anthony said.

Kelly looked at Anthony. He chuckled. "Well, then, I guess this interview is over. You should go contact your lawyer, Mr. Anthony," he said. He gestured toward the door.

Anthony looked at the door, then back at Andersen.

"You sure?" he said.

"By all means, Mr. Anthony," Kelly said. "Go call your lawyer. When you're done, just meet us back here and we'll keep talking if you're willing."

Kelly glanced over his right shoulder, toward the observation window. Anthony swallowed hard. Kelly's eyes were cold as ice, but he was smiling. He seemed relaxed in his chair. Anthony stood.

"Can I have my cigarettes back?" he asked.

" 'Fraid not," said Kelly, still smiling.

"Shit," said Anthony and started for the door.

With unbelievable quickness, Kelly rose from his chair and grabbed Anthony's shirt at the neck. Anthony's head slammed against the wall. Kelly twisted his t-shirt until Anthony could feel it biting into the sides of his neck. Kelly's face was very close to Anthony's. He could see the pores in the man's nose.

"Now you listen to me very carefully, you piece of shit," Kelly said in a new and nasty voice. "You call your lawyer and you're going to find yourself in a world of hurt. Right now, we've got you on federal serial child abuse charges based on those photos. That's bad enough. Five to ten for sure. Maybe fifteen. And that's hard time in a federal lockup. You decide to be a pain in the ass and we'll charge you with everything in the goddamned book and throw in a few extra charges. Aggravated assault and battery on a minor. That's a state felony. That's another ten-to-twenty right there. So now you're looking at fifteen to forty. You're what, thirty-four? You wanna be fifty before you breathe free air again? Huh?" Kelly jerked on Anthony's t-shirt neck.

"Hell, even if you get some liberal asshole judge, we'll have you in court so often that you won't be able to hold a job and every fucking dime you have will go to some dickhead lawyer just to keep you out of the big house. You'll never smoke dope again because if you try to buy it, we'll nail you and the guy you buy from. You'll have more cops following you around than Al Capone. And everyone in town will know that you beat the shit out of your kid. Now."

Kelly stepped back and smoothed Anthony's shirt. "Now. We have some hard evidence, photos, courtesy of a very observant high school gym teacher. You … you have two choices, Mr. Anthony. You walk out of here and make that call or you sit back down and we have a talk. If you're smart, you talk."

Kelly straightened his tie. His eyes narrowed as he looked at Anthony. Anthony noticed that the uniform in the room was looking at the floor and the other FBI agent had taken an interest in the room's ceiling tiles. Officially, neither had seen anything.

Without warning, Kelly's palm struck Anthony in the forehead, slamming his head back against the cement-block wall. It hurt. Anthony shook his head to clear the stars.

Kelly walked back to his chair and sat down. He centered his tie on his chest. He glanced back at the blue-tinted window. Anthony realized that he had assumed the same posture as he had during their earlier talk.

"So, Mr. Anthony," Kelly said in a conversational tone, "did you get ahold of your lawyer?"

Anthony licked his lips. "I ... maybe I want to ... talk a little more first," he said.

Kelly turned to face him. "Well, that's excellent, Mr. Anthony," he said. "I'm glad that you're being so cooperative."

Kelly's eyes followed Anthony as he walked from the door and sat down in his chair.

"You sure I can't have my cigarettes?" he asked.

Kelly's face took on a look of surprise. "Your cigarettes? I'm sorry. I have them right here." He pulled them out of the inside of his jacket and placed them on the table.

Anthony grabbed the pack and pulled one out. He stuck it in his mouth and by instinct felt for his lighter in his breast pocket. Just as he remembered where his lighter was, Kelly leaned forward, lighter in hand, a flame flickering at its top. Anthony lit the cigarette, inhaled, exhaled gratefully and looked at Kelly.

"OK, Mr. Kelly, I understand," he said. "Maybe we can talk a little more."

"Maybe we can," Kelly said, drawing a stack of photos from his inside jacket pocket. "Let's go back to last Saturday."

Anthony looked into Kelly's eyes, then down to the ashtray. He tapped the ash off of his cigarette.

"OK," he said. "Jeez. I didn't know that … hitting your kid was something that the FBI cared about," Anthony said.

"Oh, we take child abuse very seriously," Kelly said, moving his chair closer to the table. "Kids are the future of this country. Everyone's got a stake in kids doing well. Surprised you haven't heard about that."

Chapter
One Hundred and Eight

Feeling free of constraints because she didn't plan to run again, Cindy voted her conscience for the rest of her term, irritating the leadership of both parties. After her miraculous victory on the child abuse law, she was considered to be nearly inviolable and was generally left alone. She was occasionally asked for help with votes, but both sides knew not to take her support for granted. They asked; she considered, then voted as she saw fit.

When re-election time rolled around, the Democratic Party of Pennsylvania came to her, hat in hand, asking her to be their candidate. She agreed and, to her surprise, won a second term. She spent most of it protecting her child abuse bill from being watered down or repealed. She spent a lot of time on the road, speaking to groups about child abuse. Everywhere she went, she spoke about Defendkids dot org, urged people to join the group and give it money.

Six years passed quickly. By then she was being called "the child abuse senator." She pushed through some modifications to her original child abuse bill, responding to criticisms from the FBI, police departments and district attorneys. She was often cited as a child abuse expert, although she never made the claim herself.

As her second term ended, the Democrats asked her to run again, and she agreed – but made it clear that her third term would be her last. The Republicans threw a smart but callow young man against her, a dedicated Young Republicans type. She drew blood in a debate by pausing, removing her glasses and saying that she was worried about the "bright-eyed young men from wealthy families who march only to the tune of one band and who forget that there are people less privileged than they." After the debate, his response to the news media about the remark came off as peevish and disrespectful.

He was too smart to make many more mistakes, but he never quite recovered from the rapier she had stuck in him during the debate. Although he spent nearly two dollars for every one of hers, she beat him by 14 points. Pundits used the term "sound spanking" in referring to the young man's defeat by the lady senator with a librarian's demeanor. He didn't appreciate the humor.

After 18 years in the Senate, she quit, saying that it was time for those with newer ideas and more energy to take over. She retired quietly to her farm in northern Maryland, living simply on her federal lawmaker's pension.

For years afterward, petitioners came, seeking her prestige to attach to their bill or their cause. Most often, they were treated to tea and a pleasant hour of conversation and then they found themselves back in their cars, driving away, uncertain of her support for their cause but certain that they had just spent time with a remarkable human being.

In her retirement, she surrounded herself with children. She volunteered at the pediatric ward of the large regional hospital. She founded a new chapter of the Make a Wish Foundation and gave it money generously. She was asked – and agreed – to join the board of directors of Defendkids dot org.

She took a position as a child advocate with the national Court Appointed Child Advocate program, representing in court children who were abused and neglected and who had no one else to speak for them. Many times, her Senate-floor-trained voice rang though local courtrooms.

"Your Honor, I speak for this child," she would say, rising.

In her advocate role, she made sure that the courts considered the effects on young children when decisions were made in divorce, custody, abuse and adoption cases. Her recommendations were often followed; her assertions were rarely doubted.

She quietly accepted at her farm exceptionally difficult children, the ones who were trapped in the system and considered to be lost causes emotionally or mentally. Many but not all responded to her attention. She helped the ones she could and returned them to the child welfare system with noticeable improvements in attitude and outlook. Others that she could not help nonetheless left her farm with the feeling of an opportunity lost. For some of them, it was the first and last time that they would feel that way.

Her headaches continued and grew worse. One day, eight years to the month after her retirement, her silver-haired physician gave her the news. It was a tumor. Surgery was possible but difficult. If it was malignant – and he was sure that it was – there would be rounds of chemotherapy and radiation treatments. There were some new drugs on the market that restricted the growth of the blood vessels that fed tumors; perhaps they would buy her some time.

She waved it all away.

"I've spent enough time in hospitals, thank you, James," she said to her doctor who was called doctor by the staff and called Jim by his family and friends. "I think I'll just go home."

And she did.

In time, she required the care of an in-home nurse. Charlie and her nurses took on more household chores as she forgot about them. She would forget to eat, except for her afternoon tea. Slowly, her memories began to fade. A parade of old friends – Pannington, Harold Kaufmann, Bobbi, Dr. Jacobi, Caldwell, even Evelyn – left in tears after she greeted them with a big smile but no hint of recognition.

Every morning without fail, rain or shine, her nurse would wheel her out to the front porch of the old farmhouse and she would sit quietly, humming scraps of songs and paging through worn and tattered books with colorful covers. She preferred to sit in the sun if there was any; if not, she sat where she could see the corner of the barn and the hills behind it.

Her nurse noticed that she often read from a set of slim, battered books bound in pink and yellow. The nurse, a devoted and caring woman, noticed the titles of the books and thought them rather juvenile. She wrote it off to the affection for the past that often afflicts the seriously ill and elderly. Many of the books were worn, as if they had been read over and over. Cindy always smiled as she read them. The nurse sneaked a peek at one. She couldn't understand what Cindy saw in them – they were simple child's fairy tales. There was nothing in them that could entertain the average reading adult for more than five minutes. One title did strike the nurse, perhaps because of its alliteration: The Princess Who Ran for President.

"Ma'am, you could have run for president," the nurse said to Cindy one fine June morning when birds were singing just for the joy of it and the house was creaking as the morning sun, slanting across the fields, warmed its boards. "You know that people like me would have voted for you in droves. I bet you'd have won. There's a lot of people out there who think…" The nurse paused, caught in an expression of emotion she hadn't intended. "There's a lot of people who think that you're a very wonderful person," she finished firmly, as if it needed to be said.

Cindy gave the nurse a big smile and said, "Why, thank you."

One day she told her nurse shortly after breakfast, "I think I'll take my nap early today." The nurse helped her upstairs to the big bed and fussed over her for a few minutes. Cindy asked that a book be brought up.

"Please bring me the one called The Princess Who Ran for President," she asked.

The nurse smiled. She brought it up a few minutes later and placed it on Cindy's lap, under one of her frail hands. Cindy was resting quietly, propped against the headboard, her eyes closed, her mouth open slightly. Late morning sun streamed through the windows, making the yellow curtains glow.

"Are you OK then, Miss Cindy?"

Cindy stirred and opened her eyes. She felt the book under her hand and glanced at it.

"I'm fine. Please go down and see to the children when they arrive. Come and get me once they're here."

The nurse closed the bedroom door softly and went downstairs to read on the sunny porch.

Three hours later, with the children shrieking in the yard, chasing each other, the birds singing and the sun warming the porch, the nurse went upstairs.

"Miss Cindy?" she said, rapping twice and then opening the door slowly.

She wasn't surprised by what she found. Her tears came immediately.

At the bedside, she said, "Oh, honey. Oh, Miss Cindy. I'm so sorry."

But she knew that there was no reason to be sorry, no reason at all.

The president declared a national day of mourning. All flags on government buildings were to be flown at half-staff. A former president, the one who had signed Cindy's child abuse legislation, emerged from his elegant Chicago home and called a rare press conference.

At a podium set up in the town square of his hometown, he put on his reading glasses, cleared his throat, shuffled his papers and began to read.

"I wish to speak to you today of Senator Cindy A. Phillips. Senator Phillips did more for the children of this country than any single person has ever done," he said, his eyes on the page. "She single-handedly changed the way the nation views its most precious resource, our children. Because of her brave and determined efforts, child abuse today is seen as the serious crime that it is, and the laws against it are properly and justly enforced by the Federal Bureau of Investigation. It is with great sadness that I –" He stopped.

He looked up from his pages at the four dozen news media representatives before him. They were silent, pens poised above paper, cameras held steady, micro-recorders extended. The former president shuffled his papers back into a pile. He cleared his throat again.

"Sometimes you have to … deviate a little from the prepared text and speak from the heart," he said, smiling. He took off his reading glasses.

"Miss Cindy, as she was known on the Hill, is simply one of the most remarkable women I have ever known. She was a woman of strong faith. She was determined that this country would view children the way she did – as something that you just couldn't replace and that deserved the full protection of the authorities of this great nation.

"Miss Cindy was what some people call a force of nature, and I'd say that's an accurate description of her. She knew her destiny and she knew what she had to do and she did it. Against all the roadblocks that the town on the Potomac can throw in the way of your goals, she just kept fighting. I think she did it because she knew deep in her heart that she was right. She knew that she just had to work hard enough to get the rest of us to see it the way she did. I never knew her to have a moment of doubt and I never knew her to take a day off. She walked her talk and kept her promises, which is pretty rare in Washington, D.C. She took kids into her home. She gave her time and money to helping kids that no one else wanted to help. She never let up."

He paused and looked down, then up again.

"I'm sure I'm being politically incorrect when I say this, but she was a great mother to every single kid in this nation who didn't have one. Every single kid whose parents ever beat them or neglected them or just plain didn't care. If she could have taken them all into her home, she would have. She was the conscience of this nation."

He paused and shook his head.

"So this nation will miss her. I will miss her. Now, I know that there's a lot of lawmakers up on the

Hill who are glad she's not hanging around their offices any more, bugging them to listen to her big plan. But I know that in their hearts, when they set all the politics aside, they'll miss her too. Because we all know what she did. She made this nation a better place. That's a damned hard thing to do.

"Thank you, ladies and gentlemen. I won't be taking any questions."

He turned and walked quickly from the podium.

The headlines read:

SEN. PHILLIPS PRAISED AS 'CONSCIENCE OF THE NATION'

Chapter
One Hundred and Nine

At her grave is a simple rectangular gray stone, straight on the sides with a gentle arc across the top. Engraved on it are two cupped hands holding children at play. The inscription reads:

> *And they were bringing children to him, that he might touch them; and the disciples rebuked them. But when Jesus saw it he was indignant, and said to them, Let the children come to me, do not hinder them; for to such belongs the kingdom of God. Truly, I say to you, whoever does not receive the kingdom of God like a child shall not enter it. And he took them in his arms and blessed them, laying his hands upon them.*
> *~ Mark, Chapter 10, 13:16*

Afterword

The original version of this novel contained verbatim copies of news stories written about horrendous cases of child abuse. Copyright and legal restrictions prevented their inclusion in this novel, but you, the reader, can find your own. Unfortunately, they are not hard to find. All you have to do is type "child abuse" into your favorite news search engine. Scroll through the thousands of hits and pick one. I guarantee you won't have to read many before you find one that completely appalls you.

The central idea of this novel – that child abuse should be a federal crime, enforced by the FBI – is not mine. Its genesis was in a Bob Greene newspaper column I read many years ago. Yes, I know what happened to Bob Greene. I'm also not convinced that expanding the federal government's power is a good idea. This novel is an exploration of that idea, regardless of the idea's shortcomings and the failings of its originator. No solution to a problem as large and complex as child abuse is going to be perfect.

Defendkids.org is not a real organization, but it is a website dedicated to the publicity of this novel and lowering the American public's tolerance for child abuse. It contains links to the websites of organizations that work to prevent child abuse.

Right now, there are children out there, as this novel says, crying and wondering why the world is filled with pain and not love. You can do something about it. Please volunteer to help organizations in your community that work to prevent child abuse and help its victims heal. Any effort on your part will make a difference.

Acknowledgements

I must thank John Hooper, who taught me about transformation of the negative into the positive. John, I finally have something to say. I hope it was worth the wait.

I thank Tom Gibb, who was never able to see me as anything other than a writer. I regret that you did not live to see this novel in print. That's my fault.

Thank you to my sister-in-law Michele Tyson, who along with Bob Greene, sparked a change in my perception of child abuse. She did it with one simple question: "Why do people get so upset about abuse of animals but not children?"

And of course, I must thank my wonderful wife Karen and my children R.J. and Helena. I never knew what I was missing.